THE
BOARDINGHOUSE
BRIDES

★

Finally a Bride

Vickie McDonough

BARBOUR
PUBLISHING

ISBN 978-1-62416-723-2

All scripture quotations are taken from the King James Version of the Bible.

This book is a work of fiction. Names, characters, places, and incidents are either products of the author's imagination or used fictitiously. Any similarity to actual people, organizations, and/or events is purely coincidental.

For more information about Vickie McDonough, please access the author's website at the following Internet address: www.vickiemcdonough.com

Cover design: Faceout Studio, www.faceoutstudio.com
Cover photography: Steve Gardner, Pixelworks Studios

Published by Barbour Publishing, Inc., P.O. Box 719, Uhrichsville, Ohio 44683

Our mission is to publish and distribute inspirational products offering exceptional value and biblical encouragement to the masses.

 Member of the
Evangelical Christian
Publishers Association

Printed in the United States of America.

To preach deliverance to the captives,
and recovering of sight to the blind,
to set at liberty them that are bruised.

LUKE 4:18

Chapter 1

Jacqueline Davis had done a lot of daring things in her life, but this deed had to be the most foolhardy. She held up her skirt with one hand, holding her free arm out for balance, and slid her foot across the roof's wooden shakes. The mayor's chimney was only a dozen more steps away. She peered down at the ground far below, then yanked her gaze upward when a wave of dizziness made her sway. She sucked in a steadying breath. If she fell the two stories to the packed dirt below, *she'd* become tomorrow's news instead of the story she intended to write about the mayor's latest scheme.

She just had to find out what he had up his sleeve. Weeks had passed since she'd landed an exciting story for Lookout's newspaper. She had to get the scoop—whatever the cost. Maybe then she'd have enough clippings in her portfolio to land a job in Dallas as a reporter and finally leave Lookout.

The sweat trickling down her back had nothing to do with the bright April sun warming her shoulders. A moderate breeze whooshed past, lifting her skirts and almost throwing her off balance. Her petticoat flapped like a white flag, but she was far from surrendering. She swatted down her skirts and glanced around the streets, thankful no one was out yet. "Oh, why didn't I don my trousers before trying this stunt?"

5

"Because you reacted without thinking again, that's why." She scolded herself just like her mother had done on too many occasions to count. Would she never learn? Sighing, she carefully bent down, reached between her legs, pulled the hem of her skirt through, and tucked it in her waistband. Holding her arms out for balance, she righted herself again.

The hour was still early, but with the mayor's house resting right on the busy corner of Bluebonnet Lane and Apple Street, she couldn't exactly stand outside his parlor window, listening to the meeting he was holding inside. If the two well-dressed strangers hadn't ridden right past the boardinghouse while she'd been sweeping the porch, she'd have never known of their arrival.

Her knock on the mayor's door for permission to listen in and to take notes had resulted in a scowl and the door being slammed in her face. Scuttlebutt was running rampant around town that Mayor Burke had some great plan to bring new businesses to Lookout. He was up to something, and she meant to be the first to find out what it was.

She slid her left foot forward. Listening through the chimney opening was her only alternative. She just hoped the men's voices would carry up that far. Sliding her right foot forward, she held her breath. Her task must be completed quickly before anyone saw her.

"Jacqueline Hamilton Davis, you come down from that roof right this minute—or I'm calling off our wedding."

Jack jumped at Billy Morgan's roar. She twisted sideways, swung her arms in the air, wobbled, and regained her balance on the peak of the house. Heart galloping, she glared down at the blond man standing in the street beside the mayor's house and swiped her hand in the air. "Go away!" she hollered in a loud whisper. If she'd told him once, she'd told him a dozen times she had no intention of marrying him.

Her foot slid toward the chimney. She had to get there right now or Billy's ruckus would surely draw a crowd, and she'd have to climb down without her story.

A high-pitched scream rent the air. "Don't fall, Sissy!"

Jack lurched the final step to the chimney and hugged the bricks. She peered down at her five-year-old sister and swatted her hand, indicating Abby needed to leave, but the stubborn girl just hiked her chin in the air. Abby was so dramatic. She'd even practiced her screams until she could blast the shrillest and loudest screeches of all her friends. Parents no longer came running when the young girls practiced their hollering. Jack shook her head. It would be a shame if any of them ever truly needed help one day and Abby screamed, because not a soul in Lookout would come to her aid.

She peered down to see if Billy was still there, and sure enough, the rascal stood in the middle of the dirt road with his hat pushed back off his forehead and his hands on his hips.

Uh-oh. Across the street, her ma carefully made her way down the front porch steps of the boardinghouse—the bulge of her pregnant belly obvious even from this distance. She shaded her eyes with her hand as she looked around, probably checking on Abby.

Jack ducked down behind the chimney. With her ma so close to her time of birthing another baby, she didn't want to cause her distress—and finding her twenty-year-old daughter on a rooftop would certainly set Ma's pulse pounding.

Movement on Main Street drew Jack's attention.

She peered over the bank's roof to the boardwalk on the far side of the street. *Oh, horse feathers!* Now her pa was heading out of the marshal's office and hurrying toward her mother. He probably thought she'd drop that baby right there in the street. Their last child, two-and-a-half-year-old Emma, had been born in a wagon on the way back from Denison, almost a month early.

She glanced down at Billy, who stood with his hands on his hips, shaking his head. Her ma was looking down Main Street now. With precious few moments before the jig was up, Jack stood on her tiptoes, concentrating on her task. She listened hard, trying to decipher the muted words drifting up the chimney. The strong scent of soot stung her nose, but all she could hear was the faint rumble of men's voices.

She glanced back at the far edge of the roof, trying to decide whether to return to the tree and shinny back down or wait until her mother and stepfather went back inside. Would Billy give her away?

Jack heaved a frustrated sigh. Even if he didn't, Abby would surely tattle. She peeked at her sister. Abby ran toward their mother, her finger pointing up at the mayor's roof. *Oh fiddlesticks.*

Why did they have to come outside before she concluded her sleuthing? And now, thanks to Billy's caterwauling, a crowd was gathering on Bluebonnet Lane.

She quickly studied the town from her vantage point. This was the perfect spot to view any events taking place in Lookout and garner the news, but it was also dangerous. How could she manage to take notes and still keep her balance? Perhaps she could talk Jenny into building a platform with a fence around it atop her newspaper office so they could view the city whenever community events were happening.

8

"Jacqueline! Oh, my heavens. What are you doing up there?" Her ma splayed her hand across her chest. Abby stood beside her, looking proud that she'd gotten her big sister in trouble.

Jack held tight to the edge of the chimney and laid her forehead against the bricks. She was as caught as a robber in a bank vault on Monday morning. She turned to head back, but her skirt snagged on the chimney bricks and pulled loose from her waistband, causing her to lose her footing. Her boot slipped, shooting her leg forward and raining wooden shakes on the people below. They squealed and scattered then gawked up at her once they were a safe distance away. Jack tightened her lips to keep from giggling. She shouldn't, she knew, but she'd never seen Bertha Boyd move so fast. That woman had to be as wide as a buckboard.

Jack's fingertips ached from clinging to the bricks, and a streak of blood pooled on her index finger from a scrape. She supposed she should admit defeat, even though the thought of it left a nasty taste in her mouth. She stared across the roof and swallowed hard. Going back wouldn't be as easy as moving forward, not with so many people watching.

The warm spring breeze blew across the rolling green hills, and she tried to hold her skirts down lest the folks below see something they shouldn't. Oh, why hadn't she worn bloomers? Or better yet, trousers?

Her foot slipped again, and she reached behind her, grasping hold of a brick jutting out of the chimney. Maybe going sideways would be easier. Facing the crowd, she balanced on the peak of the roof. She slid one foot to the left and then the other. *Just concentrate. Don't think how many people are down there. Don't think how disappointed Ma is.*

"Take it slow," Ma yelled.

Loosening her death grip on the brick, Jack slid her foot sideways. The wind lifted her skirts again, and she dropped one hand, hoping to contain them. She swayed forward and swung her free arm for balance and regained it. Had the wind been this gusty when she'd first crossed the roof?

She dared to peer down at the crowd again and saw Billy Morgan staring up with a big grin on his face.

Wonderful.

Just wonderful.

"Want me to come get you?" Without waiting for an answer, Billy strode forward until she could no longer see him.

She didn't need his help, and if he gave it, she'd never hear the end of it.

As it was, she'd never live this down. And right now, her plan didn't sound half as good as it had when she'd concocted it after the mayor slammed the door in her face. She heard a scratching noise off to her left and slowly glanced that way.

"Stay where you are, Half Bit. I'm coming out to help you."

Jack rolled her eyes, then realized the action made her dizzy. Relief that Luke had beaten Billy to the rescue made her legs weak—and that was the last thing she needed just now. "I can get down by myself, Papa. Although I sure would like it if you'd make that crowd go away."

She heard him snort and then chuckle. "Your mother is spitting mad. What in the world were you thinking?"

She slid another foot toward her stepfather. "You'll be upset if I tell you. It's probably best if you just tell her that I wasn't thinking. She'll believe that."

Luke coughed, but she thought it was more to

hide another laugh than because he had something caught in his throat. "Slide on over here—carefully. No young lady in a dress belongs on a rooftop."

"Are you saying it would have been all right if I'd worn my bloomers?" She scooted her foot another three inches and looked up to see how much farther it was to the tree. The wind tugged at her skirt as if purposely trying to make her fall.

"You know that's not what I meant. Just be careful. On second thought, I'm coming out there."

"No, I got up here, and I can get back down. Besides, these shakes are half-rotten, and I doubt they'd hold your weight."

"Take it slow and easy then. I don't want you getting hurt."

Abby let out another bloodcurdling scream as Jack glided her left foot along the peak. The sole of her shoe slipped on another loose shake and shot out from under her, the right foot following. Like a child on a sled, she slid down the roof on her shame and mortification. Luke lunged for her, stretching out his arm, but he missed. The last thing she saw before going over the side was his frantic brown eyes.

A sudden jerk jarred her whole body, and she stopped sliding. Her hips dangled over the edge of the house. She heard a tear, felt a jolt, and then she hurled toward the ground.

She flapped her arms like a winged bird but gained no altitude. Abby's scream rent the air. The ground rose up to meet her like an oncoming locomotive. Billy lunged sideways, reaching for her. They collided—her head against his chest—and landed in a pile in the street. Searing pain radiated through her leg and head.

Jack lay there for half a second before she realized she was on top of Billy. She let out a screech that

11

surpassed Abby's and rolled sideways, ignoring the pain in her leg, fighting fabric to gain her freedom. Struggling to catch her breath, she stared up. Her mother's anxious pale blue eyes blurred from two to four. "I'm all right, Ma."

Laying her aching head back against the dirt, she closed her eyes. If she wasn't dead in the morning, she could just imagine the headlines in tomorrow's newspaper: MARSHAL'S DAUGHTER ATTEMPTS TO FLY.

Noah Jeffers slowed his horse at the creek bank and lowered the reins so Rebel could get a drink. He stretched, then dismounted and walked around, working out the kinks from his long ride. He'd experienced many blessings during his month-long circuit of preaching to the small towns of northeastern Texas, but he'd be glad to be back home.

After a few moments, he led Rebel away from the water and hobbled him in a patch of shin-high grass. He removed the horse's bridle and hung it on a tree stem where a branch had broken off. He rummaged around in his saddlebags and pulled out the apple, cheese, and slice of roast beef that Mrs. Hadley had sent with him this morning when he'd left for home.

Settling under a tree, he bit off a hunk of apple and watched the creek water burble over the rocks. Shadows from the trees danced with the sunlight gleaming on the water in a soothing serenade. A rustling caught his attention across the creek, and he tensed, but then a mallard with seven ducklings waddled into view. Noah smiled, enjoying the tranquil scene. The mother led her tiny crew into the water and drifted downstream.

Peace settled over him. He finished his lunch then leaned his head against the trunk and thought about all the folks he'd met during the past month. Most had been more than friendly, offering him a bed if they had a spare and three meals a day whenever he was in a town. Yes sir, he'd eaten well—for the most part. But he missed his bed—and Pete. A yawn pulled at his mouth. He'd take a short rest then head on home—

A scream yanked him from a sweet dream, and he sat up, listening. He rubbed the sleep from his eyes. Had he just dreamed that he heard someone yell?

"Help! Somebody help me!"

Noah bolted to his feet at the child's cry and searched the trees to his left. "Where are you?"

"Over here. Help!"

He plunged through the brush alongside the creek and ducked under a tree branch. The undergrowth thinned out, and he noticed a girl no more than six or seven hopping beside the creek a short distance away. A half-dozen men's shirts and lady's blouses lay drying on bushes.

The girl saw him and ran in his direction, her untidy braids flopping against her chest. "Please, mister, my brother—" She pointed toward the creek. "I cain't swim."

Noah's heart tumbled. He saw no sign of anyone in the quiet water. Dropping to the ground, he yanked off his boots. "Where'd he go in?"

The girl's face crumpled. Tears ran down her freckled cheeks, and red ringed her blue eyes. "I don't know. He was sitting on the blanket while I was doing the wash. He must have crawled in when my back was turned."

Crawled? That means a tiny child—one who can't swim a lick. Noah plunged into the creek. It was deeper than he'd expected. The warm water hit him waist level. He bent down, running his arms back and forth as he turned in a circle. Nothing.

13

"Ma will turn me out for sure," the girl wailed from the edge of the creek. "Oh, Benny. Where are you?"

Noah ducked his head below the surface, hoping to search underwater, but his thrashing had stirred up too much mud. He moved forward several steps and hunted some more, swiping his hands through the water. His heart pounded as his dread mounted. "Help me, Lord. Where's the boy?"

He stilled for a moment and gazed over at the tattered blanket where the child had been. If he'd crawled in from that point, he'd most likely be upstream a bit. Noah quickly pulled his legs through the water then ducked down. Stretching. Reaching.

His left hand brushed something.

Fabric?

He lunged forward, snagged the cloth, and tugged. A frighteningly lightweight bundle rose up to the surface. Noah turned the limp baby over, grimacing at his blue lips.

"No!" The girl collapsed on the bank, her face in her hands. Her sobs tore at his heart.

Noah lifted the tiny boy by his feet as he once saw a father do at a church social when his young daughter had fallen into a lake. He waded toward the bank, whacking gently on the baby's small back.

On shore, Noah laid the child over his forearm and continued smacking him. "Please, Lord. Don't take this young boy. He has his whole life ahead of him."

Water gushed from the boy's mouth; then he lurched. He gagged and then retched. He clutched Noah's arm and coughed up more water. When the worst had passed, Noah turned him over. Benny's eyelids moved. He jerked, then gasped and uttered a strangled cry.

The girl jumped up and hurried to him, hope brimming from her damp eyes. "He ain't dead?"

Goosebumps charged up Noah's arm as tears moistened his eyes. The boy, no more than six months old, quieted and stared up at him with blue eyes that matched his sister's. His wet brown hair clung to his head.

"C'mere, Benny."

The boy heard his sister's voice and lunged for her, wailing again to beat all.

Noah smiled, then lifted his gaze heavenward. This was as close to a miracle as he'd ever witnessed. "Thank You, Father. Blessed be Your name."

∾

Stirred up from the day's events, Noah rode all night. The next morning, he put Rebel out to pasture then headed inside the house he shared with his mentor, Pete. He set his saddlebags across the back of a kitchen chair and glanced around the tidy room. It was good to be home again.

Pete shuffled in from the parlor. "Noah! Thought I heard someone in here, but I weren't expectin' it'd be you."

Noah hugged the older man. "I rode all night so I could get home sooner."

Pete pulled out a chair and dropped into it. "Howd'ya like being a circuit rider?"

Needing time to think on his response, Noah walked over to the stove and felt the side of the coffeepot. He pulled two mugs from a shelf, poured the dark brew, then placed one cup in front of Pete and sat down, holding the other one. "It was all right. Met a lot of nice folks."

Pete stared at him with an intense gaze. From the first day they'd met, Noah had never been able to pull the wool over the old man's eyes. "What're you not tellin' me?"

Noah's stomach clenched at the memory of

the baby in the creek, but he told the story. "Mrs. Freedman is a widow. She'd been sick and was slow to recover, which was why the girl was doing the wash and caring for the baby. She offered to let me stay the night in her barn, but I was anxious to get home." He rubbed his bristly jaw and eyed Pete, knowing his mentor would find this next piece of information humorous. "Just as I was fixin' to head out, she told her girl to give me a piglet as a thank-you for saving Benny."

The old man's lips twitched, and his eyes danced. A chuckle rose up from deep within, making Pete's shoulders bounce. "Wish I'da been there to see your face when they gave you that critter."

Noah scowled. "It's not funny. You know I can't abide pork of any kind—dead *or* alive."

"What'd'ya do with it? Turn it loose?"

He shook his head. "I might despise pigs, but I couldn't turn the thing loose and let a wolf or coyote get it." He looked into his mug and swirled the coffee. "I gave it to the next family I came across. They were mighty glad to have it."

"How many of them folks that you stayed with fixed bacon or sausage for breakfast?"

"I don't want to talk about that." But there was something he needed to discuss. "I'm not sure that I'm cut out to be a traveling preacher."

Pete sipped his coffee. "How come?"

He shrugged. "I think I'd rather be a minister in a small town where I could shepherd folks instead of just dropping a sermon and riding on, not knowing how folks are until I come around again the next month." He'd traveled from one place to another as a kid and didn't cotton to doing that again. He hadn't lived in the same place more than a couple of years until he moved in with Pete. One thing was certain: With the exception of the pork he was often offered, he had eaten plenty of

16

good home cooking on the circuit—something he and Pete often lacked.

"Well. . .that's more'n you knew last month."

Noah nodded. The older man had a way of putting things in perspective. "Yeah, I guess you're right."

Pete stared at him for a few moments, and Noah wondered what he was thinking. "Got me a letter whilst you was gone."

"Who from?"

"Thomas Taylor."

Noah stiffened, tightening his hold on his cup, remembering the man from the town he wanted only to forget. "Why would Reverend Taylor write to you?"

"So you know him, huh?"

Noah nodded. Was Thomas Taylor still the minister in Lookout, or had he moved on? Was *she* still there?

"We've writ to each other for years. Thomas used to be a student of mine."

Noah stood so fast that the chair fell back and banged against the floor. He picked it up and pushed it under the table. "How come you never told me about that?"

Pete shrugged one shoulder. "Didn't see how it mattered."

He gripped the back of the chair until his knuckles turned white. "It matters."

His mentor shook his head. "What happened in Lookout is over and done with. You've gotta let go of the past, son. It'll eat a hole in your belly and ruin your future."

"I've tried. Nothing I do washes that town from my mind."

"Just what was it that the town did to you?" Pete scratched his temple. "I don't recollect you ever sayin' much about it."

Noah stared out the window. Of all the places he had lived, Lookout was the one that had left the worst taste in his mouth. It was the one place he'd never talk about much to Pete. He didn't understand himself why the memories of that town bothered him so much, so how could he explain it to his friend?

"Well, anyhow. Thomas is takin' a leave of absence. His wife's ma is doin' poorly, and they're traveling over to Fort Worth to tend her. He didn't know how long he'd be gone, so he asked me to take his place."

Watching Rebel roll on his back in the grass of the pasture, Noah thought how lonely this place would be without Pete. And he'd have to eat his own cooking again. "You gonna do it?"

Pete didn't respond, and when Noah heard the chair creak, he turned from the window. His friend stood with his hands on the back of the chair, staring at the table. Generally, that meant Pete was sorting something out in his head. Noah waited.

"Actually. . ." The old man looked up, his expression unreadable. "I prayed 'bout it and feel you're the one who's s'posed to go."

"Me! You can't be serious." Noah thought up a hundred reasons why he couldn't go. At twenty-three, he was far too young and inexperienced to pastor a church, as much as he might desire to. And he wasn't married. Nor had he been to seminary. The only credentials he had was the knowledge he'd gained from Pete's years of teaching him the Bible, a mail-order certificate he'd received after completing a series of lessons on the scriptures, and years of hard living before he came to Christ.

"Serious as a prairie wildfire durin' a drought."

Noah ran his hand through his hair, remembering all the things that had happened in Lookout. "I can't do it." He couldn't go back there. Not when so many memories of the place still haunted his dreams. "I won't."

Pete harrumphed. "You just said you'd prefer to shepherd a flock in a town rather than ridin' a circuit. Well, here's your chance to do that."

"No fair using my own words against me."

"All I'm asking you t'do is pray about it. Will you do that?"

Noah stared at the scratched wooden floor and heaved a sigh. The old man didn't know the meaning of playing fair.

Chapter 2

Jack lay on her side, squinting out the window—directly at the mayor's house. The bright light caused an ache deep in her head, but it wasn't as bad now as it had been when she'd first fallen. Closing her eyes, she willed her blurry vision away. She'd been in bed for three days now, and neither the doctor nor her mother would let her get up. Sweat dampened her cheek where it lay against her arm. If she didn't get out of this room soon, she'd go plumb loco.

Yesterday, between headaches, she'd spent the afternoon trying to think of a story angle, even though she hadn't heard a peep up on the mayor's roof. What could he be planning? Mayor Burke wanted Lookout to grow, despite the fact many of the town's residents preferred to keep it small. She exhaled a sigh. She needed to get out of this bed.

Looking around the bedroom she shared with her two sisters, she pretended it was all hers. The pale floral wallpaper that the bedroom had been decorated in when she first moved in after Shannon O'Neil had married ten years ago had been stripped off and painted a soft green. Floral curtains had replaced the spring green ones, reminding her of a flower garden. But that had been many years ago, and now the room needed to be redone. Perhaps she'd talk to her ma about painting it lavender, even though the room had always been called "the green room."

"Ugh!" She smacked the mattress. How could she be so bored that she was actually redoing her room?

She heard a noise, and then the bed creaked and the mattress tilted. A small body crashed into her back, sending sharp pain spiraling down her leg. Jack sucked in a breath. Her younger sister's giggles softened the throbbing ache. Jack rolled over on her back, wincing at the stabbing in her head. "What are you doing in here, Emmie?"

The sweet urchin patted Jack's stomach. "No no, sleep. The sun camed up."

Jack stroked Emma's wispy blond hair. "I'm sick—sort of."

Emma scowled, her little brows dipping. She turned and reached toward Jack's injured knee, which the doctor had wrapped in a bandage. Emma patted it. "Sissy gots a owee."

Jack's mother rushed in the door—as much as she rushed these days—relief evident when she spotted Emma. "What are you doing upstairs, young lady?"

Emma fell back against Jack's arm. "Me sick."

Her ma bit back a smile and crossed the room. She felt Emma's head. "Oh my, if you're so sick, I guess I should put you in your own bed."

Emma elbowed Jack's chest and shot upward to sit. "Me all better now."

Jack grinned at her ma. "Me better now, too."

Her mother shook her head and smiled, her light blue eyes twinkling. "What am I going to do with you two?"

Emma stood and bounced on the bed. Gritting her teeth, Jack turned her head so her mother wouldn't see her pain.

"That's enough, Miss Emma." Ma picked up her youngest daughter and set her on the floor. "Let's go back downstairs." She patted Jack's hip. "Do you need anything?"

"I'd like to go downstairs. I'm going batty being unable to move or see anyone."

Her mother pressed her hand against her rounded stomach. "You know I can't help you down, and Luke's not home right now. Besides, the doctor said to stay abed for a week."

Emma grabbed Abby's doll off her bed and hugged it.

Jack placed her arms behind her head and sighed. "I know, but I'm bored to death up here. I need something to do."

"Oh, that reminds me. I brought you something." A smile twittered on Ma's lips. She reached into her apron, pulled out a newspaper, then crossed her arms. "Now that you're feeling better, would you mind explaining why you haven't told me you were getting married?"

"What?" Confusion clouded her thoughts as she grasped for a memory of a wedding proposal. "I'm not getting married. What are you talking about?"

"Hmm. . .must be that head wound causing you to forget." Ma tossed the paper on the bed. "By the way, the new minister is arriving sometime today. I've got to get the pies out of the oven and then see to his room."

"Me get pie!" Emma shot out of the room, leaving the forgotten doll on the floor.

"Oh, no you don't, little missy. Don't you touch that stove." With a fist pressed into the small of her back, Ma trudged out the door, leaving Jack in silence again.

She scooted up in the bed, trying to ignore the pain in every part of her body, and unfolded the newspaper. Her heart jolted, just as it had when she'd slid off the mayor's roof. The skin on her face tightened, and the blood drained from her face as she read the headline: BILLY MORGAN SAVES FIANCÉE'S LIFE.

Jack's mouth went dry, and the words on the paper blurred as her hands started trembling. "No!"

The whole town would think she was marrying Billy Morgan.

Not in a thousand years.

Not if he were the only man in Texas.

She laid her head back and closed her eyes. This was the worst thing to happen to her since Butch Laird painted *Jack is a liar* all over the town's buildings, ten years ago.

"How will I ever live this down?"

She heard Abby giggle and clomp up the stairs just before she entered the room with Tessa Morgan and Penny Dempsey. Abby leaned against the doorframe. "You got guests, Sissy."

Tessa trounced in, a smile twittering on her lips. "You're marrying my brother? When were you planning on telling me? You know that means we'll be sisters, Jacqueline."

Tessa twisted back and forth, obviously proud of herself. For years she had tried to get Jack to see Billy's virtues, but as far as Jack was concerned, he didn't have a single one. The only reason he turned her head at all was because of his handsome looks, with that white blond hair and those deep blue eyes. But good looks alone weren't nearly enough to persuade her to marry him. She knew too much about him. Had seen his ornery side too many times.

Penny glanced at Tessa, then sent a sympathetic look at Jack. "Congratulations. . .I guess."

"Penny!" Tessa whacked her friend on the arm. "You sound as if you're sad. I think it's perfectly wonderful that Jacqueline is marrying Billy."

23

Jack groaned and bounced her head against the wall, stopping when a fist of pain clutched her head. She gazed at her sister, still lingering at the door, then lifted her finger. "Out, Abby."

The child swung back and forth, her blue skirts swaying like a bell. "It's my room, too."

"Yes, but I have friends visiting, and I'm stuck in bed, so we have to stay in here. Please go downstairs."

Abby stared at her for a moment, then noticed her doll on the floor. "Oh, Nellie. Did you fall out of bed like Sissy fell off that roof?" She rushed over, picked up Nellie, and hugged her.

"I didn't fall." Jack realized the ridiculousness of that statement the moment it left her mouth. "I just... uh...slipped."

Abby's eyes glimmered, and Jack knew she hadn't fooled her five-year-old sister. Abby stuck out her tongue at Jack and flounced out the door.

Tessa shuddered and dropped onto Abby's bed. "For heaven's sake. I'm so glad I don't have any little brothers or sisters. They can be such a pain in the neck."

Jack twisted her lips to one side, knowing that's probably exactly what Billy thought of Tessa. Her own siblings irritated her at times, but she loved them fiercely and would protect them for all she was worth. Tessa also annoyed her on many occasions, but she and Penny were her best friends, the only women her age in town. Tessa would be disappointed, but Jack had to set the record straight. "I am *not* marrying Billy."

Tessa's surprised gaze darted to her. "But—but, the paper says you are."

It was Jack's turn to smirk. "You can't believe everything you read in the newspaper." While she tried hard to be accurate in the stories she wrote, she knew the paper's editor, Jenny Evans, sometimes stretched the truth to make the news more interesting and to sell more papers.

"Billy will be heartbroken. You know he's in love with you." Tessa's bottom lip pushed out in a pout that didn't look good on a grown woman. She tossed her curls over her shoulder. "I don't know why you don't like him. He's comely, isn't he, Penny?"

Penny was wise enough not to step in that quagmire, Jack was certain. Her friend's eyes lit up unexpectedly. "I'll tell you who's truly handsome."

"Who?" Jack hated that she leaned forward the same as Tessa.

"The new reverend."

Tessa gasped. "You haven't seen him. Why, he isn't even in town yet. Besides, what's so interesting about an old minister?"

"Did too. I saw him get off the stage and walk over to the Taylors' house just before you came out of the store. He's so tall." Her dreamy gaze sparkled, and she touched Jack's arm. "He's even taller than your stepfather. And he certainly isn't old."

Luke was a good six feet two and the tallest man in town with the exception of Dan Howard. "What color is his hair?" Jack asked.

Penny shrugged. "I don't know. He was wearing a hat. Dark brown. Maybe black. But I can tell you one thing: he's young—and he was alone."

Tessa perked up. "Just because he was alone doesn't mean he's not married. Was he wearing a ring?"

Penny shook her head. "No." Her cheeks turned as pink as the tiny flowers on her gray dress. "At least I didn't notice one."

Tessa leaned forward, blue eyes blazing. "You looked, didn't you?"

Her words were an accusation, not a question, Jack noticed.

"So what if I did?" Penny hiked her chin. "It's not like there are many marriageable men our age in this dumpy town." Penny leaned against the wall and studied her fingernails. "If it weren't for you two, I'd go crazy. Half the time I wish we'd never moved here."

"Well, if Jacqueline doesn't want Billy, you can have him. One of you has to marry him. I don't want anyone else for a sister-in-law."

Jack glanced at Penny and noticed her friend's shudder. Penny wanted to marry Billy as little as she. Billy rarely helped his ma at the mercantile. He merely wanted to have fun. Only Tessa was blind to her brother's lack of motivation where work was concerned, probably because she hated laboring just as much.

"I'm telling you both right now: I claim first rights on the reverend. I think I'd make the perfect minister's wife." Tessa fluffed her skirt and twirled back and forth, then lifted her brows when neither woman commented.

Jack worked hard to keep a straight face. Tessa was the most spoiled person she knew. She couldn't imagine her lowering herself to tend the sick or take food to the poor like a minister's wife would surely do. She just about had her amusement under control when a completely unladylike noise erupted from Penny. Tessa glared at her, and Jack's giggle worked its way out.

"Really, Penny, you sound like a retching donkey." Tessa tossed her curls over her shoulder again and scowled as she looked at Jack. "You're laughing, too? Just what's so funny?"

After being cooped up for days with nothing to amuse her, Jack couldn't help letting her laughter break forth. Her head ached, but it was worth it. "Oh, Tessa, you'd be miserable as a pastor's wife. You know they don't make much money and have to serve the whole community. How would you get by without all your fripperies?"

"Well! I can see what you two think of me. I'm not nearly as shallow as you think." Tessa spun around and stalked out the door, stopping in the hall to glare at them. "Some friends you two turned out to be." She stomped off down the stairs.

Penny shook her head and wiped her eyes. "I didn't mean to hurt Tessa's feelings, but I couldn't keep from laughing. She's the last person I could ever see as a minister's wife."

Jack felt bad, even though she couldn't rid her mind of the humorous picture of pampered Tessa serving beside the pastor. "I know. The thought is beyond absurd, but I do feel bad for hurting her feelings."

A loud knock sounded downstairs. With her bed next to the window at the front of the house, Jack knew whenever a visitor arrived. She recognized the squeak of the front door that her ma had been hounding Luke to grease, and the word *reverend* drifted up.

He was here!

She hadn't thought about it earlier, but why wouldn't he be staying at the parsonage? And until Penny had mentioned him being young, she hadn't thought much about the man's arrival.

A sharp screech echoed from the hall, footsteps pounded up the stairs, and Tessa flew back into the room. "He's here! Right in your entryway."

"How do you know it's him?" Penny asked, her eyes dancing.

"Because he's the tallest man I've ever seen, and he's young, and he has black hair."

Penny nodded. "That does sound like him." She

tiptoed to the door and looked out. "Did he see you galloping up the stairs?"

"I did not gallop, and no, he didn't see me. At least I don't think he did." Tessa skirted Penny, standing just outside the door. Jack wished she could get up and sneak a peek.

"Why do you suppose he stopped at the boardinghouse?" Penny asked.

Tessa glanced over her shoulder and lifted her index finger to her lips. "Shh! I can't hear," she whispered loudly.

Jack crossed her arms and scowled at Tessa's back. Penny suddenly sucked in a breath and backed up. Tessa let out an "eek!" and scurried back to Jack's bedside.

"They're coming upstairs." Penny pinched her cheeks, turning them a rosy red. "Maybe your ma asked him to pray for you."

"Actually, he's staying here." Jack's insides twisted as she glanced down at the pale blue bed jacket covering her nightgown. She pushed herself up straighter. "He can't see me like this. Quick, close the door."

Tessa scorched her with a narrow-eyed glare. "He's staying *here*?" She frowned and ambled across the room, seemingly in no hurry. Jack flipped the sheet over her legs and pulled it all the way up to her neck.

She heard her mother's voice as she came up the stairs. Three heads jerked toward the doorway.

"Hurry, Tessa!" Jack's heart pounded, as if something monumental was about to happen, but what was so special about meeting a new pastor? She didn't want a new one. She liked Reverend Taylor's thought-provoking messages, and his wife was one of the kindest women she knew.

"This is our second story." Her ma's voice drifted into the bedroom. "Our children have rooms on this floor, and if we have any women boarding with us, they reside here. There's a third story where you'll be staying, as well as any other men who arrive."

Tessa gave the door a half-hearted push, then spun around, walking back to the bed. "You're such a lucky dog. I'd be jealous if you hadn't said you don't plan to marry."

Ever so slowly, the door drifted open. Jack saw the back of her mother's dress. The door drifted back toward the wall and made a soft thud. Jack's heart pummeled her chest. All three women seemed to hold their breath in unison.

A surprisingly tall man with black hair glanced in as he passed the entrance to the room. He held his hat in one hand and a satchel in the other. His dark brows lifted as he noticed the trio of females staring at him. His eyes widened for a second, then he yanked his gaze away. Suddenly, it flew back to Jack, setting her heart pounding as if she'd run a long race. His steps slowed, and for the briefest of moments, she felt as if they alone were connected. She swallowed hard.

A tiny smile lifted the corners of his lips; then he jerked his head forward again and strode out of sight.

Penny glided over to Abby's bed and dropped down. "Oh my. He's so handsome."

Tessa flopped down and bumped Penny's shoulder. "Heavens to Betsy, I think I'm in love."

"Get in line." Penny stared at the door as if she could conjure up the man again.

Shaking her head, Tessa frowned. "I already claimed him for myself."

Penny gazed at Jack with a knowing look. Heat raced to Jack's cheeks, and she broke her friend's gaze. Had Penny noticed the way the man stared at

29

her? Downright scandalous behavior for a minister, if someone asked for her opinion.

Jack laid her head back, feeling exhausted but also exhilarated. Irritated but intrigued. Why should one look from a handsome man set her heart to throbbing? Perhaps she'd simply had too much excitement today.

On second thought, the investigator in her went on alert. She had the oddest feeling that she'd seen the man before.

Tessa preened again. "Did you see how he had to take a second glance at me?"

Penny's gaze shot across the room to Jack's. "Yes, he couldn't take his eyes off of you."

Heat scorched Jack's cheeks, irritating her even more. She never blushed.

"I don't suppose you'll be able to attend the social this Saturday, what with your leg hurt and all," Tessa said. "I'll make sure to greet the new minister and welcome him to Lookout. Who would have thought he'd be our age?"

"I don't think he's our age. He looks a bit older—in his mid-twenties maybe, and I'm not going if you aren't, Jack." Penny smiled at her. "In fact, I'll come and keep you company since you'll probably be all alone if your family goes."

"Ma will stay home, and Papa will stay with her unless there's some kind of problem in town. Besides, I should be able to leave my bed by then."

"But you won't be able to leave the house yet." Tessa stood, straightened her skirt, and flounced to the door. "I'm going to the dressmaker's shop. I'll need something extra special to attract that man."

After Tessa left, Penny shook her head and giggled. "I declare, that girl and her high ideas. If she was the parson's wife—well, I can't even imagine that."

Jack grinned. "Tessa is one of a kind, that's for

certain. But she's a good friend."

Penny lifted her brows. "Hmm. . .I saw the way that man looked at you. He didn't even notice Tessa and me. He must like redheads."

Jack squealed and tossed a pillow at her friend. Penny dodged it, giggling. "I do not have red hair. It's auburn."

"Don't matter what color it is—that minister couldn't take his eyes off you."

Jack fingered the edge of the sheet, remembering how she used to cower in the corner whenever her first father went on a drunken rampage. She never wanted to feel afraid like that again. "It doesn't matter. I'm not interested in gaining a man's attention. I don't ever plan to marry."

Penny gasped and hugged the pillow. "Stop saying that. One of these days, you'll meet some man who'll sweep you off your feet, and you'll regret those words. I don't know why you feel that way, anyhow."

"Nope, I won't." Jack shook her head. "You don't know how things were when I was little and my first pa was alive. He was just plain mean and a liar to boot."

Penny crossed the room and placed the pillow behind Jack. She rested her hand on Jack's shoulder. "I'm sorry you had to live through that, but my pa was the kindest man on earth, just like Luke is. You've lived with a good man for a pa for a long while. You need to bury your past, so that it doesn't affect your future."

Jack crossed her arms and stared at the dust motes floating on a ray of sunshine that had crept into her room. How could anyone who hadn't lived through what she had empathize with her deep-set fear? Not even having a kindhearted stepfather had driven it totally away. She was afraid to believe it was possible to have a marriage like her ma and Luke had. What if the dream never came true? "You don't understand."

Penny smiled gently. "I know, but I'm praying that God will help you. I'd better head home. Mama will be wanting my help with the chores."

Jack watched her friend leave. Penny was sweet, but she didn't understand the scars an abusive father could leave on a child.

She laid her head back, thinking of the handsome pastor. He was young. And why had he stared at her? Had her ma told him about her injury, making him curious?

The investigator in her sensed there was more to him than one glance could take in. But one thing was for certain: If Tessa wanted him, she could have him.

Jack had no desire to chase after a man. As long as she never married, a man couldn't hurt her.

Chapter 3

Noah followed Mrs. Davis into the tidy room.

"I hope you'll be. . .comfortable here, Reverend. . . Jeffers." Her chest rose and fell as she struggled to catch her breath. Leaning against the door, she supported her large stomach with one hand while the other was splayed across her chest. She looked as if she could give birth any moment.

Noah felt a warm flush creep up his neck at the thought. "Would you care to sit down for a moment?"

"No, but thank you. Those stairs get steeper every day." She smiled and glanced away as if embarrassed to hint at her condition. "My eldest daughter has been tending these rooms lately, but her injury has her in bed all week. My husband and I are delighted to have you staying with us."

"This is far more than I expected, Mrs. Davis." His gaze scanned the two-room suite. The walls were painted a light blue, and white curtains with small navy flowers fluttered at the open window. A dark blue sofa rested along one wall, with a nice-sized walnut desk against another, and a table with two chairs beside the third wall. He could see one corner of a bed covered with a colorful quilt through the doorway of the other room. "I'm not sure I've ever stayed anywhere this fine, ma'am."

Mrs. Davis beamed. She'd aged some in the years

he'd been gone from town, but she was still a pretty woman. "I'm glad you like it. I serve breakfast at seven, dinner at noon, and supper at six. Be sure to let me know if you have an aversion to any particular foods and if you get hungry and would like a snack. I like to satisfy my guests."

He smiled and set his satchel on the sofa. "Do you need help getting downstairs, ma'am?"

She swiveled her hand in the air, then laid it on her chest again. "Thank you, but I hobble up and down these steps all day. I do need to get back downstairs, though. I don't dare leave my son, Alan, watching his sisters for long. That's a recipe for disaster."

She ambled out the door, and he followed. "Might I ask a question before you go?"

She stopped and nodded, her pale blue eyes kind but assessing.

He needed to think how to word things without letting her know just how much he knew about her family. His heart hammered in his chest. He hated deception, but he wasn't yet ready to reveal his true identity. He'd recognized Jacqueline the moment his eyes had connected with hers. She was no longer the ornery child he remembered, but a beautiful young lady who'd sent his pulse soaring. He prayed nothing was seriously wrong with her. "I. . .uh. . .happened to notice a woman in her bed on the second floor when the door blew open as I was passing." He warmed his face to admit he'd looked in the room, but he hadn't expected anyone to be in there, much less three young women. "I'm assuming that was your. . .uh. . .daughter. Could I inquire if her injury was serious?"

"Yes, you may." Mrs. Davis nodded, but her gaze held a gentle scolding. "That's my oldest daughter, Jacqueline. She fell off—" A rosy hue colored her cheeks, and she looked away for a moment. "I suppose

I should just tell you, because you're sure to hear from someone else—or read about it in the newspaper. My eldest daughter is. . .umm. . .rather. . .lively. She's a reporter for our town newspaper, and for some reason, she was on a rooftop, trying to get a story, when she fell off." She rushed out the words as if they were difficult for her to admit.

Noah's stomach tightened. Jack could have easily broken her neck. "Is she all right?"

"She will be. She has a concussion, a twisted ankle, and she wrenched her knee. I daresay it won't slow her down for long. I fear my Abby is going to be just like her."

"I'll pray for her swift recovery." And to gain some common sense—although the Jack he knew rarely exercised that particular character trait. She was ruled by her heart, by impulse, more than her head.

"Thank you." She moseyed toward the stairs, then turned back. "I forgot to tell you, but the washroom is that door at the end of the hall. We recently installed indoor plumbing." She smiled, as if proud of that fact. "Please let me know if you need anything."

He nodded, relieved that she hadn't recognized him. "I will. Thanks." He watched her carefully make her way downstairs; then he strode back into his room and shut the door. The grin he'd been holding back broke loose. Jack had been on a roof. It sounded as if she hadn't changed all that much. He shook his head, but inside, he was delighted that she hadn't lost her spunk.

Noah crossed to the bedroom and looked around. This place was nice. Even better than Pete's cabin. He dropped onto the bed and laid back with his hands behind his head, remembering how Jack had stared into his eyes earlier. Had she recognized him as one of her old schoolmates?

No. There'd been curiosity in her gaze but not recognition. Besides, he was no longer the chubby youth he'd been when he lived in Lookout. He heaved a sigh. How was he going to face her every day at every meal? Pastor Taylor had offered him the use of the parsonage while they were gone, and that's where he had expected to stay, but the mayor thought he'd be more comfortable at the boardinghouse with his meals prepared each day.

Mayor Burke had no idea how difficult it would be. If Noah had known he'd be staying here, he just might not have come.

He stared up at the ceiling. No, that wasn't true. God had made it clear that Lookout was where He wanted him.

He rolled onto his side and heaved a heavy breath. Lookout, Texas, was the last place he'd ever expected to be again. Nothing good had ever happened to him here.

∽

Jack hobbled around her room, testing out the crutches Luke had borrowed from the doctor. They pinched her underarms, even through the fabric of her dress, but they meant mobility and a chance to leave her room. Luke leaned against the doorframe, watching her. A hammering resonated in her head like Dan Howard pounding a horseshoe on his anvil, but she shoved away the pain. If Luke knew about it, she'd be back in bed before she could bat an eyelash.

She forced a smile. "Well, what do you think?"

Luke grunted and watched her. "I think you should still be in bed, but I doubt you want to hear that."

She grinned at his candidness. "Oh, c'mon, Papa. I'm going loco stuck in this room."

"I kind of thought you might like hiding up here."

She frowned. "Why?"

"Oh, I don't know. Maybe because you and Billy Morgan are headlining the newspaper this week."

Her mouth suddenly went dry. "It's all a horrible mistake."

"You're saying you're not marrying him?"

She gasped. "Eww! No! You should know I'd never marry that hooligan. He reminds me too much of Butch Laird, and well, you know how I feel about him."

"You don't know how glad I am to hear that, Half Bit. I was worried you'd taken leave of your senses." Luke forked his fingers through his hair and blew out a loud breath. "Morgan isn't the kind of man I want you associating with, much less marrying, even if his sister is one of your good friends."

"Have no fear. Jenny took advantage of something Billy said when I was on that roof, but there's no backbone to it. He never actually asked me to marry him, and I would never agree if he did. I don't care what Tessa says about him."

Luke relaxed. "Good. God has a special man out there for you. It's worth waiting until he comes along."

Jack snorted a laugh. "I'll probably be an old spinster by then."

"I didn't realize you were in a hurry to wed."

"I'm not, really. I just see how happy you and Ma are, and part of me hopes I can find that for myself. But the other part fears getting close to a man. What if he turns out like my first father?"

Luke pursed his lips and glanced at the ceiling. "There are good men and bad in this world; you know that. Trust God to bring you the man He has for you when the time is right. And pray about it."

"I will, but don't think this talk of marriage is

going to make me forget what I really want to know. Will you talk Ma into letting me come down for supper?"

He narrowed his eyes. "Are you sure you're not just wanting to eat downstairs because the new minister will be there?"

All manner of thoughts dashed through her mind. The memory of that brief connection she felt when their gazes had locked buzzed in her mind. He was so tall and good looking. So young. She'd expected an older man to replace Reverend Taylor, not someone just a few years older than she. How could he have enough life experience to be a decent pastor?

Luke's brows lifted when she didn't respond to his questions. A knowing smirk twisted his lips.

She leaned heavily on her crutches, her knee ranting at her for being on her feet, and lifted a hand. "It's not what you're thinking. Tessa has already claimed him, and Penny is besotted, although I don't see how they both can have the same man. We might have to have another bride contest." She grinned, hoping the reminder of Luke's mail-order bride fiasco before he married her mother would lighten him up.

"Now who's changing the subject?" Luke's penetrating brown eyes stared into hers. He pushed away from the door and crossed his arms over his chest. "I was a soldier for a decade, and I've been a marshal and your stepfather for another ten years. You can't pull the wool over my eyes. What are you up to, Half Bit?"

She resisted the urge to squirm and instead focused her attention on backing up and sitting down. Her leg was beginning to throb. There was no point in trying to fool her perceptive pa. She exhaled loudly. "Jenny Evans came to visit this afternoon. She knows I'm chafing at the bit to get back to work and suggested that I do a story on the new minister, being as how he's staying here and all."

Luke lifted his chin, and she knew then he believed her. "That's not a half-bad idea, just so long as you don't push yourself too hard. A concussion is something to take seriously, not to mention your knee injury. With all the antics you've pulled over the years, I can't believe you've never broken a bone." He shook his head. "And I hope you learned your lesson." His chin went down again as he stared at her. "No more rooftops."

"I've already decided that. I know what I did was stupid, but I was desperate, and it was the only way I could think to listen in on the mayor's meeting."

"And why was that so important? All he and the town leaders ever talk about from what I hear is town stuff."

Jack shrugged. "Jenny seemed to think Mayor Burke is up to something. Besides, he was talking to two well-dressed strangers, not the town board."

Luke leaned back against the wall. "I saw those men and wondered why they weren't staying at the boardinghouse. I know Burke's been trying to bring more businesses to town, but that's no secret."

"Jenny said something about a gambling hall."

"Has she got evidence?" Luke straightened. "That's not anything we want in Lookout. It's bad enough having the saloon. Maybe I need to have a talk with Mayor Burke."

Jack toyed with the crutch's wooden handrest. "No evidence that I know of, but there is something else. Jenny's received unofficial word that the railroad may be adding a spur out this way."

Luke's countenance brightened. "That's great news. Sure would cut down on my being away when I have a prisoner to take to Dallas. I'm surprised I haven't heard anything about that."

"It's in the very early stages of development—if it's true at all. I was hoping the mayor would mention something about that in his meeting."

"Ah, now I understand why you'd risk your neck. That would be some story if you could get proof and be the first to write about it."

Jack nodded. "Yeah, but I don't guess that's going to happen with me laid up like I am."

Luke crossed the room and took the crutches from her. "Well, don't be so down in the dumps. This week of bed rest will be over before you know it. And I'll talk to your ma and see if she'll let you come to dinner tonight, since it's our first family meal with the new minister. If she agrees, I can carry you downstairs."

"I'd appreciate that, Papa." She nibbled her lower lip, not wanting to voice her other thought. Still, if Luke hadn't thought of it yet, he soon would. "What will happen to Garrett's business if the railroad comes here? I mean, he can still deliver freight from the depot out to area ranches, but it seems it would cut his business sharply since he would no longer be needed to pick up deliveries in Dallas. It would be much quicker for them to come by train."

"Hmm, I hadn't thought of that. I'll talk to him about that. He's been thinking of making some changes anyway. Might be a good time."

Jack leaned forward. "What kind of changes?"

"Ah, no you don't." Luke grinned and tweaked the end of her nose. "I'm not one of those ogling, loose-lipped sources you can bat your long lashes at and get to spill the beans. If and when Garrett decides to make a change, you'll find out like everyone else."

She lifted her wrapped leg onto the bed, scooted up against her pillows, and faked a glare. "No fair.

Why'd you say anything if you weren't going to tell all? You know how curious I am."

"That I do." He placed the crutches in the corner behind the door. "Maybe hiding those there will keep your sisters from messing with them."

"I doubt it."

Luke chuckled. "Me, too. I'd better get back to work. See you later."

"Don't forget to talk to Ma about supper."

Luke waved. "I won't."

She leaned her head back and closed her eyes. Having Luke become her papa was one of the best things that had ever happened to her. He was easier to talk to at times than her ma, who worried too much.

Shifting her thoughts to the minister, she wondered what his name was. A man that large had to have a strong name like Sam or Duke, but then Duke hardly sounded like a pastor's name. Max would have been perfect, but that had been the name of her and Luke's dog. The old mutt had been dead more than two years, and she still missed him.

On second thought, she hoped that wasn't the preacher's name. He'd have to be very special to deserve the same name as her beloved dog.

∽

Fragrant aromas emanating from the kitchen two stories below his room pulled Noah away from his studies. His stomach growled, reminding him that he hadn't eaten since breakfast. He stood and stretched then strode to the bedroom window that gave him a bird's-eye view of Main Street.

Lookout had certainly grown since he was last here. The town had been shaped like a capital E before, but now it spread out almost clear to the Addams River. If he had to guess, his best estimate was that it had tripled in size. Pretty unusual for a town so far away from the nearest train depot. But folks in Texas tended to congregate wherever the water was, and Lookout had the river on two sides.

Feminine squeals burst into his thoughts, and he glanced down, his gaze landing on the porch roof. Jack's room was directly below his. He could hear high-pitched laughter emanating from her open window and wondered what she and her friends found so amusing. He didn't like the thought of her hobbled to a bed. She was like a butterfly that needed to be free—free to flit from flower to flower, brightening the world with her beauty.

"Mercy!" He sounded like a poet or something. He'd best stay focused and remember that Jack had done her fair share to get him in trouble more than once. He'd tried to be her friend, but as a young girl, she'd lied, connived, and partnered with those two male friends of hers to pull tricks on him. He ran his hand through his hair and paced into the parlor. Hadn't he given all those bad memories to God? Hadn't he forgiven Jack?

If just the briefest glance had him warring with his thoughts again, what would happen if he ever talked to her? How could he minister to the townsfolk when half his thoughts centered on Jack?

He'd never been clear about what he felt when she was near. He'd longed to be her friend more than once, but he'd hated her, too. Her lies had gotten him in trouble, both with the marshal and with his own pa.

But maybe she'd changed.

He certainly hoped so. Back in the bedroom, he knelt down and rested his head against the quilt. It smelled clean and fresh—of sunshine. Had Jack made the bed with her own hands?

"Ugh! Help me, Father. My job is to minister to this town. To make up for my past offenses here by making retribution for what I did before I knew You. Help me, Lord, to stay focused and to treat Jacqueline Hamil— uh—Davis like any other woman I encounter."

But she wasn't like any other he'd ever known— and that was the problem.

She intrigued him. Riled him. Made him want to throttle her—kiss her.

He bolted to his feet and ran his hand through his hair. "I can't do this."

Bending, he yanked his satchel out from under the bed and opened it. He hurried to the dresser and snatched up his undergarments and tossed them at the bag. Then he caught his reflection in the mirror above the chest of drawers.

He stared at himself. No longer was he the beaten-down son of a cruel drunkard. He was the son of a King. The King.

What kind of man was he if he couldn't handle one feisty redhead?

Heaving a sigh from deep within, he gathered his things and shoved them back in the drawer. Pete was counting on him. So was Pastor Taylor and the town of Lookout. Maybe even Jack needed him.

No—he couldn't think that. He'd focus on the town. Not everyone here knew God. Folks needed to hear the Bible—needed to hear about God's love. He closed his eyes, determination overcoming his doubts. He'd studied years for this moment, and Pete thought he was ready. He *was* ready.

He tucked in his shirt, then combed his hair and headed downstairs. He wouldn't let his eyes stray as he passed her room. Hadn't Mrs. Davis said Jack would be in bed a week? At least he'd have several days more than he'd first expected to get used to seeing her regularly. By the end of the week, he'd be ready to face her.

He had to be.

Chapter 4

Dallas

Carly Payton dabbed her eyes with her handkerchief, then blew her nose and shoved the fabric square back into her pocket. She washed her hands and returned to her task. Her heart ached today as much as it had that first day she'd been locked up in the Lookout jail for bank robbery. She missed Tillie. She thought back to the funeral Reverend Barker had spoken at only an hour ago. Shaking her head, she placed cookies one by one onto Tillie's favorite platter. A man shouldn't have to preach his wife's funeral, especially a man who'd been married to that woman for fifty-two years.

Now it would be her job to care for the elderly pastor and to offer words of comfort to him as he and Tillie had when she'd first come to live with the Barkers. Carly walked down the hall, carrying the platter in Tillie's stead and trying to keep it from shaking. A number of people from the church had come to offer their condolences to Reverend Barker, but she never knew how they'd treat her. Few had accepted her like the Barkers. Not even the "good" church people. Tillie had said to give them time, but she'd waited four years and still didn't feel a part of the small community church. At the sound of raised voices coming from the parlor, she quickened her steps. Why would anyone be arguing with the pastor today?

She forced a smile as she strode into the room.

Every head swiveled toward her, but instead of finding a welcoming smile, she encountered six pairs of glaring eyes. An uncomfortable silence reigned. All that remained of the earlier crowd was the church's three elders and their wives. Mrs. Harding, wife of the head elder, stared down her long, pointed nose at her. Swallowing hard, Carly ducked her head, skirted around the two men standing in the parlor's entrance, and set the platter on the coffee table. She checked the coffeepot and hurried out of the room, finally exhaling the breath she'd been holding.

"It's not proper for that woman to live here, I tell you," a female voice spat.

Carly halted just outside the parlor door. Were they talking about *her*?

"I have to agree with Gertie, Bennett." Carly recognized Mr. Harding's voice. "I tolerated you letting that ex-convict live in your home when your wife was alive, just because Tillie needed the help, but with her gone now, you need to get rid of that jailbird."

Carly clutched the doorframe to the kitchen. They wanted Reverend Barker to turn her out? How could they broach such a topic on the day Reverend Barker buried his wife? Who would take care of him? Who would fix his coffee just how he liked it with a spoonful of sugar and two mere droplets of milk?

Tears stung her eyes, and her throat clogged. "Please, Lord. No."

She slipped back into the kitchen, where she and Tillie had spent so many wonderful hours together, baking and talking about God and the scriptures. For four years she'd lived in the Barkers' home, after finally leaving the prison she'd been locked away in for six long years. Carly pulled out a chair and slumped into it. Her heart felt as if it had been dragged behind a runaway horse. Foolishly, somewhere along the line, she'd come to think of this place as home. After all, she'd lived here longer than she had any other place—except prison—and she could hardly call that horrid place home.

How could she have let her guard down? Other than coming to know God and living with the Barkers, nothing good had ever happened in her life. She was stupid to have hoped life would continue on as it had when she knew Tillie was so ill. Lifting her head off her arm, she looked around the cheery kitchen. She should have been better prepared for this day.

Perhaps if she proved herself indispensible, Reverend Barker would let her stay and not bend to the will of his elders. She pushed up from the chair and hurried outside to pump a bucket of water. Then she dumped it in the stove's reservoir to heat. The beef stew was already simmering for their supper, and all she had left to do was mix up a batch of biscuits.

A short while later, the front door banged, and Carly jumped. Had those busybodies finally left?

She dusted off her hands and shoved the biscuits into the oven. Recognizing the pastor's shuffling, she turned, her heartbeat running like a chicken chased by a fox. Reverend Barker stopped just inside the kitchen door, his gaze searching the room as if he expected to find Tillie there. His eyes downcast, he stood silently, his shoulders bearing more of a burden than they should have.

Carly pulled out his chair. "Come sit down, sir. It's been a long day."

He nodded and ambled forward, dropping hard into his chair. She'd rarely seen him so listless. He'd loved his wife dearly and had to be missing her. Why didn't the church elders realize this and let him be, at least for today? Quickly she fixed him a cup of coffee, adding just the right amount of sugar and milk, then set it before him. His wrinkled hands wrapped around the cup, and he sighed. "Have a seat, if you will."

Carly lowered herself to the edge of her chair. Her chair—had she ever actually had one to call her own before living here?

Her legs quivered, and she pressed her hands into her lap, hoping to make them stop.

"I reckon you heard them. They didn't make any effort to soften their voices."

Carly nodded and swallowed hard. How could she think of herself when he had lost so much today? She reached out and laid a hand on his arm. "We don't have to talk about those things today. You've had enough stress for the day already. Why don't you take a nap until supper's ready?"

He rested his hand over hers, and she studied the differences. Hers was smooth and lightly tanned from working in the garden, while his skin was thin, creased, spotted, and showed his blue veins. They were so different, yet she loved him as if he were her own grandfather.

He glanced up with tears in his eyes. Her lower lip wobbled at seeing him so distressed. "You know I care for you like you were my own daughter?"

She nodded but couldn't swallow the lump in her throat.

"The elders don't think it's proper for you to stay here now that T–Tillie is gone." He looked away and brushed his damp cheek with his shoulder. "I don't want you to go, but being the minister here, I have to maintain a presence that is above reproach. I can't be a stumbling block to others by having an unmarried woman living in my home."

Carly blinked, trying hard to keep her tears at bay. She was a stumbling block?

He squeezed her arm. "I don't want you to go. You understand that, don't you?"

47

She nodded. "B–But. . .who will take care of you?"

"I've always relied on the Lord, and He won't fail me now."

"But you also had Tillie. Who will cook your meals and clean your clothes?"

He gave her a teary-eyed, tight-lipped smile. "I think it's best if I go live with Maudie."

Carly jumped up, no longer able to keep from moving. She paced to the open back door and stared out at the garden she and Tillie had spent so many hours cultivating. She'd never see its harvest now, but her thoughts were more for him than herself. He'd spent the past thirty years living in this house and ministering to this town. He was too old to be forced into such a change. Didn't the elders give a fig about him after all he'd sacrificed for them? "You'd have to give up your ministry if you moved to San Antonio to live with your daughter."

He took a sip of coffee and shook his head. "I can minister anywhere for the Good Lord, and to be honest, I just don't think I can live in this house without my Tillie." He swiped his eyes again. "But I'm more concerned with what will happen to you. I told the board they would need to provide you with a train ticket to wherever you'd want to go and a month's wages. And Mrs. Wilcox said you could stay with them until Thursday, when the train comes." He fell back against the chair, his arms dangling beside him as if spent.

Carly's thoughts turned to Mrs. Wilcox's son. The man had made it clear that he wanted her for his own, but she couldn't stand him. Just the way he looked at her made her want to go jump in the nearest horse trough and wash off. Hugh Wilcox couldn't hold down a job and preferred drinking and hanging out in the saloon to attending church and doing the Lord's work. She'd had her fill of such men during the days she was forced to live with her brother and his outlaw gang. Never again would she put herself in such a position. She shook her head. "I have a little money saved. I'll pack my things and get a room at the hotel."

He pushed to his feet, looking far older than she'd ever seen. "But that will use up some of your funds. You should take up the Wilcoxes on their offer."

She shook her head. "I can't abide living under the same roof as Hugh Wilcox."

"Ah, now I understand." He trundled to the kitchen doorway and looked back at her. "I'm sorry, Carly. You have to know this isn't what I wanted."

She pressed her lips together and nodded. "I know. I'll pack while supper is cooking and then leave right after we eat and I clean up in here."

He nodded, then disappeared down the hall.

Carly leaned her head against the back-door jamb and closed her eyes. "What do I do now, Lord? Show me where to go."

She had lived in many places, but she had no desire to see any of them again except one. Lookout. Rachel still ran the boardinghouse there, and the woman's letters had been the only thing besides God's fortitude that had helped her make it through those horrible years of prison.

Could she return there? Would the townsfolk welcome her back or take the first opportunity they could to get rid of her like the elders had?

"Where do I go, Lord?"

Lookout. You'll find what you seek there.

Carly stared out the door. Was that God speaking to her? Or was that only her own wishful thinking?

And just what was it she desired?

A permanent home.

People who cared about her.

Someone to love.

Dare she hope she could fulfill all her dreams in Lookout, Texas?

At the bottom of the steps, Noah stopped in the entryway and glanced into the parlor, finding it empty. The front door suddenly burst open, and a young boy ran in, colliding with him. The dirty child bounced off Noah's leg, stumbled, then righted himself.

"Sorry, mister."

Noah smiled and shook his head, then closed the door. "That's all right."

The boy turned into the kitchen without so much as a second glance. Noah wasn't certain if he should follow him, go on into the dining room, or wait in the parlor. He hadn't stayed in many boardinghouses before.

A high-pitched scream reverberated down the hall, and Noah took a step toward the kitchen.

"Alan Michael Davis, don't you touch those biscuits until you wash up! Abby, stop screaming in the house."

Even though he couldn't see the boardinghouse owner, Noah recognized Mrs. Davis's voice coming from the kitchen's open doorway. So the boy was one of hers. He'd seen the woman's two little girls when he'd arrived, but not her son. He must have been at school.

"But I'm starvin', Ma."

"You get yourself outside and wash up, young man. Dinner is ready."

Mrs. Davis had her hands full, from the sound of it. Too bad Jack was laid up.

Noah's mouth watered at the scent of fresh-baked biscuits, something he and Pete didn't often have. A man could only eat so many pancakes and corn bread.

He walked to the parlor and looked around, his stomach complaining at his turning away from the kitchen.

He studied the tidy room. The walls were papered in a blue-and-white floral pattern. Two dark blue sofas lined the east and west walls with a pair of deep red wingback chairs facing one of them and a low table in front of the other. A piano sat in the far corner, and ivory-colored curtains fluttered on the afternoon breeze. He'd stayed in a half-dozen or more homes while riding his circuit, but he'd never gotten comfortable. Moving from house to house reminded him too much of his childhood—of never staying in one place for much more than a year or so.

He shook off the unwanted memories. Could he get comfortable in this house? He peered over his shoulders at the stairs that led up to Jack's room. Not likely. Not with *her* living here.

He checked his pocket watch and ambled to the dining room, standing in the doorway. The toddler Mrs. Davis had been holding on her hip when he first arrived was seated in a child's chair, munching on half a biscuit. The cute, blond little girl with pale blue eyes like her mother's studied him for a moment, then grinned and held up her biscuit.

"Bicket."

"Is it good?" he asked.

She nodded and grinned, revealing tiny teeth. The child was obviously used to having strangers in her home. "Bite?"

"No, thanks. I'll wait for the rest of the folks."

Mrs. Davis entered, carrying a huge platter covered with a towel. The fragrant odor of meat teased his senses. She set the heavy load on the buffet lining the wall to his right. She smiled and used her wrist to move the hair from her eyes. "Afternoon, Reverend. Dinner

51

will be served in a few minutes. How's your room?"

"It's far more than I expected." Heat rushed up his neck when she lifted her brows. "It's nice. Very nice. I didn't know I'd be getting two rooms."

"I'm glad you like it. Be sure you let me know if there's anything you need. Did I mention the fresh towels in the washroom?" She fanned her flushed face and continued when he nodded. "Why don't you go ahead and take a seat?"

He glanced at the twelve empty chairs and felt odd sitting before anyone else.

"Mama, me thirsty." The little girl pounded on the table with her spoon.

Mrs. Davis hurried over, picked up a cup that had been wisely set out of the child's reach, and gave her a drink. "We have one other boarder—a businessman who's in town to meet with Mr. Castleby—but I'm not certain if Mr. Cameron will be taking dinner with us or if he's dining with our bank president."

"Ow! Mama! Alan pinched me." The young blond girl Noah had seen earlier trotted into the dining room with her brother right behind her.

"I did not. I just squished a bug on her arm."

The girl glanced down, licked her finger, and wiped it across her arm. "Nuh-uh, you pinched me."

"Not on purpose." The boy glanced up at his ma with brown eyes that resembled the marshal's.

Noah studied the three children. They were an interesting combination of their parents. The boy more resembled his father with his dark hair and eyes, while the youngest girl was the spitting image of her mother, and the middle child seemed to have received traits of both parents. He'd never before considered being a father, and his thoughts immediately shifted to the auburn-haired beauty upstairs.

Noah shook his head, trying to rid his mind of

the vision of Jack sitting in her bed. The boy peered up at him with an odd look on his face.

Mrs. Davis sighed. "Reverend, I don't believe I introduced my younger children to you." She patted the boy's head. "This is Alan. He's seven. The older girl is Abby, who is five, and this is Emma, who's two and a half."

"We call her Emmie." Abby reached out and snatched a piece of biscuit from in front of Emmie. The toddler squealed, then threw the hunk of biscuit she'd been munching at her sister.

"Children! Enough."

Emmie's lower lip puckered at her mother's scolding, but the other two children didn't react at all. "Abby, fetch the bowl of biscuits I made. Alan, go fill the glasses with water."

Noah watched the children do their mother's bidding, but the second she turned her back, Abby stuck her tongue out at her brother. Noah bit back a grin. So this is what he'd missed by not having siblings. He wasn't quite sure if he was relieved or not.

"I'm sorry, Reverend. I sincerely love my children, but they are a handful. They know I'm not at my best with this baby on the way, and they take full advantage."

Noah swatted his hand in the air. "It doesn't bother me, ma'am. In fact, I've never been around small children much and"—he stared at her, wondering if he would offend her—"well, I find it entertaining and informative."

She lifted her light brown brows again and gave Emmie another piece of biscuit. "Informative?"

"Yes, ma'am. As a pastor, I need to know a little bit about everything. I counsel people who are having problems sometimes, and seeing the, uh...natural side of children's behavior is eye-opening."

"How so?" She cocked her head.

"Um. . .well, I didn't expect them to be so devious, even when they're young—and I hope that doesn't offend you. I saw the same thing at the home of a family I stayed with that had seven children."

"No, it doesn't offend me at all. As much as I wish my children were perfect, I haven't had one that is. All of them have been lively. Emmie is probably my mildest-mannered child." She stroked the toddler's wispy blond hair. "So, have a seat. I need to fetch the rest of the food so we can eat. Luke should be home any minute."

"Is there anything I can help you with?" His gaze shot to the large container of biscuits Abby carried into the room. Her mother took the bowl and set it on the buffet.

"Thank you, but no. Everything is dished up and just needs to be brought in here." She turned and shuffled back to her kitchen.

Noah wondered how long she had before her baby was due. Surely it must be soon. He looked around the table, trying to figure out where he should sit. Did the children have their favorite spots? He finally settled opposite Emma and watched her munch on her food. She caught him staring and gazed back. Suddenly she lobbed her biscuit across the table, and the wet, gooey substance hit his cheek, clung there for a moment, then dropped into his lap.

Emma giggled, then searched the empty space in front of her. Her lower lip came out again. Noah didn't know what to do with the goo in his lap. He glanced in the kitchen, then grabbed it and tossed it back. Emma's eyes lit up, and she snatched back her treat and shoved it into her mouth.

Good thing he'd changed out of his travel clothes earlier and was wearing clean pants.

The front door opened and shut, and Noah

expected to see the marshal. Instead, he heard quick footsteps hustle up the stairs, a knock, and then the creak of a door. Mrs. Davis returned with a large steaming bowl, which she placed beside the platter. His mind was running rampant, trying to guess what she'd cooked. He suspected she must be an excellent cook since she ran a boardinghouse and her family looked well-fed.

Abby followed with two small bowls filled with butter. She placed one at each end of the table then took a seat next to Emma. The five-year-old grinned at him. "We're eatin' pot roast. Don'tcha just love that?"

He nodded, and Mrs. Davis returned to her kitchen. A loud thump pulled Noah's gaze to the hall door. His pulse took off like a race horse at the sound of a starter's gun, and he shot to his feet.

There stood the marshal with Jack in his arms. Her eyes widened when her gaze collided with his. The air left Noah's lungs, and he pressed one hand against the table to steady himself. He couldn't look away for the life of him. Her medium green dress looked lovely with her reddish-brown hair. And—he took a second quick glance—bare toes peeked out from under the hem of her dress.

"Could you pull out a chair for me, Reverend?"

Noah jumped into motion at the marshal's request. He yanked out the chair beside him.

"I usually sit on the other side of Emmie so I can help feed her if she needs it," Jack offered.

"Oh." He hurried around the table, pulled out that chair, and stepped back.

Jack's gaze connected with his again, but for the first time close up. He could see the deep blue coloring and her curious stare. He forced himself to look away and hurried back to his seat. Feigning interest in the floral design of his empty plate, he kept his head down, afraid to look up now that Jack sat almost directly across from him.

His hands shook as badly as they had the first time he ever preached a sermon on a street corner. Why did she affect him like she did? Why couldn't he treat her like any other woman of marrying age? How would he eat with her right there?

Come to think of it, his appetite had fled.

Chapter 5

Jack peered over her shoulder at her stepfather as he entered the kitchen. How could he leave her alone with their guest?

Rearranging her skirts, she swallowed the lump in her throat, wondering why it bothered her so much. She'd never had a problem chatting with their visitors before, but remembering how she couldn't take her eyes from the new minister's the first time she saw him, she felt her cheeks warm. How could she have shamelessly gawked at him like that?

She peeked up, glad to see he was watching Emmie as she reached for Abby's spoon. Abby scowled at her little sister, snatched the spoon from the youngster's hand, and put it on the far side of her plate. The pastor's lip pressed tight, but the corners of his mouth turned up. His black eyes glimmered with humor—eyes that were more intriguing than those of any man she'd ever met. His thick, dark hair refused to lie in place, instead falling forward onto his tanned forehead. And he was so tall. His gaze flicked to hers, then darted away.

Alan set a glass of water beside her, and she picked it up and took a sip. Had the reverend noticed her staring? What was wrong with her?

"Alan says you're the new preacher." Abby tossed out a glare like it was a challenge. Alan set a glass next to Reverend Jeffers and glanced up with a worried look. He scowled at Abby and went back to the kitchen.

"I don't like going to church," Abby said.

Jack choked on her water and erupted into a fit of coughing. Her gaze whizzed across the table at him, and his concerned look didn't help any. She cleared her throat several times and focused on her sister. "Abby, that's a dreadful thing to say, especially to our new pastor. You apologize right now."

"No, it's all right. I appreciate Abby's honesty." He lifted a hand, palm facing outward. "I realize sitting through a church service can be difficult for youngsters." He smiled, but it did little to put her at ease.

"Have you been a minister long?" she asked.

"A little over a year."

"Mary's ma says you're too young to be a preacher." Abby tossed a sideways glance at Jack then smirked. "And you ain't got no wife, neither. Preachers gotta have wives."

He looked at Jack as if asking who Mary was. She reached across Emmie's lap and squeezed Abby's arm. "We don't repeat gossip." She gave her sister a gentle shake. "You just sit there and be quiet. You're being very rude to our guest."

Jack cast him an apologetic glance, relieved that he looked more amused than upset. "I'm sorry. Abby can be rather. . .um. . .outspoken." His lips quirked up in a smile. Then his gaze moved past her, and she heard footsteps. Her parents took their places at the table, as did Alan, who brought the last two glasses of water.

Luke looked over at Reverend Jeffers. "Would you care to ask the Lord to bless our food, Reverend?"

He gave a brief nod. "I'd be happy to." He bowed his head, and the others around the table followed. "Heavenly Father, we thank You for this delicious-smelling meal and for the hands that prepared it. We ask that You bless this food to the nourishment of our bodies, and I ask Your blessing on this household and this town. Amen."

"Good. He don't pray them long-winded prayers like Pastor Taylor did." Alan jumped out of his chair and snagged a biscuit off the buffet.

"Son, don't talk poorly of Pastor Taylor," Luke said. "He's a good man. And set that biscuit down. You know we allow our guests to go first."

Alan flopped back in his chair. "Sorry, Pa, but I'm starvin'."

"Please, Reverend, help yourself." Jack's ma held her hand toward the buffet.

The minister looked down at his plate. "Thank you, but it doesn't seem proper for me to go before you ladies and the children."

"I knew I was gonna like him." Alan grabbed his plate and jumped up, but her papa snagged her brother's arm and pressed him back onto his chair.

"Since the pastor has expressed his wishes, we'll let the ladies go first, Son."

Alan scowled into his plate, while Abby grinned. Jack could almost hear her sister's taunting, "Na–na–na–na–na! I get to go before you."

"That's kind of you, Reverend." Her mother stood, took her dish and Jack's, then soon returned with both plates filled with food.

Jack wondered how she'd manage to eat so much pork roast, green beans, and potatoes with *him* sitting across the table. And just why did that bother her so much?

She'd already decided she wasn't going to chase after him like some schoolgirl with her first crush. Tessa had made it clear that she meant to lasso the poor, unsuspecting man.

With her head lowered, she watched him through her lashes. He waved and smiled at Emmie while he waited on her siblings to fill their plates. Finally, he followed Luke to the buffet. While his back was turned, she took the opportunity to study him. Luke was a solid six feet two, so Reverend Jeffers had to be at least six feet four. His shoulders were even broader than Luke's, but he wasn't husky for a large man, nor was he a string bean. In fact, he looked well-muscled—a man more used to physical labor than studious pursuits. As far as she could tell, Noah Jeffers was close to perfect. She exhaled a heavy sigh then noticed her mother watching her. A smirk danced on her ma's lips, and a knowing gleam lit her eyes.

Appalled that her ma must think she was attracted to the man, Jack shook her head and stabbed a bite of meat.

The minister returned with a full plate and a contented smile and sat down. She imagined a man his size had a big appetite.

"This sure looks delicious, Mrs. Davis." He poked some green beans with his fork and took a bite.

"Thank you," her ma said. "Pastor Taylor didn't tell us much about you when he mentioned you'd be taking his place. So, where do you hail from?"

"Emporia, ma'am."

"Isn't there a sawmill in Emporia?" Luke set his plate down and reached across the table for the butter.

"Yes there is. They cut a lot of wood there, but most of the lumber is shipped by train to Houston." Using his fork, the minister lifted one corner of his meat, which he'd covered with the red-eye gravy her ma had made.

Intrigued, Jack watched him. His brow crinkled, and he leaned down, as if to sniff his food, then glanced up and caught her watching. Quickly he cut a bite of meat and shoved it in his mouth. He chewed it a few times, and she'd have sworn—if she swore—that he turned three shades of white before he all but turned green. His cheeks puffed out as if he'd belched. A panicked look engulfed his handsome face as he glanced one direction and then the other. Suddenly he leapt from his chair and rushed out of the room.

"My heavens." Her mother looked at Luke. "What do you suppose that was about?"

Luke shook his head and glanced at his plate. He blew out a sigh. "Don't know, but I'll go check on 'im."

"If'n he's done eatin', can I have his food?" Alan reached over to take the pastor's biscuit.

Her ma snapped her fingers. "Don't touch that. I'm sure he'll be right back." Then she glanced over and met Jack's eyes. Her brows lifted.

Jack shrugged. "That was the strangest thing I think I've ever seen."

Noah's stomach swirled and cramped, and he bent over the porch railing and heaved. Once he retched, his belly settled. With his hands spread apart, he leaned on the railing, his head hanging. What a fool he'd made of himself. How could he go back in there?

"You all right, Reverend?" Mr. Davis stopped a few feet behind him.

"I'm sorry, sir." He straightened, pressing a hand to his stomach, and turned. "I guess I should have told your wife that I can't eat pork. It's just that I thought your daughter—the middle one—said it was pot roast."

Luke smiled. "Abby sometimes gets confused on the meat we're having. If it looks like a roast, it's a pot roast to her."

Noah rubbed his hand across his mouth, making

a mental note to look the meat over better before taking any in the future. "I hate to think I hurt your wife's feelings. I feel bad about that."

"Think nothing of it. Rachel's run this place for close to fifteen years. She's used to people having particular tastes or not being able to tolerate certain foods."

"I just don't want her going to any extra effort on my behalf."

Luke clapped him on the shoulder. "Don't worry about her. She's a good-natured woman and wants to please her guests." He stared at Noah; then his brows dipped. "Have we met before? There's something familiar about you."

Noah's heart jolted. He wasn't ready to tell people his true identity. What would the marshal say if he knew who he actually was? Would he kick him out of his home? Out of town?

A wagon rolled to a stop in the street, and the marshal turned his attention to it. He smiled. "When'd you get back home, Garrett?"

Noah studied the man in the wagon, grateful for the reprieve. He fully intended to answer the marshal's question, but he needed more time first. He had things to do in this town—to make recompense for injuries he'd caused in his youth.

"Afternoon, Luke. I just rolled into town. I suppose you've already had your lunch."

Luke shook his head. "We've just started eating. C'mon in and join us."

Noah recognized Garrett Corbett, the older of the marshal's two cousins. The man glanced down at the mess Noah had made in the grass, then back up. His brows lifted. "Is Rachel trying out a new recipe? Or did Jack cook?"

Luke chuckled and shook his head. "Neither.

This here's our new parson, Reverend Jeffers." Noah extended his hand toward Garrett.

"I'd appreciate it if y'all would call me Noah."

"Nice to meet you, Reverend." Garrett nodded. "Just let me take the wagon around to the freight office and tend to my horses; then I'll wash up and come back." He clucked to the horses, and they plodded forward.

Luke waved and turned to face Noah. "Are you ready to go inside now?"

Noah hung his head. How could he face Mrs. Davis after his uncouth flight from her table? How could he face Jack?

"Don't be worrying so much, Noah. You're not the first in this house to air their paunch."

"I hope I didn't make your wife feel bad. The beans I ate were delicious."

Luke crossed the porch and opened the front door. "C'mon. Rachel will be fine. I'll explain to her."

"If you could show me where a bucket and the water is, I'll take care of"—he motioned toward the porch rail—"uh. . .that."

Luke shook his head. "No need. I'll tend to it. Just come on back inside."

Noah nodded and trudged across the porch. He hadn't been here a full day yet, and he'd already made a fool of himself. If only Abby hadn't said the meat was pot roast, then he wouldn't have taken any. He hated wasting food, but there was no way he could eat two bites of that pork—much less that large slice he'd taken. He could only hope Mrs. Davis would forgive him.

Jack watched Noah Jeffers wolf down his food—everything, that is, except his meat. Whatever had bothered him earlier no longer affected him. Perhaps he didn't like the flavor of the meat, or maybe something had gotten stuck in his throat.

"When is your next trip to Denison, Garrett?" Her mother pulled a biscuit in half and buttered both sides then handed one to Abby and the other to Emma.

"I was thinking about headin' that way in a day or two." Garrett stabbed a bite of meat and shoved it in his mouth. "Why?"

The parson turned his head away, looking pale again. Jack glanced down at her slice of pork. Was something wrong with it? She hadn't noticed that it tasted odd. She cut a bite and lifted it to her nose and took a quick sniff. Fine. No, not fine, it smelled downright tasty. She put the bite in her mouth, relishing its delicious flavor.

"I have a package that needs to be picked up at the train depot in Denison, and I wondered if you could get it for me."

Garrett nodded and forked some green beans into his mouth. "Sure thing. Do you know when it's supposed to arrive?"

Jack thought of Garrett Corbett as more of an uncle than her stepfather's cousin. Even though he was close to forty, he was still a handsome man with blond hair and eyes that often gleamed with mischief. She loved his blue eyes. If only hers were that vivid hue that put her in mind of a robin's egg instead of being so dark a blue.

"Yes, it should be there in two days."

Luke stared at Ma then lifted his brows. Jack glanced at her mother in time to catch her smothering a grin. What was that about?

She couldn't think of anything her ma had ordered. They had just celebrated Luke's birthday, and nobody else had one for a few months, so it couldn't be a present. She spent the rest of the meal contemplating that mystery. The reporter in her just couldn't let it go.

Alan stood up first. "Can I be excused?"

"*May* I," Abby stated like a little teacher.

"I asked first," Alan whined and curled up his lip at Abby.

"You may both take your dishes to the kitchen," her papa said. "Alan, fetch a bucket of water and set it on the front porch. Abby, you can help your ma clear the table and clean up."

Abby scowled and glanced at Jack. "What about Sissy?"

Her mother wiped Emmie's face with the towel tied around the girl's neck. "You know Jacqueline can't be on her feet yet. She needs to rest her knee. In fact, she shouldn't even be downstairs so soon after her accident." She cast her husband a mock glare.

Luke shrugged. "She's all right, Rachel. I'll make sure she takes things easy."

Jack's mother sighed. "Fine. I suppose it won't hurt her to rest on the sofa or even sit in a rocker on the porch for a bit."

Luke grinned and winked at Jack. She couldn't help smiling back at him. They were shameful to gang up on her ma, especially when she was going to birth a baby in the next few weeks, but Jack had to get out of that bedroom. How else was she going to get a story about the parson?

She peeked over at him. He was listening to Garrett tell a story about a duck that hitched a ride on his freight wagon. She smiled at Garrett's animated expression and his arms, which flapped like wings. Emmie giggled at him and lifted her arms up and down.

"Well, I need to get the wagon unloaded."

All three men stood at once. Luke picked up his plate, as well as Garrett's and Mr. Jeffers's. "Have you heard anything from Mark lately?"

Garrett swigged back the last of his water and set the glass down. "Yep. He and Shannon are talking about maybe moving back here."

"Truly!" Jack's ma hurried back into the dining room. "It would be so nice to see them more often."

"I don't know if they will, but they're considering it since Lookout is growing so much. Dallas is gettin' really big now, and Shannon wants to raise the children in a smaller town." Garrett lifted his hat off the corner of his chair and set it on his head. "I just don't know if we have enough call for a lawyer here, though."

"The closest one I know about is in Denison, and you know that's several hours' ride away. Some of the folks who live in the small towns around Lookout may need one on an occasion." Luke wrapped his arm around Rachel's shoulders.

Garrett stretched and scratched his belly. "The food was great, as usual, Rachel. Thanks for letting me invite myself to dinner."

"Anytime." She smiled.

Garrett held his hand out to the minister. "Nice to meet you, Reverend."

"It's Noah, and a pleasure to meet you, too."

"I guess I'd better carry Half Bit back to her room, although I don't know if I can manage after eating all that good food." Luke kissed Ma's head and winked at Jack. "Maybe you could sit in the parlor for a spell until my food has time to settle."

Jack bit back a grin. "I could manage that for a while."

"Oh! You two." Ma gently swatted Luke's stomach. "You're not fooling anyone with that act of yours." She pushed away from him and grabbed the bowl of beans off the buffet.

"Ma, Alan spilled water on the floor and got my shoe wet."

Ma rolled her eyes. "I'm coming."

Luke reached down and hoisted Emmie into his arms. He nibbled her neck, eliciting a giggle from the toddler.

A melancholy smile lifted the parson's lips. He pushed away from the chair's back he'd been holding on to. "I reckon I'll go back upstairs and study my sermon some more."

Jack jumped up, immediately regretting her quick action as a sharp pain clutched her knee. She tried not to grimace but must have failed because Luke set Emma down and hurried to her side. She gazed back at Noah Jeffers, who stared at her with compassion in his obsidian eyes. "Actually, I was wondering if I could interview you for the town newspaper—the *Lookout Ledger*."

Chapter 6

Noah followed the marshal as he helped Jack make her way into the parlor. Things would have been a whole lot quicker if Noah had scooped her up in his arms and carried her, but that would hardly seem proper. He paused at the stairway that held his escape and glanced up to the second floor. The last thing he wanted was a newspaper article about him.

"You're not thinking of running out on me, are you, Reverend?" Jack's expressive tone alerted him that she'd had her eye on him and wasn't about to take no for an answer.

He resisted tugging at his collar, which suddenly seemed too tight against his throat. Sighing, he strode into the parlor as the marshal slid a chair toward the couch.

Jack discreetly lifted her injured leg onto the seat and rearranged her skirts. "Would you mind bringing me some paper and a pencil, Papa?"

"I don't mind, but be nice to him, Half Bit." The marshal flashed Noah a teasing grin. "We don't want the parson leaving town before we get to hear him preach."

Noah thought they all might just be better off if he did leave, but he kept his thoughts to himself. Doubt was something he frequently battled. Pete had told him often to not belittle his efforts, because Noah prayed hard and studied God's Word before preaching a sermon; and if his message was God-inspired, then disparaging himself was also demeaning the Lord. He perched on the end of a chair across the room from the couch where Jack sat, bouncing one leg.

His gaze ran around the large parlor, but it kept stopping at Jack, no matter how hard he tried to not look at her. She'd matured from a rowdy tomboy who preferred overalls to dresses into a lovely young woman, but the ornery gleam still sparked in her pretty eyes—eyes the color of blueberries. She flipped her waist-long hair, which was tied with a yellow ribbon, over her shoulder. He couldn't be certain until he saw her in the sunlight, but he thought that it had darkened over the years, looking more brown than red. His fingers moved, as if to reach out and touch her creamy skin, which held the faint hint of the sun. He sighed again and looked out a nearby window. Coming to Lookout had been a bad idea. If only he could convince the Lord of that—then maybe he could hightail it back to Emporia.

Jack's gaze flitted to his then back to the doorway. She fidgeted with her skirts and tugged at the cuff of each sleeve. "I wonder what's keeping Luke."

His brows lifted. "You refer to your father by his first name?"

Jack's cheeks actually pinked up. "Luke's been my stepfather for ten years now, but he's the only father I've ever cared for. I guess I sometimes call him Luke because that's how I referred to him before he married my ma."

Noah leaned back, his hands holding on to the arms of the chair. He knew that, but she didn't know he did. Maybe he could get some answers to his own questions. "So, I'm guessing that you didn't care much for your real father."

69

Jack's eyes flashed, and he recognized the spunk that had often gotten her in trouble in past years. She lifted her nose in the air. "I hardly see what that has to do with anything."

He offered her a placating smile. "We are who we are because of our past, Miss Ha—uh. . .Davis." Sweat beaded on Noah's forehead at his near miss. He'd almost called her Miss Hamilton—the name he'd known her by previously. He'd have to watch himself and be extra careful around her.

Jack's narrowed gaze pierced him, but he forced himself to sit still and return her stare. The marshal strode back into the room, paper in hand. "Here you go."

Jack took the items without breaking Noah's gaze. His heart thumped harder. The marshal glanced from her to Noah and back. He scratched his hand, then rested his thumbs in his waistband. "You want me to stay, Half Bit?"

Finally she looked up at her stepfather and offered a cordial smile. "No, thank you. That's not necessary—that is, unless the parson is afraid to be alone with me." She wielded her smile like a weapon.

A bead of sweat trickled down Noah's spine, but he forced himself not to move. He was not without the means of affecting an unabashed female when the occasion warranted. He planted a smile on his face— his best feature next to his dark eyes, so he'd been told—and when the marshal glanced at Jack again, Noah winked at her.

Her mouth opened wide, and the marshal spun back toward him, obviously wondering what he'd missed. Noah resisted chuckling and affected a straight face then rubbed his eye. "Your daughter is safe with me, I promise, Marshal."

The man stared at him for a long moment then

gave a quick nod and spun on his heel, leaving the room.

Jack leaned forward, her lids lowered halfway, her blue eyes cold as ice. "Are you in the habit of winking at single females, Reverend?" Her snide tone left no doubt that she'd taken offense.

"I beg your pardon." He rubbed his eye again, and she blinked. Confusion wrinkled her brow, and she stared at her blank paper.

"Um. . .never mind. I must have misconstrued your actions." She scribbled something on the paper. "So tell me, Reverend, where do you hail from?"

"Emporia, like I said at the table."

"And have you always lived there?"

He swallowed hard and stared at the top of her head while she wrote some more. Too soon she glanced up and lifted her brows. His heart flip-flopped at her direct perusal. "Uh. . .no, not always."

"Where else have you lived?"

He straightened, knowing he'd have to divert her train of thought if he was going to stay truthful—and he fully intended to as much as possible. "I fail to see what that has to do with anything."

Her mouth quirked to one side in an enticing manner, and he focused on the bottom of her bare foot, which faced him where it lay on the chair. How could her feet be so small?

"Where did you receive your ministerial training?"

"From the man who took me in after my father died. His name is Pete Jeffers."

Her gaze darted up from her notes. "You changed your last name?"

He nodded.

"Isn't that a bit drastic? I mean, was your original last name so awful you couldn't abide it?"

He lifted his brow at her question and turned the

cards on her. They were more alike than she realized. "Was your original surname so awful *you* couldn't abide it?"

"What?" Her expression blanked out, and he knew the moment she realized what she'd asked. "Oh dear. I suppose that did sound rather crass." Her pinks grew rosy, and she chuckled. "My birth name was Hamilton, but after Luke married my ma, I chose to use his surname. It wasn't my name that was awful, Reverend Jeffers, but rather my father."

He'd remembered hearing scuttlebutt about James Hamilton, but the man had died before Noah first came to Lookout. His fist tightened to think that Jack's father could have hurt her so badly that she'd still be bitter today. "Have you found it within yourself to forgive your father, Miss Davis?"

She straightened rigid as a newly cut piece of lumber. "I hardly see how that's any of your concern."

"I'm your pastor now. It's my duty to minister to you, and if I notice an area that you need help in, I feel I should do my best to assist you in overcoming it. An unwillingness to forgive eats away at a person, Miss Davis. It does more damage to the one who carries the weight of not forgiving than it does the person who originally committed the deed."

Her face wrinkled up. "Nevertheless, I'm the one asking questions today." She scanned her paper then tapped a line with her pencil. "You said you received your training from this Pete Jeffers. Has he had any formal training as a minister?"

Noah shrugged. "You know, I don't think I ever asked him. Pete lives his life as a witness to those around him. I never doubted that he loved God with all his heart and had dedicated his life to serving others and helping them find peace in the Lord. He knew his Bible from end to end. He taught me as much as I could learn in the years I lived with him. I felt God calling me to minister to His flock. What other training is required?"

Jack heaved a sigh. Was the man being purposefully vague? He had deftly deflected most of her queries like a skilled outlaw evading a judge's questioning.

"Let me ask you this," he said. "What college did you graduate from to become a reporter?"

Her mouth opened, but she didn't know how to respond. Did he know she hadn't been to college? But how could he? Were her interviewing skills so lacking that he picked up on it?

He smiled. "Ahh. . .so you didn't. What gives you the right to drill me on my credentials?"

Jack narrowed her eyes. This man was unlike Reverend Taylor in just about every way. "You have effectively avoided answering most of my questions. Do you have something to hide, Reverend?"

For the briefest of seconds, Jack was certain he blanched, but then he smiled.

"What an imagination you have, Miss Davis. Perhaps you should be writing novels instead of newspaper articles."

Indeed. She'd worked at the newspaper off and on longer than her ma had been married to Luke. Jenny Evans had taught her well how to interview and to read people and catch deception. But what could a minister have to hide? Maybe she was too suspicious. Or maybe she was imagining things that weren't there because she wanted so badly to score a big story to offer a Dallas paper.

Jack scanned her list of questions again. She had precious little information for an article. "You never mentioned where you grew up."

He shrugged again. "Here and there. My folks never stayed in one place for long, and after my ma died, it only got worse."

Jack wanted to grit her teeth and scream at the evasive answer. She studied the man. His eyes were so dark that she couldn't tell if they were deep brown or black. Shouldn't a minister have caring, blue eyes instead of ones so dark and mysterious they threatened to suck you in like a whirlpool?

Yet they weren't unkind eyes. There was something compelling about them. Compelling her to believe in him. Compelling her to trust him.

Her mind flashed back to another time. Another place. Another set of dark eyes begging her to believe. But just that fast, the memory was gone.

She shook her head. What was that? Who was that?

Reverend Jeffers leaned forward. "Are you all right, Miss Davis? Your mother said you'd recently had an accident. Maybe you are pushing yourself too hard." He reached his hand out as if to touch her then pulled it back into his lap. "We can continue this interview some other time if you need to rest."

Her mind swirled as it had right after she first fell off the roof. Maybe she wasn't ready to be working again. She closed her eyes and leaned back against the sofa, trying with all her might to grasp hold of the memory that had assaulted her. It was too late.

"Do you need a drink, Miss Davis? Should I fetch your mother?" At his concerned voice, she opened her eyes again. His worry seemed real. Maybe she was searching for a story where there wasn't one. She glanced down at her questions a final time, then a new one popped into her mind. "Have you ever been to Lookout before?"

There it was again. That brief, frantic look before

he schooled his expression. He leaned back and crossed his arms, a smile on his lips—a smile that looked decidedly forced. "That would be rather ironic, wouldn't it? Can't you just see the headlines? TOWN DELINQUENT RETURNS AS NEW PASTOR."

He shook his head and chuckled, as if he'd cracked the funniest joke in years.

Jack studied him until he sobered and glanced into the hallway at the stairs again.

The new minister was hiding something.

She was certain.

Chapter 7

Carly once again checked the engraved pocket watch that had belonged to Tillie. She snapped the cover closed and ran her thumb over the swan figure etched into the silver, encircled by two curved branches, thick with leaves. Reverend Barker had said he wanted her to have something by which to remember Tillie. The watch would always be her most cherished possession, but she didn't need it to remember. Tillie Barker would always hold a special place in Carly's heart.

She placed the watch in its velvet drawstring bag and put it in her handbag. Lifting her hand to shade her eyes, she scanned the rolling hills to the west. The telegram she'd received from Rachel said that Garrett Corbett would pick her up. She placed a hand against her jittery stomach. Would the man remember her?

She hoped that Mr. Corbett and the town had forgotten all about her association with the Payton Gang. She hadn't thought of her brother in a long while but allowed a moment to reflect on how her life had changed. Ty was long dead now. He hadn't been a good brother, but he had protected her from his gang members, and for that she was grateful. If only they'd had parents to love and nourish them like the Barkers had cared for her, then surely things would have turned out different.

She searched the green hills again, then sat back

down on the depot's bench in the shade. Though only late April, the sun shone down with a vengeance, heating the still air. But then, even if it had been winter, she'd probably still be sweating just because of her nervousness. Her foot jiggled relentlessly as she wondered what she'd face in Lookout.

Rachel had written her that the town had grown a lot in the past ten years. That meant there would be many newcomers who wouldn't know her story and how she'd pretended to be one of the mail-order brides who'd come to town, hoping to marry the marshal, although in truth, she'd had more sinister plans. None of the mail-order brides the Corbett brothers had brought to town ever had a chance, least of all her. The marshal had long ago lost his heart to Rachel, but he had a quagmire of bitterness to work through before he realized that.

Carly sighed, leaning her head against the wall. She yawned and closed her eyes. She'd worried so much last night that she hadn't slept much. Would she be welcomed in the town? Would she be able to find work to support herself? Would people remember that her brother had attempted to rob the Lookout bank? She heaved another sigh. The Bible said to not worry about tomorrow because today had enough cares of its own—and wasn't that the truth?

"All right, Lord, I'll try to not be concerned about my future, and will place it in Your hands."

God had brought her so far—out of the life of crime her brother had forced her into, out of prison, out of sin. She would give her future to Him, and at least for today, she'd try not to worry.

Garrett crested the hill, and the outlying buildings of Denison came into view. The horses must have sensed an end to their journey, because they picked up their pace. The wagon creaked as it hit another rut in the road and bounced out.

How many times had he made this drive from Lookout to Denison? Garrett shook his head. Too many to count. But with news of a railroad spur coming to Lookout, he might be facing the end of such trips.

He stretched, trying to work the kinks out of his back, and chuckled to himself. His horses could probably make this trip alone, if only someone on the other end could load the freight and head the animals back toward Lookout.

Rubbing his hand along his jaw, he considered his future. If the spur did come through as the mayor said it would, he'd be out of business, for the most part. Yeah, he could pick up deliveries at the depot and take them to surrounding ranches, but his profit would be cut way down. He'd been trying to decide what else he'd like to do, but so far nothing came to mind.

Duke flicked his long tail, gaining Garrett's attention. He loved both of his stock horses. He hated the thought of putting them out to pasture, especially when there was a need for good work horses in the county, but he doubted he could part with the two animals, which had been so faithful. Sitting up straighter, he allowed a thought to take wing. Maybe he could raise stock horses. Farmers and ranchers always needed quality animals. He rubbed his jaw, getting excited for the first time in a long while.

He drew the horses alongside the depot and pulled back on the reins. "Whoa there."

Smiling, he hopped down and jogged up the steps and into the depot.

The clerk glanced up and nodded. "Howdy, Garrett. H'aint seen you in a while."

"Virgil." Garrett nodded. "Ain't been here in a while. Been back and forth to Dallas, hauling wood and freight for a rancher who's building a new house."

"Guess you won't be doin' that much longer, what with the new rail spur going in over to Lookout." Virgil's prominent Adam's apple bounced up and down over the man's black string tie. The cuffs to his white shirt were faded a dingy gray, matching the clerk's eyes.

Garrett shrugged. "Haven't exactly decided what I'll do yet. Got some ideas I'm kickin' around, though. I'm supposed to pick up a package for Rachel Davis. You know where it is?"

Virgil scowled and riffled though a pile of papers. He turned and studied a stack of crates behind him then spun back around, smiling. "Ah. . .you had me goin' there fer a minute." He squealed out a laugh that resembled a cat choking, and his bald head bobbed up and down as he fought to regain his composure.

What in the world? Garrett couldn't think of a thing he'd said that the man would find humorous.

The clerk swiped his eyes on his sleeve and pointed out the window to the waiting area. "You'll find yer package out there on the bench."

"Thanks." Garrett glanced back at the man a final time before exiting. It was far too early for the man to be drinking, but Virgil's behavior sure seemed odd. And why would the clerk leave a package out where just anyone could pick it up—unless it was so big Virgil couldn't carry it himself. Garrett flexed his arm muscle as he opened the door. He'd manhandle the load alone, just to show Virgil what he was made of.

The door banged shut, and a woman on the bench jumped. Garrett glanced around the platform for the package, then swung back for a look at the woman. Her gold-colored dress was wrinkled, and her hair was pulled up tight in a stark bun at the back of her head and covered with a straw hat tied down with a sash. She stretched and yawned. His gaze immediately landed on her chest, where the fabric of her dress pulled tight as she locked her hands together and stretched again. She rubbed her eyes, then stared at him.

Embarrassed and feeling guilty to be caught watching her, he spun around and walked to the other end of the deck but found no crates of any kind. He lifted his hat and scratched his head. What was Virgil up to?

"Mr. Corbett?"

Garrett pivoted again and studied the woman's face. She looked to be in her late twenties and was fairly pretty with her black hair and unusual light brown eyes. She had all the right curves for a woman, even if she was on the thin side. But how did she know his name? The woman's eyes narrowed, but she didn't look away. There was something oddly familiar about her. Had he stumbled across her path before?

"You are Garrett Corbett, correct? Or are you Mark, perchance?"

Now she really had his attention. How did she know his brother? "Who are you, lady?"

She flinched as if he'd slapped her, making him regret his harsh tone. "I received a telegram from Rachel Hamilton saying you would be by to give me a ride to Lookout. Did she neglect to inform you?"

"*You're* Rachel's package?"

She blinked, confusion marring her features. "What?"

Garrett lowered his head and stared at the floorboards. Now that odd look Rachel and Luke had exchanged at the dinner table made sense. They'd set him up. But why? Who was this woman? And why would Rachel not just tell him he was supposed to pick her up?

The woman turned back toward the bench and snatched up a worn satchel. "Never mind. I'll find another way to get to Lookout. Sorry to have imposed on you."

Garrett opened his mouth to reply, but nothing came out. He was still trying to figure out what Rachel was up to when the lady opened the depot door and scurried inside. She walked up to the counter and said something to Virgil, who glanced through the glass at him and pointed. The woman shook her head. Virgil shrugged, and the lady stood still for a minute, then spun toward the front door and walked outside.

Why wouldn't Rachel tell him he was to pick up a woman passenger? He could think of only one reason—she had something up her sleeve.

The window in the depot door rattled when Virgil yanked it open. "What did you say to that lady? H'ain't you gonna give her a ride? Makes no sense for you not to when yer goin' right back to Lookout. You are, h'ain'tcha?"

Garrett nodded.

"Then why you standin' here? That lady waited for you nigh on two hours. Git on out there and give her a ride."

Garrett bristled at Virgil's scolding. "What's it to you?"

The clerk shook his head. "What's wrong with you? Did she say something that set you off?"

Rubbing the back of his neck, Garrett shook his head. What *was* wrong with him?

He didn't like people getting his goat or pulling the wool over his eyes—and yet he couldn't quite decide if Rachel had. His feet moved forward before his mind clicked into gear. He had been rude to the lady—not intentionally—but rude all the same. And he was returning to Lookout, so he had no excuse for not giving her a ride.

He didn't waste time responding to Virgil but charged out the door and searched the road that ran past the depot. Skirts swinging like a church bell, she marched down the road that led out of town. Was the fool woman going to walk all the way to Lookout?

Garrett climbed back into the wagon, released the brake, and slapped the reins against the horses' backs. "Giddyap, there!"

The wagon jolted forward, nearly tossing him into the back. Guiding it in a wide circle, he finally sat and focused on his target. The gal had stopped and looked one way and then the other. She set her satchel down, untied her bonnet strings, and then retied them and picked up her bag again. As he drew near her, she turned and gawked at him, then spun around and started walking faster.

He pulled up beside her and tugged on the reins to slow his team. "I'll give you a lift to Lookout."

"No thanks," she tossed over her shoulder. "I can find my own way. I don't need your help."

"Whoa there, Duke. Daisy." He wrestled with the horses, which weren't ready to stop, seeing as how they'd just started their trip home, but they finally came to a halt. He jumped down and hurried after the confounded woman. Couldn't she see he was trying to help her?

Garrett caught up and reached for her bag. She spun around, yanking it from his grasp, and glared at him. He held up his palms. "Whoa, lady, I'm just trying to help."

"So, now you want to help. Well, you're too late. I told you I'd find another way to Lookout."

Garrett shoved his hands to his hips and couldn't

hold back a grin. "Like walking?"

"What?" She swirled around and looked down the road. Only a few dilapidated buildings littered the lane. "Uh. . .that train man said the livery was this way and that I could rent a buggy there."

"Ah. . .I see." Good thing he came to her rescue or she might have been wolf bait come nightfall. "The livery is the other direction, ma'am."

Surprised flickered in her eyes, and she looked back toward town. She spun around again and marched back in the direction she'd just come. All this swirling was making him dizzier than doing do-si-dos at a square dance. But no female, no matter how irritating she might be, was going to get him into trouble with Rachel. His cousin's wife just might get it into her mind not to allow him to eat at the boardinghouse any more, and a near-forty-year-old bachelor could only eat so much of his own cooking. He hurried after her again.

This time, he wasn't taking any chances. Garrett caught up with her. "Stop! Right now."

The woman scowled at him and kept on walking.

"I aim to give you a ride to Lookout whether you want one or not, so stop walkin', you hear?"

If she did, she sure didn't obey well. Garrett ran past her, turned, and halted right in her path. She had no choice but to stop, go around, or knock him to the ground, and given that he was a good half-foot taller than she and twice her breadth, he doubted the last choice was much of an option. Then he noticed the satchel flying toward his face.

Carly gasped as her travel bag collided with Mr. Corbett's head. The man staggered backward then fell flat on his rump. She couldn't help the giggle that rose up in spite of her irritation. The man was more of a pest than a wasp nest in a privy.

He hopped right back up and glared at her, his lovely robin's egg blue eyes flashing. "What was that for?"

"I don't like to be pushed around by men."

He stepped closer. "I didn't push you."

She leaned toward him. "You know what I mean. I don't like to be bossed around. I've had enough men telling me what to do to last me a lifetime."

He flung his arms out to the side. "Well, I'm sorry, lady, but there are no women here to assist me."

She gasped. No women indeed. "Then what am I?"

He blinked. "What?"

"You said there were no women around, so I just wondered what you considered me?"

His gaze traveled from her eyes downward. She hiked her chin. His stance relaxed a smidgen as a cocky smile tugged on one side of his mouth. "I never said you weren't a woman. You've just got me all— all—discombobulated."

Carly sighed at his confused expression. He was like a little boy in a man's clothing—only he was all man. In the ten years since she'd last seen him, his shoulders had gotten broader, but his blond hair hadn't grayed at all. She knew he must be pushing forty, but he looked as if he could take on a man half his age. Maybe she'd been unwise stirring his ire. "Did Rachel send you to get me or not?"

He leaned in again but this time didn't look so menacing. His warm breath touched her cheeks, sending tingles up and down her spine. "She asked me to pick up a *package* at the depot. A *package*, not a *woman*."

"Oh." No wonder he'd been so confused. Why would Rachel say such a thing? Had she gotten mixed up on the date she was arriving and actually meant for Mr. Corbett to pick up something she'd ordered? "Maybe she also had a package that needed picking up."

He shook his head. "Virgil said she didn't. He just motioned me outside and said my *package* was out there. No wonder he was about to bust his gut laughing."

"I don't see anything funny about the situation." Carly rubbed her hand across her face. Making him feel guilty about the situation wasn't very Christlike. "I'm sorry. I just assumed that when you saw me, you decided you no longer wanted to give me a ride—and that made me mad."

"Why would I care about who you are? I've never met you before."

Taken aback by his lack of recognition, she moved away from him. Was it really possible that he didn't know who she was? Obviously, Rachel hadn't informed him. If he didn't know, then maybe the rest of the town wouldn't remember her either. But they would once they heard her name. And so would he.

She strode over to the wagon, tossed her satchel in the back, and climbed up. It was best he didn't learn the truth until he was too far along to turn back.

Chapter 8

Noah glanced down at the note again. Was he doing the right thing? Would his apology be as effective done anonymously rather than in person?

Well it would have to be, because that was the only apology he could offer at the moment. He shoved the paper in his pants pocket and entered the mercantile. All manner of aromas tickled his senses, from coffee to spices to pickles to leather. Pushing his hat back on his forehead so he could see better, he gazed at the crowded shelves and colorful displays.

A pretty woman with dark hair tucked up in a neat bun smiled at him as he glanced around the store. "Good morning. I'm Christine Morgan, and this is my store. Can I help you find something?"

Noah lifted his hat. "A pleasure to meet you, ma'am. My name's Noah Jeffers."

"Oh!" The woman's hand flew to her chest. "You must be the new minister."

"Yes, ma'am. I am that." At least for the time being. Once people learned his true identity, he might be tarred and feathered and sent away on foot—barefoot. "I don't need much and thought I might just look around to see what all you have."

She nodded. "Take your time. I'm not going anywhere."

Noah meandered down one aisle and up another

until he found the pie tins. He peeked over his shoulder at Mrs. Morgan. How could an unmarried minister living in a boardinghouse explain purchasing pie pans?

He blew out a deep breath. Well, there was no getting around it. There were two styles of pans: one a blue granite with white specks and the other a plain silver pan with wavy edges. He looked around the store, glad that no other customers had come in, and tucked two of the silver pans under his arms. Heat warmed his neck, and he shook his head. A grown man buying pie plates. Paying retribution was going to hurt more than his money pouch.

He picked out a new comb and then stopped at the ready-made shirts. He needed a new white shirt for preaching in, but that would have to wait until he'd earned his first wages. Mrs. Morgan watched him approach, and her brows lifted when she caught sight of the pans.

"What do you plan to do with those?"

Noah shrugged. He didn't want to tell a lie, but neither could her tell her the truth.

"I guess they might make good collection plates for the church," she said.

He turned them over and knocked on one. "They might at that."

She tallied up the items and wrote something in a small ledger book. Noah paid her the required sum and picked up his purchase. "Will I see you and Mr. Morgan in church this Sunday?"

She glanced out the open door for a moment then faced him again. "There is no Mr. Morgan. My Jarrod died years ago, Reverend."

Noah winced. He'd have to be more careful addressing people he didn't know in the future. "I'm sorry for your loss, ma'am."

She swatted her hand in the air. "It was a long time ago. I will be at church Sunday, along with my daughter, Tessa, and my son, Billy, if I can get him to come. It's getting harder and harder these days."

"I'll pray for Billy, ma'am. That God would get a hold of him like He did me. Don't give up hope."

Her sweet smile warmed Noah's insides. "If there's ever anything I can do for you, Mrs. Morgan, please let me know. I'm staying at the boardinghouse."

She nodded. "Thank you for your generous offer. You may have already met my daughter, I believe. She's a good friend of Jacqueline Davis."

Noah's heart quickened just hearing Jack's full name. It was a beautiful name, and he'd never understood why she preferred being called by a boy's name. "I don't think I have met your daughter yet, ma'am, but I look forward to it."

Mrs. Morgan leaned back against the counter, a gleam sparking in her blue eyes. "Tessa is close to your age, and she's quite a pretty girl. She has my blue eyes and her father's blond hair."

A warning bell clanged in Noah's mind. This wasn't the first time a young woman's mama had tried to get him to notice her daughter. He smiled and stepped toward the door. "If she looks anything like you, ma'am, I'm sure she is." He tipped his hat and hurried outside, certain he'd seen a blush rising to Mrs. Morgan's cheeks.

Maybe he shouldn't have made that last comment. When was he going to learn to think before he spoke? The Morgans hadn't lived in Lookout when he was last here, so he'd never made their acquaintance. Was Billy older or younger than his sister? Either way, he must be a grown man. Suddenly, the vision of the young ladies he'd seen in Jack's bedroom that day he'd first arrived entered his mind. Had one of those visitors been Tessa Morgan?

Noah ventured away from the boardinghouse and down the street. He passed the marshal's office but didn't stop. Luke Davis hadn't asked him again if he'd ever been in Lookout before, and for that he was grateful.

He passed the stage depot and then the café, where his steps slowed. After living much of his life without decent food to eat, the scent of something baking always gave him pause. He inhaled deeply, wondering if Polly Dykstra still managed the café that held her name. The older woman had been kind to him, allowing him to chop wood for her in exchange for a meal or occasionally a pie. His mouth watered, even though his belly was still filled with Mrs. Davis's delicious cooking.

Pushing on, he noticed that the saloon had been moved to the far end of Main Street and several new businesses had been erected. A dentist office sat where the old saloon had been, and Noah noticed a sign on the door. He crossed the street, dodging a wagon, and loped up the steps. Squinting, he read the sign. CHECK AT THE SALOON IF I'M NOT HERE. Staring down the street, Noah couldn't help wondering if the dentist also worked at the saloon or spent his time drinking. Either way, he wasn't too sure he'd contact the man if he ever needed a tooth pulled.

He continued his tour of the town, making note of the other new buildings and businesses. At some point, he ought to stop in each one, introduce himself, and invite those working there to church. Pastor Taylor had told Noah in a letter he'd written about the church that only about one-half of the town attended services at his church, which was the only one in town. Noah sent a prayer heavenward. "Lord, help me to make a difference in this town while I'm here. Give me a chance to redeem my early years before I knew You."

He paused at the end of Apple Street and stared past the houses lining the lane. A half mile northeast of town was the site of his old home, a shack really—if it was still standing. Part of him longed to go see if anything remained, but another part didn't want to have anything to do with his past. He kicked a rock and sent it skittering across the dirt road. Most of his memories were bad ones, anyway.

The pie plates under his arm slipped, and he pressed his arm tight against his body to keep them from falling. They'd reminded him of the task he still had to complete. His heart pounded harder the closer he got to the mayor's house. What if someone saw him and asked what he was doing? How could he respond without telling a falsehood?

Lord, I believe in my heart that You want me to make restitution for my past deeds, so give me the courage to complete this task.

∽

Jack moseyed into the store and searched the building, disappointed to find it empty except for Mrs. Morgan. She was certain she'd seen the parson enter when she'd glanced out her bedroom window a few minutes ago. There was nothing particularly odd about a minister going into a mercantile, but her reporter instincts sensed Noah Jeffers was up to something.

"Morning, Jacqueline." Mrs. Morgan smiled. "It's good to see you up again. I hope you're feeling better after your fall."

Jack grimaced at the mention of her plummet off the mayor's roof. She'd been halfway surprised he hadn't marched over to her house to lecture her about respecting people's property. The fact that he hadn't confirmed in her mind that he was working on some big plan for the city. She just had to discover what it was. She leaned against the counter and took the weight off her injured leg. "I'm still a bit sore, but I'm getting better. Thanks for asking."

"If you're looking for Tessa, she isn't here. She ran out the door, mumbling something about needing to go to Penny's for a while."

"No. Actually, I was wondering. . . . Didn't Noah Jeffers come in a little while ago?"

Mrs. Morgan nodded, picked up a feather duster, and started swiping the cans of vegetables on the shelf behind the counter. "Yes, he was here about ten minutes ago. Bought a few things and left. He's a nice young man, and quite handsome with that dark hair and eyes, don't you think? Tessa can't quit talking about him."

Jack wasn't about to admit that she did indeed find Reverend Jeffers attractive, much to her consternation. Shouldn't a minister be plain looking so a woman wouldn't waste time dwelling on his features instead of his message? Why, the man had even invaded her dreams. How was she to fight something like that? Forcing her frustrations aside, she smiled at Tessa's mother. "Yes, she made it clear to Penny and me that she intends to marry him."

Mrs. Morgan's blue eyes widened. "She never said a thing about that to me. Isn't it ironic that I just gushed about her attributes to the parson?"

Jack pursed her lips. The poor man hadn't been in town two days, and the Morgans already had him in their sights. At least she hoped she was no longer in Billy's. A shudder wormed its way down her back.

Mrs. Morgan paused. "Tessa told me that you don't plan to marry Billy." She nibbled her lower lip and stared out the door. Finally she met Jack's gaze again. "I can't say as I blame you, although I was hoping to welcome you into the family. Billy has always been a handful, and now that he's far bigger than me, I don't know how to handle him."

Jack shifted her feet, uncomfortable talking about Billy with his mother. From the day the Morgans first moved to town, she'd known Billy was a wild child. He seemed to pick up where Butch Laird left off when he left town. She hadn't been very kind to the lonely youth. She'd thought Butch a big bully but had had second thoughts after she'd talked to him once. It seemed the boy who stank like pigs wanted to make something more of his life than his father had. What had happened to him?

She shook Butch from her mind and refocused on Billy's mother. The poor woman looked to be at her wit's end. "Maybe you could get Reverend Jeffers to talk to Billy. There's not all that much difference in their ages, I imagine."

Mrs. Morgan's expression brightened, and she stood taller. "Why, that's a wonderful idea. Do you think he'd do it?"

Jack shrugged. "I don't know why not. He seems nice enough." Secretive, but nice.

"I may come over and talk to him this evening, if you're sure he won't mind."

"It's part of a minister's job to counsel folks who need help, isn't it?"

Mrs. Morgan nodded. "Yes, I do believe it is."

A shadow darkened the doorway, and Christine Morgan glanced past Jack, her face erupting into a brilliant smile. The woman—who had to be in her late thirties—reached up and tucked a loose strand of hair behind her ear, then licked her lips. She dropped the duster on the floor and quickly shed her apron.

Interesting.

Jack slowly turned to see who had so effectively snagged the woman's interest that she'd primp and grin like a schoolgirl. A tall cowboy stood in the doorway, his gaze equally riveted to the store clerk's. Jack smelled a romance in the making.

Mrs. Morgan hurried toward the door. "How can I help you, Mr. Kessler?"

Jack ambled down an aisle and paused in front of the ready-made dresses. She picked up the hem of a dark rose calico and pretended to be studying it. A person with better manners would leave and give the lovebirds some privacy, but she wouldn't become a full-time reporter if she didn't do a little snooping. Besides, neither Mrs. Morgan nor Mr. Kessler seemed to notice she was still there.

Something tickled the back of her mind, and she struggled to grasp hold of the thought. Suddenly, as if someone had turned on one of those electric lights she'd read about, the memory was revealed: Rand Kessler had once asked her ma to marry him—so she'd heard. Then she remembered that he used to come around for a while but had stopped after Luke returned to town.

Jack eyed him over the skirt of the dress. She'd heard Garrett talk about him over dinner before. The man owned a large ranch a few hours' ride from Lookout, if she was remembering correctly. She dropped hold of the dress and fingered the trim on a dark green one that she actually liked. Pants were still her preference, but she rarely got to wear them now that she was grown up. Her ma nearly had apoplexy the last time she'd donned them, and that wasn't a good state for a woman carrying a baby to be in.

Mr. Kessler must have suddenly remembered his hat, because he yanked it off. His tanned cheeks and ears had a reddish cast to them. He was nice looking for such an older man. Jack guessed him to be in his midforties—far too old to come courting.

"It's a pleasure to see you in town midweek, Mr. Kessler." Mrs. Morgan leaned back against the counter, flashing a wide smile at him.

"I. . .uh. . .had some business to tend to at the freight office, but Garrett wasn't there."

"I saw him ride out earlier this morning, just as I was opening the store. Must have gone to pick up something, because his wagon was empty."

Mr. Kessler shrugged. "Don't matter none. I just left him a note."

"Oh well, good thing your trip wasn't wasted."

A smile tugged at one corner of the man's mouth. "It's never a waste when I get to see you, Christine."

"Oh!" Mrs. Morgan fanned her face with her hand. "What a nice thing to say."

"It's just the truth, ma'am." He curled the rim of his hat and glanced down.

Jack grimaced. If things got any more syrupy, she just might retch. Why did perfectly normal people become fools when romance came calling? Even big, tough ranchers who would never back down from a fight or could break the wildest bronc became sweet like honey when they fell for a woman. Would a man ever act like that toward her? Did she even want one to?

A movement out the window and across the street snagged her attention. She strained her eyes to see who was walking toward her, past the mayor's house. Her pulse picked up its pace. Noah Jeffers! What reason would he have to walk between houses? Most normal folks stuck to the boardwalks. The sun reflected off something under his arm. He ducked down—or did he bend to pick up something? Then he turned onto the alley and disappeared behind the bank. Intrigued, Jack started to follow but held her ground, hating to miss out on whatever happened in the store.

"I was wondering. Would you. . .ah. . .consider going with. . .ah. . .me to the social this Saturday? That is if you're not going with someone else already."

Sucked right back into the blossoming romance, Jack abandoned all thought of following the minister. How much trouble could a man of God get into, anyway? She lowered the skirt of the green dress, wishing she had something to write notes on. If Mrs. Morgan didn't answer the man fast, Jack feared he'd be buying a new hat before he left.

Mrs. Morgan's hand flew up and rested on her chest. "Why, I'd be delighted, Rand."

The grins on their faces reminded Jack of when her ma and Luke had first gotten married.

Mr. Kessler slapped his crumpled hat back on his head. "That's great. I'll pick you up a little before six, and I'd like to purchase a bag of that horehound candy and another of the lemon drops."

With his difficult chore over, Mr. Kessler seemed business-minded once again. Mrs. Morgan bagged the candy and set it on the counter, quoting the price. He dropped several coins into her hand and pocketed one bag of candy and handed her the other. "This is for you. I recall how you mentioned that you loved lemon drops."

Mrs. Morgan clutched the surprise gift to her chest. "Why, Rand, that's so nice of you. I'm much obliged."

He nodded, spun on his heels, then stopped just outside the door and glanced back. "See you on Saturday."

Mrs. Morgan watched the door for a long while then lifted the bag of candy with both hands and held it to her nose. She closed her eyes, and Jack imagined she must be inhaling the tangy scent of the hard candy. After a moment, the store owner hurried to the back room, and Jack took that opportunity to dash out the door. When a pain charged up her leg, she slowed her steps and carefully made her way across the dirt road, dodging the horse flops.

The newspaper was due out tomorrow, but if Jenny hadn't filled up all the space, just maybe she could post a brief vignette about shopping for love in the mercantile.

Noah hurried down the street, thankful that nobody was out and about, then skulked past the east side of the mayor's house. As he passed under a window, he could hear a woman humming. His heart quickened again. He ducked down, scurried past the window, then slowed his steps as he came to the back of the house. The Burkes had a large back porch, and Mrs. Burke had often left her pies on a table there to cool. They'd been much too conveniently located within easy reach for a poor boy who never got to eat home-baked goods. Noah winced, remembering the two pies he'd stolen from that same porch.

Pulling the note and a dollar from his pocket, he glanced around again, then tiptoed across the grass and onto the porch. He all but dropped the pie plates on the table with the note and dollar, then hightailed it back across the yard and onto Bluebonnet Lane. He quickly headed for the church. His heart thrummed, matching the thumping in his ears, and he licked his dry lips. His legs wobbled like jelly. Peering over his shoulder, he was relieved not to see anyone following him.

Never had doing a good deed felt so. . .devious.

One down, about a dozen more to go.

Chapter 9

After picking up a load of supplies for Dan Howard, the livery owner, Garrett drove the wagon back toward home. His passenger hadn't uttered a single word for the past hour. At least she wasn't one of those gabby gals who yakked a man's ear off.

He'd never admit it to anyone, but he rather liked having a pretty female by his side. At some time or another, he had started thinking more about settling down and starting a family, and at nearly forty, he couldn't afford to wait much longer. He actually envied Luke and Mark. Both were married and had children, while he'd been content to work and have fun in life. But living alone wasn't fun anymore.

And did he want to leave this world one day and not leave behind children—his legacy?

He let the idea simmer in his mind. Yeah, he was ready to marry. The problem was there was no woman in Lookout who snagged his attention enough that he'd want to spend the rest of his life with her.

The woman beside him gasped, and he reached for his rifle. Her hand shot out and grabbed his arm. "What is that?"

Pulling the rifle into his lap, he scanned the prairie but saw nothing except grasses and colorful wildflowers waving in the light breeze. "I don't see nothin'."

She tugged on his sleeve, sending tingles up his arm. He shook them off as if they were pesky flies and followed the way her finger pointed. "Over there. I've never seen a bird so blue. What is it?"

Garrett relaxed, hearing the trill of the bird that sat twenty feet away atop a bush. He'd half expected she'd seen an outlaw. He'd encountered few of them during the years he'd been hauling freight, but you never knew what to expect, so he had to stay alert. "That's an indigo bunting."

She turned to him, gazing at him with curiosity, not anger. He'd never seen light brown eyes like hers before, yet they seemed oddly familiar. Had he known someone else with similar ones?

Her teeth brushed over her lower lip in an enticing manner, stirring Garrett's senses. He forced himself to look away. How could a woman who'd efficiently fueled his temper an hour ago—a woman whose name he didn't know—stir him in a way no other woman had in a long while?

"Um. . .why is it called an indigo bunting when it's so blue? Isn't indigo a purple color?"

Garrett shrugged, frustrated with himself for noticing so much about the woman. "I don't know. Maybe the guy who named it was color-blind or something."

Her brows dipped, and she turned away. "You knew the name of the bird. I just thought you might know more about it."

"Well, you're wrong. I just happen to know the name because I got bored one night and thumbed through one of the books my brother left behind. There were gray and white pictures of the bird, and the book said it was a dark blue, so I guess indigo is a dark blue."

"The lady I lived with used a deep purple fabric

in a quilt she was making and always called it indigo. That's why I thought that."

Garrett grunted. He was a man. What did he care about colors? Other than to notice a woman in a pretty dress. "I'm sorry your brother moved away." She caught his gaze again and narrowed her eyes. "He was always the nicer of you two."

Garrett scowled at the intended slur. Here he was offering this nameless woman a ride, and she had the gall to insult him! "How do you know my brother? And how do you know my name?"

Her bold gaze melted, and she returned to watching the prairie. The wind picked up a strand of her hair and tossed it about. "I lived in Lookout for a short while, but it was a long time ago."

He searched his mind but still came up empty. "How do you know Rachel Davis?"

"I stayed at Hamilton House."

Garrett let that thought stew. Rachel's home and boardinghouse hadn't been called Hamilton House for almost ten years, not since shortly after she married Luke. Rachel didn't want the name to constantly remind Luke of her first husband, so she asked the townsfolk to quit calling it that. It had taken awhile for folks to get out of the habit, but most people now just referred to it as "the boardinghouse" or "Rachel's place."

Garrett wasn't one to play games unless he was the instigator, and the woman's evasiveness was starting to wear thin on his nerves. "Why don't you just tell me your name and get it over with?"

She sucked her lips inward, as if that could keep her from talking, but she finally heaved a sigh of resignation. "It's Carly. Carly Payton."

Garrett stared at the landscape, rolling the name over in his mind. Carly was an unusual name—a pretty one at that. "Well, Miss Payton, nice to meet you."

She looked at him as if he'd gone loco. "We've met before."

"When? The name does sound a bit familiar."

She uttered a very unladylike snort and shook her head.

Garrett didn't like her mocking him. Was she telling the truth about her name or just stringing him along? Suddenly, like the headlight of a locomotive coming ever closer in the dark, his mind grasped hold of the name, and realization hit him upside the head. She was that outlaw bride! The gal who'd pretended to be one of the mail-order brides that he and Mark had ordered for Luke years ago before he married Rachel. The sister of the man who'd kidnapped Rachel and tried to rob the Lookout bank. That was her—the criminal who'd been sent to prison for her unlawful deeds.

He pulled back on the reins, set the brake, and jumped down. The horses snorted. One pawed the ground, but he ignored them. Pacing through the knee-high grass, he tried to wrap his mind around something else. That look Rachel and Luke had exchanged at the dinner table suddenly took on meaning. He stared at Miss Payton, and it made complete sense. Rachel was aiming to match him up with that outlaw lady.

Not today.

Not tomorrow.

Not ever.

He wouldn't fall for Rachel and Luke's scheming, and if he wasn't already closer to Lookout than Denison, he'd turn the wagon around and take the jailbird back.

She watched him but said nothing. Yeah, she was pretty, and yeah she'd stirred up his senses, but he would never lower himself to marry an ex-convict—a woman who'd robbed banks and ridden with an outlaw gang. What kind of mother would she be to his kids?

"I'm sorry. If I'd known it would upset you so much to ride with me, I would have found another way to get to Lookout." She swiped her eyes and turned her body so that her back was to him.

Great. Just great. He flung his arms out to the side, then hauled them back down and slapped his thighs. Now she was trying to use tears to weaken him.

Well, it wouldn't work.

He climbed back onto the buckboard. Suddenly a shot rang out, and a fire like Hades itself seared his shoulder. The surprise and the force of the blow knocked him back, and he fell to the ground. The sky blackened before turning blue again. He could hear riders galloping closer and tried to sit, but the pain nailed him to the ground.

"Are you all right?" Miss Payton stood. Her frantic gaze leapt from him to the riders and back.

"Go!" He swatted his good arm in the air. "Get out of here."

"I can't leave you. Get on up here and hurry!"

"No time." He might not like the woman, but neither did he want to see her suffer at the hands of robbers. 'Course, she might just know the men and be in no danger at all. Maybe those fellows were a welcome-home party. He huffed a cynical laugh, then peered under the wagon to see how far off the riders were. Not far at all.

Two more bullets pinged off the side of the wagon. Miss Payton ducked. She seemed to be wrestling with indecision. Then she steeled her expression and snatched up his rifle. She spun around and shot both men out of the saddle with just two shots.

Garrett's mouth hung open, and he struggled to

make sense of what he'd seen. Not even Luke could shoot like that, and he'd been in the army for a decade. He lowered his head back against the ground. Grass tickled his ear and cheek, making his face itch. How could a woman shoot so well?

Maybe it was God's protection. He stared up at the sky and thanked his Maker. He believed in God, but he wasn't as faithful to pray or even attend church as he should be. Realizing how he could just as easily be lying there dead instead of wounded made him conscious of things he rarely thought about.

Miss Payton climbed down and hurried toward him. "Are you hurt bad, Mr. Corbett?"

"Where'd you learn to shoot like that?"

She shrugged and leaned over him, checking his wound. "If I bind it, do you think you could make it to Lookout? It's closer than Denison, right?"

"Yeah." He nodded, still impressed with her coolness under fire and the fact that she refused to leave him. He couldn't help thinking if the situation had been reversed, he might well be racing toward home, with her lying alone on the prairie. "Who taught you to shoot?"

She nibbled that lip again, making his belly turn somersaults. "My brother, Tyson. I picked it up real fast. He said I was a natural."

"I'm duly impressed."

A shy smile tilted her lips, and she hurried back to the wagon and started yanking garments from her satchel. When she came to what looked like a nightgown, she used her teeth and ripped off the six-inch-wide ruffle along the bottom. Rushing back to his side, she tore off a smaller square and folded it in quarters. She knelt beside him and dabbed the square against his wound.

Garrett hissed at the burning pain but sat still,

letting her tend him. With her head bent, he could smell the floral scent of her hair. She must have washed it recently. It was black as a raven's wing. The wisp that had pulled loose fell across his cheek, taunting him.

He didn't want to like her.

Didn't want to be drawn to her.

When he thought of marrying, he wanted a woman people respected. He had worked hard to gain the town's esteem after his wild years as a rowdy youth, and that was important to him. He wanted to wed a gal who could cook, sew, keep house, and raise children. Thinking back to the bride contest a decade ago that had been held to determine which mail-order bride would make Luke the best wife, he remembered that Miss Payton—or Miss Blackstone as she'd been called then—couldn't cook or sew. What good was she to a man? Other than to shoot bandits out of their saddles.

She pulled tight on the two sections of fabric, and Garrett gasped at the stinging it caused.

"Oh, stop being a baby. He just grazed your arm."

"Try getting shot and see how you like it, lady." He grunted when she tightened it again.

She stood and walked back to the wagon. "I have been. Twice. And I can tell you, it's not the worst thing I've endured."

He shook his head. Surely she didn't say she'd been shot before. The bullet wound must be affecting his head somehow. Carefully he stood, taking a moment to shake off the dizziness. He needed to check on the two men she'd shot and get them tied up before they came to—if they were even alive.

By the time he made it to the wagon, he felt as if he'd been breaking mustangs all day. How could one shot that only winged him affect him this much?

Maybe the blow his head took when it collided with the packed dirt was making him woozy—that and thoughts of marriage and Miss Payton all in the same sentence. This was all Rachel's fault.

Miss Payton headed toward their attackers, frayed nightgown and rifle in hand. He shook his head and followed after her. She'd never be able to overpower even one of those men if he came to.

By the time he finally got to where the men had fallen off their horses, she had one unconscious man tied up and was working on the other. He bent down and tugged at the man's bindings, not a little impressed with the good job she'd done. A grin teased his mouth when he noticed she'd tied the man up with pink fabric that was covered in tiny red roses and had wrapped his head wound with the same. Suddenly his smile slackened, and he glanced at his own wound. A groan erupted that drew her attention.

"You all right?"

He nodded and strode across the grass toward the closest horse. He'd have to get these bandages off before he got back to Lookout, or he'd be the laughingstock of the town.

Chapter 10

Noah's stomach still churned, and his legs hadn't fully quit wobbling, but the pie plates had been delivered, and he felt better for having completed that task. He walked around the church, praying for his congregation and making mental notes of things that needed repair. The outside of the white building was in decent condition but could use a new coat of paint, and a cracked window needed replacing.

He still found it hard to believe that God had entrusted this church and its people into his care. Who was he? Nothing but a rowdy kid who'd met God and changed his ways. He'd grown up some, too, but he felt inadequate in so many ways to shepherd a flock of believers.

Pete had told him numerous times not to dwell on his doubts but to shove them away and trust God. Mentally, Noah packed his insecurities back in a box and refocused on the church. The shin-high grass needed cutting before Sunday services. He walked around back, hoping to find a lawn mower, but he didn't. He'd have to ask Marshal Davis about that.

He strode back to the front of the church, eager to see inside. This building had also served as the schoolhouse when he lived in town, not that he had fond memories of those years. The other children had made fun of him because he'd been fat and smelled bad. His pa had been of the opinion that a man only needed a bath once a month, and with his ma dying when he was young, nobody had taught Noah otherwise—until he met Pete. He certainly hoped Mrs. Davis didn't mind him taking several baths a week. He shivered at the thought of how filthy he used to be and promised himself to never be that way again.

Slowing his steps near the front door, he noticed a large man waddling toward the church. Something about him was vaguely familiar. Noah crossed the churchyard and met him under a tall oak that had only been a little more than a sapling when he was last here. "Morning."

The man slowed, his chest heaving from his exertion. He leaned one hand against the tree trunk and struggled to catch his breath. "I'm Titus—Burke. Lookout's mayor. You the new preacher?"

Noah nodded. "Yes, sir. I'm Noah Jeffers." The mayor had always been a heavyset man, but now he was as wide as an ox. His dark hair, which used to be parted in the middle and stuck down, had thinned, and what was left had been brushed forward in an ineffective attempt to cover his bald spot.

"Sorry I haven't come to the boardinghouse sooner to meet you, but I've had some pressing business to attend to." The mayor pushed his wire-frame glasses up on his nose with one thumb. "Aren't you rather young to be a preacher?"

Noah shrugged. "I don't reckon age has much to do with sharing God's Word with folks."

Mayor Burke harrumphed. "You're wrong. How are you going to counsel people with problems when you haven't had time to experience things yourself? You married?"

"No, I'm not. And you might be surprised to

know of the trials I've endured. You don't have to be old to have experienced the bad things in life."

The light breeze taunted the mayor's hair, lifting it up and setting it down in a different place. The long, thin hairs looked odd, but Mayor Burke smashed his hand down on top of his head and pressed them back into submission. Noah suspected the strong-willed mayor browbeat some of the people in town the same way, but he wasn't going to become one of them.

"Look, Mayor, I had a wonderful mentor—a godly man who dearly loved the Lord, who personally instructed me in the ways of God for a number of years. We studied the Word for hours a day. I'm not perfect by any means, and I may be younger than most ministers, but I feel God called me here to fill in for Pastor Taylor, and I plan to do the best job I can. All I ask is that you give me a chance to prove myself."

The mayor studied him as if taking his measure, then finally nodded. "Fair enough. Ray Mann, our church board director, told me about you and gave his recommendation. My missus and I'll be sittin' in the pews come Sunday."

Noah nodded, and the mayor turned and made his way back across the street. Noah had talked with Mr. Mann when he first arrived in Lookout and was relieved to know the man had given him his approval. Releasing a huge sigh, he glanced up at the sky. "I sure need Your help here, Lord. Equip me to do the task You've set before me."

Hot, musty air met him as he stepped inside the church building, so he left the door ajar. Walking the center aisle, he remembered his school days and noticed all the changes. Gone were the chalkboard, desks, maps, and schoolbooks, replaced by a podium and skillfully constructed pews. He'd never attended church when he lived here previously, but the building was still familiar. A colorful array of lights danced on the floor just past the podium from the sun shining in the large stained-glass window. That was new. The window depicted several scenes of Christ's life, and he rather liked the idea of it being behind him when he preached, almost as if God was looking over his shoulder.

His stomach swirled at the thought of standing before the town that he'd once despised and telling its inhabitants about God's love. Memories of fights he'd been in flooded his mind. Yeah, he'd started some, but he'd been blamed for many more that he'd never participated in. He became the scapegoat, and the teacher never believed him when he proclaimed his innocence. He dropped onto the first pew, head in his hands.

Did those former students still live in town? Would they be the very people he'd minister to in a few days? In spite of believing God had sent him to Lookout, he felt so inadequate.

He knelt on the hard floor and placed his elbows on the pew. "Help me to forgive those who wronged me in the past, Lord, even as I ask that the people I wronged will forgive me. Give me strength and guidance. Don't abandon me, Father. I need You now more than ever."

He clenched his hands together. Everyone he'd ever loved had abandoned him. His mother had died when he was a young boy, but even before that, his tiny little sister had passed on. Then his father had died when he was fifteen, not that he shed many tears over him. Even Jack had turned on him—although they'd never been friends. It ate at his gut to think she might have been afraid of him, and she'd have been justified. Like his father, when his temper reached its limit, he spewed on whoever was nearest, and the flame of his anger had scorched Jack more than once. At one time, he'd fancied himself in love with her, but she'd made it clear that she couldn't stand him. If she knew his real identity now, would she give him half a chance to prove he was a different person?

Noah muttered a groan. He wasn't here to think about her. He had a purpose. He was no longer the lonely boy who craved a friend and wanted to prove he could be a better man than his drunken father.

If he could just keep his thoughts off of Jack, he'd be all right.

But the question remained: How could he do that?

"So, what do you think about my story idea?" Jack watched Jenny Evans. She'd told the newspaper editor about what she'd overseen at the mercantile and couldn't wait to set pen to paper.

Jenny squeezed her lower lip together with her thumb and index finger, as she often did when deep in thought. "Hmm. . .it's interesting, but I'd hate to do anything that might scare Rand Kessler away. Catherine Morgan could use a husband, and Rand has wanted to marry for years."

Disappointed, Jack leaned back against the counter. She hadn't considered that her story might scare Rand away or otherwise affect the budding relationship. "What if we did the story but kept it anonymous? What if we said something like, 'A certain town widow was seen cavorting with a local rancher'?"

Jenny slowly nodded. "I like it. But be careful how you word the story so it's not too obvious who you're talking about, and *cavorting* is a word that could be taken the wrong way, so try to think up a better one."

She tapped her pencil against the desktop. "And maybe you should say *cowboy* instead of *rancher*—or just say *man*."

Staring at the ceiling, Jack contemplated Jenny's wise suggestions. "I can do that."

"Good. Then write it up, and get it back to me as soon as possible. I planned to start printing the papers this evening."

Jack nodded. "I'd hoped to have something about the new minister for you, but he's not very talkative."

Chuckling, Jenny grinned. "Well, that's something different—a preacher who doesn't have the gift of gab. Now that's a rarity. I just might have to come and hear him preach, given his messages are likely to be short."

Jenny had misconstrued what she'd tried to say, but Jack kept that thought to herself. She wasn't quite ready to admit to others that she suspected the preacher of harboring secrets.

"I'm glad to see you're healing quickly and that you didn't get hurt too bad trying to get that story on the mayor."

"Thanks. I'm still sore in places, especially my knee, but it could have been a lot worse. I don't know what I was thinking going up on that roof in my dress." Suddenly she straightened. "And just where did you get the idea that I was engaged to Billy Morgan?"

Jenny grinned again and leaned back in her chair with her hands clasped behind her head, elbows sticking up. "Billy told me, and others repeated what he'd said about not marrying you if you didn't come down."

"Well, you should have checked with me first." Jack crossed her arms and pinned a stern glare on Jenny. "I am not now nor ever have been engaged to Billy Morgan. That's just an odd fancy he's got."

Jenny shrugged. "You might change your mind in

110

a few years. He's a nice-looking young man."

"Yeah, but he's a sponger. He only helps his mother when he has to and then gallivants around town, getting in trouble. It's like he doesn't want to grow up. I don't want to marry that kind of man."

"Guess I'll have to print a retraction, but it did make interesting news." Jenny's shameless grin proved she wasn't sorry about what she'd done. "So just what kind of man would you want?"

An image of Noah Jeffers shoved aside all other pictures of the men she knew. Jack shook her head to rid him from her thoughts. She just found the man attractive, that was all. "I don't know that I'll ever get married. I've told you how I want to move to Dallas and be a big-city reporter."

Jenny straightened and leaned forward, her arms resting on her desk. "Don't forget I used to live in Dallas."

"Why would you leave there to come to a small town like Lookout?"

Jenny seemed to be pondering her response. "For one, I had a broken heart and needed to get away from the man who canceled our engagement. And two, men run the bigger towns, and women often have a harder time breaking into their world. I'd worked for some Dallas editors—all men. A few were nice, but most resented a woman working in their realm. I longed to start my own paper, but it would have been nearly impossible for me to do so in Dallas and to have to compete with the other already-established publishers."

Jenny had always encouraged her to seek her way in a man's world, so it took Jack off-guard to know her friend left Dallas rather than stay and compete for what she wanted. "Well, I don't see that there's much for me here. Besides, I don't plan to start my own newspaper, I just want to get a job where I can report the news and support myself."

"Have you talked this over with your mother?"

Jack nibbled on the inside of her cheek. Her mother would never want her to go. Luke wouldn't either, but he'd probably be more understanding. And how could she even begin to discuss such a topic when her ma was fixing to have another baby?

Jenny smiled. "I can see that you haven't." She stood, walked around her desk, and gently took hold of Jack's shoulders. "Big towns seem exciting and glamorous, but if you have no family or friends there, they can be frightening and lonely. I don't want to lose you here, but whatever you decide, you know I'll support you and help however I can." Jenny pulled her into a light hug then released her quickly. "Well, I'd best get the typesetting done if we're going to have a newspaper any time soon."

"I'll go find a quiet place to work on my story." Jack grabbed a pad of paper and pencil and hurried out of the office, probably just as embarrassed as Jenny at her rare show of affection. Jenny was a tough lady and rarely needed anyone, so it seemed. Maybe she'd just gotten her heart broken and no longer trusted men.

Hobbling down the boardwalk past the bank, she glanced across Bluebonnet Lane at the boardinghouse. If she went home, the kids would pester her, and she wouldn't finish her story in time. Her gaze traveled down the lane to the church. She loved sitting there when the place was empty, watching the sun shine through the lovely stained-glass window, but her knee was already aching.

With a sigh, she started across the road toward home. A sudden screech coming from her bedroom window halted her steps.

"Maaa! Alan hit—"

Jack turned toward the church. If Alan and Abby were fighting again, home was the last place she'd find any quiet. Taking it slow, she made her way down the street. She paused when she noticed the church door open, but this wasn't the first time someone had forgotten to close it. She stepped inside and shut the door. Instantly peace filled her. She dropped onto the nearest bench and blew out a breath. The ankle she'd twisted ached, and her knee throbbed. Doc Phillips had said that knee injuries could be slow to heal, but she'd hoped he was wrong. Hobbling along like someone's great-grandmother wasn't her normal speed.

She turned sideways on the bench and lifted her injured leg to the seat. After pulling up her skirt and petticoat, she rubbed her kneecap for a few minutes. When the pain lessened, she finally pulled out her paper and stared at it.

How could she slant the story without people guessing who she was referring to? Several ideas popped into her mind, but nothing was exactly what she was looking for.

"Hmm. . .maybe I should concentrate on the title first." She tapped her pencil against her mouth and stared at the colorful glass panes. She'd been so excited when the town decided to install the stained-glass windows after a tornado had blown through town and broken many of the clear panes in the church.

Shaking her head, she closed her eyes and tried to concentrate. Maybe "Shopping for Love" would work. But no, that might make people think of Mrs. Morgan since she ran the only mercantile in town.

Hmm, maybe "Lassoing Romance." There were many ranchers and cowboys in the county, so people wouldn't likely figure out who the man was. Or what about "Be on the Lookout for Cupid"?

She couldn't help giggling at the clever way she

incorporated the town name. She scribbled it down before she forgot it.

A loud sound—as if someone were sawing wood—echoed through the church, and Jack froze. Her gaze darted to the front, then the sides and back of the building. Her heart pounded so hard she thought it might break through her skin. *What in the world?*

She concentrated on listening, but also remembered the open door. What if some wild animal had wandered inside? But she'd never heard a creature that made such a sound.

For several minutes she sat frozen, listening to her heart pound in her ears, then finally shook her head. Maybe she'd imagined the noise or it had come from outside. She glanced down at her paper, determined to get her story written.

Spring is in the air. New creatures are being birthed on ranches across the rolling green hills of the countryside, and romance has come to town. A certain lonely widow has been seen in the company of an equally forlorn rancher.

Remembering what Jenny had said, she scratched out *rancher* and changed it to *cowboy*.

She closed her eyes again and willed the words to come. Writing articles was generally difficult at first—until her creative juices started flowing.

A loud snort ricocheted through the building. Jack jumped, and her pencil flew out of her hand and rolled under the pew in front of her. Her frantic gaze traveled the room. The only thing she knew that made a sound like that was a pig—and if it was in the church, it must be a wild one. She pulled up her legs and stood on the bench seat, her whole body shaking. Luke had warned her about wild pigs. They were mean and could tear a person apart.

She glanced at the door. Could she make it outside before the creature got to her?

Would her knee hold up if she tried to run?

Could wild pigs leap up onto pews?

A deep moan made her jump again.

If the creature was wounded, it would be even meaner. Her heart raced like a runaway horse, and she found it hard to breathe. Her gaze flew to the stained-glass window and the image of Jesus standing in the boat, calming the seas. "Could You calm a wild pig, Lord? Please?"

She lifted her skirts and sidestepped along the bench, keeping careful watch on all the aisles. She'd never been one to scare easily and hated feeling helpless. If she could just get close enough to the door. . .

A huge figure rose up at the front of the church, and Jack couldn't squelch the scream that would have made Abby proud. A man spun around, wide-eyed, and stared at her. He frowned, then rubbed his eyes. "Ja—uh. . .Miss Davis?"

Jack's knees bent, weak with relief. She giggled, mortified to have squealed like a pig and to be caught standing on the pew by the minister, no less. What would he think of her?

What did it matter?

Like a flame to kindling, her embarrassment sparked her irritation. "Why were you hiding up there like some child and making those weird noises? You scared me half to death."

He ran a hand through his messed-up hair, causing it to stand up in an enticing manner. Creases lined one cheek. His neck and ears turned beet red, and his shy grin did odd things to her stomach, which still hadn't settled from her fright. "I was praying. Guess I fell asleep."

"Those were snores I heard? Well, I pity your wife."

He walked toward her, hanging his head, a saucy

grin on his lips. "I don't have a wife, remember?"

She did, but he would soon acquire a spouse if Tessa had anything to say about it. "Yes, well, you won't have one long if you do marry and you snore like that every night."

He stopped at the end of her aisle and gazed up at her with his ink-black eyes. They were so dark she couldn't even see his pupils. She swallowed hard, not wanting to admit how attractive she found them.

"Allow me to help you down, Miss Davis, since I obviously scared you half to death."

"I wasn't scared," she blurted out before she could stop the words.

His brows lifted. "Ah, so let me guess. . . ." He glanced upward. "You're standing on the pew because you were just about to dust the ceiling."

She scowled. "Don't be ridiculous."

His hands found his hips, but his impudent grin seemed glued to his face. His eyes sparkled. "Then why are you standing on the pew?"

"I, uh. . .dropped my pencil." *Oh, horse feathers.* He had her, and he knew it.

His gaze lowered as he searched the floor. He stepped to the row in front of hers, bent down, and held up her pencil. "Imagine that, it was on the floor, not the ceiling."

"Ha ha, our minister is a jokester. That should certainly liven up the services." She snatched her pencil from his hand and stuck it in her hair over her ear. Obviously she wouldn't find any peace and quiet here with this joking preacher present. She reached down to take hold of the back of the pew in front of her. Before she could touch it, his hand snaked out and grabbed hers. "Let me assist you, Miss Davis."

Her eyes collided with his. Her rebellious heart pummeled her chest again. With him so close, she found it hard to breathe, but judging by his warm breath touching her face, he sure didn't. Slowly, she straightened. He laid her hand on one wide shoulder, claimed her other one and did the same. Then his hands wrapped around her waist. As if she weighed no more than Emmie, he lifted her down, his gaze never leaving hers.

Her legs had decided to pretend they were made of noodles, and her knees refused to lock. She sank down, but his hands tightened their grip, holding her steady.

"Are you all right?"

She shrugged. That was a highly debatable topic. How could any woman be completely composed with the handsome preacher so close—and he smelled so clean. "I. . .uh. . .think I may have overdone things, walking this far on my injured knee."

He frowned, but in the next instant, he scooped her into his arms. Jack gasped, yet she was amazed at how easily he held her and how good it felt. She lifted her gaze to his—so close, she could barely breathe. His lashes were long and thick, his eyes almost pleading. Many emotions crossed his face, but she couldn't read them. Up this close, she could see the slightest beginnings of his beard starting to grow in, even though she was certain he'd shaved this morning. Would his cheek feel smooth or rough?

He glanced down at her lips. Then he blinked several times, and an icy reserve replaced the warm look in his eyes, splashing onto her like a cold bucket of self-control.

"I'll carry you home, Miss Davis."

"No, just put me down."

"But you're hurt. I don't want you to injure your leg any more than it is."

"Why do you care?"

Although he didn't respond for a moment, his eyes revealed an inner struggle. Could he possibly have feelings for her?

No, it wasn't possible.

They'd only met.

Yet she couldn't help thinking she could spend the rest of her life in his arms. Tessa would be so mad if she found out.

"I'm your pastor. It's my job to care."

"I'm a reporter, and it's my job to get my story, but you refuse to answer my questions. What do you have to hide?"

"Most men in Texas are hiding something."

She wiggled her legs, and he loosened his hold but didn't set her down. "Most men in Texas aren't the only preacher in town, either."

He released her so suddenly she had to grab the back of the pew to keep from falling. "My past is my own. I've changed and am not the man I used to be, Miss Davis. God forgave me of my sins and set me on a new path. If you have a problem with me being the minister here, take it up with Him—or the church board."

He spun on his heel and marched out, slamming the door.

Jack lowered herself onto the bench. She shouldn't have pushed him, but she hadn't been prepared for her strong attraction to him. His arms felt so strong that he could shoulder any burden, yet she sensed she'd hurt him somehow. Would it have been so bad to let him carry her home?

Yes! It would. The whole town would be talking, and he just might lose his job, and she'd lose Tessa's friendship, such as it was. She found her paper and held it to her chest. How could she face him again?

But even more important, how could she discover what it was in his past that he wanted to keep secret?

Chapter 11

Carly twisted her hands as Lookout came into view. If things went as bad this time as on her last visit, she didn't know what she'd do. Jobs for unmarried women were hard enough to find, but for her, it was much more difficult. Few people wanted to hire an ex-convict.

She studied the buildings as they drew closer to Lookout. The town had grown quite a lot over the past decade. They drove past a schoolhouse that hadn't been there before and then the church. Would the members of this congregation be more accepting of her than the last?

Shaking off her worry, she glanced at Mr. Corbett. "How is your arm? I truly didn't mind driving."

"It's nothing." He gnawed on a stem of dried grass he'd plucked after he'd tied the thieves' horses to the back of the wagon. "Those fellows still passed out back there?"

Carly twisted around on the seat and studied the two robbers that they'd thrown over the horses and bound. One man's head was lifted, but thankfully it was turned away from her. The other man didn't look as if he'd moved a muscle. She sincerely hoped she hadn't killed him, even though they'd probably planned to rob them. She knew well how individuals with a tainted upbringing could change when God got ahold of them, and she muttered a brief prayer for their souls.

The wagon slowed, and she turned to see the boardinghouse. The light green, three-story home with white trim looked exactly the same. The porch railing, with its white spindles, still encircled the house, and even the rocking chairs survived, awaiting someone with a few minutes to relax. She swallowed hard. Rachel would welcome her with open arms, but what about the marshal? He'd been the one to arrest her and take her to Dallas all those years ago, once he learned she was a wanted outlaw, pretending to be one of the mail-order brides who had come to marry him.

What if he *had* picked her and they'd married? Would she have actually gone that far? All she'd wanted was the chance to get away from her brother and stop living an outlaw's life. Her plans to find out about gold shipments had failed, but she'd made some good friends—one in particular. She was counting on that friend to allow her to live in her home for the time being.

Shoring up her nerves, Carly thought about the past. She knew in her heart that back then, she *would* have married the marshal if given the chance, even with the constant threat of him figuring out she was a member of the Payton gang—albeit a reluctant member. Nothing was more important to her than having a home and people who cared about her. Even her own brother had wanted her around only so he could use her to his advantage. A sharp pain stabbed her heart. At least he could never hurt her again.

The wagon stopped, and she heaved a sigh. Time to find out how things would be. If the marshal was uncomfortable around her, she couldn't stay. Rachel had saved her life by leading her to Christ, and Carly wasn't about to cause her strife in her own home.

"What are you so antsy about?" Mr. Corbett set the brake, then looped the reins around the wooden handle.

Carly's heart leapt into her throat. "What makes you think I'm nervous?"

He grinned, revealing his straight white teeth. "Oh, maybe it was all the squirming you've done ever since Lookout came into view. Or maybe it was because you grabbed hold of my arm and wouldn't turn loose."

Carly gasped. "I did no such thing."

His head bobbed up and down. "You did. Wanna see the marks your fingernails made on my skin?" He winced as he moved his injured arm and started unbuttoning the cuff of his sleeve.

"That isn't necessary. I apologize for causing you so much trouble, Mr. Corbett. Thank you for the ride." She stood and reached over the seat to retrieve her satchel, but when she turned back, he tried to take it from her.

"I'll carry that."

"No, please let go. You're injured, and I'm quite capable of handling it myself." She gave it a sharp yank, but he didn't let go.

His interesting lips curved up in a grin that would probably melt the heart of a less determined woman. This man had interfered in the lives of too many women. She wasn't about to let him mess with hers. Such as it was.

"A gentleman always assists a lady."

Since when were the ornery Corbett brothers gentlemen? Carly tugged again on the handle, confused by his sudden desire to be her champion. Back on the prairie when he'd learned her name, he couldn't get away from her fast enough. She mulled over how to retrieve her satchel from his tight grasp. Surely she could out-tug a man weakened by a bullet wound in one arm. Maybe she just needed to distract him. "So, now I'm a lady? That ain't what you thought earlier."

His grin faded, and his gaze turned serious. "That was before you saved my life with your fancy shooting."

Dread churned in her belly like bad stew. "You ain't gonna tell no one, are ya?" Carly winced. Whenever she got upset, she tended to fall back into speaking how she used to—before Tillie taught her proper grammar.

His brows lifted up to the edge of his hat. "Why not? That's something to be proud of. Not many men can shoot that good, much less a woman."

Much less a woman. For some odd reason it hurt her to learn he was one of those men who thought women inferior. She wouldn't argue that men were stronger, but she had learned to be clever and resourceful just to survive. He watched her with those intriguing eyes. If he expected her to thank him for his offhanded compliment, he'd be waiting a long time.

She heard the front door to the boardinghouse open behind her, and Mr. Corbett's gaze darted past her shoulder. She took that moment to give another hard, two-handed jerk, and the bag not only fell free of his hand, but it sailed backward out of hers as well.

"Hey! Watch it."

Carly spun around from the momentum and nearly toppled across the nearest horse's rump. She swung her arms, struggling to regain her balance and not fall off the wagon. Mr. Corbett grabbed her arm, steadying her, and she saw Marshal Davis standing in front of the door, holding her bag against his chest, one brow lifted, an odd expression playing on his face. The sun glinted off the badge pinned to his shirt, and Carly dropped onto the bench seat. So much for making a good first impression.

Mr. Corbett chuckled and glanced up at the sky. "I've heard of it raining cats and dogs, but satchels? We'd better hurry up and get inside before any more fall from the sky. I've already conked my head once today, and that's enough." He held his hand toward Carly. "After you, Miss Payton."

The marshal set her bag in a rocker near the front door and strode forward. Carly's heart raced as if she'd just robbed a bank and was being pursued by a posse. She attempted to swallow the big lump in her throat, but her mouth was so dry she was about to spit cotton. Rachel's husband hadn't changed a whole lot except for looking a bit older. He was still a handsome man, but she'd hardly expected his welcoming smile or the lack of condemnation in his brown eyes.

He stopped next to the wagon and raised a hand. "Rachel's half beside herself from excitement to see you again. She's been baking all morning."

Steeling herself, Carly allowed him to help her out of the wagon. He released her hand, and she glanced up at him. She'd forgotten how tall he was. Mr. Corbett had to be close to six feet, and the marshal was at least two inches taller. He smiled at her then glanced at his cousin, still standing in the wagon. His smile dimmed as he looked at the two men tied to their horses. "What happened to you, Cuz, and who are they?"

Mr. Corbett hopped down and winced when his feet hit the ground. He grabbed his arm and gritted his teeth so hard that Carly could see his jaw tense. "They shot me."

"Shot? How bad is it?" The marshal glanced at Mr. Corbett's arm.

"I'll make it. I guess they'd planned to rob us, but they didn't count on—"

Carly cleared her throat, and both men's eyes

swerved toward her. If she was going to be arrested because she used a weapon after the prison warden instructed her to never touch one again, she at least wanted to see Rachel first. "Would you mind if I go inside while y'all tend to those men? I'm anxious to see Rachel." *And to get away from you two.*

The marshal nodded. "Of course. My apologies, Miss Payton. I know you've had a long journey." He offered his arm, and she let him help her up the stairs. "Rachel's been holding lunch until you arrived."

"Lunch?" Mr. Corbett lifted his nose and sniffed. "Did someone mention food?"

"You're as bad as my kids." Marshal Davis shook his head and grinned. "And what's that on your arm? I didn't realize pink calico was the new style in arm bands."

Sticking out his elbow, Mr. Corbett flicked the loose fabric where Carly had tied a knot. His ears were red, but instead of acting embarrassed, he grinned. "Yeah, well, I'm not the only one wearing it. Them two probably need to have the doc look them over."

Carly resisted shaking her head. The man had been a joker when she'd been here before and never seemed to take anything seriously—except for when she'd told him her real name. He'd been more flustered than a rooster who had seen his last hen served up for someone's dinner. He hadn't cracked any jokes then. Still, she owed him a debt. "Thank you, Mr. Corbett, for giving me a ride here, in spite of the fact that you weren't expecting me."

The marshal grinned. "That was Rachel's idea. How'd you like her surprise?"

Mr. Corbett frowned at Carly, then mumbled something about seeing to his horses.

"You don't like it so much when the joke's on you, huh?" Chuckling, Marshal Davis grabbed her satchel, then opened the door. He paused and looked back at his cousin. "I'll take Miss Payton inside and send Alan over to fetch Doc Phillips. Then I'll help you with those fellows and the team. And I want the doc to check your arm." He opened the door and pushed it. "After you, ma'am."

Carly slipped past him, her stomach awhirl, and stepped into the boardinghouse. Fragrant aromas emanated from the kitchen, and she felt almost as if she'd stepped back ten years. The only difference she noticed right off was that the parlor walls had been painted light blue. Several toys littered the floor, as if a child had just hurriedly left the room. The marshal set her satchel on the hall tree bench, then strode toward the kitchen. He disappeared through the doorway, and Carly heard a high-pitched squeal.

Rachel bustled out of the kitchen and chugged down the hall like a locomotive building steam, her light blue eyes sparkling. "I'm so glad you're finally here." She pulled Carly into an awkward embrace. Then she stepped back and patted her belly. "Oscar here gets in the way of things at times."

Lifting one brow, Carly stared at her friend. "Oscar?"

Rachel laughed. "That's what Luke called our first baby before it was born, and it just stuck. They're Oscar while they're in my womb, but once they come out, they get a name of their own."

Carly had never heard of such a thing, but then she hadn't been around many women carrying babies other than the few who had visited Tillie. "It's so good to see you again."

Rachel nodded. "You, too. I'm glad you finally decided to come and stay with us."

The back kitchen door banged, and a boy charged out of the kitchen and down the hall, followed by the marshal. A girl of about five or six raced after him. Alan and Abby, Carly assumed. They were just as Rachel had described them in her letters.

"Gotta go, Ma. Papa needs the doctor."

Rachel's gaze jumped from her son to her husband. "Are you hurt?"

Marshal Davis shook his head. "Not me—Garrett and two men he shot."

Carly bit her lip to keep from correcting him. Maybe Mr. Corbett would keep her secret, but she doubted it.

"I'm goin' with Alan," Abby said.

The boy skidded to a halt. "Nuh-uh. Tell her to stay here, Papa. You said *I* could go."

Marshal Davis lifted a brow. "I'm the one who gives orders around here, Son, not you. Take your sister, but hurry back. Your ma has the food ready."

The boy's shoulders sagged, but his sister's grin illuminated the room. Carly smiled at the child. Alan's medium brown hair and blue eyes favored his ma, while Abby—if she was remembering right from Rachel's letters—had blond hair and her father's eyes.

"I'm gonna beat you." Abby lunged for the front door.

"Nuh-uh!" Alan charged after her, nearly knocking Carly down.

"Slow down and stay clear of the horses and wagons," Rachel hollered.

Carly watched the two children fight to get out the door first and shook her head. Rachel had written to her about the rambunctious children, but Carly hadn't believed they were so wild until she saw it with her own eyes. They reminded her of Jacqueline.

"Garrett's hurt?" Rachel asked. "How bad?"

The marshal glanced at Carly as if asking her to

respond. "Not too bad. God must have been watching over him, because the bullet just grazed his upper arm. It's a deep gouge but should heal all right if Mr. Corbett doesn't overuse his arm for a while."

"Let's sit a minute while you tell me what happened." Rachel looped her hand around Carly's elbow and tugged her into the parlor as the marshal headed for the door, eating one of Rachel's biscuits.

Carly relayed the story, leaving out the part about her shooting their attackers and also the part about Mr. Corbett's reaction to finding a passenger at the depot instead of a package. If he wanted them to know of his shock, he could tell them.

Rachel shook her head. "I think that's only the second or third time a Corbett Freight wagon has been attacked before. At least you got the men, so they can't hurt anyone else. And Garrett truly seems to be all right?"

Carly nodded. "He's in some pain, but he wouldn't let me drive the wagon, and he was joking some."

"That sounds like him. Stubborn as Luke." Rachel shook her head and blew out an exasperated breath. Then she took Carly's hands. "I was so sorry to hear about Tillie and how you had to move out of the Barker home. I know you enjoyed living there."

Carly shrugged and pulled her hands back to her lap. "I do miss Tillie—and the reverend—but I can't say I miss that town much."

"Were the people unkind?"

She studied the braided rug at her feet, remembering how many of the church folks shunned her. "Some, but not all."

Rachel clutched Carly's hands again, drawing her gaze up. "I'm sure things will be different here. You can start over. I'm so excited to have you here."

Carly smiled, trying to stir up her enthusiasm to

match Rachel's. "But I must find work, and who'll hire an ex-convict?"

Blinking, Rachel stared at her, looking confused. "Didn't you receive my last letter?"

Carly searched her mind, then shook her head. "The last one I got arrived about a month ago. Then your telegram that said, 'Come.'"

"I wrote you after you told me that it looked like Mrs. Barker was failing. Oh, Oscar is kicking me." She leaned back and rubbed her hand across the right side of her stomach.

Carly wondered if she'd ever get to experience being a mother—to feel her own child move and kick within. At twenty-eight, she was well into spinsterhood. She smiled as she held her hands tightly together to keep from fidgeting.

"Anyway, before Oscar interrupted, I was going to say that I wrote and asked you to come and help me."

"Of course I'll help. You know you don't have to ask after all you've done for me. I imagine you must get exhausted tending this big place and cooking and caring for your family, especially now with the baby so close to coming."

"Thank you. I'll admit it is harder when I'm this far along in my pregnancy." She turned and stared out the window, her cheeks pink, as if embarrassed to talk about such a delicate topic. "Jacqueline is a lot of help most of the time, but this week she's been in bed after. . .uh. . .taking a fall. She's getting up and around some now, but I don't want to have to depend on her all the time."

Carly's stomach growled at the delicious scents drifting through the house, and she placed her hand against it. "Is she still writing stories for the newspaper?"

"Yes." Rachel pursed her lips. "But that's not the

worst of it. She wants to move to Dallas and write for a larger paper. She doesn't think I know, but I overheard her talking with her friends one day."

Carly knew how hard it would be on Rachel to have her eldest daughter move away, not just because Rachel wouldn't have help, but more so because of Jack's hankering after adventure and getting into trouble. "I'm sorry. That worries you, doesn't it?"

Rachel nodded and pushed up out of the chair. "Yes, it surely does. But she's a grown woman now, and I've got to trust God to take care of her." A smile flitted across her lips. "Don't tell her, but I've been praying the Lord would bring a nice young man to town who will steal her heart and make her forget about Dallas."

Carly stood and picked up her bag. "And has He?"

"Perhaps." With eyes dancing, she waggled her brows. "Let me show you to your room so you can freshen up before we eat."

Carly followed her friend up the stairs, remembering so many things from the past. Leah, the blond mail-order bride who'd come to marry Luke, had stayed in the first room on the left, while Shannon, the Irish bride, had the one to her right.

"My girls stay in the green room now, and we divided your old room in half. Alan stays in one side, and we use the other for stage drivers who occasionally overnight here, but with the expansion of the railroad, I don't expect stagecoaches will be around much longer." Rachel opened the second door on the left.

"Too bad there isn't a train that comes to Lookout." Then she could have avoided that uncomfortable ride with Mr. Corbett, and he wouldn't have gotten shot.

"I hope you'll be comfortable here." Rachel pulled back the blue and white gingham curtains and lifted a window. "Of course, in exchange for your help, your room and board is free. I know you'll need some extra for expenses, and if we have lots of customers, I'll gladly pay you a small salary."

"I never expected you to pay me." Carly set her satchel on the bed and glanced around the cozy room painted white. A lovely wedding quilt in various shades of blues and white covered the bed. "I offered to help you because you're my friend, and if it hadn't been for you, I probably would never have met the Lord."

Rachel wrapped an arm around Carly's shoulder. "The help I need goes beyond the bonds of friendship. I basically need someone who can take over and run the boardinghouse after I have the baby—at least for a few weeks."

Carly smiled. Maybe things were finally looking up for her. "You've got yourself a helper."

Chapter 12

Jack stared at her image in the long mirror at Dolly's Dress Shop. The bottom of the fitted bodice of the dark green dress angled down to form a V at her stomach, accentuating her narrow waist. The neckline also tapered to a V and was edged with wide lace, which lay across her shoulders. The short sleeves ended just above her elbows, but six-inch lace attached to the cuffs flounced across her lower arms. The full overskirt swirled when she twisted from side to side, but a stabbing pain in her knee made her grimace.

"What's wrong? The dress looks lovely with your coloring." Dolly Dykstra stared at her in the mirror, concern etching her features.

"Oh yes, I love it. But I twisted too far and made my knee hurt."

Tessa hiked her chin and fluffed her curls. "Your ma says you should still be abed."

Jack glanced at Penny, who rolled her eyes. Stifling a smile, she glanced back at the mirror. She actually looked pretty. She still loved donning britches, but she had to admit, if only to herself, that she was learning to enjoy dressing up.

"Don't you just love the shirred-up bottom of the green fabric and how it reveals the lace-trimmed underskirt?" Penny's eyes grew dreamy as if she imagined herself in the gown.

"I do love it, Mrs. Dykstra." Jack smiled at the older woman. "You outdid yourself."

Dolly puffed her chest and smiled, her chubby cheeks a bright red. Jack was glad she had ordered the dress, but she wasn't sure, as fancy as it was, if it would be suitable for a church dress. She'd hoped to be able to use it for more than special occasions.

She might look pretty at the Saturday social, but she sure wouldn't be dancing. An image of Noah Jeffers flashed across her mind. Would he be disappointed? Would he even be at the dance?

"I plan to wear a beautiful pale copper and soft sea-green brocade tea dress that Mother ordered from Boston," Tessa announced. "It has pearl buttons. There was even a very similar dress on the cover of *Ladies' Home Journal*." Tessa hiked her chin and planted a smile on her face, obviously proud that her dress was much more elaborate than Jack's.

"I'm sure it will be lovely." Jack ignored Tessa's barb, as she did most times Tessa had to prove whatever she had was better than someone else's. She'd long ago decided if she wanted to be friends with her, she'd have to overlook Tessa's need to put herself above others. Jack didn't care. She despised hot, fancy dresses and much preferred the cooler calicos.

"That pine-green color looks beautiful with your reddish-brown hair." Penny stood off to the side, along with Tessa. Jack appreciated her friend's effort to make her feel better.

"I agree." Dolly pushed her large frame up from her chair and tucked a strand of gray hair behind her ear. "If you could stand on that crate for me, I'll measure the hem, and then you ladies can be off to tend to whatever it is you need to do."

Ever helpful and considerate, Penny hurried over and held out her hand, assisting Jack as she climbed onto the box. "Yes, you should finish here, so you can rest your leg. We want it well so you can go to the social tomorrow."

Tessa swirled sideways and back, her blue skirts swishing. "I thought you weren't going."

Jack shrugged. "I changed my mind." Or had Noah Jeffers changed it for her?

Tessa's blue eyes sparkled, and her face took on a dreamy expression. "I can hardly wait to dance with the new minister. I'm sure he's an excellent dancer."

Penny scowled and glanced sideways, shaking her head. "How do you know he'll come? Reverend Taylor never did."

"Oh, I just know. Reverend Taylor was married, but a handsome man like our new parson has to be looking for a wife, and I plan to be there for him." Tessa picked up a fan from a nearby display and snapped it open. She held it across her face, leaving only her blue eyes showing. "I'll make myself irresistible."

Penny coughed and held her hand over her mouth, eyes dancing with mirth. Jack stared at her own image again. She was tall and lanky, where Tessa was shorter and had much fuller curves. Didn't men prefer women with curves? And blond hair?

She shuddered. What did it matter? She didn't want to attract a man. Then why was she going to the social?

"Hold still, Miss Jacqueline," Dolly said. "I know you like to be moving constantly, but if you want a straight hem, don't move."

Jack forced herself to stand quietly, even though her knee was screaming at her. She'd have to spend the rest of the day off of it. Maybe she could work some more on her story about the reverend. And maybe if he showed up, she could wheedle some more answers from him about his past.

She thought back to their encounter at the church several days ago. She'd never seen a man with such dark eyes who wasn't an Indian or Mexican. Noah's skin was nicely tanned but didn't have the coloring of those other races. And he was so tall. And strong. She heaved a sigh, drawing Penny's gaze. The young woman lifted her brow and grinned, as if she could read Jack's mind. She turned her face away, staring at Dolly's crowded store, and hoped her friend hadn't seen her blush.

Bolts of fabric lined the shelves of one whole wall, with all manner of sewing tools, thread, and buttons lining the drawers of a glass-topped credenza. The place was small but well-organized.

"All right, missy, you're done. Take care of the pins when you remove the gown."

Jack slid behind the dressing screen, undid the practical front buttons, and let the garment pool onto the floor. As she put on her navy skirt and shirtwaist, she couldn't help the envy that surged within her. Would Tessa turn the reverend's eye with her fancy dress and beguiling ways?

Something else bothered her even more.

Why did she care?

Jack stood on the boardwalk outside of Dolly's store, glad to have her final fitting complete. She'd return tomorrow morning to pick up her dress, just in time for the evening social. A whack sounded to her right, and she turned to see what it was.

Tessa tugged her arm, pulling her attention back. "Let's go over to Polly's Café and have some pie."

Jack shook her head. "I've got to head home. Emmie will be waking up from her nap soon, and I'm watching her and the other children so Ma can rest."

"Oh my. . ." Penny heaved an exaggerated sigh. She stood in the space between Dolly's Dress Shop and the freight office, looking down the alley.

Jack stepped off the boardwalk and stood beside her. Another whack echoed between the buildings. Past Dolly's purple dress shop, across the alley in Bertha Boyd's backyard, a bare-chested man was cutting wood—a very well-built man. She tried to swallow, but her mouth was so dry she couldn't even work up a good spit.

"What're you two gawking at?" Tessa shoved her way in front of Jack. "My goodness, what a fine-looking man."

"Why, isn't that the new pastor?" Penny glanced at Jack before resuming her staring.

"It is—and he's shirtless. Oh my. . ." Tessa fanned her face and started toward the alley. "I need a closer look."

Jack followed. She just might have to keep Tessa from getting into trouble. Penny trailed after them.

They stopped at the back corner of Dolly's building and lingered there. Noah Jeffers lifted the ax and brought it down hard, splitting the log in half. A memory flashed across Jack's mind of another time and another woodcutter. She winced, remembering the mean trick she and her two best friends had played on Butch Laird, the town bully. Yet Noah Jeffers was not a thing like Butch Laird, other than having the same color hair. And maybe eyes—or were Butch's brown?

Tessa leaned in close to Jack and Penny. "Have you ever seen anything so. . .so manly?"

He turned slightly toward them, picked up the half log he'd just cut, and set it back on the chopping block. Jack couldn't help noticing the dark hair that covered his chest and tapered down his flat stomach. The muscles in the minister's arms bulged as he lifted the ax again. His skin glistened with sweat across his broad shoulders when the ax hit its mark. Jack knew that watching him wasn't right, but she couldn't tear her gaze away.

"How do you suppose a preacher got so—uh— muscled?" Penny asked, without ever looking away. "And his back is so tanned. He must chop a lot of wood."

"We should go. If we startle him, he could slip and hurt himself." Jack pulled at her friends' arms. "It isn't proper for unmarried women to be watching a man without his shirt on."

"Oh, posh. Men remove their shirts around ladies all the time." Tessa tossed a glance back over her shoulder at Jack. "And are you saying it would be all right to observe him if we were all married?"

"I don't know." Penny's voice quivered. "I think we should go, like Jacqueline said."

Jack straightened, watching as the minister picked up an armload of the quartered sections and carried them to the woodpile that sat along the backside of the house. Butch would never have been able to carry such a hefty load. She shifted her feet, knowing she needed to get home. Her ma was constantly tired and needed every chance she could to rest. And the longer she stood there, the guiltier she felt.

"Back up, or he'll see us when he turns to go back to the chopping block." Tessa shoved backward, not even bothering to turn around. Penny pivoted, and her eyes went wide, just as Jack backed into a solid body.

"What are you ladies up to?"

Tessa squealed and turned, holding a hand against her heart, but she quickly pasted on her trademark smile. "Why, you scared us half to death, Marshal. Don't you know not to sneak up on a group of ladies?"

Ever so slowly, Jack glanced over her shoulder and lifted her eyes to her stepfather's. "We. . .uh. . .just left Dolly's shop and were. . .uh. . .heading home."

Luke quirked a brow and stared at her. Jack had

to work hard not to squirm. "Taking the alley is longer than just walking down Main Street." The whacking resumed, and Luke's gaze moved past her. A grin twittered on his lips. "Ahh. . .now I see what has y'all so captivated. I was wondering if you were ever going to take an interest in a man."

Jack's heart somersaulted. "No, Papa, you've got it all wrong. I. . .um, I mean. . .we. . ." What could she say that wouldn't be a lie?

Tessa suddenly screamed. Luke's hand went straight to his gun, and Jack spun around to see what had happened. Had the minister injured himself?

Tessa danced from foot to foot then jumped behind Penny. "A snake!"

Luke chuckled and stepped past them. "It's nothing but a garden snake." He picked it up and dangled it in front of them.

Tessa gasped and back-stepped, pulling Penny with her, as if she were a shield.

Jack shook her head. "It's harmless."

Tessa wheeled around and charged past Jack, holding her skirts high. "You know I despise snakes!" She disappeared around the corner in a blur of blue dress.

Luke tossed the offending critter in the tall grass growing under the back porch of the freight office. "I think it's time you ladies moved along."

Jack nodded and took one last glance at Noah Jeffers. Her heart jumped clear up to her throat. He stood there, leaning on the ax handle, watching them just as they'd watched him.

࿎

What were those gals up to? He'd heard the one woman scream and thought someone was in trouble, but then the marshal held a snake in the air. Noah chuckled. It sure wasn't Jack who'd let out that squeal. A little ol' snake wouldn't daunt her any.

But why had she and her friends been in the alley?

His mind flashed back to another day and time. He glanced at the stacked wood, relieved to see it was all still there. Old Mrs. Linus and her sister, Mrs. Boyd, had been delighted to meet him and duly impressed when he offered to chop some wood for them as a courtesy. The tea they'd offered him had been as tasty as the tiny cucumber sandwiches they'd fed him, but that delicious stuff they called fudge had been his favorite. He'd chop wood every day for another taste of that sweet treat.

He set another piece of wood onto the chopping block, but a motion in the corner of his eye caught his attention. The marshal ambled toward him, wearing his trademark denim pants and light blue cambric shirt. The sunlight glimmered off the badge on his chest, and Noah couldn't help noticing the gun that hung low on his hips. Noah's pulse sped up, and he worked hard to look casual. It made no sense that this man should cause him to be nervous, but he did.

"Afternoon." The marshal nodded his head.

"Marshal." Noah held his tongue, figuring the lawman would speak his mind without any prompting.

He pushed his hat back off his forehead. "Were you aware you had an audience?"

Noah's gaze darted toward the ugly purple building. They'd been watching him? He reached for his shirt.

Marshal Davis chuckled. "Too late for that."

Noah tossed it back across the tree branch since his job wasn't finished. "How long had they been there?"

"Not long. I saw them come out of Dolly's shop and then duck down the alley. I wondered what they were doing and followed." He shook his head and looked away for a moment. "You're new around here, so you probably haven't yet heard that my daughter can be a handful."

Though he knew just which daughter the man meant, he said, "You have more than one daughter, sir."

Luke Davis grinned again. "Good point, Reverend. I was referring to my eldest. She's actually my stepdaughter, but I think of her as my own. That feisty little Abby, though, sure is giving Jack a run for her money."

Noah nodded. He'd seen traits of Jack in her sister. "Do you think you could call me Noah or even Pastor, instead of Reverend? I'm uneasy with that title."

The marshal nodded. "I can do that." He hooked his thumbs in his pockets and stared at Noah.

Struggling hard not to squirm, he picked up his ax and leaned on the handle. He could see the marshal was working up to something. *Don't ask. Not yet.*

Luke's mouth twisted sideways. "I reckon I should warn you about those three gals. My Jack's never shown a great interest in men. I imagine that's the fault of her first father." Luke stared off in the distance, a muscle ticking in his jaw. "Let me just say he wasn't a kind man."

Noah had heard a few rumors about James Hamilton when he previously lived in town, but being just a kid, he hadn't thought on it much. Besides, the man hadn't sounded all that much different from his own pa. He was well aware of the issues that surfaced when a kid lived with a cruel father. Could that be why Jack had always acted so tough?

"Anyway, what I'm trying to say is that I don't think you have to worry about her or Penny, but I'd watch out for that Tessa Morgan. If she sets her hat for you, well. . .just consider yourself duly warned."

Noah had seen the blond gal looking at him more than once, and she always tried to weasel up next to him if she saw him alone. He swallowed hard, then looked Jack's stepfather in the eye. "I didn't come here looking for a wife, Marshal."

"Luke."

Noah nodded. "God sent me here to share His Word with the people of Lookout."

Luke pursed his lips. Then a wry smile tugged at his mouth. "I once thought God sent me back to Lookout for a certain reason, too, but things turned out far different from what I'd planned. Don't close any doors on God. He may have more for you here than you ever expected."

Noah's heart leapt before he lassoed it back under control. Maybe he could find a home here and the friends and respect he craved. But Pastor Taylor would eventually return to town, and then Noah would no longer be needed. Yeah, he could start another church, but he wouldn't do that. The parishioners would most likely stay with Pastor Taylor anyway.

"Well, guess I'll be moseying along. Have a good day. . .Noah."

Noah's grasp tightened on the wooden handle as he watched the marshal walk away. He exhaled a sigh of relief, knowing he'd dodged another bullet. He turned the log on the chopping block to get the best angle, then lifted the ax, just as the marshal spun back around. The man strode toward him with purpose. He eyed the ax and slowed his steps.

Noah lowered the tool and waited. Sweat ran down his temple, but he didn't swipe at it.

Luke shook his head. "I've been a marshal for ten years and was a soldier for another decade before then. One thing I've learned is to trust my gut, and it's screaming that we've met before." The marshal's gaze hardened, but he didn't look unkind. "Noah Jeffers isn't your real name, is it?"

Chapter 13

Jack and Penny's quick steps echoed along the boardwalk as they passed a moseying couple. Jack glanced over her shoulder just as the man and woman turned into the newspaper office. She blew out a heavy breath and allowed her steps to slow.

Penny copied her and peered back toward Dolly's shop. She patted her thin hand against her chest. "I don't know how you keep from having curly hair."

Jack stared at her friend. "What?"

Penny swatted her hand in the air. "The marshal is so stern. He scares me so badly my hair curls."

Shaking her head, Jack couldn't help grinning. "Luke may act tough, but he's just a big, lovable puppy."

"Nuh-uh." Penny stiffly shook her head, her eyes wide. "I'd better head back home before Mama comes looking for me."

Jack waved. "See you tomorrow."

Penny walked backward down Bluebonnet Lane. "You gonna dance with the minister if Billy doesn't hog you?"

"No. I doubt I'll be dancing at all since my knee still hurts."

Penny shrugged and turned around, then continued down the lane at a quick clip.

"Well, now, that disappoints me."

Billy. Jack closed her eyes and took a calming breath. He was more annoying than a bad case of poison ivy. Forcing a cordial smile, she turned to face him. "H'lo, Billy."

His passionate gaze raked her from head to toe, a slow smile stealing across his mouth. "Sure am glad you didn't kill yourself when you fell off that roof."

"So is my ma." Jack resisted rolling her eyes at her dumb response.

Billy scowled and leaned against the boardwalk railing, crossing his arms. "What's that nonsense about you dancing with that new minister?"

"Nothing." Jack's ire simmered. It was none of his business who she danced with. "I won't be dancing with anyone because my knee is still tender."

"I've been looking forward to this social just so's me and you can kick up our heels a bit."

"Sorry to disappoint you. I need to go." She started across the street, but he intercepted her, blocking her way.

Irritation flickered in his blue eyes. He forked his fingers through his white blond hair. "Hold on now. Surely you could dance with me a little bit."

She glanced at the store and boardinghouse, half relieved no one was watching and half disappointed. Where was Luke when she needed him?

She'd told Billy over and over that she wasn't interested in him, but he failed to believe her. "I'm going to the social, but I won't be dancing. My knee is all right for walking, but I can't dance and risk twisting it and doing more damage. The doctor said it may take a long time to heal."

"Then why are you bothering to have that new dress made?"

She could hardly tell Billy she hadn't been all that interested in the dress her ma had ordered until Noah

Jeffers came to town. Jack lifted her brows. "How do you know about that?"

"Tessa told me."

Ahh, Tessa. She'd probably bragged about how much nicer her own dress was and how it had come all the way from Boston.

He stood with his hands on his hips, staring down at her. She couldn't deny he was a handsome man, and that was part of the problem. He thought he could flash his dimpled smile and get every gal in town to swoon. Well, not her. She never swooned.

"Why don't you ask Velma Tate? She'd love to go with you."

He snorted and looked as if he might gag. "She's fat."

Jack crossed her arms. "She is not. Besides, she's really nice and likes you a lot."

"Well I don't like her. You're my fiancée. It wouldn't look right for me to take some other gal."

Gritting her teeth, Jack leaned in close. "I—am—not—your—fiancée. And stop telling people that I am. You hear?"

His smile returned. "Oh, Jacqueline, are we having a lover's spat?"

"Oh!" Jack stomped her foot. The sharp pain that grabbed her knee like a bear claw instantly caused her to regret the action. She bent down, rubbing her knee through the fabric of her skirt and petticoat. "We're not lovers. And I thank you kindly not to ever say that again."

"You all right?" He had half enough sense to look repentant.

She straightened but kept the heel of her sore leg off the ground. "No, I'm not, thanks to you."

"I didn't make you stomp your foot."

Jack rolled her eyes. Men were so dense. A dog barked behind her, and she heard a harness jingle. She stepped to the side of the road and looked to see who was coming. A farmer she didn't recognize tipped his straw hat at her. His black-and-white dog sat on the seat beside him, wagging his tail. Jack smiled and waved at the man.

Billy scowled as the wagon passed them. "Who's that?"

"I don't know. I was just being friendly."

He stepped up close to her and brushed his fingers through the hair that hung into his eyes. "How come you ain't more friendly to me?"

She hated hurting people's feelings, but she was also getting tired of Billy's possessiveness. "Maybe because you won't take no for an answer. I'm not interested in marrying you, Billy. Or courting, either. I don't ever plan to marry, so you're wasting your time." As soon as the words left her mouth, an image of Noah Jeffers chopping wood invaded her mind.

"You're just too high and mighty, Miss I'm-the-marshal's-daughter." Billy's childish, singsong tone set her nerves on edge.

"Luke doesn't have anything to do with us."

The door on the boardinghouse flew open, and Alan stepped onto the porch. He shaded his eyes with his hand; then he saw her and waved. "Emmie's awake and wants out of bed. Ma said I should come find you, Sissy."

"I'm coming." She looked at Billy again. "I've gotta go."

A muscle in his jaw ticked, and he glared at her, his eyes as cold as ice. "Most girls in this county would be happy to dance with me. You just be ready come tomorrow night, or else."

Jack shoved her hands to her hips and leaned toward him. "Or else what?"

"You don't wanna find out." Billy spun on his heel and marched back toward the mercantile his mother owned.

Jack watched him go. She wasn't one to scare easily, but something in the tone of Billy's voice set her senses on alert. What would he do if she didn't dance with him? Hurt her? Or one of her siblings?

Besides her father, only one person had ever scared her like Billy just had, but he was long gone. Too bad Billy wasn't also.

Noah's hands sweated as he stared at the marshal. He found it hard to swallow, as if the man had his fingers around Noah's throat, but he couldn't lie—he wouldn't. All he could do was tell the marshal the truth and hope the man believed that he had changed. That he wasn't the troubled youth he'd once been. *Please, Lord, don't let him send me packing. I'm not done here yet.*

The marshal's eyes narrowed, and Noah broke his gaze and stared at the woodcuttings spread across the grass where he'd been working. If he had to leave Lookout now, his heart would resemble those chips— splintered and scattered.

"I am with you always."

Noah lifted his head, resolve coursing through him as God's words strengthened him. The Lord had sent him here on a mission, and Luke Davis couldn't keep him from it.

He caught the marshal's gaze again and nodded. "Yes, sir, we've met before."

Luke's jaw quivered, as if he was clenching his teeth. "When—and where?"

Noah glanced away again. "Here. Ten years ago."

The marshal's eyes lifted to the sky, and he seemed to be searching his memory. His brow dipped, and his mouth twisted to one side. His eyes suddenly widened. "You're not part of the Payton Gang, are you?"

Noah shook his head, surprised the marshal

hadn't figured out the mystery yet.

"Nah, you're too young. How old are you, anyhow?"

"Twenty-four."

The marshal didn't seem in any big hurry to remember, so Noah waited, hoping he'd get distracted like the last time he asked. Finally, he shook his head. "I can't recollect who you are."

Noah kicked a chunk of wood, knowing his time was up. "Noah is what my ma named me. It's my real first name, but my pa hated it and refused to call me that. Said it wasn't a manly enough name for his son. I did change my surname, though."

He tightened his fist on the wooden handle as unwanted memories of his past assailed him. Of all the times he took a beating because he didn't do something fast enough for his pa or when he burned the meal or came home late. "My pa was a lazy man and a mean drunk. We were living up near Emporia when he died. I was fifteen and old enough to be on my own, but a kind man named Pete Jeffers took me in anyway and taught me how to be a real man, and he taught me about God's love."

Noah leaned the ax against the chopping block. If the marshal got upset when he heard the truth and took a swing at him, he sure didn't want either of them to get hurt on the ax blade. "Pete was the only real father figure I ever had, and it just seemed the right thing to adopt his name."

The marshal nodded. "Sounds a whole lot like Jack's story and mine. She uses my last name now."

Hope spread through him. Maybe this man did understand. "Yeah, it does. Anyway, my real last name was. . .Laird." He attempted to swallow the lump in his throat. "And everyone knew me by Butch."

For a moment, the marshal's face remained passive. Then he scowled. "Butch Laird! You're Butch

Laird? That bully who caused Jack so much trouble?"

Remorse weighted down his shoulders. "Yes, sir."

The marshal stepped closer, his gaze narrowed. "You don't aim to cause her any more problems, do you?"

Noah blinked, not the least bit surprised at the vehemence in the marshal's expression. The man had no idea how much trouble Jack had caused him by her lying and trickery, but he had no desire to be vindicated. The past was past. Why was it so easy to forgive her and not his own father? "No, sir. Nothing could be further from my mind. I came here to do the Lord's work—and to make restitution for the bad things I did in the past. I'm not like I used to be, sir. Let me prove to you—and the town—that I've changed."

Marshal Davis relaxed his stance and stepped back. After a few moments, a grin crept onto his face, both surprising and relieving Noah. "Would those two new pie plates Mrs. Burke said magically appeared on her back porch have anything to do with your making restitution?"

Noah shrugged and tried to keep a straight face, but he felt his lips quirk up on one side. "Maybe. The scriptures say that when you give, your right hand shouldn't know what the left hand is doing."

The marshal nodded. "All right. I hear you. But I do have to say that was the first time I responded to a complaint about intruders, only to discover they left something instead of taking stuff." He smiled then rested his hands on his hips and stared at the ground. "There's one thing I do need to ask—were you the one who painted *Jack is a liar* all over town that day you left?"

He'd all but forgotten that stupid deed and deeply regretted painting those words, but he'd been so angry. Jack had lied about something he no longer remembered, causing him to spend two days in jail, only to return home and take a beating from his pa for being gone so long and not being there to cook his meals. They even packed up and moved because his pa said he was getting into too much trouble, and they needed a fresh start. He stared at his fingers. It had taken days for that red paint to wear off his hands, a constant reminder of his stupid, impulsive deed. "Yeah, I did that, and I can tell you I've regretted it ever since."

Jack's father stared into his eyes, as if judging how truthful his words were. Finally, he nodded. "I believe you mean that."

"I do. If I could do it over, I'd do things differently."

The marshal placed his hand on Noah's shoulder, warming his skin and his heart. "You had a hard time of things, son, and I want you to know that Jack told me the truth about everything after you left."

Noah stared at the man, shocked all the way to his toes. "She did?"

"Yep. I'm sorry I was so hard on you back then, but I believed that little squirt. I never dreamed she'd tell me a falsehood."

"She could be convincing."

"And she had those two friends of hers always backing up whatever she said. It was your word against theirs. I'm sorry that I didn't take you more seriously." He yanked off his hat and smacked it against his leg. "I feel like I let you down, son. I'm sorry for not believing you."

Overhead, a robin chirped a cheerful tune, oblivious to the turmoil Noah was experiencing. He never expected the marshal to apologize and didn't quite know how to take it. He'd always been the one blamed whenever there was trouble, and no one had ever taken his side on things, even when he was the one who'd been wronged. "It's all right. I understand."

Luke Davis locked gazes with him. "I reckon you had more character back then than I gave you credit for."

A place deep within Noah sparked and glowed as he saw respect blossom in the marshal's eyes.

"I don't remember you ever tattling on Jack."

He shrugged. "It wouldn't have done any good. Nobody believed anything I said."

"Is that why you haven't told people who you are?"

Was that the real reason? Or could it have something to do with Jack? He lifted one shoulder and dropped it again. "Maybe. Do you think anyone would come to church if they knew the old town bully, Butch Laird, was preaching?"

"You've got a point, but you might be surprised. Lots of new folks who never heard of Butch Laird have moved here and attend church, and plenty of others would come out of curiosity."

Noah watched a dog slink over to someone's trash pile a few houses down and snitch a piece of garbage. The mutt carried it over to a nearby tree and lay down in the shade, chewing on his find. He'd felt just like that unwanted creature when he'd previously lived in Lookout. "You honestly think if folks knew they'd give me a chance?"

The marshal set his hat back on his head, then rubbed his chin with his forefinger and thumb. "Some would, some wouldn't. But you'll never know for certain unless you come clean."

Noah wiped his sweaty brow with his forearm. "I plan to tell folks, but I'd hoped to wait a month or so and let them see me for who I am now. I'm a new creation in Christ, Marshal. I can assure you, I'm not like I used to be."

Marshal Davis nodded. "All right. I appreciate your being honest with me. But there's one thing I have to know: How does Jack figure in to all of this?"

At the mention of her name, his heart bucked, but she wasn't the reason he'd come back to Lookout. "When Pete first told me about the letter he'd received from Pastor Taylor, I closed my ears and wouldn't listen. Lookout was the last place I wanted to be."

The marshal grinned. "I reckon we've got more in common than we first realized. I felt the exact same way about returning here, but look what God did for me. He let me marry the only woman I ever loved, we've got four great—albeit ornery—kids with another on the way, and they're all healthy and smart. I'd have never dreamed all that could happen to me, but God has greater plans for us, son, than we can ever imagine."

Noah closed his eyes, accepting the man's encouragement into his heart. Growing up the way he had, not ever seeing anything good coming from his life, had been discouraging. Pa had beat him down both physically and verbally. Other kids had gotten him in trouble for things he'd never done. It was only by the grace of God that he was standing here. "Thank you, sir. I appreciate the encouragement."

He nodded; then an odd expression engulfed his face. "I just had a thought—that's why you won't eat pork, isn't it?"

"Yeah. Living on a hog farm, I ate pork three meals a day. Oft times it was all we ate. I just can't stomach it anymore."

"I noticed." The marshal grinned. "Well, I reckon I've kept you from your work long enough. All I ask is that when you feel the time is right that you tell Jack before you reveal your identity to the rest of the town. She'll probably need some time to work through that." He glanced down the alley for a moment. "She was real sorry after you left and told me that she had wanted to apologize for lying about you on more than one occasion."

"She actually told you that she lied?"

"Yeah." He nodded. "The deception ate at her until she couldn't hold it in any longer, and she had to come clean. Jack has a good heart, but she sometimes buries it deeply to protect it. Her other pa was cruel and had no problem hitting women. It's no big surprise that Jack has trouble trusting men. I've been trying for ten years now to fix the damage James did."

Noah wasn't sure if he should confess his current thoughts, but the marshal might as well know the whole story. "Though she did anger me at times, I always admired her spunk. I had a little sister for a few years who wasn't scared of anything, but she took sick and died. I suppose Jack reminds me a little of her. I just wanted to be Jack's friend, but she never gave me a chance." Bertha Boyd stuck her head out the back door and stared. She must have recognized the marshal, because she quickly ducked back inside.

The older man clapped his hand on Noah's shoulder again. "Jacqueline's changed—somewhat. Give her another chance, but just don't break her heart."

Noah snorted a sarcastic laugh. The marshal gave him far more credit than he deserved if he thought he'd have any influence over Jack's heart. "Hurting her is the last thing I want to do, but I seriously doubt you have anything to worry about on that account."

A strange look passed across the marshal's face. "Don't be too sure of that."

"What do you mean?"

"I've seen the way she looks at you."

Noah frowned. "What do you mean?"

"The Lord sure works in mysterious ways." The marshal grinned and shook his head. "Sorry, Noah, you're gonna have to figure that out on your own."

Chapter 14

Dressed in his Sunday preaching suit, Noah sat on the boardinghouse's front porch, trying to decide if he ought to go to the social or stay back and study his sermon some more. He tapped the edge of the chair in time with the lively music playing in the vacant lot next to the church.

Across the street at the mercantile, a buggy pulled to a stop, and a tall man climbed out and took the steps to the boardwalk two at a time. The door flew open, as if someone had been standing there waiting for him. Mrs. Morgan stepped out, looking pretty in a rose-colored gown, followed by her daughter in a fancy dress in a brown and light green fabric. Both women's hair had been piled onto the crown of their heads, although the daughter also had blond ringlets hanging down from her topknot. Dainty bonnets adorned their heads.

Noah shook his head, glad that he was a male and only had to comb his hair. How did they manage to keep all their tresses up with just a handful of hairpins?

The trio crowded into the buggy and drove down the street. Several groups of people wandered past the boardinghouse dressed in their finery. Men escorted their ladies, who were decked out in almost every color of the rainbow. They reminded Noah of a field of spring wildflowers. What color would Jack's dress be?

He gripped the end of the armrest. Would she even come?

He'd seen her limping around the house this afternoon, but knowing she'd been watching him work without a shirt, he'd not been able to meet her gaze. He couldn't help wondering why she'd been staring and if she'd liked what she saw.

He sighed and shook his head. "Forgive me, Father. Keep my mind set on things above, not things on earth."

Closing his eyes, he prayed about Sunday. Prayed that he would preach a sermon that would touch hearts. Prayed that he wouldn't be so nervous that he'd mess up like he'd done the first few times he'd preached.

He kept his head back and eyes shut as he prayed for the Davis family. *Thank You, Lord, for Luke's support. Bless Mrs. Davis, and let her baby be delivered safely. And Jack. . .I don't even know what to say. Touch her heart, and draw her closer to You.*

He heard rustling and peeked out one eye. Alan and Abby Davis were hunkered down, tiptoeing around the side of the house. Quiet giggles filled the air like the sweet scent of pies cooking.

"He's asleep." Abby giggled again.

"No he ain't," Alan said. "He's just resting his eyes like Papa does when he's tired."

"Nuh-uh, he's sleeping."

Noah couldn't help letting out a fake snore as he peeked out one squinted eye.

"See! I told you." Abby shoved her brother's shoulder.

Curling his lips, Noah tried not to smile. Both of these children reminded him of Jack, even though he hadn't known her when she was so young.

He faked another snore then fluttered his lips as

153

he blew out a breath. Childless laughter sounded to his right.

"Oh, dear."

That was no child's voice. His eyes flew open and landed on an emerald-green skirt. Jack's skirt. He bolted out of the chair, and his hat flopped off his lap and rolled across the porch floor. Squeals of laughter echoed beside the porch.

"I wasn't sleeping. I was just playing with your brother and sister."

Jack lifted her brows as if questioning if he was being truthful. Her dark blue eyes sparkled, and her auburn hair had been pinned up in a fashionable style that revealed her slender neck. His gaze traveled down her pretty dress, skimming past her bodice to her narrow waist and her flared skirt. Sometime in the past ten years, Jacqueline Hamilton Davis had blossomed from a coltish tomboy to a beautiful woman.

He lifted his gaze and smiled, receiving a shy grin back. A becoming rose red stained her cheeks. Her neck was lightly tanned, but the skin on her shoulders, which was normally covered by her shirtwaist, was a creamy white that just ached to be touched. He reached for the basket that hung on one of her arms to keep his hand busy and shoved the other one into his pocket. He shuffled his feet. He'd never known how to relate to Jack when she was a spunky young girl, but he felt even more discombobulated with this very pretty, feminine version. *Help me, Lord.*

Noah forced his gaze on the younger Davis girl. Instead of using the stairs four feet away, Abby climbed up the porch spindles and shinnied over the railing. "Yes, he was. I heard him snore'n."

"Me, too." Alan clambered up beside his sister, and both children dropped onto the porch floor with a light thud.

"You mean like this?" He snorted like a pig and bent down, gently poking Abby's belly, sending her into another fit of the giggles.

As he straightened, he picked up his hat and set it on his head.

"Were you waiting on me?"

He shrugged, not sure if he was or wasn't. "Guess I just didn't want to go down there alone."

The disappointment on her face made him pause. Had she wanted him to escort her?

Jack turned away and pointed at her siblings. "Back inside, you two. Ma said it's time for your baths. There's church tomorrow."

"Ahh. . .do we have to go? Church is boring."

"Abby Louise Davis. I don't ever want to hear you say such a thing again." She wagged her finger in front of the child, as if she were Abby's mother. Noah cocked his head, realizing how nice an image that was.

Abby crossed her arms over her chest and frowned at her big sister. "I don't want no bath."

"Me neither." Alan licked his finger, then swiped it across his shin below his short pants and held it up. "See, I ain't even dirty."

"Alan! That's horrid behavior—and don't say *ain't*. Both of you get into the house this instant, or I'm getting a switch to tan your hide."

Both kids glared at her with arms crossed but finally relented and stomped inside. Jack closed the door and swung back around to face him, bringing with her the fragrant scent of flowers. "I sure hope I was never half as bad as they are."

Noah couldn't help the gleam in his eye. The truth in his opinion was that Jack had been twice as bad as her siblings, but he could hardly say that.

"What?" She tilted her head, exposing her soft neck. The perfect spot to place a kiss.

155

Noah took a step back, stunned at his train of thought. He couldn't allow her to tempt him. "Uhh. . . nothing." He cleared his throat. "Are you the only one of your family going to the social?"

"Luke's helping Carly—uh, Miss Payton—bathe the kids and put them to bed, so Ma can stay off her feet. I imagine he'll mosey down to make sure things are going all right. He likes to keep a close eye on public events. You never know when some cowpoke will cause trouble."

He'd never before considered how the marshal was always on duty, much like a minister. Did that interfere with his family life?

"So, will you escort me to the social, Reverend?"

He tugged at his collar and stared down the street to where the crowd had gathered. Maybe some folks wouldn't think it proper for a minister to attend a square dance social. "Maybe I should just stay here and work on my sermon for tomorrow."

"Horse feathers." She pulled his arm down. "Don't be a stick-in-the-mud. This is a good time to get to know some of your parishioners before you preach to them."

Did she actually want him to go? Her eager expression and sparkling eyes hinted that she did. But in his heart, he knew that if she knew his real identity, she'd flee back to the house as fast as she could.

Jack held on to Noah's solid arm and tried to ignore how much her knee ached. She'd been on it far too much the past few days, but she'd had things to do to get ready for tonight, and she'd tried to help her ma as much as possible. With the baby due anytime, her ma tired much quicker and had less patience with the children. Having Carly here to help sure was a blessing.

"So, does the town have these get togethers often?" Noah's deep voice rumbled beside her.

"This is the first one of the year. We have them the last Saturday of the month from April to September. These socials are the remnant of the Saturday Socials that the Corbett brothers started years ago."

"Corbett—as in your pa's cousin?"

"Yes, him and his brother, Mark." Jack smiled up at him. "You haven't been here long, so you probably haven't heard the story about the mail-order brides they ordered for my papa."

She felt him stiffen and glanced up. He smiled but had an odd look on his face. They passed a passel of buggies and horses lining both sides of the road. Up ahead, lively dancers were enjoying the do-si-do of the Virginia Reel to guitar and fiddle, while others stood around the refreshment tables and in small groups, talking with friends and neighbors. Jack scanned the busy area for Billy and allowed some of the tension in her shoulders to flee when she didn't see him.

She sure hoped he didn't show up. "Anyway, when Luke first returned to Lookout, he'd just become a Christian and felt God told him to come back and forgive my ma for marrying another man when she'd been engaged to Luke. His cousins thought if he had another woman in his life, he'd forget about Ma, so they ordered some mail-order brides. Even though they wrote to several, they thought only one would show up, but instead, three did. And so someone decided to have a contest to see which gal would make Papa the best wife." She glanced up to gauge his reaction and was surprised that his face remained passive. Maybe being a man, he didn't like to hear romantic stories. Why should that disappoint her?

She shrugged and continued her story. "Some things happened to make Papa realize he still loved my ma, and they got back together, which made me the happiest kid in the world."

He smiled down at her, his dark eyes intense, as if her happiness mattered to him. Her heart did a somersault, and she worked to keep her breathing under control so she could finish. "Needless to say, there were several brides left over after Papa chose Ma to marry. The Corbett brothers started hosting Saturday socials in order to find husbands for Miss Bennett and Miss O'Neil."

"And did they?"

Jack nodded and slowed her steps, not quite ready to share him with the rest of the crowd. "Sort of. Shannon O'Neil married Mark Corbett. Garrett hired her to work in the freight office, so she and Mark saw each other every day, and somewhere along the line, they fell in love."

A soft smile tugged at Noah's lips. "Good for them. Will they be here tonight?"

Jack shook her head and searched the crowd for Penny and Tessa. "No, they're living in Dallas right now. Mark is a lawyer."

"What happened to the other bride?" Noah held his hand out toward two empty chairs that rested against the wall of the church.

Jack sat, grateful to rest her leg. "Leah Bennett married Dan Howard, who owns the livery. I suspect they'll be here tonight."

He looked the crowd over, almost as if searching for the couple, but that was silly since he didn't even know what they looked like. She studied his strong profile. His nose was straight and not overly big. Most of the time, his sleek black hair was combed back, revealing his broad forehead, but when he'd been chopping wood, his hair had draped down across it. A vision of him working, his bare chest shiny with sweat, flashed across her mind. She touched her hand to her cheek. Was she actually blushing? What was it about this man that caused her to behave like a silly schoolgirl with her first infatuation with a boy?

"Something wrong?" He glanced down with concerned eyes. "Are you in pain?"

"I'm fine. Just wish I could dance, is all." Oh! Was that a lie?

No, but it wasn't the whole truth either. Whenever he was around, she was far from fine. Her heart beat faster, she couldn't catch her breath, and her legs turned into liquid like melted butter. The truth hit her as hard as if she'd been run down by a herd of stampeding cattle. She liked Noah Jeffers. No, more than liked him.

Wringing her hands, she wished someone would walk over and talk to her. She needed a diversion from her wayward thoughts. She couldn't like the minister. It wasn't part of the plans she'd made for her life.

"Uh, what do I do with this basket?"

"I'll take it to the refreshment table." Jack started to rise, but Noah's hand to her shoulder halted her. His warm, gentle touch set her rebellious heart thrumming, and she peered up at him. His gaze collided with hers, and she felt as if they were connected. Alone, though in a crowd. The music and conversation faded. His fingers moved ever so slightly, brushing across her skin and sending delicious chills scurrying down her spine. She swallowed the lump in her throat. Then he glanced toward her shoulder, scowled, and yanked his hand away.

"You. . .uh. . .sit. I'll um. . ." His words sounded hoarse—huskier than normal. Noah cleared his throat as he looked across the crowd.

"They're cookies. Just deliver the basket to one of the food tables, and the ladies there will take care of them."

He nodded but didn't look back at her. She watched

him walk a few feet before Tessa intercepted him.

"There you are, Reverend." Tessa glided up to Noah and looped her arm possessively around his. "I hope you saved me a dance."

With his back to her, Jack couldn't hear his response, but if Tessa's fake pout was any sign, he must have turned her down. She knew that shouldn't make her happy, but she smiled anyway. Maybe the preacher was immune to Tessa's wiles.

Tessa clung to the preacher as though they were a couple, as they wove in and out of the crowd. Several more people stopped them before Noah made it to the table and relinquished Jack's basket to Polly Dykstra. He glanced back toward Jack, and she quickly looked to the side, not wanting him to catch her watching.

Two guitar players and a fiddler filled the air with their lively music, while a small group danced a quadrille. The women's dresses swirled around their partners' legs, and smiles lit up each face. Jack tapped her foot in time with the music. How ironic that she never really cared about dancing, but the one time she might have enjoyed it, she was unable to participate.

"There you are." Penny straightened her peach-colored skirt as she sat down. "I was beginning to think you weren't coming after going to so much effort to get that new dress. It's the perfect color for you."

Jack blew out a sigh, fluttering her lips. "Thank you, but I might as well not come. I can't dance with anyone."

Eyes glimmering, Penny leaned over close to her ear. "I noticed you had an escort—and a very handsome one at that."

Jack shook her head and chuckled. "He's not my escort. In fact, if I hadn't come out onto the porch just when I did, I fear he would have fallen asleep on the front porch or else scurried back up to his room."

"He didn't want to come?"

Jack shrugged. "I think he's just nervous about meeting so many folks."

Penny leaned back in her seat. "You'd better keep the parson close by, or Tessa will steal him from you."

"She can have him. I've no designs on him." Now why did those words leave a bad taste in her mouth?

Penny gasped. "Surely you don't mean that. I've seen how he looks at you."

Jack's pulse sped up. "What do you mean?"

Her friend's mouth puckered as if she knew a special secret, and she wiggled her brows. "Like you were the prettiest filly in the corral, that's what."

"Penny! You're comparing me to a horse?"

Her friend giggled as she watched the dancers. "No, of course not. But I just figured that's what a man might think."

Jack shook her head, but her gaze sought out Noah again. "I'd make as good a pastor's wife as Tessa would." She couldn't help following that train of thought. Jacqueline Jeffers actually had a nice ring to it. If Noah's light touch on her shoulder sent butterflies swarming in her stomach, what would his kiss be like? She closed her eyes trying to imagine it. He'd lean down, his dark eyes burning with passion; their lips would touch lightly, then press harder as he pulled her to his chest. She fanned her warm face.

"Why, Jacqueline Davis, whatever are you thinking about? You have the oddest smile on your face."

Jack's eyes popped open at Tessa's question. Then her gaze darted to Noah, who stood a few feet away. She'd been so lost in her fantasy that she hadn't heard them return. She could hardly answer that question, could she? "I. . .uh. . ."

Noah held a mug out to her. "I thought you might be thirsty. We got a drink ourselves, but I wanted to bring you this—since you can't walk much, you know." He glanced at Penny. "Sorry, ma'am, I would have brought you a drink, too, if I'd known you were here."

"That's all right." Penny ducked her head, then glanced sideways at Jack, giving her a knowing grin.

"This is my friend, Penny Dempsey, and Penny, this is Reverend Jeffers." Jack waved her hand toward Penny and then Noah. "You already know he's staying at the boardinghouse."

Penny nodded. "A pleasure, Reverend."

"The pleasure's all mine, Miss Dempsey." Noah smiled at Penny.

"And you've already met Tessa Morgan, I see." Jack took a sip of her cider.

"Oh, yes. We're getting along famously." Tessa leaned against Noah's arm and batted her lashes at him.

Noah's gaze darted to the woman who all but hung on him then to Jack, as if pleading for her help.

"Why don't you sit with us, Tessa?" Jack patted the empty chair on her right. "I'm sure Reverend Jeffers would like to meet more people from the town."

Tessa scowled at her and shook her head. She twisted her finger around a yellow curl hanging from her topknot and gazed adoringly at the bewildered minister. "I intend to dance with the reverend."

"I. . .um. . .don't plan to dance, Miss Morgan."

Tessa tucked her chin down, stuck out her lower lip, and batted her lashes. "Surely you don't want to disappoint one of your parishioners, do you? My mother owns the mercantile and gives quite generously to the church."

"Tessa!" Jack pushed up from the chair, knowing she needed the advantage of height to persuade her friend to leave the poor man alone. "I hardly think you'll convince Reverend Jeffers to dance with you by blackmailing him with your mother's tithes."

"Well, fine." Tessa shoved her nose in the air. "If he doesn't want to dance with me, plenty of other men will." She spun around, her skirts swishing in a mass of copper and sea-green brocade, and marched over to the refreshment table. In a matter of seconds, she sidled up to a trio of young cowboys and started weaving her web.

"Uh, thanks for rescuing me." The parson's neck and ears were the color of a ripe strawberry.

"I'm sorry about Tessa." Her friend's behavior embarrassed Jack.

"She's not used to men turning her down." Penny shook her head. "I think I'll go see what there is to eat. See you later." She waved at Jack but ducked her head as she passed Noah.

"Penny seems nice." Noah's deep voice floated to her amid the harmony of the guitars and fiddle.

"She is, though she's shy around men."

Noah grinned. "I noticed. Your other friend doesn't have a timid bone in her body, does she?"

Jack shook her head. "No, she doesn't. Tessa sees what she wants and goes after it, no matter who is in the way or who gets hurt."

"I hope she doesn't end up being the one to get hurt one day."

"Me, too." Jack located Tessa and watched her dance with a handsome cowboy. Tessa's head was cocked, a brilliant smile on her face. She seemed to have already forgotten about her quest to win Noah's heart. Jack smiled up at him. "Why don't I introduce you to some folks? It will make things easier tomorrow if you meet some of them tonight."

Noah nodded and held his hand out to help her up. He mumbled something that wasn't clear over the ruckus of the crowd and the music, but it sounded as if he'd said, "Nothing will make tomorrow easier."

Chapter 15

Garrett stood off to the side of the crowd, sipping a glass of apple cider and watching the dancers. He wasn't even sure why he'd come. The social was more for younger folk than a man a few years shy of forty. How had life sped by so fast?

A picture of Carly Payton snatching up his rifle and taking down those two outlaws bounced around in his head. He'd been spitting mad to learn who she was, and it goaded him to be in debt to such a woman. Even worse was admiring her quick action, her calm in the face of danger, and her impressive shooting skills. He didn't want to like the woman and hated how she'd invaded his dreams ever since he'd delivered her to Rachel.

He forced his thoughts off the jailbird and watched Jack introduce Noah Jeffers to several couples who attended the church. She and the parson looked good together, but he couldn't imagine a rambunctious, adventure-loving girl like her ever being happy with a peace-loving minister.

"Didn't expect to see you down here, Cuz." Luke smacked him on the shoulder with his palm, scaring him right out of his thoughts.

Garrett held out his near empty cup and gave Luke a mock glare. "Hey, watch out. You nearly caused me to spill my drink on my clean shirt."

"Well, we can't have that, can we? Then you'd have to do laundry twice this month." Luke chuckled and shook his head. "You need a wife."

Thoughts of marriage had been heavy on his mind of late, but he wouldn't tell Luke for fear of being teased to death. "Paying the Widow Schwartz to wash my clothes is a whole lot cheaper than a wife."

"Maybe so, but not nearly as much fun." Luke waggled his brows and shoved Garrett with his elbow.

He shook his head but was happy for his cousin. Luke had returned a somber man from his years as a soldier, even though he had become a Christian. The unforgiving spirit that ate at his heart almost stole his future, but God had intervened and brought Rachel and Luke back together. Garrett hated to admit he was jealous of the life his cousin had now. "If I could find a good woman like Rachel, I just might consider settling down."

Luke's eyes widened, and he pushed his hat back on his forehead. "I never thought I'd hear you say those words."

Garrett shrugged. "Don't go telling Jack, or next thing I know, it'll be in the newspaper."

"It would serve you right. Maybe you can get your own mail-order bride."

"No thanks." Garrett watched the dancers. Most of the men who weren't frowning from focusing on their dance steps had big grins on their faces. They actually seemed to be enjoying themselves.

Luke, too, surveyed the crowd, but Garrett knew he was searching for troublemakers. Though Luke was a family man with another child on the way, he took his job seriously and never seemed to be off-duty. Fortunately, Lookout was a peaceful town most of the time.

Leaning back against the church wall, Luke

crossed his arms. "You know, there's a perfectly fine woman staying at the boardinghouse who'd be a good match for you."

The sip of cider he just took came spewing back out. A man dancing nearby cast a glare his way. Garrett coughed and waved an apology. "You can't be serious."

"What's wrong with Miss Payton?"

Garrett stared at his cousin as if he'd taken leave of his senses. "She's an ex-convict."

"So?" Luke's cool gaze needled him.

Pushing away his guilt, he formulated his argument. "If and when I marry, I want a decent woman, not one who was an outlaw and a jailbird."

"You disappoint me, Cuz."

Garrett straightened and crossed his arms. Why didn't Luke understand that he wanted a decent woman for a wife? "Why? Because I want to marry a good woman who can teach morals to my children?"

Luke pushed away from the wall. "Miss Payton *is* a good woman. She paid her debt to society, but even more important is that she's a new creation in Christ. She's given her heart to God. What more could you want in a wife?"

"Oh, I don't know. Maybe one that didn't spend six years in prison."

Luke glared at him. "You're a fine one to be talking."

"What does that mean? I've never been in jail."

"You look at life as one big joke. You and your brother ordered me not one but three mail-order brides, and almost caused me to lose my job and the woman I loved."

"But you didn't, did you?" Garrett forced a smile. He and Luke had rarely ever been at odds with one another, and he didn't want his cousin to know how much his lack of support hurt. "You still have both, and a passel of kids to boot."

"So could you if you weren't so stubborn." Luke stalked over to where Jack and the preacher were talking to Polly and Dolly at the refreshment table.

Garrett shook his head. Luke ought to know not to push him where women were concerned. He may be a joker and a tease, but he'd never felt truly comfortable with a woman. For some reason, they scared him. They seemed so delicate and sensitive that he feared he'd unwittingly hurt them.

He remembered all the times his own ma had watched his father leave home to spend the evening at the saloon. She carried her pain like a broken flower that refused to die. Had she known that his pa sometimes went upstairs with the saloon gals?

Garrett swigged down the last few drops of his cider. Not a soul, not even his brother, knew that he'd never been with a woman. Though in the eyes of God that was a good thing for an unmarried man, it was embarrassing for a man his age to admit.

He couldn't shake loose the image of the time he'd gone looking for his pa and found him laughing and chasing a scantily clad floozy up the saloon stairs. He caught her and jerked her into his arms, embracing and kissing her. Garrett's stomach churned. His mother had been home tending Mark, who was sick, and finishing the chores his pa should have done.

All that was in the past, but he never wanted to hurt a woman like his pa had, so he had steered clear of them for the most part. But loneliness was a powerful motivator. Garrett's foot kept pace with the lively guitar and fiddle music. He thought of his empty house and dreaded being alone for another night. Maybe it was time he seriously pursued finding a wife. Didn't the Bible say that "he who finds a wife finds a good thing"?

Carly Payton again intruded into his mind, but he

cast her out. She might be pretty and able to shoot well, but she wasn't marrying quality.

Jack ate a slice of applesauce cake and watched Christine Morgan dance with Rand Kessler. When the couple had first arrived, they'd acted awkwardly toward one another, and their movements had been stiff. But now they both had relaxed and were talking and smiling. Romance was in the air.

Her gaze drifted to where Noah stood talking with Luke and the mayor. If her papa knew anything about the mayor's big plans, he wasn't sharing the information with her. Now that she was feeling better, she needed to resume her quest, but how could she find out what he was up to?

Her first thought was to sneak into his house or office, but after the roof fiasco, she knew she shouldn't press her luck. The mayor had been furious about her being on his roof, but he had backed down when Luke told him he'd repair the broken shakes for free.

"Well, it's good to see you're waitin' on me."

Jack stiffened as Billy drew up beside her and placed his arm around her waist. She swerved away from his grasp. "Stop it!"

"A man has a right to cuddle his fiancée." His stern glare dared her to disagree.

She glanced toward where Luke had been, but he was no longer there. Noah looked to be patiently listening to some kind of admonition from the mayor, nodding his head at the shorter man.

"Now don't you look pretty." He leaned close and tilted her face so she had to look at him. "And you smell as good as that fancy perfume Ma sells."

"Thank you, Billy, but you need to understand that I am not your fiancée, and calling me that over and over won't make it so." She tried to pull loose of his hold, but he only gripped her tighter. If she wasn't hindered by her sore knee, she might have just hauled off and kicked him.

"Got you a present." He dangled something shiny in front of her face. When she didn't react, he pulled her arm up and pressed it into her hand.

Her first thought was to ask him where he got the money for the shiny silver bracelet with floral engravings. It was beautiful, but how could Billy afford such a thing? She never saw him in the store, other than helping unload crates of freight whenever Garrett had a delivery and could cajole him into assisting him. She stared at the expensive jewelry, turning the silver band so that it reflected the evening sun. Nothing she owned equaled the gift, but she couldn't keep it. She held it out to him. "I can't accept this."

Billy yanked it from her hand. "Can and will. I want my gal to look better'n all the others in town." He flipped the jewelry over her wrist and quickly secured it closed, even though she tried to pull away.

"Billy, I said—"

"C'mon, we're having that dance." With his arm behind her back, he forced her forward.

A stabbing pain in her knee from fighting Billy made her stumble. He hauled her up and kept her close to his side. They moved toward the dozen couples who glided to a slow waltz. Maybe she should just go along with him and get it over with, but it galled her to let him win. The only other choice she had was to pretend to faint, but she'd never swooned once in her life and didn't want folks thinking she was a weak woman. Nor did she want to get her new dress dirty. Her final option was to call for help. As they made their way into the dancers, she searched for Luke. *Horse feathers*. He was gone.

Christine Morgan and Rand Kessler glided past them. Tessa turned up her nose at Jack when she caught her eye. She'd get no help from her. Billy loosened his grip and turned to face her.

Jack glared up at him. "You'd better enjoy this dance, Mr. Morgan, because it will be the only one you'll ever get."

He yanked her against his chest. "Oh, I'll enjoy it, but it won't be our last."

Gritting her teeth, Jack tried not to wince whenever she had to move to the right. Billy held her improperly close. As he turned, she caught the minister's gaze and sent him a look that made him straighten. She lost sight of him on the next turn, then came around again and found he was gone.

Suddenly Billy halted and glanced over his shoulder. "You ain't cuttin' in, Preacher."

Noah stepped up beside Billy. "Miss Davis has an injured knee and has no business dancing."

Billy narrowed his eyes. "It ain't no concern of yours."

"I disagree. I'm the one who escorted her to the dance, so it's my responsibility to watch over her." Though his expression remained passive, the sternness in his gaze showed he wasn't intimidated.

Dancers whirled around them as the musicians played "The Blue Danube," but they were starting to stare. Jack tried to back away from Billy, but he only tightened his grip. He sliced a seething glance her way before bull's-eyeing in on Noah.

"I'm a man of peace, mister, but I haven't always been. I'm asking you to please turn loose of the lady." The tone of Noah's deep voice made the order more menacing, and his no-nonsense glare backed up his words.

"Just who are you, anyway?" Billy demanded.

"I'm Noah Jeffers, the new pastor."

A confused look passed over Billy's face, then he tilted his head back and laughed. His hand that rested on Jack's waist loosened, and he swiped it across his eyes. Noah slipped in between her and Billy, grabbing Billy's wrist. He yelped and let go of Jack's hand. She stepped to the side so she could see around Noah's tall body. If Billy was finally going to be put in his place, she wanted to watch. The dancers closest to them also slowed to a halt, as if not to miss the action.

"Hey, that hurts." Billy scowled at Noah and rubbed his wrist.

"Maybe you should have considered that it hurt Miss Davis when you forced her to dance."

Billy's face instantly changed from wounded indignation to fury. He hauled back and struck Noah's cheek with his fist, driving him backward. Noah regained his balance and dabbed at the cut below his eye. He stared at the blood, and his gaze darkened. He frowned. Jack held her breath, seeing the evident anger on the pastor's face.

"C'mon, *Reverend*. If you want her, fight for her." Billy held up his fists and danced on his feet like a boxer.

Christine Morgan stopped dancing and hurried to her son's side. Rand Kessler stood behind her, a silent support. The music squeaked to a stop as did the rest of the dancers. Mrs. Morgan reached out to touch her son, but he jerked away, his fists still in fight mode. "Billy, what's going on here?"

"Stay out of this, Ma. That new preacher wants to steal Jacqueline away from me, and if he wants her, he'll have to fight me for her."

Mrs. Morgan glanced at Noah, a shocked look on her face. "Is that true, Reverend?"

Jack watched Noah's angry expression soften as

171

he regained control. Her heart ached for the position he'd been put in just because he tried to help her. Maybe she should explain things. "No, Mrs. Morgan, it isn't true. I told Billy I didn't want to dance tonight because my knee still hurts. Reverend Jeffers came to my aid because Billy wouldn't listen to reason and forced me to dance with him—and that's the honest truth."

Mrs. Morgan studied Jack's face, then the reverend's and her son's. She lowered her head and shook it. "Go home, Billy."

"No, I ain't letting him steal my fiancée."

"I don't belong to you, and I have no idea where you got that notion." Jack gritted her teeth to keep from saying something she'd regret. "I am not your fiancée." She looked around the curious crowd that encircled them. "Everybody, hear that? I have no intention of marrying Billy Morgan."

Billy lowered his fists, looking both hurt and angry. "I don't know why I give a hoot about you. Half the time you don't even dress like a lady, and you run around in pants like a man." He turned as if to leave, then ducked his head and charged Noah. Billy rammed his head into the preacher's belly, and both men went down.

Sitting on Noah's stomach, Billy pummeled his face with both fists. Noah held up his arms, protecting himself, but not fighting back.

"Billy!" Mrs. Morgan gasped, lifting her hand to her mouth. "Stop it."

"Wallop him, Preacher," a voice called out from the crowd. "Show him you ain't no coward."

Jack's heart pounded harder with each fist Billy planted. Why didn't Noah fight back? Surely it was all right for a preacher to defend himself.

Suddenly, Noah roared and shoved upward. Taken

off guard, Billy was flung backward and rolled feet over head. Noah jumped up, far more agile than most men his size, and stood with his fists up. His chest heaved; blood trailed down his cheek from a cut over his eyebrow. He swiped his face with his white sleeve, leaving an ugly red stain on the once spotless fabric.

Billy lurched to his feet and charged, fury burning from his eyes like blue fire. The men in the crowd cheered the preacher on, but Jack heard women praying for him to stop. Noah drew back his right fist then brought it forward with a mighty force. It collided with Billy's cheek, knocking his head sideways. He staggered, then dropped to his knees and shook his head.

Noah, with fists still lifted, seemed to wake up from his stupor and glanced around. A frantic look crossed his face, and his arms fell to his side, as if suddenly boneless. Desperate remorse flooded his face, making Jack's heart ache. Was he sorry for defending her?

Rand Kessler, who stood half a foot taller than Billy, stepped away from Mrs. Morgan and took hold of Billy's upper arm. "That's enough fighting, young man."

"Let me go! You ain't my pa." Billy struggled but couldn't overpower the hardy rancher, who pulled him through the crowd and out of Jack's view.

Noah bent over, hands on his knees, head hanging down, breathing deeply. Dirt and grass covered his backside. Hadn't he told Jack that was his only suit and shirt? What would he preach in tomorrow?

"Are you all right, Reverend?" Mrs. Morgan asked. She pulled a handkerchief from her sleeve and handed it to him. "I'm so sorry. My son can be hotheaded at times."

Noah straightened, took the hanky, and held it

against his cheek. He offered Billy's mother a pain-filled smile. "No, I'm the one who's sorry."

"You had to defend yerself, Parson," someone behind Jack yelled. Cheers of agreement battled those of condemnation.

"A preacher oughtn't to fight," came another voice off to Jack's left.

Noah lifted his hands, stilling the crowd. "I want to apologize to y'all." He pursed his lips and glanced at Jack. "Fighting is never the right choice, and I'm sorry that I was a bad example."

Murmurs sounded all around, both negative and positive.

"Let me pass, y'all here. Move out of the way."

Jack groaned inwardly as she recognized Bertha Boyd's voice. She was in no mood to tolerate the busybody tonight. What could she want?

Everyone knew Bertha only came to the socials to fill up on the latest gossip first and then the refreshments. Men and women backed up, clearing a wide path for the large woman.

Bertha stopped right beside Jack and Noah. "I want y'all to know what a good man our new reverend is. He spent two and a half hours yesterday chopping wood for me and Aggie. And he did it all out of the goodness of his heart." She nodded her head so vigorously, her three chins wobbled like a turkey's wattle.

Heads nodded and murmurs circled the crowd.

"I was happy to do it, Mrs. Boyd." Noah smiled, but Jack caught his grimace. He lightly touched his swollen cheek. The damaged skin around his right eye was puffing up so badly she could barely see his pupil.

Jack stepped forward, ready to be free of the crowd. "If y'all will excuse us, I need to get home and off my leg, and Reverend Jeffers needs his wounds treated."

"I'll go after the doc." Hiram Stone, a man who'd recently moved to Lookout, took off at a jog.

"I don't need a doctor," Noah called after the man, who either didn't hear him or ignored him.

With the action over, people drifted away, and the music started up again. Some of the men found their women and ambled back to the area in front of the musicians to dance, while others said their good-byes and headed for their buggies or horses.

Jack limped over to where Noah stood alone and looking crestfallen. "I disagree about the doctor. That cut on your brow may need to be stitched up. C'mon. Let's go home." Jack took hold of his elbow and led him across the field.

"I made a royal mess of things." Noah shook his head. "It wouldn't surprise me if nobody showed up at church tomorrow."

"Don't be so hard on yourself."

Noah stopped in front of Ray Castleby's home and stared down at her as if she'd gone loco. "I'm the town's minister, Jack. It's my duty to keep peace and lead by example, not fight with a hotheaded man upset over unrequited love."

"Oh and because you're a pastor, I guess you don't believe in defending a woman's honor. What if your wife were attacked by outlaws, like Garrett and Miss Payton were? Would you defend her and shoot the man who was about to attack her?" Jack shoved her hands to her hips.

"That's ridiculous. It's a theoretical situation that may never happen and has no bearing on this conversation."

"Fine, then. See your own self home, *Reverend* Jeffers." Jack stomped off, more livid than she could remember. She hadn't asked for his help. Yeah, she was grateful he had put Billy in his place, but she wouldn't be responsible for his being upset. He was the one who chose to fight.

Guilt nibbled at her heels as she left him standing in front of the bank president's house. It wasn't as if he couldn't find his way since the boardinghouse was within view, but the honest truth was he *had* come to her aid. And he had tried hard to not fight back and allowed Billy to pummel him far too long. Remorse battled her irritation. Tomorrow, battered and bruised, Noah would have to stand before the people who showed up and preach his first sermon. Many would support him, but others would oppose him.

She clenched her teeth as she climbed up one step to the front porch and then another, fighting the pain in her knee. Glancing back, she could barely make out Noah's tall form standing in the growing shadows at the edge of the glow cast from buildings along the street. She couldn't solve his problems. She could barely work through her own.

Her hand connected with the doorknob, and the bracelet on her wrist glimmered in the light from the parlor. *Horse feathers!* She'd forgotten about it in all the ruckus. She'd have to return it and dreaded seeing Billy again. But keeping it would give him the wrong idea.

She looked again to see if Noah was coming. Something niggled at the back of her mind. As if someone had turned up the flame of a lantern, the thought burst to light in her mind.

The preacher had called her Jack.

Chapter 16

After allowing the doctor to tend his wounds, Noah sat on the front steps to the boardinghouse, his face in his hands. Remorse weighed so heavily on him that he didn't have the strength to climb the stairs to his room.

He'd lost the respect of the townsfolk before he even won it in the first place.

He'd jumped out of the frying pan and into the fire.

This was a catastrophe. If only Pete were here to offer his sage advice.

But Pete wasn't, and Noah needed to take his burden to God instead of his mentor anyway. "I'm sorry, Lord. Sorry for not showing the love of Christ to Billy Morgan. Sorry for fighting instead of being a peacemaker."

He stared down Main Street, deserted now that everyone had gone home from the social. Some folks had waved as they drove past him, but the stern glare of others left him unsettled. Unable to find peace in his heart. He'd been right to stand up for Jack, hadn't he?

She'd sent him a panicked look when dancing with Billy Morgan that seemed a cry for help and stirred up within him a fierce desire to protect her. He hadn't wanted to fight—just to help Jack. But all he'd done was upset her and half the town. He'd be lucky if anyone showed up in the morning to hear his first sermon.

The quiet evening soothed his aching heart, and the stiff north breeze that had stirred up left a chill on his cheeks. The only sounds were insects buzzing around, crickets in the grass, and the distant revelry of the saloon. The noise of children inside the boardinghouse had fallen silent. Somewhere nearby, a dog barked.

Noah sighed. He generally felt closer to God outside. He bent his head in prayer, hoping to find peace and some direction for tomorrow.

"You're looking mighty down in the dumps."

Noah jumped at the sound of Luke's voice. The tension that was finally leaving his neck and shoulders returned in full force. He'd been wallowing so deep in doubt and despair and begging God's forgiveness that he hadn't heard the marshal's footsteps. "I thought you'd gone to bed."

"Naw. I tucked Rachel in earlier, then took a final tour of the town. I don't like to turn in until things quiet down." Luke let out a low whistle. "Looks like you'll have a shiner tomorrow. You want me to get you a slab of meat to put on it? Got some down in the root cellar. The cold might help with the swelling."

"Thanks, but no. It'll be all right, I reckon."

Luke nodded and hopped up the steps, opened the front door, and turned down the lamp in the parlor that threw some light on the porch. Then he took a seat on the steps next to Noah. "I don't know about you, but I sometimes find it easier to discuss things in the dark."

He could argue the point that the night wasn't fully dark with the half moon in the western sky, but he held his tongue. The truth was he could use someone to talk to.

"I heard all about what happened at the social. Sorry I wasn't there, but I'd come back to check on Rachel." Luke shook his head. "That Billy Morgan has been trouble since the day he arrived in town. It's time someone put him in his place."

"I shouldn't have hit him."

"Why did you?"

Because I lost control of my temper. "I didn't want to, but he had me down and wouldn't quit punching me. I finally got tired of it—no, the truth is, I went berserk. Something in me snapped, and I came up fighting."

"A man has a right to defend himself."

Noah shook his head. "This wasn't defending. This was revenge."

Luke was quiet for a moment. "You didn't know Billy when you lived here before, did you?"

"No, he must have come after I left."

Luke rubbed the stubble on his jaw, making a bristly sound. "Then how could it be revenge?"

Noah clasped his hands tightly together and wrapped them around his knees. He hated talking about his past—remembering how rotten his childhood had been—but the marshal already knew some of his story. "I'm sure you remember what my pa was like. He wasn't a nice man."

"Yeah. I had a few run-ins with him before you two left town. He'd drink too much, then start fights."

"Uh-huh. And he'd come home like that, and any little thing could set him off. I had more beatings as a child than I could count."

Luke rested his hand on Noah's shoulder. "I'm sorry about that, son. A man should love his children, teach them right from wrong, not be cruel to them."

"I think Pa blamed me for my ma's and sister's deaths."

"How so?"

Tears burned Noah's eyes, but he batted them away. The day his sister died was one of the worst in his life. "Pa had gone hunting when they took sick. I wanted to go for the doctor, but I couldn't leave them alone. Zoe wasn't even two years old yet, and Ma was too sick to care for her. When Pa came home and found them dead and me alive, something in him broke. He was never the same. The beatings started soon after that."

"I'm sorry, Noah. You did the best you could, I'm sure."

Noah crossed his arms. "I don't know. I can't help wondering what would have happened if I'd gone for the doctor when they first took sick."

"You can ask a million 'what ifs,' but it won't change anything."

"I know. I just wish I'd been the one who died instead of them."

Luke lifted his face toward the sky. "They're safe in the Father's arms now and will never know pain again."

"Yeah, I take comfort in knowing that. I told you all that because I want you to understand. When I was about fifteen, a year and a half after we left Lookout, my pa came home drunk and broke one night. He was spittin' mad that he'd lost what little money he had in a poker game, and he intended to take out his frustrations on me. Well, it had finally dawned on me that I was a whole lot bigger than him and stronger, too. I'd been working some, chopping wood for folks, and I decided then and there that I would never be beaten again."

"I see. So when Billy had you down on the ground, that fighting instinct kicked in."

Noah nodded, thankful the man understood. "Yeah. I know that as the town's shepherd, I'm supposed to be a good example to my flock, but I really bungled things tonight. Maybe it would be better for everyone if I pack up and head back to Emporia."

Luke draped his arm loosely over Noah's shoulders. "Don't hang up your fiddle yet. You told me God sent you here. Do you feel like you've fulfilled the work He wanted you to do already?"

Noah barked a laugh. "What work? I've been here less than a week."

"Well, there's your answer then."

"What is?"

Luke leaned forward and looked at him. "God sent you here for a purpose. You haven't completed the task, so leaving now isn't an option."

"Oh. I see what you mean." As much as he'd like to take the easy way out, Noah knew he wouldn't. "Guess I'll have to stand up there tomorrow and eat some crow."

"Like I said, there's nothing wrong with a man defending himself, and from what I heard, it all started when you stood up for Jack and made Billy stop forcing her to dance. Yeah, maybe you lost control in the fight, but you were defending yourself and an innocent woman. In many people's eyes, you'll be a hero."

"You didn't see the looks of disappointment I got from other folks."

Luke stood and stretched. "You'll never please everyone, Noah. I learned that long ago. So start with pleasing God and being obedient to your calling, and trust God to deal with the people."

Noah stood, feeling like an old man in his battered body.

"You need to get a good night's sleep." Luke opened the front door and held it for Noah to enter. "I, for one, am looking forward to hearing your sermon."

Noah allowed a small smile. "Yeah, well, don't set your standard too high."

They were finally done talking. Jack pulled her pillow out of the window and listened to the creak of the stairs outside her door as Noah climbed them. She hadn't heard much of what was said, since the men had talked mostly in low tones and Abby's loud snores filled the room, but she'd gotten the odd feeling that Luke knew far more about Noah than she did.

How was that possible?

Had they talked before?

Why would Noah open up to her papa and not to her?

One thing she *had* heard was a woman's name— Zoe. Who was she? Could the parson have a gal he left behind somewhere?

The cool breeze blowing in her window sent goose bumps racing up her arm, and she reached over and lowered the sash. Jack sat there, staring into the dark room, scowling and nibbling one corner of her lower lip. It shouldn't bother her that some woman might have already claimed his heart. In fact, it didn't.

What bothered her was that she hadn't been able to get her story. Being a lawman, Luke was fairly tight-lipped, but if she waited for just the right timing, maybe she could get him to tell her something more about Noah Jeffers. At any rate, tomorrow he'd preach his first sermon, and that alone should give her enough fodder for an article.

Lying back, she smiled. For a woman with skills and wiles, there was always a way to reach her goal.

Chapter 17

Carly dipped the last plate into the rinse water and laid it on the stack on the table. "Is there anything else that needs washing?"

Rachel set the dish she'd just dried on the stack of clean plates and leaned back in her chair, resting her arm across her large belly. "I don't think so, but the dining table may need to be washed off."

Ringing out the rag, Carly noticed Rachel lay her head back against the chair and close her eyes. "Is Oscar misbehaving this morning?"

Rachel's lips curved up in a soft smile. "Not so much. I just can't believe that breakfast is barely over, and I already feel the need for a nap."

Carly wiped down the kitchen counters, then rinsed the dishcloth and wrung it out again. "Well, why don't you go lie down? I can finish drying the plates and silverware."

"I still need to dress for church and fix the girls' hair." With obvious effort, Rachel forced herself to sit up and dry another dish.

"Nobody will think bad of you if you were to miss church, considering you will be having a baby any day. I can fix your daughters' hair."

"It's not as easy as it sounds. Emmie isn't too hard since her hair is too short to braid. Just brush it, but trying to plait Abby's hair is about as easy as lassoing a cloud."

Chuckling, Carly found a dry towel and quickly started drying the silverware before Rachel could object. Her friend had offered her a job helping her, but that wasn't such an easy task. Rachel was so used to doing everything that instead of waiting for help, she just went ahead and did things. Carly was going to have to be on her toes and stay alert if she was to be any help around here.

Thinking of braiding Abby's hair reminded Carly of her last visit when Rachel would struggle to get Jacqueline to sit still long enough for her to fix the girl's tresses. "Is Abby much like Jacqueline?"

Rachel set the last dried plate on the pile and rolled her eyes. "Far more than I wish she was."

Remembering how young Jack had shed her dresses and donned her worn overalls every chance she got made Carly realize just how long she'd been away. Jacqueline had grown from a spunky ten-year-old who preferred fishing with her two male friends over school or housework, to a lovely young woman. She ambled into the dining room and washed off the table, chairs, and the buffet. She glanced around the clean room, a feeling of satisfaction rising within her.

A bird's cheerful song wafted in on the morning breeze, fluttering the white lacey curtains, reminding her of Tillie's house. She wondered how Pastor Barker was getting along without his wife or her to care for him. Had he moved in with his daughter yet?

Carly breathed a wistful sigh. She'd thought of the old couple as caring grandparents, even though she wasn't their kin. They'd treated her far better than she'd expected when she first arrived as a newly released convict. Her past hadn't mattered to them any more than it did to Rachel, but in truth, she wasn't family. She had no family.

And wasn't that just as well?

As she walked back into the kitchen, she thought about her brother. Tyson was dead now, God rest his soul, and she couldn't help feeling relieved. Yeah, he'd let her live with his outlaw gang and kept the men away from her with his vile threats, but he'd used her. Forced her into a life of bank robbery, stealing from hardworking people and being on the run. Thank the Lord those days were behind her.

She hung the dishcloth on the edge of the sink and looked at her friend. Rachel again sat back with her eyes shut. Carly reached down, taking her arm. "C'mon, it's back to bed for you."

"No, no. I wasn't sleeping. Just resting my eyes."

"I've heard that line before." Carly chuckled, helping Rachel to her feet. A streak of jealousy raised its head when she stared up close at the bulge the baby made beneath Rachel's apron. She squelched the snake of envy and guided Rachel to her bedroom. "When did you say your baby is due?"

"Not for another week or two." Rachel lay back on her quilt and released a sigh. "I think you're right about not attending church, although I hate missing Reverend Jeffers' first sermon and sitting with you."

Carly pulled a brown knitted coverlet off the back of a nearby chair and laid it over Rachel's legs. "I'll be fine, and so will the minister."

Rachel's pale blue eyes filled with concern. "I feel so bad that Noah has to preach his first sermon in town with that black eye. It looks atrocious."

Carly couldn't help comparing Noah Jeffers to Reverend Barker. Other than both being Christians, they were nothing alike, as far as she could tell in the short time she'd been at the boardinghouse. "Maybe it'll keep him from fighting again. I can't imagine Reverend Barker from my old church ever getting into a fight."

"Just remember, our reverend was trying to help Jacqueline. He never expected to get into a fight, from what Luke told me. I, for one, appreciate him standing up to Billy Morgan. I've known that young man since the first day he arrived in Lookout and stayed here with his mother and sister, and he's always been trouble."

"Now that he's been publicly put in his place, maybe he'll straighten up." Carly pushed away from the doorjamb she'd been leaning on. "Better round up your girls and make sure they're dressed, then finish getting ready for church myself. You have a nice rest, and don't worry. Jacqueline and I will handle things."

"Thank you, Carly. . . ." Rachel's words were already slurring together as sleep claimed her. "I 'ppreciate. . .you."

Carly left to take a final glance around the kitchen then hurried upstairs. Hopefully Jacqueline would have the younger girls dressed by now. At the top of the stairs, she tapped on the door. Childish squeals echoed from the other side.

"Come in."

Pushing the door ajar, she peered in. "I came to fix the girls' hair."

"I was just getting ready to do Abby's." Jacqueline cast a quick glance at Carly, then grabbed Abby, who attempted to chase after Emmie. "Oh, no you don't. Hold still and let me fix your hair. You don't want to look like a scarecrow, do you?"

"I do if it means I can stay home from church." Abby kicked at Emmie's ball as it rolled toward the bed. Emmie screeched and ran after it.

"Abigail Louise Davis! You don't mean that."

Abby nodded, pulling her hair free from her big sister's hand. "Uh-huh. I told that preacher I don't like church. It's boring."

Her deep blue eyes sparkling with humor, Jacqueline shook her head while braiding Abby's hair so fast, her hands almost blurred. She glanced up. "My sister is a heathen, Miss Payton."

Carly couldn't help the grin that pulled on her lips. "Won't you please call me Carly?"

Jacqueline lifted her brow and gave her a schoolmarm look. "Only if you'll call me Jack."

"Ma don't like that name," Abby said.

"Well, it's my name, and I can have folks call me what I want." Jack tugged gently on her sister's braid. "Hold still while I tie the ribbon."

Arms crossed, Carly leaned against the door and watched Jack patiently tie the ribbon on the wiggly girl. What would it be like to have a sister? She'd heard her ma had birthed another baby when Carly was two, but it hadn't lived. Glancing up at the ceiling, she offered a quick prayer that God would watch over Rachel and see that her baby was delivered safely.

"Is Papa back yet?" Jack asked.

"No. Your friend Tessa came to the door just after you came upstairs after breakfast. Said something about the mercantile being robbed."

Jack's eyes widened. "Truly? When did that happen?"

Carly shrugged. Emma toddled over to her and lifted her hands, and she picked up the child. "I don't know. Miss Morgan said the family came downstairs early and found the back window broken and a number of things missing."

"That's horrible." Jack tapped her sister's shoulder. "You're done. Now try to keep your dress clean."

Carly picked up a small brush off the chest of

drawers and brushed Emma's hair then set the girl down. "It looks like you have things under control here, so I'd better change into my church dress."

Jack nodded and stood, smoothing out the skirt of her delft blue dress. Her pretty auburn hair wasn't piled up on her head like it had been last night but rather was tied with a blue ribbon and hung down her back to her waist. The gangly wild child had grown into a beautiful young woman.

In her room, Carly shed her apron and calico and donned her yellow gingham church dress. She stared at her hair in the tall oval mirror that hung on one wall. She had never gotten used to pinning it up as Tillie had shown her, but the ladies at her old church always wore theirs that way. Turning sideways, she looked at her long braid. Dare she try wearing it hanging down as Jack had?

Finally she shrugged. What did it matter? She wasn't trying to impress anyone—and yet the moment that thought fled her mind, a picture of Garrett Corbett in his Sunday best replaced it. From the parlor window, she'd seen him walking to the social the night before. He had probably been relieved to see that she hadn't shown up.

Snatching up her brush, she shook out her braid and brushed her hair. It wasn't as long as Jack's, having been kept short while in prison, but it had finally grown to the middle of her back. She tied a ribbon and looped it into a bow at her nape, then turned sideways to see how she looked. Some might actually think she was pretty. She pinched her cheeks, then found her Bible.

With one hand on the doorknob, she considered the day's importance. Today she would either be received by folks in the town—or rejected. If they hated her, what would she do?

She breathed a prayer, "Please, Father, let them accept me."

Noah leaned over the hitching post at the back of the church property and retched. After a few moments of misery, he dabbed his mouth with his handkerchief. No amount of preparation ever eased his stomach before preaching a sermon, and this was by far the most nerve-racking situation he'd ever encountered.

He glanced around, glad that no one had shown up early, then strode toward the water pump. The cool liquid tasted delicious but didn't sit well in his belly. He gazed up at the sky through the canopy of trees overhead. "Father, I ask that You settle my stomach. Help me to rectify the damage I did last night, and enable me to share the message that You've laid on my heart."

A wide yawn slipped out, and he covered his mouth. He'd slept little last night. The fight with Billy and then the disagreement with Jack weighed heavily on him. Doubts swirled through his thoughts like debris in a tornado. Would anyone recognize him as the former town bully? Would the church people be angry that he'd gotten in a fight? Would they be receptive to his message? Would they even show up?

Clutching his well-worn Bible against his heart, he opened the church door and stepped inside. Immediately the peace of God flooded him and calmed him. The morning sun peeked through the storm clouds overhead and glimmered through the stained-glass window, creating colorful patterns of light that danced on the floor and walls. Closing his eyes, he murmured a prayer of thanks to the Lord for His presence.

He opened all the windows, then sat down on the

front row, read several psalms, and scanned his sermon again. By the time he was done, buggies were driving past the windows and parking in the lot next door.

Noah blew out a breath and went to greet his parishioners at the front door. A man he didn't recognize walked up to the entrance with his wife and two adolescent boys. The man smiled at him, but when the woman glanced up, her happy expression turned to shock. She halted so fast, one of her boys ran into her back.

"Hey, Ma, whatcha stoppin' for?" The boy backed up a few steps, nudging his brother with his elbows. Both youths glanced at him in unison, and their mouths dropped open.

Noah smiled. He'd seen his ugly purple eye in the mirror this morning, as well as his puffy cheek and eyebrow. He probably looked like some kind of monster that children conjured up in their creative minds. "Good morning, and welcome. I'm Noah Jeffers, the visiting minister."

"Uh. . .we'uns is the Cauldwells," the man said. "I'm Jethro, and this here's my wife, Maisy, and our boys Samuel and Josiah."

"Ah, good Bible names, I see. It's a pleasure to meet y'all." Noah held his hand out to the man.

Mr. Cauldwell glanced up, frowned, and then shook Noah's hand. "D'you have some kind of accident or somethin'?"

Noah winced. He'd hoped word had gotten around town, so all he'd have to do was repent to the crowd and not have to explain things. "No, sir. I mean, I suppose it was sort of an accident."

"Either it was or it weren't. Which is it?" Mrs. Cauldwell pushed her wire-rimmed glasses up her thin nose. Behind her boys, another couple waited to enter.

"Since I'm going to have to explain myself, if you wouldn't mind being patient for a short while, I'd prefer to give the details just once, rather than having to tell each person as they enter."

Mr. Cauldwell glanced at his wife, then nodded. "I reckon we can wait. C'mon boys."

Mrs. Cauldwell followed her husband, but the boys stopped in front of him. The older one leaned toward him, his brows wiggling. "That's a mighty fine-looking shiner, Reverend. You oughta be proud of it. I hope you gave the other guy what for. Anybody who'd fight a preacher deserves a thrashing, right, Sammy?"

His brother nodded his agreement; then both sat on the third row with their parents. The next couple had similar expressions of surprise on their faces. He'd seen them around town but had yet to meet them.

"I'm Noah Jeffers. Welcome."

The man nodded a greeting, but his wife huddled close as if she feared Noah. Just the thought made him wonder again if he shouldn't pack up and leave. What was God thinking in giving him a church to pastor?

"I'm Earl Hightower, and this here's Myrtle, my spinster sister."

Noah wasn't sure why the man felt the need to inform him his sister was unmarried since she had to be at least ten years his senior. He smiled. "A pleasure to meet you both. Come in and have a seat."

Agatha Linus hurried through the door. Her sister was still making her way across the street at a snail's pace. "Sorry I wasn't here earlier to practice the hymns, Reverend Jeffers. But I had to wait so I could help Bertha down the stairs. She doesn't handle them too good these days, what with her rheumatism being so bad and all. Should I play the two songs we decided on when we last talked?"

"That sounds perfect. Thank you, ma'am, and maybe I could come by your house this week and look over those stairs. Might be something I could do that would make things easier for your sister." Noah smiled at his organist, relieved that she had arrived.

"Wonderful! We'd love to have you visit again—and this time you won't need to chop wood." Agatha took her place on the organ bench and began to softly play a hymn.

Noah walked outside to the middle of the road, where Bertha Boyd rested on her cane, huffing hard. "Might I assist you into the church, Mrs. Boyd?"

"I'd be grateful. . .Reverend. This walk. . .seems longer. . .each time I. . .make it." She held one hand to her chest and struggled to catch her breath. The skin on her cheeks and throat jiggled with each breath she took.

Holding out his arm to her, he smiled. Bertha Boyd talked more than any woman he'd met and was the biggest woman he'd ever seen. Like Jack, the top of her head barely reached his shoulders, but Mrs. Boyd was a half-dozen times bigger around than the woman who refused to leave his mind. He'd learned a long time ago that Mrs. Boyd had the gift of gab and lived to gossip. Breathing hard, she leaned her weight on his arm and waddled into the church. She collapsed in the pew closest to the door and waved a thank-you.

"I say any Texan has a right to defend himself, pastor or not."

"A minister shouldn't oughta be fightin'."

Noah's attention was pulled back to the door by the raised voices. Two men he recognized as the bank tellers wrestled each other to get in the door first.

"Good morning, gentlemen." He considered

asking them to lower their voices as they entered God's house but chose to take another route.

Both ceased the shoving and gazed up at Noah. One man smiled, and the other scowled. Behind them, a family with a large number of children waited quietly.

"Jess Jermaine, Reverend." He slipped in the door. "A pleasure to meet you."

The other man hurried in, head down, and slunk to a nearby pew.

"Don't pay him no never-mind. He's a passa—uh, passa—"

"Pacifist?"

Mr. Jermaine shook his head and removed his hat. "Yeah, that's it. He thinks nobody should ever fight." Mr. Jermaine leaned closer. "But he's from Boston. Them city folks don't know that a man who doesn't defend himself in Texas just might'n live to see the sunset. You did the right thang last night, Pastor."

Remorse again gutted Noah. If he hadn't fought Billy Morgan, people's minds would be on God this morning and not whether the pastor should or shouldn't have defended himself.

A familiar-looking man almost as tall as he held out his hand for his wife to enter. Noah recognized the blond woman as one of the boardinghouse brides the Corbett brothers had brought to town a decade ago. She'd lost the marshal's hand, but it looked as if she'd been highly successful in attracting another man and raising a large brood of children.

The woman smiled, her blue eyes shining. "It's a pleasure to meet you, Reverend. I'm Leah Howard."

Noah shook her fingertips. Then she motioned for her children to come in. They were like stair steps, from a young woman about Jack's age to a baby she held in her arms, an even combination of boys and girls. The man watched them scurry past, a proud smile on his face.

"That's quite a family you have there."

"Yes sir, we've been blessed by the Lord, for sure." He held out his hand. "I'm Dan Howard. I own the livery."

"Of course. The day I arrived, you were receiving a load of hay, so your assistant helped me. Isn't that him?" Noah nudged his chin toward the tallest boy, still standing in the aisle.

"Yep, that's our oldest son, Ben. He's a good help."

"How's my horse doing?"

Mr. Howard smiled. "Good. We feed him ever' day, give him fresh water, and put him in the pasture each morning."

"I wasn't questioning your care, Mr. Howard. I've neglected to exercise him like I should and feel bad about that."

"Davy, my thirteen-year-old, is real good with horses. He'd be right pleased to ride yours around town if'n you'd like him to."

Noah smiled. "I'd be obliged."

Mr. Howard nodded and took his seat beside his wife. His family took up two whole pews.

For the next ten minutes, people filed in, greeted Noah, and took their seats. As his pocket watch hit the top of the hour, Noah headed for the front, trying to shake his disappointment that Jack and her family had failed to come this morning. Was she still angry with him?

On second thought, maybe her not being present was a blessing. He cared deeply that his parishioners would receive him as their pastor and friend. But it mattered immensely more what Jack thought—and that idea threatened to shatter his tenuous peace. Grasping hold of the podium, he stared at the crowd and determined to shut Jack from his mind—at least for the next hour.

He glanced at Agatha Linus and nodded. The woman began a flowery introduction of "At the Cross." He smiled. "Would you please stand and join me in worship to our God?"

Most of the crowd rose to their feet, leaving Bertha Boyd and a few old folks and youngsters still seated. Noah closed his eyes, offered a final, quick prayer that God would speak through him and that the congregation would forgive his actions of the previous night, and then joined in the singing:

"At the cross, at the cross where I first saw the light,
And the burden of my heart rolled away,
It was there by faith I received my sight,
And now I am happy all the day!"

Chapter 18

Carly quickened her steps as voices lifted in song emanating from the church filled the muggy air with a beautiful serenade of praise to God. Time had gotten away from them, and the last thing she wanted was to go in after the service had started and receive the scolding stares of those already seated—the very people she hoped would accept her.

"Horse feathers. We're late." Jacqueline hoisted Emma into her arms and hurriedly shooed her siblings along like a mother hen.

"Horses ain't got no feathers." Alan shook his head, his short legs pumping fast to keep up.

"Goodness, Alan. Where'd you ever learn to talk like that?" Jack grabbed Abby's hand to keep her from dashing back home to her ma. "C'mon."

"Yeah, don'tcha know *ain't* ain't a word?" Abby stuck her tongue out and made a face.

"Abby! Stop that. You two better behave, or you'll get no pie today." Both kids frowned but settled down at Jack's warning.

Carly wondered how Rachel would manage having another child when the ones she already had were so rambunctious. Hopefully the new baby would take after Emma, who seemed to have the most docile character of the bunch.

The open doors of the church looked more like a monster's mouth ready to swallow rather than welcome her. Now that they had arrived, a part of Carly wanted to rush back to the security of the boardinghouse to stay with Rachel. But if she were there, Rachel would feel obligated to stay up and talk, and the poor woman needed her rest. And Carly desperately needed to hear an encouraging message this morning.

Thunder sounded to the west, and she glanced up at the gray sky. Even the heavens looked unsettled today. The air hung heavy with moisture, and sweat already dampened the back of her dress.

At least she'd met the new minister and had shared several meals with him and the Davis family. He seemed kind and accepting of her; then again, he didn't know about her past. But with him being new, wouldn't most of the church folk be focused on him and whether his sermon passed muster and not concerned about a new woman in town?

They entered the doorway and shuffled down the aisle to the closest empty row. Emmie squealed when she saw the reverend and waved. "Howdy, Pas'er."

Most folks nearby chuckled, but a few cast stern glares their way. Reverend Jeffers grinned, even though singing, and waved his fingers at the toddler. Carly sat down and bit back her own smile. Jack had her hand wrapped securely over the girl's mouth and had leaned over to whisper something in her sister's ear.

Carly joined in the third verse of the song, which she'd learned at Reverend Barker's church:

> "Was it for crimes that I had done;
> He groaned upon the tree?
> Amazing pity! grace unknown!
> And love beyond degree!"

Carly's heart clenched, and she closed her eyes. Jesus had suffered on the cross partly because of her own sins. *Forgive me, Lord.* She knew in her heart that He had pardoned her, but remembering the price Jesus had paid for her salvation kept her humble. She had much to be thankful for. God had freed her from prison and given her peace—at least most of the time. And He'd blessed her by making it possible for her to live in Lookout again with her dear friend who had told her about salvation. God's faithfulness was truly great. She prayed again that He would open the townsfolk's hearts toward her and that He'd give her the home she'd never had before.

She rearranged her skirt and smiled at Alan, who sat next to her. From behind, she heard the loud whispers, "Outlaw. Convict."

Her heart clenched, and her hope wilted like a daisy in a drought. She closed her eyes as the pastor prayed. *Help me, Lord.*

She simply had to make a stand here in Lookout, because she had nowhere else to go. Either people would accept her, or they wouldn't. If their scorn was the worst she had to face, then she could endure. *But please, Lord, don't let things get any worse.*

Footsteps shuffled down the aisle, and someone squeezed into the small space between her and the edge of the pew. She scooted closer to Alan then glanced over to see who had just arrived. Garrett Corbett stared down at her with those intriguing blue eyes. Her hands started sweating, and she yanked her gaze away. *Oh, Lord, why'd he have to sit here?*

Jack scooted to the end of the pew so that Carly could move over and not have Garrett crowding her. She probably should have mentioned that he often sat with her family and then came over for Sunday dinner.

Agatha Linus started playing the chorus of "What a Friend We Have in Jesus," and the pastor started singing, his deep voice clear and surprisingly on-key. She pulled Emma back against her, hoping the warmth of the room would put the toddler to sleep, and continued listening. Who would have thought Noah could sing so well?

His handsome face looked dreadful. His black eye had all but swollen shut, and his other cuts were puffy and red. She wondered why he hadn't worn the bandages the doctor had put on his wounds last night. Maybe he wanted folks to know he had nothing to hide.

If that was the case, why wouldn't he talk about his past with her? The fact that he refused to stirred up her investigative senses and made her want to discover his secrets. But what if he was hiding something that could hurt the town? Didn't people have a right to know that?

What if he was a reformed train robber? Her gaze immediately shifted past the children to Carly. She'd been an outlaw, but God had changed her. So if He could change an outlaw into a kind, God-fearing person, He could change anybody.

But not Butch Laird.

Jack glanced to her right and gazed out the open window. Where had that thought come from? She hardly ever thought of her old nemesis these days. She had a hard time believing even God could change a fat, pig-stinking bully like him, but in her heart, she knew that He could.

She hadn't treated Butch kindly, either, but had ganged up on him with her two childhood friends. She'd even lied about him. But at least she'd come clean on that and had told Luke the truth. Jack remembered going to Butch's home to wallop him for the words he'd painted on the town's walls, but when she saw the shanty he lived in, her anger had fled, and she had the overwhelming urge to apologize. She'd never been certain which she'd actually have done, but he'd been gone. Had left town and never returned. Where was he today? Was he still alive?

Shaking thoughts of Butch from her mind, she concentrated on the words she was singing:

> *"Have we trials and temptations?*
> *Is there trouble anywhere?*
> *We should never be discouraged—*
> *Take it to the Lord in prayer."*

Jack ducked her head. She didn't pray half enough. She was always doing things she thought was right, but she needed to seek God more.

Emmie's eyes rolled back, and her lashes lowered. She'd open them wide for a moment, and they'd drift closed again. Leaning down, Jack placed a kiss on her sister's head. When was the last time she'd prayed for her siblings?

Abby shoved Alan, and he pinched her leg. "Ow!" Heads swerved in their direction.

Jack leaned over. "I'm warning you two. No pie."

Abby scowled at Alan and leaned on Jack's left arm. Her right arm was already going to sleep. Maybe she should talk to the reverend about starting some kind of Sunday school program for the young children to attend during the service.

"Thank you kindly, Mrs. Linus." Noah Jeffers nodded at the piano player as she left her bench and proceeded to the pew where her sister sat. The pastor cleared his throat and held on to the podium so tightly that Jack could see the white of his knuckles. He stared out at the congregation.

"I tried to introduce myself as each of you came in this morning, but I apologize if I missed anyone. I'm Noah Jeffers, and I'm filling in for Pastor Taylor while his family is out of town."

He lowered his head, pursed his lips, then looked back up with resolve. Jack wondered if he was as nervous as he looked. Preaching to a crowd for the first time would be difficult enough, but to be doing so battered and bruised. . .

"Last night, I had the misfortune to be in a fight."

Jess Jermaine leapt to his feet. "A man's got a right to defend himself, Preacher. Everyone saw that you tried hard to not fight that Morgan boy."

"Not when he's the pastor, he don't." A man Jack hadn't met before jumped up. "A pastor oughta be a man of peace."

"Gentlemen, please. Have a seat, and let me continue." He stood quietly while the two men stared each other down, then finally sat. "I want to apologize to y'all. I don't condone fighting."

Jack sucked in a breath. He was apologizing for defending her? She held Emmie so tightly the child began to fuss. She forced her arms to relax. Was he sorry for what he did?

"I can't deny that this is a rough land and men sometimes have to take actions to protect themselves and their families. But as your current pastor, I should have tried harder to resolve last night's situation without fighting. For that, I apologize. That's all I want to say on the matter now, but if you feel it necessary to talk more, come and see me at the boardinghouse at your leisure."

He looked down and opened his Bible. Heat scalded Jack's cheeks. She stared down at Emmie's little fingers, feeling rejected and foolish. Everyone would have been better off if she'd just stayed home last night instead of attending the social when she had no intention of dancing. Then Billy wouldn't have created a commotion, and Noah Jeffers wouldn't have had to sully his reputation and suffer for her sake. The sooner she left town, the better it would be for everyone.

"I thought a fitting verse to start with this morning would be Matthew 5:46: 'For if ye love them which love you, what reward have ye? Do not even the publicans the same?'" Noah walked away from the podium and stood at the front of the pews. "Y'all know that a publican was a tax collector?"

Several heads nodded.

"Good. Well, we all know that nobody likes a tax collector."

Chuckles echoed across the room.

"Jesus is saying here that even men we might not like love their wives and children—people who love them. It's a simple thing to love people who care about you. But it's far harder to love a person who, say—pokes fun at you for something you did or said. And what about that man who cheated you last month? How easy is it to love him?"

"Downright impossible," Mr. Cauldwell shouted.

Reverend Jeffers looked at the man. "Maybe so, but it's what our Lord is instructing us to do. It's not easy. I'm proof of that. Last night I failed to show love to an angry man, and I'm the minister. But God doesn't always call us to do the easy thing."

Jack thought about that. In some ways, leaving Lookout would be very hard. Yeah, she might actually have a room to herself, but she would miss seeing her brother and sisters grow up, and the new baby wouldn't even know her. She stared out the window at the cloudy sky. Wind battered the trees, signaling a coming storm that mirrored the one going on inside her. Could she sacrifice all that for the opportunities and adventure she could have in Dallas? Would moving be worth the cost?

"Let's read a bit farther." Noah's words pulled her attention back to the front.

"Matthew 9, verses 10–13 says, 'And it came to pass, as Jesus sat at meat in the house, behold, many publicans and sinners came and sat down with him and his disciples. And when the Pharisees saw it, they said unto his disciples, Why eateth your Master with the pelicans and sinners?'"

Andy's head jerked up. He'd been sitting there quietly unraveling his sock. "What's a pelican?"

Jack shushed him and glanced at Carly, who shrugged, an embarrassed grin teasing her lips.

Old Mr. Carpenter, who always sat on the second row because he couldn't hear well, turned to his wife. "Did he say pelican?"

Poor Opal Carpenter held up her finger to quiet him, but the old man lifted his ear horn. "Eh?"

"Hesh up, Henry," the old woman said.

Chuckles rebounded around the room.

Noah cleared his throat, looking a bit confused. Jack couldn't help feeling sorry for him. Did he know about his faux pas?

He continued reading. " 'But when Jesus heard that, he said unto them, They that be whole need not a physician, but they that are sick. But go ye and learn what that meaneth, I will have mercy, and not sacrifice: for I am not come to call the righteous, but sinners to repentance.' Jesus chose to fellowship with the poor and lowly, but He was the son of a king—the King. Instead of demanding fine clothing, a feast, and jewels, He lived a life of poverty, so that He could be an example and reach those nobody else cared about."

Noah slowly paced back and forth across the front of the church. "Remember the parable of the two sons? The father told one son to go and work in the vineyard, but the son said no. Later he repented and went and did as the father asked. But the father went to his second son and told him to go to work. That son said he would but then failed to go."

He paused and looked over the congregation. Jack swallowed hard, knowing she was more like the second son than the first. Much of her life, she'd shirked her chores, preferring to be with her friends than help her ma. Remorse ran through her.

"So let me ask you a question. Which of the two sons did the will of his father?"

"The first," someone behind Jack shouted.

"Perhaps." Noah shrugged one shoulder. "Jesus said, 'Verily I say unto you, that the publicans and the harlots go into the kingdom of God before you.' It seems a harsh statement, doesn't it, folks? We strive all our lives to work hard, raise enough crops or make enough money to feed our families and provide for them, and all of this is good. But God looks at our hearts."

Noah remained silent for a moment and stared at the crowd. Jack ducked her head when he glanced her way. "What is your motivation, folks? Are you working hard to be the richest man in town? Or are you just trying to care for your family and serve God?"

Noah looked down at the floor and stood with his hands in his pockets. "I've never been a rich man, nor particularly care to be. But I can tell you that I've lived about as low as a man can go."

Jack perked up. Was he going to share something about his past? "My pa wasn't a kind person. Oh, he was all right until my ma and little sister died, but then he fell off the wagon. He was a mean drunk, and

I was the one he took his anger out on."

Jack sucked in a breath.

"It's hard for me to believe that Jesus would have sought out my pa before...say, Pastor Taylor."

Jack's heart clinched at the pain etched on Noah's face. She'd once had a mean father and remembered hiding when he'd go into one of his rages. Remembered how it hurt the few times he hit her before her mother would distract him and take his brutality instead. She'd never have expected that she and Noah would have that in common.

"I doubt my pa ever heard about God. He never taught me about the Lord. And to be honest, it would be hard for me to accept that he might be in heaven." He huffed a fake laugh. "It's a good thing I'm not God. I'm imperfect. A sinner. Just like everyone else in this room. But there's good news, folks. Jesus came to save us sinners. If we turn from our wicked ways and humble ourselves, God can make us new. Wash us clean as new-fallen snow."

He returned to the podium just as Abby slid off the bench and onto the floor. Jack motioned for her to get back on the seat, but she shook her head. Abby leaned her head against the pew in front of them and stuck her tongue out at Alan. Jack tried to shift Emmie to a different position to free up her arm, knowing an explosion was about to occur. Alan leaned forward, reaching for Abby's hair, but Carly snatched up the boy just in time to avoid a catastrophe. She hauled him onto her lap, but he shinnied off and climbed onto Garrett's, giving Carly an angry glare. Abby had already inhaled—ready to scream, Jack was certain—but instead, the girl slowly let out her breath, looking disappointed. Jack glanced at the ceiling. *Father, forgive me if I was anything like my siblings.*

Noah returned to his podium and ruffled the

pages of his Bible. "Let me close with this. 'Two men went up into the temple to pray; the one a Pharisee, and the other a pelican.'"

"What is a pelican?" Alan whispered, far too loudly.

Garrett leaned down to his ear. "It's a kind of bird."

Alan nodded. "Thought so."

"'The Pharisee stood and prayed thus with himself, God, I thank thee, that I am not as other men are, extortioners, unjust, adulterers, or even as this pelican. I fast twice in the week, I give tithes of all that I possess. And the pelican, standing afar off, would not lift up so much as his eyes unto heaven, but smote upon his breast, saying, God be merciful to me a sinner. I tell you, this man went down to his house justified rather than the other: for every one that exalteth himself shall be abased; and he that humbleth himself shall be exalted.'"

Noah closed his Bible, his gaze roving the crowd again. Jack didn't think he had any idea of the mistake he'd made. "I challenge you not to leave here today until you've made things right with the Lord. Don't be proud like the Pharisee, who boasted of his good deeds, but rather, see how you can help your neighbor or friend without expecting something in return. Shall we pray?"

Jack bowed her head, shame weighing heavy on her shoulders. She was so tied up in achieving her own dreams that she rarely thought of doing something nice for someone else, even her ma. *Forgive me, Lord.*

Thunder boomed outside, and though the prayer had yet to be completed, a number of heads swiveled toward the windows. The scent of rain filled the air, and Jack had a suspicion that many folks were going to get wet on their travels home. She couldn't help being thankful she didn't have far to go.

Alan squirmed on Garrett's lap, and the moment Noah said, "Amen," the child went slack and slid free of his captor. He crawled across the floor toward Abby. She spotted him, squealed, and scurried under the pew in front of Jack, with Alan chasing after. Jack bent and just missed snagging her brother's britches. Mrs. Abbott, sitting directly in front of Jack with her quiet trio of children, squealed and looked down. Then she turned and shot Jack a glare that could curdle milk. Jack shook her head and shrugged. *How did Ma get those two to behave?*

"Sorry," Garrett said. "I'll go after them."

Emmie sat up, her hair and the back of her dress damp with sweat. She rubbed her eyes and sniffled. "I tirsty."

"Why don't I take her back home and get the table set for dinner?" Carly smiled.

"Are you sure you don't mind? I probably should go rescue Garrett."

Carly held out her arms. "You wanna go home and get a drink?" Emmie stared at her for a moment, then fell forward. Carly stood and held the girl on her hip. "Let's go home before the rain starts." Thunder echoed through the room again, and Emmie buried her face against Carly's shoulder. They joined the crowd making its way outside.

Jack stood, stretching out the kinks in her shoulders and arms. She glanced down and gasped. The dress that had taken her nearly an hour to iron yesterday was a mass of damp wrinkles. She crossed her arms and slid out of the pew.

Mr. Abbott leaned toward his wife. "Oddest sermon I ever did hear. I don't remember reading nothing in the scriptures about pelicans."

"That's 'cause it's not there. Just a bad case of

nerves, I reckon." She flicked one finger, and her three children followed her quietly out of the church like ducklings behind a mama duck.

Her husband moseyed behind the group, scratching his head. "You know, Louise, come to think of it, I do believe pelicans are mentioned in the scriptures. Somewhere in Leviticus or Deuteronomy, but I sure don't recall any mentioned in the New Testament."

Jack glanced toward the front of the church. The mayor was forcing his way against the flow of people, up the aisle toward Noah. With such a crowd surging to the exit, she figured she wasn't leaving any time soon and started making her way to the front. If there was going to be some action, she wanted to be there.

She smiled and returned a wave from Callie Howard as she passed her friend's family. Sitting down in a pew several rows from the front, she tried not to look too obvious. Several small groups of friends and neighbors stood in clusters talking, but most of the people were leaving the building. The mayor squeezed his bulk past Agatha Linus and her sister, then strode toward the reverend with determined steps. The man sure didn't look very pleased.

During the sermon, she'd learned a bit more already about their mysterious pastor, but was the mayor going to fire him before she got a chance to write her story?

Chapter 19

Noah folded his sermon notes and stuck the papers in his Bible. He heaved a heavy sigh, glad to have his first sermon over and done with. Several people had come up front and thanked him for coming to Lookout. He glanced at the door, disappointed as most of the congregation made their way outside to their horses and buggies. He'd planned to stand at the door and send them on their way, but the threat of a thunderstorm had everyone hurrying home.

The mayor squeezed past Mrs. Linus and strode toward him. From the expression on his face, Noah was certain he wasn't happy. What could have upset him so much?

"Now see here, young man, what's all that talk about pelicans?"

Noah's heart lurched at the man's harsh attack. "What? I talked about publicans, not pelicans, Mayor."

The man wagged a beefy finger in Noah's face. "No, sir. I heard it with my own ears. You must have said *pelicans* a dozen times."

Noah's gaze darted over to where Jack sat several rows back. She watched them with obvious interest, but he didn't like the idea of her seeing him get wrung out by the mayor.

"I never heard the like of that message." The mayor's bellowing drew his attention back. Mayor

Burke's eyes actually bulged. "If you want to keep your job here, you'd better not repeat today's fiasco. Do you understand me?"

Slowly, Noah nodded. He really had no idea what the man was ranting about. Had he just heard him wrong?

The mayor stormed down the aisle, mumbling. "I knew it was a bad idea to have such a young man. . . ."

Turning his back to Jack, Noah returned to the podium and pretended that he'd left something behind. The mayor should have waited and talked to him in private, not lambasting him while people were still in the church. Had he actually said *pelicans* instead of *publicans*? Surely not. He'd wanted to speak a message that would encourage folks to be nicer to their neighbors, but he'd evidently failed.

"Don't listen to Mayor Burke. He used to fuss at Pastor Taylor, too."

Noah faced Jack, grateful that she tried to soothe his rumpled composure. She was so pretty in her medium blue dress, which enhanced the color of her eyes. The bodice was all wrinkled, but he shouldn't be noticing that and pulled his gaze back up to her face. "Did he really do that? Fuss at Pastor Taylor?"

Jack nodded. "I saw him do it several times."

"Well, if he only complained a handful of times, I'll try not to be overly concerned."

"I don't usually stay later like today, though, so I can't really say how much he criticized the sermon." Jack smiled, setting his barely settled stomach to swirling again. She was so pretty—she always had been—even when dressed in overalls.

"So, what was all that talk about pelicans? It was a little confusing."

The blood rushed from Noah's face, and his heart pounded. "What do you mean?"

"You didn't hear Alan?"

Noah shook his head. "No, but I did hear several people call out things to me. I was concentrating, though, and didn't hear everything they were saying."

Jack leaned her hip against the podium and rested her elbow on the top of the wooden stand. "I'll admit I was a bit distracted by Alan and Abby, but was that just a slip of the tongue? Or did I completely miss the point of your sermon?"

He had hoped she'd come up to tell him how his sermon had enlightened her and encouraged her, but instead, she confused him. "I have no idea what you're talking about."

Her eyes sparkled, and she lifted a hand to cover a giggle. "Oh, dear. You really don't know, do you?"

"No, and I fail to see any humor in my message."

Jack's expression turned serious. "You did say *pelican* several times."

"Great. Just great." Noah closed his eyes. How had he made such a foolish error? "No wonder the mayor was so angry. That also explains the perplexed looks on so many people's faces."

Jack reached out her hand as if to touch him, then lowered it. "I'm sure it was a simple mistake because of nerves."

Thunder exploded overhead. Jack squealed and jumped, latching on to his arm so hard her fingernails bit into his flesh through the fabric of his shirt. Her reaction surprised him. He didn't think she was afraid of anything.

"Sorry." Her gaze was directed out the nearest window where the rain was coming down in torrents. "Thunder always makes me nervous, ever since the time a tornado hit the town on the day my folks were married."

"Yeah, I know." He patted her hand, hoping to

211

reassure her, remembering that day well. Everyone had been excited about Luke Davis marrying Rachel Hamilton, Jack's ma, except maybe the boardinghouse brides who'd come to town to marry him. There had been cake afterward, but he hadn't gotten any. He'd watched from afar. Jack glanced down, her cheeks aflame, and tugged her hand out from under his.

"Huh? You know what?"

His heart quickened, and he scrambled to remember what he'd just said. "I. . .uh. . .don't like thunderstorms, either." He nearly smacked his forehead with his hand. That made him sound like a ninny. What man was scared of a storm? But he couldn't very well have said he remembered because he'd lived in Lookout and remembered the very same tornado, could he?

"Oh."

She walked over to the closest window and lowered it. "Rain is coming in on this side."

He pushed his feet into action, chastising himself for thinking of her instead of the church. *Lord, help me to keep my focus on You and the church and not Jacqueline Davis.*

Jack closed another window, and he managed to get two more shut. He searched for something to dry the floors but there was no cloth of any kind in the sparse building. He walked to the open front door to make sure the rain wasn't coming in there. Thankfully it was blowing from the opposite direction. Jack joined him, and they stood near the exit watching the rain cascading in torrents, as if it needed to water the whole world in a single day.

Noah stared down at the top of Jack's head and smiled. Her part was crooked and her long hair hung down her back in waves, tied back only with a wilted blue ribbon that sat catawampus. Along her pale neck, untouched by the sun's fingers, damp tendrils of curls clung to her skin. His fingers ached to reach out and touch her hair. They stood so close he could probably feel it without her even knowing. He balled his hand into a fist and sighed.

Jack glanced up over her shoulder, and he could see faint freckles smattered across her nose and cheeks. "It won't last long. These Texas storms blow as hard as a schoolyard bully, but they don't have any staying power."

Noah winced. He knew all about Texas storms, having spent his whole life here, but she had no idea how much her bully reference hit home. If she did, he had little doubt she'd race out in the storm rather than suffer his company any longer. He was fooling himself if he thought she'd ever be interested in him. No matter how much he'd changed.

Why had God sent him here? Was it so he could learn to control his emotions when tempted? Wasn't it so that he could make recompense for past misdeeds?

Jack leaned against the doorjamb and faced him, her arms crossed over her chest. "Was that true—what you said about your pa?"

His breath caught in his throat. Had he said too much? Jack was no common woman. She was smarter than most and, as a reporter, able to connect the dots. He swallowed and nodded. "Unfortunately, my pa wasn't a nice man."

"I'm sorry, Pastor. My first pa wasn't either." She nibbled her lip and watched the rain. "He would drink and get really angry and he even hit my ma—and me."

"Sorry. As hard as it was to take Pa's beatings as a boy—and I wasn't a scrawny lad, either—I can't imagine how much more difficult it must be for women to endure such mistreatment." He wanted to clobber the man. No wonder Jack was such a tough kid when she was younger. She had to be just to survive. Her father was already dead when he and his pa moved to town. He was glad he'd never met the man.

"We managed. I mostly ran and hid whenever he went loco like that, and other times I was already in bed, so Ma had to face him alone." She looked up. "I wish I'd been big like you so I could have protected her."

He wanted to say he was glad she wasn't, but that would hardly be proper. He wanted to say he wished he'd been around back then to protect her, but he couldn't say that, either. So he said nothing.

Jack frowned. "You gonna tell me about your past, so I can write that article for the paper?" She grinned and wiggled her brows up and down, her eyes shining. "You're not hiding any deep, dark secrets you're ashamed of, are you?"

Noah worked hard to keep a straight face. She had no idea how close to home her teasing question hit. He shrugged, hoping it looked casual. "What Texan doesn't?"

He could see that sharp mind of hers at work. She suspected something, and he knew her tenacity. She was like a snapping turtle. Once she took hold of a notion, she wouldn't let go until her curiosity was satisfied. He needed to distract her—and fast.

"Do you think maybe you could call me Noah?"

Her blue eyes widened, and her mouth dropped open a bit. "Uh. . .do you think that's proper, I mean, with you being the pastor and all?"

He shrugged. "I don't see why not. I asked your pa the same thing. I've never cared for being called reverend. I looked it up one time in a dictionary, and it means 'worthy of being revered.' In my eyes, God alone deserves that honor."

Jack nodded. "That makes sense. I reckon I could call you Noah when it's just you and me around, but it's probably not a good idea in public. At least not yet. Folks spread rumors faster than wildflowers pop up in springtime around here."

"We don't want folks spreading rumors, do we?" He grinned.

She looked embarrassed but shook her head. "So, if I call you Noah, you'll have to call me Jack."

He quirked an eyebrow feigning surprise. "That's not a very ladylike name for such a pretty young woman. What would your ma say?"

Jack sighed and crossed her arms again. "She hates it, but that's what I prefer. Even Luke calls me Jack when he doesn't call me Half Bit."

Noah remembered hearing Luke call her Half Bit on several occasions, but he wasn't sure where the man had dug up such an odd nickname. "Why don't you go by Jackie if you don't like Jacqueline, which is a pretty name, if you ask me?" Noah knew he should rein in his bold tongue before it got him into trouble, but he didn't know if he'd ever have Jack all to himself like this again.

She shrugged. "Nobody's ever called me that. I guess I liked Jack when I was young because it made me sound tougher. I always wished God had made me a boy."

"I'm glad He didn't."

Her gaze jerked up to his, and he allowed himself the pleasure of gazing into her lovely, intelligent eyes. The dark blue was streaked with lighter blues and some gray. An inner ring of pale blue encircled her pupil, as if her ma had laid claim on a small section of her eye color. Jack's cheeks flamed, and she broke his gaze, a pleasant smile twittering on her lips.

"Oh, look. The rain's let up. We probably won't get too wet if we leave now. I need to get back and help get dinner on the table."

He set his Bible on a pew, not wanting to risk it getting wet. He'd come back for it later. Then he took hold of Jack's arm, and she stiffened. "It's wet out, and the mud will be slippery. I want to be sure you don't fall."

She nodded and allowed him to escort her outside. He stopped to close the doors, and she tugged away.

"I'll race you home!" With her skirts hiked up, she dashed into the drizzle and ran for all she was worth. He smiled. That was the girl he remembered. The daring one, full of heart and gumption. He longed to chase after Jack, grab her up in his arms, and kiss her. Walking out into the light rain, he glanced skyward. Above him, the sun broke through the gray clouds, casting its bright beams on the earth, as if the finger of God was reaching out to him.

Noah heaved a sigh and slowed his steps, allowing the warm rain to wash over him. What he truly needed was to go jump in a cold lake somewhere and cool his senses.

On second thought, maybe he'd already taken leave of his senses.

Chapter 20

Carly put Alan and Abby to work setting the silverware out on the table while she placed the plates in front of each chair. Garrett Corbett stood in the entryway, one arm still in a sling and the other holding Emma. He puffed up his cheeks and widened his eyes at the toddler. Emmie giggled and poked at his cheeks with her tiny fingers. Carly ducked her head, not wanting him to see her laughing at him.

She'd been more nervous than an inmate on parole day when he'd sat down beside her in church. The space had been so narrow that his leg had pressed against her skirts, and with Alan squished against her other side, she'd nearly panicked. Thank goodness Jack scooted over, making more room. Ever since being locked in prison, she hadn't liked confining spaces of any sort.

"You're such a good girl, Miss Emmie Poo." Garrett nibbled on the toddler's belly, eliciting squeals of delight.

Carly glanced at the wall as if she could see through it to Rachel's bedroom door. She must be especially tired since she hadn't gotten up when they returned home. She lifted a finger to her mouth. "Shh. . . we need to let Rachel rest as long as possible."

Garrett made a face, showing he hadn't thought of that. "Maybe I should take her out to the porch?"

She glanced around, unsure what to do. The food was ready, but Rachel wasn't up, Luke was still gone, and Jacqueline and the pastor hadn't returned from church. With all the rain, she figured they'd decided to wait it out. "I probably should help the girls change out of their church clothes."

He nodded and handed Emma to her. Their hands brushed during the exchange, sending her heart skipping. He gazed down at her with a perplexed look on his face. She didn't want to like him, but she loved his eyes—almost the color of a robin's egg, but bluer.

"What should I do?" he asked.

She glanced around and spied Alan standing in front of the buffet and eyeing the pie. He reached up real quick-like, pinched off a piece of crust, and stuck it in his mouth. "Uh. . .Alan, do you need help changing?"

The boy rolled his eyes. "I'm seven, for Pete's sake." He stomped past them shaking his head.

Garrett grinned and leaned toward her. "Yeah, he's seven—an old man already."

"He ain't old." Abby shoved her hands to her hips. "You're old, Uncle Garrett."

Carly couldn't help laughing. "Yeah, you're ancient, Mr. Corbett."

His smile was conspiring, but his gaze serious. "Call me Garrett. Everyone does."

She swallowed hard.

"Or"—he wiggled his brows—"if you prefer, you can call me Uncle Garrett." He grinned wide, as if cracking the funniest joke in town. If the man had a serious bone in his body, it must be his little toe.

Keeping a straight face so as not to encourage him, she shook her head and gave him a schoolmarm look. She still didn't quite trust him and wasn't sure she wanted to get first-name familiar with him, but rather than disappoint him, she avoided his comment altogether. "If you could maybe stir the beans for me, I'll hurry up and get the girls changed."

"I'm a big girl. I don't need help." Abby marched out of the kitchen just like her brother had done.

Garrett shook his head. "I don't know what Luke and Rachel are going to do with another young'un. Before long, they'll have to close the boardinghouse because they'll need all the rooms for their own family." He chuckled and walked into the kitchen.

"Stay out of that extra corn bread." She wagged her finger at him then hurried upstairs. If he was anything like Reverend Barker, he'd already be wolfing down a square.

She made quick work of getting the girls changed. Abby skipped into Alan's room, and Carly carried Emma back downstairs. Garrett stood at the stove, stirring the beans, and she wondered if he had been the whole time she'd been gone.

He peered over his shoulder at her. "Looks like the rain is letting up."

"Good. That means Jacqueline and the preacher should be here soon."

She set Emma down on the floor and hoisted the heavy platter of corn bread. "You can stop stirring now."

He laid the spoon down, then took the platter from her, holding it in one hand. "Where do you want this? On the buffet?"

She couldn't help noticing the crumbs on his lips. He licked them, probably realizing she'd caught him, and then grinned, turning her insides to the consistency of hot grits. "Uh. . .yes, put that on the buffet." She followed him into the dining room, as if he couldn't do such a simple chore on his own.

"How come there's a big pot of beans and a

smaller one?" He leaned against the buffet, looking as comfortable as if in his own home.

His broad shoulders, wide from lifting crates of freight for years, filled out his white shirt. He'd already removed his black string tie and had stuffed it into his pocket, leaving a tail hanging out. His skin was tanned from years of driving wagons across the rolling hills of northeast Texas. Though she couldn't quit looking at the man, she knew him to be a rogue and a joker. She'd never truly been attracted to a man before. The men she'd known had never been the trustworthy sort. They tended to have three things on their minds most of the time—food, drinking, and women.

So, why did he weigh so heavily on her mind? Why had she dreamed about him last night?

When she didn't respond to his question, his blond brows lifted. "Oh. . .the extra pot. It seems the reverend can't tolerate pork, so I made a smaller batch for him without the meat."

"Oh, yeah. I saw what happens when he eats it. Not a pretty sight." He feigned a mock shudder. "Poor man. I can't imagine not eating bacon, or ham, or gravy with sausage." Suddenly he paused and stared at her. "Wait a minute. You cooked the beans?"

"Yes, and the corn bread, too."

His gaze dashed to the platter on the buffet and back to her. "But I thought you couldn't cook."

She shoved her hands to her hips. "Whatever gave you that idea?"

"Uh. . .well, that pie you made for Luke's bride contest wasn't worth feeding to the hogs."

It took great effort, but she resisted stomping her foot on his narrow-mindedness. "That was more than ten years ago, *Mr.* Corbett."

He shrugged. "So?"

She narrowed her gaze. How in the world could she have been attracted to this...this... "A person can learn a lot in a decade."

The bedroom door rattled, and Carly jumped. She hurried into the hall. Rachel leaned on the doorjamb, holding her lower belly and breathing hard. Carly felt Garrett standing right behind her. "Are you all right?"

Rachel shook her head. "Where's Luke?"

"I don't think he ever came back from investigating the mercantile theft. He wasn't in church."

Rachel closed her eyes and groaned. "Find him. The baby is coming."

As the rain stopped, Jack slowed her frantic pace and climbed the steps of her home. Catching her breath, she looked back down the street, halfway disappointed Noah hadn't chased after her. That would hardly be proper. He was already on the mayor's bad side, and chasing after a woman would get him fired, for sure.

And she would regret if that were to happen.

A glimmer drew her attention, and she stared down muddy Main Street where puddles of water glistened in the brilliant sunlight that had chased away the storm clouds. Looking upward, she gasped. A rainbow stretched over the town, almost as if God had sent her a prism of promise that things would work out. But just what things, she wasn't sure.

Would she get that Dallas job she wanted? Would she figure out what the mayor was up to? Would Noah kiss her?

She dropped into a rocker, stunned at her train of thought. Where had that idea come from? She didn't want to like Noah, but there was an odd connection with him that she'd never experienced with another man—almost as if they'd known each other for years. And they had similar pasts. Only someone who'd suffered such ill treatment from a parent could understand how she used to feel. In fact, she suspected, his life had been far worse than hers.

She undid the laces on her mucky high-tops and started loosening them. Her ma would have a fit if she tracked mud on her clean floors. She set them beside the rocker nearest the door then reached for the knob. The door flew open in her face, and a startled squeak slipped out. Garrett nearly collided with her, his eyes wide. "What's wrong?"

"Your ma! Gotta find Luke." He ran his hand through his short blond hair, looking more flustered than she'd ever seen him. "The doctor. Gotta get him, too."

"What happened?" Her heart pounded. Had her ma burnt herself or gotten cut?

Garrett's face blanked for a moment, and then he said, "The baby's comin'."

"Oh!" Her heart leapt. "Move out of the way, and let me by." He turned sideways in the doorway, and she slipped past him. She swatted a hand in his direction. "Go! Get Doc Phillips, and find Papa."

"I'll go for the doctor." Noah stood in the doorway, his hair flattened with dampness.

She nodded. "Go! Both of you."

Garrett grinned. "Have you found the women in this house to be uncommonly bossy?"

Noah grinned, but Jack didn't have time to analyze what that did to her insides. She had to get to her ma. Her stockinged feet padded down the hall to her parents' room, and she peeked in. Her ma sat on the side of the bed, eyes closed and breathing hard. Sweat ran down her cheek. Emma played quietly with her dolly on the far side of the bed, oblivious to her mother's toiling. Carly bent and wiped Rachel's face with a cloth.

Jack nibbled her lower lip, hating to see her mother in pain. "Ma, are you all right?"

"Ha!" Rachel rubbed her hand across the front of her stomach. "Ohh, sure." The *oh* sounded more like a moan than normal speech. "I'm perfectly fine. In fact, I just love being in pain like this."

Jack lifted a brow. It wasn't like her ma to be sarcastic. Maybe her pain was worse than with previous childbirths.

Sitting down beside her, Jack took her ma's hand and held on to it. "What can I do to help?"

"Make sure the kids eat dinner. Then put Emma—oh—" Rachel gritted her teeth, and her whole body seemed to tense. She clenched Jack's hand so tight Jack thought some bones might break. Carly backed up against the wall looking frightened half out of her wits. Evidently she'd never attended a birthing, either. "Here comes another one."

"Another what, Ma?"

"Birth. . .pangs. Ahh!" She leaned her head back and moaned. "I don't know. . .if I can. . .do this again."

Jack couldn't help smiling. "You don't have much choice at this point."

Emmie patted her mother's back. "It be all wight."

Rachel tucked in her chin and growled a long grunt. "I'm too old. . .for thi–sss."

Jack sat there, allowing her ma to hold her hand and wondering what it would be like to carry a baby. What if it were Noah's child? Heat flooded her face, and she was glad her ma was so busy or she surely would have noticed. Jack glanced at Carly to see if she'd noticed the blush, but she was focused on Ma. Jack mentally berated herself. *A decent young woman doesn't think of such things.*

Carly handed the cloth to Jack. "I'll see to the youngsters' meal and get Emmie down for her nap so you can tend your ma."

"Oh, that was a big one." Rachel leaned back on her hands, her face more relaxed, the birth pain evidently over. "Have you seen Luke? Anyone sent for the doctor?"

"Garrett is looking for Papa, and Noah went for Doc Phillips."

Carly walked to the other side of the bed and clapped her hands. "Are you ready to eat?"

Emmie glanced at her ma and Jack, then stood and fell into Carly's arms. Jack was happy that her little sister had bonded so easily with Carly. Knowing that Miss Payton was here to help her ma would make leaving and going to Dallas much easier. She wouldn't worry about her ma overdoing it as much.

Loud footsteps sounded in the hall, and Jack stood. "I'll be right back, Ma."

She nodded. "Be sure there's plenty of hot water boiling."

"I will." Jack strode out the door.

Noah stood near the parlor door as if afraid to enter any farther. He rubbed the back of his neck, his brow crinkled.

"What's wrong?"

"The doctor wasn't there. He's gone out to a ranch where a cowhand got hurt and isn't expected back until this evening. His wife was home and said she'd come over as soon as she found somebody to watch her young'uns."

Panic shot through Jack like a bullet. She knew nothing about birthing babies. What if she did something wrong and hurt the baby or her ma? The baby could die. Her ma could die. Her knees trembled. She steepled her fingers and held them against her mouth. Her mind seemed like a quagmire of quicksand, and her thoughts sank so fast she couldn't grab hold of a single one.

What should she do? She could ask Carly to watch the doctor's children to free his wife to come and assist in the birth, but who'd watch her siblings?

Noah gently clutched her hands and pulled them away from her face, a sympathetic expression enveloping his face. "Tell me what's going on in that mind of yours. How can I help?"

His calm demeanor soothed her frenzied nerves. "I don't know what to do. I've never witnessed a birthing and have no idea what I should do."

"Has the doctor's wife delivered any babies?"

Jack nodded. "I think so. I'm sure she's assisted her husband before. She has to know more than I do."

Noah pulled out his pocket watch. "How much time do you think we have before the baby comes?"

Flinging up her arms, Jack blew out an exaggerated breath at the ridiculous question. "How should I know?"

Noah shoved his watch back in his pocket. A deep red glow crept up his neck. "Maybe you could ask your ma."

Jack rolled her eyes. "Every birth is different. She won't know."

He placed his hands on her shoulders. "Calm down, Jackie."

His use of the unexpected nickname grabbed her attention.

"Let's pray and ask God for direction."

She started to open her mouth to tell him they didn't have time to pray, when his hands slid down her arms, sending chills cascading across her skin and firmly locking her lips together. He took hold of her hands and bowed his head. "Father, we ask that You give us wisdom to know what to do. Help Mrs. Davis with the delivery of this child. We ask that You protect both mother and baby and show Garrett where Luke is so he can return home. Calm Jackie, and give us direction. In Jesus' name, amen."

He glanced up as if expecting she'd already have an answer to her dilemma, but she didn't. God hadn't seen fit to reveal His plan to her. She probably wasn't worthy enough. She hung her head, but the clopping of shoes on the stairs gave her an idea. "We could ask Carly to watch the doctor's children, and you can watch Alan and the girls."

Noah's eyes went wide, and he took a half-step back. "Me? I don't know anything about children."

"Well, there's no one else to do it. You for sure can't stay with Ma, nor would I ask you to care for children you don't even know. It just makes sense. We'll ask Carly to watch the doc's kids, and you can watch ours—I mean my...uh...siblings." Jack touched her hands to her cheeks, sure they must be bright red. Had he caught her reference to "our children"?

He tugged on his earlobe, then rubbed the back of his neck. "I reckon I could watch them for a while. What would I have to do?" Carly and the children reached the bottom of the stairs and clumped down the hall into the dining room. Carly glanced at her and Noah but didn't stop or question them.

Emmie waved as Carly carried her past Jack and Noah. "I eat p'cakes."

"No, sweetie, we're having beans and corn bread."

Emmie bounced in Carly's arm. "Me like cor'bread."

A gentle smile pulled at Noah's lip as he watched her sister. Jack wondered what he was thinking. Did he wish he was a father?

Rachel groaned, and Jack jumped. "I need to get back to Ma. Why don't you sit down with the kids and eat?" She didn't wait for his answer but proceeded into the kitchen. Carly stood at the buffet, dishing up the children's plates. She glanced at Jack, and Jack explained her plan. Carly contemplated it for a moment then nodded her head. "I'd be happy to watch the Phillips' young'uns, if that's how I can be the most help."

Jack paused. "Have you ever delivered a baby before?"

Carly shook her head with vigor. "No. I've never even seen one delivered."

"Then I think the best help would be for you to watch the Phillips' children."

She placed a square of corn bread on each plate and then spooned on the beans. "I can do that. Just let me eat a few bites of beans. Then I'll run down there."

"Thanks. I'll be close by in case Noah has need of me."

Carly's brow lifted, and Jack wondered if it was because she used the pastor's Christian name. "All right."

Jack glanced up at Noah as he entered the room. "Go ahead and eat with the children. Afterward, take them back upstairs to Alan's room to play. Emmie may take a nap—or not, since she had one in church."

Noah nodded, picked up a plate, and held it out to her. "You need to eat, too."

"Just let me check on Ma first." She spun around and hurried to the bedroom that she used to share with her ma—before Luke married her and moved in. Ma was still seated, wearing her day dress, but her face was creased with pain. Jack fished a cloth out of the bucket and wrung out the water then dabbed her mother's face. "Are you all right?"

"Will be." She rubbed her hand back and forth across her stomach. "After Oscar comes."

"We should probably get you into your gown

before Mrs. Phillips arrives."

Ma's pale blue eyes lifted, looking right at her. Sweat dampened her face, and fatigue lines crinkled around her eyes. "Hank's not comin'?"

"Not for a while." Jack offered a sympathetic smile. "But Carly's going to go watch their children after she gets ours fed so Martha can tend you."

Rachel nodded. "She's a good midwife." She slowly stood, hunched over like a hundred-year-old woman. She kept one hand on her stomach as if holding the baby in. Jack fetched a clean gown and held it out, noticing the back of her ma's dress was sopping wet. "Do you want me to get you a chamber pot, or is it too late?"

Rachel shook the gown down around her legs and sat again. Jack picked up the dress and carried it to a peg.

"No. That's not what you're thinking. My water broke while y'all were at church."

Jack dropped the calico dress as if it was covered in ticks and kicked it against the wall. She wiped her hand on her skirt. "Ma–aa! What does that mean? Are you all right? Is the baby?"

"Calm down. We're fine." Rachel giggled and brushed her tousled hair with her fingers. "You should have seen how fast you dropped my dress. You've never been squeamish."

"I'm not. It was just. . .unexpected. That's all."

"Have no worries. The dress will wash clean." Rachel's smile faded. She pressed her lips together and moaned, low and long. She spent several minutes in deep concentration, never screaming like Jack had heard men say their wives had, but just maintaining that eerie keening like when the wind blew beneath a closed door in winter.

"Oh!" Ma tucked her chin to her chest. The

muscles in her face tensed, and all color fled from her skin.

Jack's heart jolted. She dropped to her knees. "What's wrong?"

"Got. . .push–ing. . .urge."

"Push what?"

"The baby. It's coming."

"Tell me what to do, Ma." She couldn't do this. Jack ran to the door, glanced down the empty hall, then hurried back to her ma's side. She needed help. "You wanna lie down? Want some water?"

"Wait!" Rachel grabbed hold of Jack's arm, nearly crushing it. Her mother's eyes squeezed shut, and her teeth clenched, lips parted. Ma strained so hard her whole body shimmied.

What's wrong? Help her, Lord. Show me what to do.

Never had she felt so helpless. So powerless. She was used to fighting for what she believed in, but how could she fight this? If she did something wrong, her mother or the baby could die. She glanced around the room. There must be something she could do. Her gaze landed on the tall stack of newspapers beside the ladder-back desk chair. Hadn't her ma mentioned needing those when the baby came?

Stretching out her free arm, she could just reach the pile without breaking her ma's connection on her other one. She pulled an inch-high stack over to her, shook them open, and began lining them over the wooden floor at her mother's feet. She kept stacking them until her ma breathed out a more relaxed breath and loosened her grip.

"Whew! Oscar is anxious—to be born." Her ma panted and rubbed her stomach. She leaned back on her hands. After a few moments, she finally looked up. "Good. Stack all but a few of those on the floor." Rachel slowly pushed up from the bed and stood.

"Lay the rest so they are half on and half off the bed, then cover them with those towels." She took a deep breath and blew it out, as if preparing for the next battle. "This quilt is old, but I'd like to protect it if we can."

Jack snatched the faded towels from the chair seat and spread several on the bed. Her mother sat back down.

"You want a drink?" Jack patted the damp skin on her ma's face.

"Can't. It makes me sick to my stomach." She rubbed her hand across the top of her stomach. "I didn't want you to have to witness this." She grimaced and ducked her head again, holding tight to the bed frame with one hand. "Hurry! Get hot water. Knife."

"I don't want to leave you."

"Go!" One brisk swat of her ma's hand in the air set her in motion.

Jack jumped up and ran into the kitchen, peeking through the door into the dining room. No one was at the table, although the dirty dishes remained. She prayed that Martha Phillips would hurry. Jack grabbed a bowl and ladled boiling water out of the pot on the stove. She found a clean knife and hurried back to the bedroom. What in the world was the knife for?

"It's coming." Her ma had slid off the bed and was squatting beside it, grunting. "Ohh. . . . Knife in water."

Jack obeyed. "What else?"

Her mother glanced down.

Jack's eyes went wide.

"Catch Oscar."

Chapter 21

Noah looked around Alan's room. What would it have been like to have had such a nice room all to himself and a bed, instead of sleeping on the dirty floor?

He cradled Emma's head against his shoulder, reluctant to put her on the bed. Sweat curled the waif's wispy hair, and her soft breaths touched his cheek like a feather. The bed sat against one wall, but with all the noise Alan and Abby were making, he was sure Emma would awaken if he stopped rocking her.

He needed to put Emma in her own bed, but everything within him shouted that it was wrong for him to enter the girls' bedroom. Ambling through the upstairs hall, he walked to the stair railing and glanced down. Why hadn't the doctor's wife arrived? Or Miss Payton returned? What could be keeping them?

He stared at the girls' closed door—Jackie's door. He snorted a soft laugh. When had he started calling her that? It fit her better now than Jack did. There was something softer about it, like she was soft.

Abby squealed, and Emma jerked in his arms. The poor toddler would never sleep unless he put her someplace quiet. He looked at the door again, remembering Jackie sitting in her bed. He couldn't have told a soul what color the room was, because he'd only been able to focus on her that day. "Forgive me, Father."

He twisted the knob and pushed on the door. A garden of beauty opened up before him. The walls had been painted a soft green, and colorful curtains covered in a multitude of flowers flapped in the afternoon breeze. His gaze landed on Jackie's bed, which sat under the front window, covered in a vivid quilt. He yanked his gaze away, feeling guilty for even looking at it.

A smaller bed sat on the wall opposite the big one, and to his right was another small bed with rails along the side. He laid Emma down on that bed. Should he cover her up? The room was warm, even with two windows open. He glanced down at Emma's chubby legs sticking out from under her dress, and he bent and touched the back of her calf. She felt plenty warm to him.

He backed away, watching to make sure she didn't awaken, and then closed the door. His heart pummeled his chest, whether from being in Jackie's room or just succeeding in getting the little girl to sleep, he wasn't sure.

Now what? He peered downstairs again but couldn't tell if anyone had come in. He moseyed back to the other children, unable to keep his mind from wondering how things were going downstairs. He had no doubt that Jackie could handle just about any situation, but would she know how to deliver a baby if need be?

Help them, Lord. Protect mother and child. Help Jackie to not be afraid.

He leaned against the doorframe and watched Alan and Abby playing checkers. The girl glanced over at him and smiled. While her face was turned, her brother snatched one of her kings off the board. Alan glanced over at him, his guilt obvious. Noah lifted his brow, and the boy scowled and looked away.

"Hey! Where'd my other king go?" Abby glanced around the floor, and when she was turned away from the table, Alan set the checkers back on the board. He frowned.

Abby turned back to the table, and her mouth dropped open. She rubbed her eyes and stared again. "I must be gettin' old, like Papa."

"Yep." Alan nodded his head, a sheepish grin pulling at his mouth.

Noah tucked under his upper lip in his effort not to laugh at the precocious child. The only children he'd spent any time around were those of his congregation whom he'd eaten meals with during his circuit-riding days.

The simple room called to him. Besides Alan's bed, there was a small table with a chair and a crate the boy used for a second seat. A half-dozen pegs lined the wall about three-and-a-half feet up from the floor and held the boy's clothing. Some mismatched pieces of wood filled another crate, and a blue-and-gray rag rug covered the center of the floor.

He wanted a home of his own. He was tired of traveling—of never putting down roots. All his life, until he'd moved in with Pete, he'd traveled from one shack to another.

Before he came to Lookout, he'd never thought much of marrying and starting a family. But how could he when he didn't own a home or land? He wasn't even sure how long he'd be in Lookout or what he'd do once Pastor Taylor and his family returned.

But the biggest issue was Jack—Jackie. He'd held a fondness for her even as a troubled youth. It made no sense to him when she caused him no end of problems. She'd lied about him, even causing him to spend two days in jail for something he hadn't done. 'Course, he'd settled up with her on that account the day he locked *her* in her pa's jail.

He shook his head. Walking away with her begging and pleading to set her free had been one of the hardest things he'd ever done, but he felt she needed to learn a lesson. Whether she did or not, he never knew. They'd moved once again shortly after that.

Noah stretched. He could use a Sabbath rest himself. He hadn't slept much at all last night, worrying over his sermon and Jackie. He yawned and toyed with the idea of scrunching up on Alan's bed.

"I won!" Abby held up two black checkers.

"Nuh-uh, you cheated." Alan leaned back against the wall and crossed his arms so hard he made a clapping sound.

"Why don't you play another game. I bet you'll win this time." Noah hoped they would agree. He had no idea how to entertain two such strong-willed children. He eyed the bed again, then crossed the room and eased down. The metal frame creaked and groaned under his weight. Slowly testing its strength, he relaxed and leaned back against the wall. Maybe he could grab a little catnap when the children played another game. He yawned and closed his eyes.

He claimed Jackie's hand, and together they strolled along the Addams River. Adolescents splashed in the pool where water collected in the spot where the river made a sharp turn and traveled on. A gangly youth swung out on a rope and dropped down into the pool, screaming a yell that would make a Comanche proud.

He led Jackie down a path to a quieter spot. Overhead, birds battled in song. Sunlight played peek-a-boo, first hiding behind a tree branch and then sprinkling its rays across the water. He turned Jackie to him and ran the back of his finger down her cheek. His breath hitched. She was so lovely. His hand trailed down the unbound auburn tresses. She smiled, love for him glowing in her blue eyes.

Contentment made every muscle, every bone in his body relax. He dug his hand into the hair behind her nape, then cupped her neck and drew her to him. Suddenly, her expression turned to horror, and she screamed his name.

Noah jerked up. Where was he? He saw the empty table and lurched to his feet. Where were the children?

He spun around, and his heart loosened. Abby lay on the end of the bed, curled up on Alan's pillow, fast asleep. But where was the boy?

"Noah!"

He jerked toward the door at Jack's frantic cry. His feet pushed forward, and he charged down the stairs. His gaze searched each room as he raced by, but there was no sign of Alan. Had something happened to him?

He skidded to a halt outside Mr. and Mrs. Davis's bedroom, his heart racing. "Jackie?"

"In here. Hurry!"

At Jack's hysterical cry, Noah rushed through the bedroom doorway, pushing aside his reservations. She held a lifeless newborn in her arms. Tears ran down her cheeks. Her plaintive gaze begged for his help. "He's not breathing! I don't know what to do!"

"Give him to me." He didn't know what to do either, but he had to do something. Jack gazed into his eyes, obviously reluctant to let go of her brother. "Jackie, let me have him. Hurry!"

She carefully passed the damp baby, and Noah swallowed hard when he saw the boy's blue lips. Making sure to keep his eyes averted from where Mrs. Davis sat on the floor, he cradled the child's face in his palm with the limp body resting on his arm. *Show me what to do, Lord.*

He held the baby so that his head was down and gently patted the soft skin on his back. Nothing happened. Visions of the young boy who'd fallen into the creek flashed in his mind. Jackie would never forgive him if he didn't help her brother. "Noah!" Jack's near hysterical plea touched a place deep within him. He could not fail her. He couldn't fail this child. He whacked the baby harder.

"Don't! You'll hurt him." Jack pulled at his sleeve.

Rachel fell back onto the bed, her eyes wide, face pale. "Lord, save my son."

Noah turned his body away and gave the child a downward shake, then whacked him a bit harder. The baby jumped, arms outstretched. He gagged, then uttered a strangled cry. Easing up, Noah continued to tap and hold the baby's head down. Jack grabbed a cloth and swiped the boy's mouth. After several more fervent coughs, a pitiful squeal that resembled a lamb's bleating filled the room and sent spears of relief straight through Noah.

Jack dropped down on the side of the bed and peered at the infant's face, tears making her eyes glimmer. "Oh, thank God!"

Noah shifted the child to his other arm, relishing the sounds of ever-strengthening wails. Dark, damp hair was matted to the baby's head. A thick cord protruded from where his navel should be, and someone had tied twine around it. Noah had never seen a brand-new baby before and sure hoped that was normal. The boy's cries magnified, and his face pinked up, then turned red. "I think he wants his mama."

He passed Jack her newest brother. His heart warmed, watching her kiss the newborn's forehead and pass him to Rachel. Noah turned and hurried out of the room, knowing he was no longer needed. He made it as far as the kitchen before he sagged against the doorframe. His whole body shook, and tears rolled down his face. "Thank You, Lord, for saving that baby."

A light touch on his back made him straighten. Jack stood there, her blue eyes glistening and tears of joy making rivers down her cheeks. "I was so scared. I th–thought he was. . .dead."

Suddenly she lunged into Noah's arms and hugged his waist. Surprise washed through him, but he shut his eyes and wrapped his arms around her. Jack's warm tears dampened his shirt. Fresh love for this woman flooded his heart. No, in truth, he'd loved her for years, even though she hadn't given a hoot about him. He was afraid to hope that God might change her heart—that she might ever come to care for him.

He couldn't fool himself. Gratitude was her motivation for this hug—and relief.

No matter, for this one moment, this single second, he savored having Jacqueline Davis in his arms.

∾

Jack couldn't quit shaking. Her tears refused to stop. What if her ma hadn't made it through the birthing? What if she'd cut the cord wrong and the baby had died?

She'd feared he had.

And if not for Noah, he probably would have, but thank the Lord, the baby seemed fine now.

She never wanted to be in such a situation again.

Jack pressed her face against Noah's solid chest and hugged him tighter. *Thank You, God, for sending Noah to help. For saving the baby.*

Suddenly she stiffened. She was hugging Noah. The preacher. Her roiling emotions had caused her to momentarily take leave of her senses.

"H'looo, Jacqueline?" came a woman's voice from the front of the house.

"In here." Jack jumped back and swiped her cheeks. She couldn't look at Noah. His arms dangled at his side, and she deeply felt the loss of their comfort.

Mrs. Phillips scurried into the kitchen. "I'm so sorry to have taken so long, but I'd just started"—she glanced past Jack, at Noah, then leaned forward— "nursing my baby," she whispered. "I couldn't very well stop, not knowing how long I'd be away. Besides, I figured I had time since babies aren't generally in a rush to get here."

Noah chuckled.

The doctor's wife glanced back and forth between the two of them. "Is everything all right here?"

Jack nodded, feeling for sure that her mother's friend thought they'd been up to no good. "We're fine, but Ma could use your help. She's in her room."

"Of course, I'll just scurry on in there." She started to leave, then looked at Noah again. "Are you doing all right, Reverend? Your face isn't hurting overly much?"

"I'm fine, but thank you for asking, Mrs. Phillips. Your husband tended me last night and did an excellent job." Noah smiled but it looked more like a grimace, since one side of his mouth didn't lift as much as the other because of the cut on his upper lip.

Mrs. Phillips nodded. "I'm glad you're doing well." She spun out the kitchen doorway then suddenly halted and peered back over her shoulder. "Someone really ought to see to Alan before he makes himself sick."

The woman disappeared, and Jack wondered what she meant. Where was Alan? Where were all the children for that matter?

"You really should have told her," Noah's deep voice quivered.

Jack worked up the nerve to look him in the face. "About what?"

"Heavens to Betsy! The baby's here?" Mrs. Phillip's loud exclamation bounced off the walls and clattered down the hall.

"About that." Noah's lips were pressed together so hard they'd turned white around the edges, but his eyes danced with mirth. At least the one that wasn't swollen shut did.

"Oh. Surprise! Surprise!" A grin tugged at Jack's mouth. "I'd better check on Alan. Do you know where he is?"

The smile on Noah's face faded, and he shook his head.

Jack crossed into the dining room and glanced around the empty table. All seats were vacant, but the dirty dishes remained and food still sat on the buffet. A loud belch pulled her gaze downward. She bent over and lifted the edge of the tablecloth. Her brother sat on the floor with a near empty pie tin on his lap, sugary juice and crumbs covering his mouth and chin. "Alan Davis, what do you think you're doing?"

She could hear Noah's chuckles behind her, and she scorched him with a glare. Obviously, he didn't realize that Alan would see that as support and it would just encourage the imp all the more. Her brother's blue eyes stared up at her from under the table. She saw the worry written there, but then they turned pleading.

"Come out from under there, and take care not to spill any more crumbs on the floor."

He slid the pie pan along the floor and crawled behind two chairs. He handed her the pan then glanced at Noah, as if looking for help.

Jack set what remained of the pie on the table and shoved her hands to her hip. "Well?"

"I was hungry, Sissy."

His whining tone was wasted on her. "Then why didn't you finish the food on your plate?"

His lip curled up, and his nose wrinkled. "You know I don't like them kind of beans."

"So you thought you'd eat a whole pie while everyone else was busy?"

His gaze dropped to the floor. "I didn't eat the *whole* thing." He pointed at Noah. "The preacher and Miss Carly both had a slice, and Abby had a *huge* one." He stuck his lower lip out.

"And you didn't?"

Alan shrugged.

Noah leaned close to her ear, and her stomach flip-flopped. "Miss Payton said he couldn't have any since he hadn't finished his beans," he whispered, tickling her ear and making it hard for her to think straight. She gave her head a little shake, hoping to recapture her thoughts. "But this is probably my fault. I—"

Jack cut a sharp glance at Noah. "No, it's not, and don't take up for him." She looked Alan in the eye again. "Since you disobeyed Miss Carly, young man, and ate pie when you knew you shouldn't have, you can just march up to your room until I talk to Ma. It would serve you right if she doesn't let you have any dessert all week."

His eyes widened. "But that ain't fair."

"Not fair." Jack snatched a napkin off the table and wiped the mess off of Alan's face.

"That's what I said."

Noah uttered a little snort, and she elbowed him in the gut. "What I meant was that you shouldn't say *ain't.*"

"Oh."

"Now, get on up to your room." She gave him a nudge on the shoulder.

"Aw. . ." Alan hung his head and trudged toward the door.

He was trying to make her feel bad, but it wouldn't work. Just as he reached the doorway, the baby let out a high-pitched shriek. Alan spun back toward her, eyes wide. "What was that?"

Jack contemplated not telling him, but she was too excited. "That was your little brother."

Alan's mouth dropped open. "The baby came?"

Jack nodded, pleased that she'd surprised him.

He gasped. "I have a brother!" He jumped up and punched his fist in the air, then turned and raced out of the room and up the stairs. "Wahooo!"

Jack grinned, and behind her, Noah chuckled. She spun around, and he seemed to struggle to contain his mirth.

"Should I not laugh at that?" He pressed his lips together, they quivered, and then he grinned.

"No, that was actually funny." Jack smiled, then forced a stern expression. "But never laugh at a child being scolded. Don't you know anything about children?"

His eyes dimmed, and he shook his head. "No, not really."

A jab of compassion pricked her heart, but then she remembered her sisters. "Hey, speaking of children, where are the girls? I just realized I haven't seen them for a long while, and that's not a good thing, especially where Abby is concerned."

He nudged his chin toward the ceiling. "Emma fell asleep not too long after dinner, so I, uh, put her in her bed." He swallowed so hard she noticed his Adam's apple move. "Then Abby fell asleep on Alan's bed."

"That was very gracious of you to watch them."

"It was an emergency. I was happy to help out."

"You helped out a lot today. You saved my brother's life."

He shook his head. "Not me. God did that."

"Well, you still helped." He was such a kind, humble man. How could he be so caring when he'd had such a rugged childhood and no example of a loving father, like she'd had in Luke? She hated seeing his handsome face marred and his eye nearly swollen shut. Her gaze landed on the damp spot on his white shirt where her tears had spilled over, and he looked down.

He lifted his hand and brushed it.

"Don't worry, it'll wash out." Jack winced when she saw the stains on his sleeves from where he held the baby. "You'd better change out of that and let me get it soaking."

One dark brow lifted.

"I'm serious. You don't want your shirt to stain, do you?"

He checked his sleeves, then shook his head. His dark hair, normally combed back, flopped onto his forehead, and Jack had a powerful urge to reach up and smooth it back in place.

"No. It's the only good shirt I've got to preach in."

"Well, go change, and I'll wash it."

"On Sunday?"

Jack heaved a sigh. "Sometimes you must do what you must. I just delivered a baby on Sunday." At the reminder of the baby's near death, her knees started shaking. Now that the danger had passed and she wasn't distracted by Noah or her brother, the realization of all that had happened made her weak. She reached out for Noah's arm.

"What's wrong?" He grabbed hold of her upper arms.

"I—I delivered my brother today." The wonder in her voice surprised even her. She started wobbling, and he yanked out a chair.

"Sit down."

She obeyed, then leaned over, resting her head in her hands. Noah patted her back. "You're fine. Your ma's fine. And the baby's fine. You did a great job today, Jackie."

The momentary faintness passed at his encouragement, and she bolted upright. She craned her neck to see his face, so high from her seated position. "Why do you keep calling me that?"

He pulled out the chair beside hers and lowered himself. His gaze connected with hers, and she couldn't look away. "I used to know someone named Jack. Someone who caused all kinds of trouble." He shrugged and looked past her. "I just think Jackie fits you better."

A feeling as of warm honey glided through her. She'd never had a man call her by a special name, and she liked it. A lot. "I guess it won't hurt if you call me that, but you probably should be prepared to explain yourself."

His gaze snapped back to hers, and he smiled. "I can do that." His black eyes—even the one barely visible—shone bright with something that looked like affection. She licked her dry lips, wondering if he actually felt something for her or if he was just feeling emotional from all that had happened. How could he when he'd known her less than a week?

But surely he must, if he gave her a nickname.

His gaze dropped down to her mouth and lingered there a moment, sending her heart bucking around her chest like a crazed bronco.

He bolted out of the chair. "I. . .uh. . .should. . ." He cleared his raspy throat and walked toward the hall. "Better get changed. . .so you can set this shirt to soaking."

Nodding, she watched him stride away, surprised

243

at her disappointment. Had she actually thought the preacher would kiss her? She shook her head at the foolish thought. He was just being kind, because that was his nature. She sighed and rested one arm on the table and leaned her head against it. What a crazy girl she was. She had no plans to be courted by a man or ever marry, and here she was getting starry-eyed over the new minister.

Surely it must just be from all the emotion swirling through her today.

Chapter 22

Jack pushed her shoe against the porch floor, moving the rocker in a gentle sway. Even though baby Andrew was only a few hours old, her mother had assured her it was fine to rock him on the porch as long as she stayed out of the sun, but she still worried. At least it was quiet out here. With the three children all excited about the new baby, sneaking outside was the only way she could have him to herself.

Andrew's head leaned back over her arm, and his tiny mouth formed an O. She lifted the flannel blanket her ma had made over his head and ears, leaving only his face peeking out. She ought to be inside, figuring out what to fix for supper, but she just had to hold her baby brother again while her ma rested up.

Jack ran the back of her finger along his soft cheek, and he smiled briefly. His chest rose and fell in quick cadence with each breath. She had a hard time imagining such a tiny thing could one day grow up to be a man like Luke or Noah. But then she highly doubted Noah had ever been so small.

She loved each of her siblings, but when the others had been born, she hadn't experienced the maternal desires that swelled through her like they did now. Maybe it was because she was older. Maybe it was due to helping deliver Andrew. Or his near death, which had drawn her and Noah closer. Butterflies fluttered in her stomach as she thought about Noah.

Her gaze lifted to the pale blue sky. Fluffy clouds created a wide shadow on Main Street. "Thank You, Lord, for saving my brother. For letting Noah be there to help. Watch over Ma, and help her heal quickly and regain her strength. And please send Papa home soon."

Her only regret of the day was that Luke hadn't been there to enjoy the excitement of his youngest son's birth. Mrs. Phillips had assured Jack she'd done just right in delivering her brother and explained that sometimes babies had trouble breathing right off. She said she'd have done the same thing Noah had to encourage the baby to take his first breath.

A dog barked across the street. Andrew threw out his arms, and his face scrunched up as if he prepared to cry. She lifted him to her shoulder and patted his back. Smiling, she remembered how she'd helped Mrs. Phillips give him his first bath, and now he was dressed in a gown her ma had stitched. She leaned her cheek against his fuzzy head, amazed at how much she already loved him.

How could she leave him and go to Dallas?

She felt as if her soul and his were stitched together. Was this anything like what it felt to be a mother?

A motion down Main Street caught her eye. She watched Bertha Boyd and her sister slowly make their way up the boardwalk. On the other side of the street, Leah Howard walked past Luke's office with several of her children following and went into the store. The mercantile was closed, so they must be paying a quick visit to Mrs. Morgan. Jack knew the names of each of Dan and Leah's children. Leah had called off her wedding with Dan when she found out he had brought his five nieces and nephews home to Lookout after his brother and sister-in-law died, but love won out. Jack knew all about most of the people in this town, like the Howards, but if she moved to Dallas, she wouldn't know a soul. She'd be all alone.

Jack leaned her head back. Why had she never really considered that before?

Ever since her fall off the mayor's roof, her life seemed to be changing. She hadn't finished a single article for the paper, and the fact that it didn't bother her like it would have in the past vexed her. What was happening to her?

Tessa strolled out the mercantile door, talking with Callie Howard. Soon Leah and her children left the store and headed down the boardwalk. Tessa ambled back inside, and Jack pursed her lips. Too bad her friend hadn't seen her and come over so she could show off her new brother. Not that Tessa would be impressed.

A wagon rounded the corner, momentarily blocking her view of the store's entrance, and when it passed on by, surprise gripped Jack. Tessa and Billy stepped off the boardwalk and walked toward her. What could Billy want? She hadn't seen him since the fight last night. That seemed years ago. She still needed to return that bracelet but had forgotten about it in all of the day's excitement.

Tessa stepped onto the porch, and her face scrunched up. "Are you holding Abby's dolly? I swear, Jacqueline, you do the oddest things."

Billy stood behind his sister, his nose swollen and black smudges resting below his eyes. He looked as bad as Noah. A smirk pulled at his lips, and he didn't look the least bit repentant. Maybe ignoring him was her best.

Jack pulled the blanket back, and Tessa gasped. "It's real? Wherever did you get it?"

Jack rolled her eyes. Given the condition her ma had been in the last few months, Tessa's question bordered on ridiculous. "Where do you think? He's my new brother."

"But I thought it wasn't due for several more weeks." Tessa's reaction fell flat.

"Babies have their own time schedule, don'tcha know?" Billy poked his sister with his elbow.

Tessa swatted him, then leaned over and stared at the precious baby. One side of her face curled up. "He's awful red, and his head has a funny shape. What's wrong with it?"

Jack sucked in a breath, flipped up the blanket, and held Andrew to her chest so they could no longer look at him. Why couldn't Tessa say anything nice? "He looks like any newborn. His head will take its normal shape in another day or two. Mrs. Phillips and Ma both said so. I think he's perfect."

Billy snorted. "A baby's a baby. Why you makin' such a fuss?"

Jack tossed him a hooded glance. "Babies are precious. You were one once, remember."

He snorted a laugh and booted the rocker rung nearest her, setting it in motion. Tessa halted it with a hand to the arm of the chair, then plopped down and straightened her dress. She huffed out a breath, crossed her arms over her chest, and laid her head back against the chair. "My life is over."

Jack sidled a glance her way. "What do you mean?"

"That robbery was the straw that broke the camel's back," Billy said.

Tessa shot him a glare. "I'm telling her, not you."

Billy narrowed his gaze in a menacing stare that didn't in the least faze Tessa. She tossed her blond curls over her shoulder. "Ma is getting married."

"Truly?" Jack's mind raced. Maybe she could write up the story before word passed around the whole county, if Tessa hadn't told many people. "To Rand Kessler?"

Nodding, Tessa set the rocker in action. Billy casually leaned against the porch railing, watching

Jack. His close presence gave her the creeps. He was a nice-looking man, but his character left something to be desired.

"Please give your mother my congratulations," Jack said.

"No, no, no!" Tessa shook her head with vigor. "I don't want to live clear out on that man's ranch. I'll never see my friends or have any fun. What will I do? It will be so boring."

Tessa's whine mirrored Abby's when she wasn't getting her way—kind of like when Butch Laird would run his fingernails across his slate in school and make all the girls squeal. Jack couldn't help wondering why Butch had been on her mind so much lately. She gave her head a little shake and tried to think of something to make her friend feel better. "I think it would be nice living on a ranch. You could ride all you wanted and have lots of peace and quiet, unlike living in a town. No music or ruckus from the saloon to bother you when you're trying to go to sleep."

Billy made a grunting sound. "That's one reason I ain't goin'."

"You have to go, Billy. You don't have a choice, and neither do I." Tessa all but stuck her tongue out at him.

Billy straightened, then bent down, placing each hand on the arms of Tessa's chair. "I'm a grown man. I don't have to go nowhere I don't wanna go."

Tessa leaned back, obviously stunned at his spiteful tone. She blinked several times. "But what would you do? You don't have a job. Ma's gonna sell the store, so where would you live?"

Billy's blue gaze darted to Jack, then away. "I have ways of gettin' money."

This wasn't the first time Jack had wondered just where he got his cash. How could he have afforded that bracelet he gave her, even with the discount he probably got from his mother? He claimed to want to marry her, but he still lived with his ma and sister. A thought came to her. "Why couldn't you two stay in town and run the store? You're certainly old enough and have plenty of experience."

Tessa tucked a loose tendril of hair behind her ear and curled her lip. "I'm sick of the store. The work is dirty—opening all those crates, dusting everyday, and people can be downright snippety."

Jack ducked her head and placed a kiss on Andrew's head in her effort not to laugh. That was the pot calling the kettle black.

"What am I going to do?"

Jack considered a different tactic. "Doesn't that cute cowboy you danced with last night work on the Kessler ranch?"

"He does." Tessa uttered a heartfelt sigh and fanned her face with her hand.

"Ma said she cain't see him no more." Billy lifted his chin, looking proud to have revealed that piece of information.

"Why not?" Jack thought the man seemed nice enough, and he was always decently dressed and polite.

"Because he's just a cowhand, that's why."

Tessa jumped up from her chair. "Stay out of this, Billy. You'll be just as miserable out at that ranch as I will." She spun toward Jack. "I'm parched. I think I'll go get something cold to drink." She waved her fingers at Jack and glided toward the steps. Suddenly she stopped and stamped her foot. "Oh, drat. I'll probably never have another cold drink if I have to move to that dreadful ranch."

Jack watched Tessa march across the dirt road and shook her head. "She sure isn't happy."

"No, but Ma seems to be."

Jack snapped her gaze back to his, surprised to

actually hear Billy say something halfway nice. "You really think so?"

"Yeah, but this move sure will cause me and Tessa problems."

"What will you do?" Andrew started squirming, so Jack patted his back. Almost instantly, he belched.

Billy cocked his head and stared at her with a contented smile that made ants crawl up her spine. With Tessa gone, she should probably go back inside, but first she needed some information about the robbery. "Did the thief steal much from your store?"

"I guess so." He shrugged and looked away. "Left a big mess, too. Dumped over the cracker barrel, then walked all over them. The marshal said there'd been some strangers coming into town of an evening lately, and he rode off to see if he could find them."

"I'm sorry. So how did the thief get in? Did he break down the door? It doesn't look damaged from here."

He shook his head. "No. Came in that storeroom window under the stairs out back. You know, the stairs that lead up to our rooms."

"Yeah. Do you know if the robbery happened last night or this morning?"

Billy shrugged. "Your pa still out hunting for the thieves?"

Jack nodded, and Billy smirked. He pushed away from the railing, pulled the rocker Tessa had sat in around to face Jack's, and sat. He fingered the cut on his upper lip, which Noah's fist had made. "Why don't you take that scrawny thing back inside and let's you and me take a walk?"

"Billy! That *thing* you're referring to is my brother." Jack stood and shot knives at him with her eyes. How could he be so rude and then expect her to follow him around like a stray pup?

His gaze hardened. "Don't you think you owe it to

me after last night?"

"Of all the. . ." *Pigheaded nincompoops.*

He flipped up his thumb, pointing it at his nose. "Look at me, Jacqueline."

She stared closely at his battered face. His nose was swollen and bent like a letter *C*, marring his near perfect features. She shoved aside a wave of sympathy. "You shouldn't have hit the minister."

"He shouldn't have butted in. I just wanted to dance with you."

Jack hugged Andrew close to her heart. She needed to get him away from Billy before he did something stupid. "I need to take Andrew inside and fix some supper."

"I just want to spend time with you." The whine in his voice mirrored Tessa's and did nothing to endear him to her.

"I'm sorry, but that's the problem. I'm not interested in spending time with you. I've tried to tell you nicely, but you refuse to listen."

His countenance darkened, and he grabbed her elbow. "You'd better—"

A man strode down Main Street, and Jack's heart leapt. Billy must have noticed, because he glanced over his shoulder. A muscle in his jaw ticked, and he stepped back, relaxing his stance and pasting a smile on his face. "Evening, Marshal."

Luke's gaze narrowed, and he looked between Billy and her. His gaze dropped. His brown eyes widened. "Do we have company?" He glanced down at his clothes and brushed a dusty patch off his knee. "Whose baby is that?"

Jack tried hard to hold back her smile, but it insisted on bursting forth. "It's your new son, Papa. Ma said his name is Andrew."

The cavalry yell that poured forth from Luke's

mouth made both Andrew and Billy jump. The baby screeched, and Billy bolted off the porch. She couldn't help giggling at the picture Billy made—like a stray dog with his tail between his legs—as she gently soothed the frightened baby. "You want to hold him?"

"Of course I do." He held out his arms, then looked down at his hands.

"Um. . .maybe you should wash up first," she offered.

"I reckon that's a good idea. How's your ma? She all right?"

Jack nodded. "She's fine. Tired and missing you, but fine." She smiled again. "Guess what?"

He shrugged and peered at his son. "Looks a bit like Abby, don'tcha think?"

"Papa, I'm trying to tell you something life altering."

His gaze bounced up to hers. "What? Did something happen while I was gone besides the baby comin'?"

"That's it. I delivered Andrew."

Luke shoved his hat up his forehead, revealing the lighter skin near his hairline, and grinned. "You're joshin' me, Half Bit."

"I'm not. Honestly."

He placed his hands on his hips. "Well. . .I'll be. Ain't that somethin'?"

"Papa!" Jack scolded.

His hand dropped to his pistol, and he glanced over his shoulder, then back at her. "What?"

Jack shook her head. "I wondered where Alan learned to say *ain't.*"

Luke shook his head and started unbuttoning his shirt as he walked across the porch. "We're not havin' that conversation. I need to clean up and see my wife and hold my new son."

Just before he stepped off the far side of the porch, Jack called, "Did you catch the thieves?"

He shook his head and broke into a jog.

Chapter 23

The bell above the freight office door jingled, and Garrett glanced up from the *Horseman* magazine he'd been scouring. Luke moseyed in, hat down low on his forehead. Garrett leaned back in his chair, lacing his hands behind his head, and grinned. "Well, there's the proud papa. How you doin'?"

"Still proud but exhausted." Luke shuffled across the room like an old man, pulled out the chair that used to belong to Mark, then fell into it with a heavy sigh.

Garrett dropped all ideas of jesting and leaned forward, arms on his desk. He rarely ever saw his cousin looking so haggard. "Is Andrew all right? I know he had a rough start, with nearly dying and all."

"Oh, *he's* doing great—at least during the day— sleeps like a baby." Luke chuckled and ran his hand over his eyes, then down his unshaven face. "Emmie was such a good baby. She slept through the night almost from the start. I'd forgotten about how Abby and Alan stayed awake like Andrew does, until Rachel reminded me." He groaned and rested his face in his hands. "I'm getting too old for this."

Shaking his head, Garrett rose and poured his cousin a cup of coffee. In spite of Luke's fatigue, he couldn't help being a bit jealous. At forty, Luke was the father of five, albeit Jack was his adopted daughter. Garrett set the cup in front of Luke, then walked to the window. He'd concentrated on building his business all these years and let time slip by. He rubbed the back of his neck. Was thirty-nine too late to get married and start a family?

"What's eating you, Cuz?" Luke slurped his coffee and smacked his lips. "Mmm. . .just what I needed."

Garrett watched the busyness on the streets as people shopped or visited. Two cowboys moseyed by on their horses. Garrett shrugged. "I don't know."

"You wouldn't happen to be thinking of a pretty, black-haired gal, would you?"

Maybe he shouldn't have been so quick to share his coffee and revive Luke. If he'd known his cousin was going to meddle, he wouldn't have. He turned and leaned back against the window frame, feigning a confused look. "What brunette are you talkin' about?"

Luke grinned, but his lips quickly transformed into a yawn. Not the least bit tired, Garrett copy-catted with a yawn of his own. His cousin scratched his chest and leaned back. "I think you know."

Ambling back to the coffeepot, Garrett took his time answering. It wouldn't do to let his cousin know he'd been attracted to Miss Payton. He took a sip of the hot brew and peered over the edge of his cup. He needed some kind of response, but what could he say when he didn't understand his own feelings toward the woman? "She's too young for me."

Luke grunted. "No, she's not. Lots of men marry younger women. It's a good idea if you want to start a family."

Watching his coffee swirl, he thought about that fact. His cousin was right, but he wasn't about to let him know. Marrying younger did make a lot of sense.

"What's your hesitation? I saw how you looked at her that day she first arrived." Luke stretched then crossed his arms over his chest and propped his boots up on Mark's old desk.

Garrett's thoughts flashed to his brother. He knew Mark was very happily married and enjoying fatherhood. He couldn't believe that his brother had been married almost a decade. Where had the years gone?

"You gonna answer me, Cuz?"

Garrett shrugged. "Marrying an ex-convict wasn't ever on my chore list. I want a respectable woman. How'd you like your kids being raised by a gal who'd spent six years in prison?"

Luke jumped to his feet so fast Garrett jumped and sloshed coffee on his sleeve. Stomping across the room, Luke's eyes fired bullets. "Miss Carly *is* a respectable woman. She had a rough life when she was young. Her ma died when she was fourteen, and she had to go live with that no-account outlaw brother and his gang—or be forced into being a saloon gal." He took a breath and continued, "She served her time for the crimes she committed and became a Christian. All is forgiven in God's eyes. So, if He can overlook her past, why can't you?"

Garrett's eyes widened, and his brows hiked up all on their own. He'd never seen his cousin this agitated, not even when he and Mark had written off to a trio of mail-order brides and they all came to town, hoping to marry Luke. "I don't reckon God has any inclinations to marry her."

"And you do?" Luke's hackles were still lifted, and his bloodshot eyes reminded Garrett of a crazed bull that he and Mark had tormented until it had charged them.

He lifted up one shoulder and dropped it. "I don't know. Could be."

Luke blinked, his expression softening. "Really?"

He ran his hand through his hair. "Good thoughts or bad, I can't seem to quit thinking of her."

"Well. . .good." Luke loosely held his hands on his hips. "You're a good man, Garrett. You'd make a great father, and you deserve to know the joys of being married." Luke grinned wide. "And trust me, there are some excellent benefits."

"I can imagine."

"Nope, I don't think you can." Luke's eyes took on a faraway stare, and one corner of his mouth curved up. "There's something real special about coming home to a woman who thinks you set the moon up in the sky. To be able to cuddle up with her soft body on a cold winter's night, and to share your dreams or just hear about how the children got in trouble."

Garrett rolled his eyes, not because he was disgusted with his cousin's soliloquy, but because Luke's sincerity embarrassed him and made him jealous. "All right, I hear you. But even if. . .say. . . I had some inclinations toward Miss Payton, I have no idea what to do about it."

Seeming pacified, Luke returned to Mark's desk and sipped his coffee. "Women want to be noticed and to feel they're special to a man. They like to receive flowers."

"Aw, Luke, I can't go walkin' down Main Street carrying a wad of flowers. Every man in town'd be laughin' at me." He didn't mind them heehawing at his jokes, but laughing *at* him was altogether something else.

"You can if you want to catch a woman. Don't forget how I stood in front of the whole town and told Rachel she was the only gal for me. Always has been."

"Yeah, well, I haven't exactly been pining my heart away after Carly Payton all these years. In fact, I'm not sure I even thought of her once the whole time she was gone."

Luke rubbed the back of his hand across his cheek. "Well, you haven't known her all your life like I knew Rach—" He yawned, his eyelids drooping. "Why don't you try prayin' about it?"

Luke folded his arms, laid them on the desk, and rested his head on top of them. Garrett stared out the window across the street to where a couple stood in front of the café. The man glanced around then leaned down and gave the woman a little peck on the cheek. She ducked her head, but Garrett could tell she was pleased. Would Carly be agreeable if he tried to kiss her?

He snorted a laugh. Probably not. She'd most likely yank a derringer from her skirt pocket and shoot him.

"Sure is nice and quiet in here. No kids running around like Indians, whooping it up and making the baby cry."

Garrett strode across the room and tugged on Luke's arm. "C'mon, ol' man. You can't sleep here. I've got a business to run."

Luke, limp as an old rope, stood and weaved a bit. "Where we goin'?"

"I have an empty house. No women. No children. All quiet."

"Mmm...sounds perfect."

Luke managed to stumble across the room and out the door, leaving it wide open. Garrett wondered if he should walk him across the street, but he didn't want to embarrass the marshal in front of the townsfolk. They might think he'd taken to the bottle, but Luke would never do that.

Garrett thought about his house. All empty. No one to greet him when he came home—unless Luke was still there. It had never bothered him all that much before, but now it sounded lonely.

He stared out the door window and down the street to the boardinghouse. Would Carly give him a chance if he approached her?

There was only one way to find out.

Noah swiped his sleeve against his damp forehead. Just a few more boards and he'd be done painting the mercantile. The memory of the angry youth who'd smeared ugly red letters all over the town resurfaced. *Jack is a liar.*

It had been a dumb thing to do, and he now regretted it, but he'd taken all he could back then and had lashed out. His pa finally sold all their hogs and forced him to leave town because he feared Marshal Davis had it in for Noah—or rather Butch. Swallowing hard, Noah dipped the brush into the paint and resumed his work.

He hadn't wanted to leave back then and had been young enough to hope that things might change. Their home hadn't been much more than a shack, but it was home. Or at least it had been for a while.

He still didn't have a permanent place to call home. Glancing to his right, he stared at the boardinghouse. It was nice—and the food was certainly some of the best he'd had in years—but having Jackie living there, avoiding him for over a week, made things awkward. He kicked at a rock on the boardwalk, sending it flying. The stone hit the marshal's office next door and made a loud clunk then dropped to the ground. Paint dribbled onto his boot top.

Noah ground his back teeth together. Why couldn't he quit thinking about Jackie?

He yanked his handkerchief out of his pocket

and swiped his boot, leaving an ugly white smear on the brown leather. Sighing, he dipped the brush then stroked the building again.

Mrs. Morgan strolled out of the shop, broom in hand. "Oh! I suppose I should wait to sweep until the paint dries."

Noah nodded. "Probably a wise idea, ma'am."

The pretty woman smiled, her blue eyes beaming. "That looks so nice, Reverend. I just don't know why you felt you had to go to so much trouble for us."

"No trouble, Mrs. Morgan. I'm glad to help out." He lifted his hat and set it back on his head. "And congratulations."

The near-forty-year-old woman swung back and forth in her purple calico dress, grinning like a schoolgirl with her first crush. Her dark brown hair, which was pulled up into a neat bun, didn't hold a hint of gray. "I guess Rand came to see you then."

"He did." Noah nodded, remembering the shy rancher who couldn't quit grinning when he'd tracked Noah down at the church Tuesday afternoon. "The wedding is set for two weeks from this coming Sunday."

She glanced down, her cheeks crimson. "I know. I'm so thankful to the good Lord for bringing Rand into my life. I can hardly believe I'm marrying again after all these years." Nibbling her lip, she glanced down the street. "Rand almost married Rachel Davis, you know?"

Noah remembered seeing Mr. Kessler sitting on the porch with Mrs. Davis years ago—back when she'd been the Widow Hamilton, but the man quit coming around once Luke came back to town. "I don't think you have to worry. Mr. Kessler is smitten—with you, ma'am. I probably shouldn't tell you, but he couldn't quit talking about you and how happy he is to finally be getting married."

Her eyelids blinked quickly, and she dabbed one corner with her fingertip. "I haven't been this happy in years." She glanced over her shoulder into the store, then leaned the broom against the wall and walked over to him. "I'm concerned about Billy and Tessa though," she said, her voice lowered. "Neither one seems keen on my marrying Rand. Nor do they want to move out to the ranch."

He hadn't counseled many women, much less a woman alone. He glanced around the street and boardwalks. Dolly Dykstra stood outside of her dress shop, hands flapping in the air as she chatted to a woman he hadn't met. There was no one else on the street this evening.

Mrs. Morgan wrung her hands together. "I don't know what to do."

Noah glanced down at the drying paint and decided helping the storekeeper was more important than painting her building. He set the brush across the open tin can. "I reckon you've talked to them."

"I have, but they get angry whenever I bring up the subject. They've both always been so stubborn. I admit I may have spoiled them, but raising them without a man to help wasn't easy."

Noah wasn't all that much older than Billy, he imagined. Three or four years at the most. What did he know about dealing with grown children—or any children for that matter? *Give me wisdom, Lord.*

"If they have no interest in living at the ranch, why not let them run the mercantile?"

She shook her head. "They don't want to do that, either. I don't like to talk bad about my own children, but the truth is they're both lazy. I found out a long time ago that it was easier to do things myself rather than fight Billy or Tessa to do them." She kept her head down. "You must think me a terrible mother."

"Not at all. It's not my place to judge you, ma'am." He started to lay his hand on her shoulder, but the mayor turned the corner just then with two other men and walked in their direction. "It just might do both of your children some good to live on the ranch and have Rand Kessler as a stepfather. He's used to dealing with hired help and probably could control them."

She glanced over her shoulder, then nodded. "I think you may be right. I just don't know if I can force them to go, especially Billy." She grabbed her broom and stepped back to let the men pass.

The mayor smiled at the men who accompanied him. "Ah, good. Gentlemen, let me introduce you to our storeowner and our minister." He waved his hand toward the only woman present. "This is Christine Morgan, who runs our only mercantile, and this is our temporary minister, Noah Jeffers. This is Mr. Humphrey and Mr. Brown. They are here in town on business."

Noah didn't miss the intended emphasis on *temporary*. He studied the men while Mrs. Morgan greeted them. Mr. Humphrey was close to six feet but almost as thin as Mrs. Morgan's broom handle. His dark hair and handlebar mustache were in stark contrast to the shorter Mr. Brown, with his white hair and neatly cropped beard. Their clothing looked store-bought and expensive. Rich city folk. When the men turned their eyes on him, he held out his hand. "A pleasure to meet you both. If you're staying in town, I hope you'll attend Sunday services."

Mr. Brown grunted, but Mr. Humphrey's eyes went wide. Then he turned to the mayor, whose head jerked back at the man's glare. "We must be on our way," the mayor hastily said. "If you'll excuse us."

Noah nodded and stepped back to make more room for the trio to pass. The boardwalk shimmied as the men's footsteps thudded across the wooden planks. When they were in front of Polly's Café, Mrs. Morgan scurried to his side.

"I wonder what kind of business they're in," she said, her hands holding tight to her broom handle. "Scuttlebutt says it's the railroad."

"I thought talk of the railroad coming here was just rumors." He glanced down at his paint can, hoping it wasn't getting too dried out.

She shrugged. "I don't think so."

"That would be good for the town."

She nodded then glanced at the can. "I suppose I should let you finish your work so you can go home."

"I'll pray for you and your children and that God will give Rand wisdom as you all become a family."

A shy smile lit her face. "Thank you, Reverend. I appreciate that." She slipped back into the store, closed the door, and he heard the bolt slide to lock it.

He bent and resumed his work, sending up prayers to God for the Morgan family and for Rand Kessler.

Awhile later, Noah slapped paint on the last board and stood back to admire his handiwork. Mrs. Morgan may not have owned the store when he'd committed his wicked deed, but at least he felt he'd done all he could to make recompense for it. He pressed the lid on the paint can. He turned toward the boardinghouse but noticed Jackie, skirts held high, hurrying down the opposite side of the street, away from her home.

He stooped down again, pretending interest in the can. Jackie slowed her pace as she approached the saloon. She glanced in all directions, but if she noticed him, she didn't act like it. Besides her, he was the only person on the street. All the businesses were closed up as tight as a spinster's coin purse, and most decent folks had gone home for the night. That was one reason he'd waited to paint—fewer people on the road meant less stirred-up dust to soil his wet paint.

Jackie tiptoed to the saloon windows and pressed her nose against the glass. It wasn't likely she could see through the dingy, smoke-covered panes that he'd noticed once or twice as he'd passed by. She tiptoed to the swinging doors, pushed one open a little, and peered inside. Noah stood. After a few moments, she darted to her right and around the far corner of the building, waving her hand in front of her nose.

What in the world?

He scratched the back of his head. He never paid much attention to the Wet Your Whistle, but he couldn't imagine what would cause Jack to slink down the street like a wolf on the prey and peek inside such a place. A man stumbled out and tottered to his horse, which was tied to the hitching post in front of the saloon. After four tries, he managed to mount the poor critter. Noah shook his head. Not even dusk yet, and the cowboy was already drunk. After the man rode out, barely staying in his saddle, Jack reappeared and hurried to the double doors again.

Noah lifted the brush up and down, close to the wall but not touching it, so she would think he wasn't watching—but he was. His curiosity had definitely been piqued.

Jack jumped back, then darted around the left side of the building. The saloon owner burst through the doors, sending them flying against the wall. He shoved his hands to his hips, looking back toward town. Noah set the paint and brush just under the porch steps, so they'd be out of the way, and broke into a jog.

He didn't know what that ornery gal was up to, but he intended to find out.

Chapter 24

Jack's heart pounded as she raced around the side of the saloon. Holding her hand over her mouth, she tried to quiet her cough. How could those men stand being in that smoky, smelly place for hours?

She leaned against the rough wood, willing her heart to slow down. This was just another of her harebrained ideas that was probably nothing but an effort in futility. She ought to run back home before she was missed, but she knew she wouldn't. There was a story here, she could smell it.

If she hadn't been outside hanging Andrew's diapers on the line to dry, she wouldn't have noticed the mayor and his two companions strolling down Bluebonnet Lane. Her heart had pounded as she followed to see where they were headed. She hadn't even known that those men—the same ones who'd been at the mayor's home the day she climbed on the roof—had returned to Lookout. They had stopped at the end of Bluebonnet Lane, past Elm Street, where there was nothing but a few houses, then open prairie all the way to the Addams River. The mayor had waved his hand, almost as if offering the land to the men.

They must be going to build something, but what? The town could use many types of new businesses, but the way the mayor was keeping this project such a secret made her suspicious.

Something banged hard against the wall she leaned on, and she jumped. Night was falling. She needed to finish her task and get away from this vile place before Luke saw her or something bad happened. Her papa had warned her to stay clear of the Wet Your Whistle, even during the daytime. He didn't need to warn her about being here at night.

Pushing her feet into action, she tiptoed to the end of the building and peered in both directions. No people were out, but crickets and lightning bugs already heralded the coming darkness. She'd seen the mayor and his friends at the bar; then they'd headed upstairs. She surmised that there must be a private meeting or maybe gambling room the men planned to use. She swallowed hard as she worked her way around to the back stairs. She sure hoped the men hadn't come here with pleasure in mind.

The first weathered stair creaked from her weight. She winced and held her breath. Her fears were silly—who could hear a faint squeak over the ruckus coming from the saloon? The tinny piano music did little to mellow out the loud chatter, groans, and hollers from the men inside the building. And if the noise was bad, the stench was horrid. Unfortunately, she was downwind of the saloon's privies, and she suspected half the folks who ventured out of the building to use them never made it that far.

She hiked her skirt up farther and hurried quietly up the steps. She reached the landing, but she didn't dare go inside. The line had to be drawn somewhere. Her mother would be proud that she was finally learning to set some boundaries for her behavior.

To her left, the two windows on the rear of the saloon were dark, but light flowed from the ones to her right. She reached up toward one of the open windows, but it was too high and too far to her right to grasp. Jack glanced around, making sure no one was about, then lifted her skirt and climbed onto the landing's railing. Too bad she hadn't had time to don her bloomers.

Deep voices echoed from the window. "It's good in theory, but if the railroad fails to come here, we'll have wasted a small fortune."

"That's true, and we will also lose the faith of our investors."

Jack didn't recognize either voice. She held on to the railing support that ran up the side of building. She glanced down, barely able to make out the ground below in the growing darkness. If she fell that far, she could well injure her knee again, and the pain had just barely stopped biting her with its sharp teeth.

She shook off her apprehension like a winter cloak. This was nothing compared to walking on the mayor's roof.

"I understand, gentlemen, but I just received a certified document stating that the Katy Railroad will definitely be building a spur track from Denison to Lookout and on farther west. Construction of the rails is set to commence in a few weeks."

Jack's heart soared at the mayor's declaration. She'd gotten her scoop! The railroad was coming to Lookout, and she was the only one who knew except for these men. She needed more details and to find out what they planned to build. Maybe it was the depot. But no, wouldn't the railroad company take care of that?

She held her breath and leaned sideways to reach the window frame three feet away. Her right foot slipped, flailing, unable to find a place to land. Her fingertips latched on to the window casing, keeping her from falling. She managed to get her foot back on the railing, but now she leaned precariously to the right.

One man stood and walked toward the window. Jack sucked in a breath and leaned her head away from the light. If he looked out, he'd see her fingertips on the window's frame.

Sprawled out like she was, she felt like a newborn foal that had just stood up for the first time. Good thing night had come, or anyone below would have a clear view of her unmentionables.

"I'm not convinced this town has need of a hotel," Mr. Mustache, as she had dubbed the man, said.

Hotel?

They planned to build a hotel in Lookout?

Why. . .that would put the boardinghouse out of business. How could they compete with a brand-new hotel? Irritation at the mayor seared her belly and flared her nostrils—definitely not a good thing, given her closeness to the privies. She scrunched her nose shut on the inside, just like she did when she changed Andrew's messy diapers, but that did nothing to quell the fire burning in her gut.

No wonder the mayor had been so devious and wouldn't let her listen in on his conversation with these men. Mayor Burke had once planned to buy the boardinghouse and make it his home back when her ma thought Luke would marry one of the boarding-house brides. But when Luke picked her, she canceled her plans to sell out and move away. The boardinghouse was far bigger and fancier than Mayor Burke's present house, and he'd always admired her home. Was that his purpose? To drive her family out of business so they'd have to move and sell the boardinghouse? Of all the. . .

"Our surveyor should arrive within the week."

"I'm not sure where we will put him," Mayor Burke

said. "There's not another bedroom at my house."

"Perhaps he could stay at the boardinghouse and investigate our competition." Mr. Mustache chuckled.

The mayor snorted. "Mrs. Davis's place won't be much of a threat to your establishment. That minister is the only boarder she has now. At the rate she's birthing babies, it won't be long before she's filled the house with children and won't have any more rooms to let."

Jack sucked in another gasp, trying to keep quiet. Her fingers were starting to ache, as was her knee, bent in an unnatural manner as it was. She tightened her grasp on the window frame, halfway wondering how she was going to get back on the landing.

A drunk in the doorway mumbled something incoherent and fumbled with the screen door latch. Suddenly it flew open, banging into her hip and sending her flying.

For a fraction of a moment, she hung only by the fingertips of her right hand. Her body swung far to the right. Her fingers slipped. Her frantic heart tried desperately to escape her chest.

She would not fall.

Not again.

Help me, Lord.

She forced her trembling left hand up to the frame and grabbed on. Her boots slipped against the fabric of her petticoat as she tried to gain a foothold. If the men so much as glanced her way they'd see her hands. Her breath came in little gasps. The ache in her fingers intensified.

"Well now, what've we got here? Eh?" The man responsible for her precarious position leaned over the rail and grinned. The light shining out the window illuminated him. Several days' worth of sparse whiskers coated his cheek and chin, looking like mange on a dog. He belched, sending a putrid stench Jack's way.

She couldn't do a thing. *Go away!*

If she so much as whispered, the mayor would hear her. And what would he do if he found her spying on him a second time?

The drunk swatted at her arm. "Come over hear and give ol' Harvey a smooch. Yer a purty little thang."

"Git!" the mayor yelled.

Jack plastered her cheek against the building. Her fingers slipped. If that man didn't leave soon, she was in serious danger of falling. The drunk leaned over—and Jack hoped and prayed he didn't choose that moment to spew the contents of his belly all over her.

"C'mere." He snagged hold of her sleeve, then lost his balance and tilted over the rail. "Whoopsie-daisy."

She closed her eyes, expecting him to knock her off her perch. When no collision occurred she peered out of one eye. Relief made her weak—and she sure didn't need any more weakness—to see he had righted himself on the landing.

"I said get out of here. Can't decent men have a meeting in quiet?" the mayor yelled. Footsteps sounded in Jack's direction.

Yikes! Fall or get caught?

Neither option was favorable.

The drunk regrouped and took another swipe at her but missed. She hoped he'd attract the mayor's attention so he wouldn't notice her.

Falling was better than getting caught. Jack let go.

The mayor slammed the window shut.

Jack hurled downward, her skirts snapping like a flag in a windstorm.

∽

"Tell us another story, Miss Carly." Abby sat on her bed in her nightgown, bouncing her legs.

"Not tonight, sweetie. Emmie is already asleep." She lifted the toddler off her lap and held her tight against her chest as she stood. She kicked out her skirts and carried Emma to her bed.

"Puh-leasse." Abby held out her doll and danced her across the quilt.

"Shh...I said no." She pulled a sheet over Emmie and placed a kiss on her head. Oh, how she'd grown to love these children. If she had to leave and move on one day, her heart would break.

"Miss Carr—llyy, I gotta go."

She turned toward Abby, putting her hands on her hips like she'd seen Jacqueline do. "Are you telling the truth?"

Abby nibbled her lip, then looked down at the floor.

"That's what I thought. Lie back now. It's time to sleep."

The girl did as told, but her frown proved she wasn't happy about bending her will. Suddenly her gaze turned apprehensive. "But Sissy's not home. I'm scared to go to sleep without her."

Carly laid the sheet over Abby's body. Was she really afraid, or was this another bedtime stalling tactic?

"Abby, you know that's not true." Luke walked into the room, making it seem smaller.

"But Papa..."

"No more talking. Time to go to sleep." He leaned over and kissed Abby's cheek. "I love you, punkin."

Carly left the room and started down the stairs. Luke turned off the bedroom lamp and followed behind her, chuckling. "That one is such a fireball. Reminds me of Jack when she was younger, although I didn't know her at Abby's age."

Carly didn't miss the regret in his voice. "I have

to admit, I can't yet tell when she's pullin' my leg or bein' truthful."

Luke joined her in the entryway, shaking his head. "Neither can I, and I'm her father—and a lawman. And Alan's almost as bad."

"I never realized how difficult raising children can be." She'd probably never have any of her own. She ducked her head and studied the floor. A large ant crawled out from under the hall tree. Before she could even reach in her pocket for her handkerchief, Luke squashed the intruder.

"Raising children can be hard at times, but it's worth all the effort." A soft smile tugged at his lips.

Carly continued to be amazed at how he'd welcomed her into his home, given their past history. How he entrusted the care of his children to her. He didn't seem to hold any animosity toward her for her past.

He glanced down, his brown eyes anxious. The sun had ironed permanent creases in the tanned skin beside his eyes. His brown hair, the color of a pecan shell, had touches of gray at the temples and sideburns. "I wonder if I might ask a favor of you."

"Of course. Anything."

His smile turned him from a rugged lawman to handsome. "I'd like to get Rachel out of the house and take her for a short walk. Would you mind tending the baby and keeping an ear out for the children?"

"I'd be happy to." She loved holding the baby. It was her first time to be around one other than at church or when a young mother would visit Tillie.

"I'd be much obliged. We won't be gone long. I know Rachel is tired, but the fresh air will do her some good and maybe even help her sleep." He glanced at the window beside the front door. "Hmm...I wonder where Half Bit is. Do you know?"

Carly shook her head. "No, she was hanging up the diapers last time I saw her. Come to think of it, she didn't come in afterward."

He strode toward his bedroom. "Rachel and I can look for her. I'm sure she just got distracted chasing a rabid boar or trying to interview a cattle rustler for that paper." He shook his head and turned into the bedroom.

Rabid boar? Carly chuckled. She remembered all the stories about Jacqueline that Rachel had written to her while she was in prison. Those letters and Rachel's encouragement had kept her going when things seemed more than she could bear.

She walked into the dining room, turned up the lamp, and checked to make sure everything was in place. A light breeze blew in the window, but a flash of lightning pulled her across the room. If a storm blew in, she didn't want the floor to get wet. She shut the window and stared out, waiting for another flash.

Footsteps sounded behind her, and she turned. Luke strode in with Andrew on one arm. The baby's head rested in his father's hand, while the tiny body lay across Luke's forearm. Andrew looked so much smaller when Luke held him.

"Here you go. Rach' said he still needs to be patted since he just finished his supper." Luke handed her a clean diaper and waited while she draped it over her shoulder then passed his son to her.

"Take care of him."

"I will." Cuddling the baby, she walked around the table, satisfying herself that all was in order and no food had been overlooked on the floor. Then she turned down the lamp. In the dimly lit parlor, she sat in the rocking chair and patted the baby's back. She liked sitting in the dark. It was a habit she'd developed in prison, not by choice but because the lights were turned off shortly after supper.

In the dark, she'd been able to pretend she was somewhere else—anywhere except the hot cell she'd been locked in. She closed her eyes and laid her head back. Andrew squirmed, pumping his legs, and uttered a squeak.

Footsteps echoed down the hall. Luke and Rachel stopped at the front door. He opened it, but she turned toward the parlor.

"Andy's fussing. Maybe I should stay." Rachel nibbled her lower lip and took a step in Carly's direction.

Luke snagged her arm. "Nope. C'mon, Mama, Andrew is fine, your other little chicks are in the coop, and now the rooster wants to take a walk with you."

Rachel laughed and took his arm. "Why, you have such a way with words, Marshal Davis."

"Yep."

The door closed, leaving Carly alone. She loved how Luke and Rachel teased one another and joked. Loved the affection brimming from their eyes whenever one stared in the other's direction. She loved it, but it only emphasized what she'd never have.

No man wanted a convict for a wife. The women in prison had told her as much, not that many of them seemed to care if they married. And neither had she until she'd come back to Lookout and observed how a couple in love lived.

Now she wanted it all. A husband. A home. Children.

She glanced up at the dark ceiling. "Help me to turn loose of those dreams, Lord. They only cause me anguish."

Andrew jerked and screeched. Carly stood and bounced him up and down. She glanced at the front door. How long would Luke and Rachel be gone?

What should she do if the baby had a problem?

She walked down the hall, bouncing little Andrew and patting his back. The baby stiffened and wailed. If she didn't get him quiet, he might wake the other three, and she wasn't sure she was ready to handle all four children at once.

"Shhh, little fellow. You're all right." Her crooning helped but the moment she stopped, he kicked out his legs, and she nearly dropped him. "Hey now, settle down. Your mama will be back soon."

A knock sounded, startling Carly. She stared at the front door, knowing it wasn't locked. Who could be knocking at this hour?

Whoever it was pounded harder. Maybe there was a problem and someone wanted the marshal. She hurried to the door, baby crying, and peeked outside. Garrett Corbett's oh-so-beautiful blue eyes stared back, illuminated by dim light in the parlor. June bugs and moths flittered around the porch lantern. "Well, c'mon in before you let all the bugs inside."

He hurried through the door, shut it, and yanked off his western hat, revealing a sweat line that darkened his blond hair. "That wasn't exactly the greeting I was expecting." He flashed a teasing smirk. "What's wrong with Andy?"

"Sorry. And I don't know. He was fine until Rachel left. I'm supposed to pat him until he belches, but it's not working." Tears blurred her view of her guest. She wasn't qualified to care for a baby.

"Let me see him."

She tightened her grip on Andrew, raising her voice to be heard over his frantic wails. "What do you know about babies?"

"Watch and learn." He lifted Andrew out of her arms and carried him into the darkened parlor. He perched on the end of a chair, then set the baby on his lap. Holding the baby upright with his neck and head supported, Garrett patted circles on the baby's back. Andrew continued screeching.

"You're gonna wake the other children. Let me have him back." Carly reached for him.

Andrew stiffened suddenly, then a huge belch erupted from the tiny child, followed by a white arc of sputum.

"Ah!" Garrett spread his legs, but not fast enough. The milky white steam spread across his left leg.

Carly couldn't help the giggle that worked its way up. Garrett stared at his pants, unable to take his eyes off the stain. She covered her mouth and bent over, laughing harder than she had in years.

"It's not funny." He glared up at her.

"Yes it is. You should have seen your face." She yanked the diaper off her shoulder and handed it to him.

"Here, take this scoundrel. I try to make him feel better and he does *this* to me." He passed Andrew to her and attacked his pants with the diaper. "That's no way to say thanks, kid."

"At least he's quiet now."

Garrett grunted and held up the nasty wad of cloth. "Got another one of these?"

"Yes, just a minute." She turned up the lamp then hurried back to Rachel and Luke's room and laid Andrew in his cradle, hoping he'd be happy for a few minutes. In the kitchen, she grabbed a towel, dunked it in the water bucket, and took it to Garrett.

He scrubbed his pants like a man trying to wash away his sins. She noticed a spot on the floor and stooped down beside him to mop it up with a dry towel. His hand stilled, and she glanced up and found him watching her. She swallowed hard and stood. He copied her, which left them only a few feet apart.

Carly cleared her throat and backed away,

wondering at the odd sensations surging through her body. "Did you. . .uh. . .need to see the marshal?"

Garrett shook his head and kept gawking at her. She glanced down to make sure she didn't have a button unfastened or some food on her bodice. She'd never been comfortable staring men in the eye. Generally, she saw things in their gaze that she didn't want to see, and that scared her.

"Um. . .well, did you need to talk to Rachel?" she asked.

"No."

Perplexed, she looked up. "If you came to see Jacqueline, she's not here."

"I didn't."

Carly shoved her hands to her hips. "All the children are in bed, so what are you doing here?"

The tiniest of smiles lifted his lips. "I came to see you."

"Me?" She blinked, trying to remember if there was something she was supposed to give him or tell him, but nothing came to mind. "Whatever for?"

His smiled faded. "I thought you might like to take a walk."

"A walk?"

He nodded.

"Why?"

He shrugged one shoulder.

"It's getting ready to storm."

"No it's not."

"Yes it is. I saw lightning."

He stepped closer, and she tried to back up, but her calves bumped the coffee table.

"The storm is moving away from town," he said.

"Oh. Well, how do you know?"

"I've lived in Texas my whole life. I know."

"Oh." Unable to hold his steady gaze, she glanced

around the room. Why was he here again?

"So, do you wanna?" He held out his palms as if to hold her hand, begging her with his eyes to agree.

But those eyes made her mind go foggy, as if a cloud had taken up residence in her head. She placed her hands behind her back to avoid touching him. "Want what?"

"To go for a walk."

She shook her head. It would be completely inappropriate for her to walk with him in the dark. People would talk, and it could damage her reputation—such as it was. Besides, she couldn't leave the children unattended. "I can't."

"Oh." He shoved his hands inside his pockets. "All right. Guess I'll go then."

The light in his eyes dimmed. She watched him shuffle to the door, shoulders drooping, and a spear of regret stabbed her. Why would he want to walk with her? As far as she knew, he didn't even like her.

"Rachel and Luke aren't home, and neither is Jacqueline, so I can't go."

He spun back around. "You mean you would if you could?"

She shrugged. In truth, she would like to go, but she couldn't wrap her mind around why he'd want to. "I guess so. I just don't understand why you'd want to take a turn around town with *me*."

"Why wouldn't I?"

She stared at him. Had he been eating loco weed? "You know."

He shook his head. "Know what?"

Carly rolled her eyes and sighed. "You could hardly get off that wagon fast enough when you first learned who I was that day you brung me back here. Now you wanna walk with me in front of the whole town? I'm confused."

He scratched his blond hair and looked a bit perplexed himself. "I guess I've changed my mind."

"About what?"

"You."

"Why?"

His gaze flitted across her face, then her hair, and back down, as if he actually was attracted to her. She held her breath, not quite able to believe it might be true.

"You're different, and I—I kind of like it."

"Kind of?"

He flung his arms out sideways, making her jump. "Yes! No! Why are you making this so hard?"

"Making what so hard?"

He stared at her then suddenly spun away and stomped toward the door. "Never mind."

"Wait? Where are you going?"

"Leaving?" He yanked open the door.

"Why?" He had to be the most confounding man in the world.

He tossed a wounded glance over his shoulder. "I knew this was a bad idea."

Carly stomped her foot. "What is?" she all but yelled.

"Trying to court you."

"Court me?" Her voice rose to a high squeak. Could he actually be serious? Or maybe this was one of the pranks he was well known for pulling.

He must have noticed something change in her expression because he turned back toward her. "Didn't I make it clear that I want to court you?"

Carly laughed and shook her head. "No, you just asked me to take a walk."

"Isn't that the same thing?" The daft man looked honestly bewildered.

"Uh. . .no, it isn't." Carly shook her head, then

felt her cheeks warm. She peeked at him, looked away, then glanced back. She'd learned to be wary of Garrett Corbett ten years ago, back when he and his brothers had ordered the mail-order brides for Luke. He had a reputation for being a prankster, but since she'd returned to Lookout, he seemed different—as if he'd finally matured. Did she dare risk trusting him, even though she was attracted to him now?

She'd watched him play with Rachel and Luke's children. He was always gentle with them, but fun, and he made them laugh. He made her laugh when she watched them play.

Maybe he'd changed as much as she.

Maybe God would actually make her dream of marriage come true. "Uh. . .yes, I would be interested in. . .um. . .courting."

Garrett's wide grin was worth all the frustration of the past few minutes. He reached out and nearly shook her arm off, as if they'd sealed the business deal of the century. "Good," he said, then looped his thumbs in his pants pockets. "Good."

Rachel pushed the door open, stepping inside alone. Her cheeks were rosy and her eyes dancing. "Who's courting?"

Chapter 25

Jack closed her eyes and braced for the hard landing, praying only that she didn't reinjure her knee or fall into a pile of broken liquor bottles.

"Oompf!"

The masculine grunt took her by surprise as rough hands flailed around her skirts. Her back smashed into a hard body. Strong arms fumbled around her waist then found purchase, crushing her back against a solid chest. Her feet dangled in midair. She didn't know whether to scream or be relieved or just enjoy the fact that she was still alive and uninjured.

Then the arms tossed her up and whirled her around. She squealed but then squelched the sound almost as soon as it left her mouth. She caught Noah's familiar scent as he once again stopped her fall. He lowered her gently to the ground.

"What—do—you—think—you're—doing?" Noah's warm breath bathed her face, and she allowed herself to relax in spite of his harsh tone.

"Let's go," she whispered and pointed up at the open window above them.

The drunk leaned over. "Hey, li'l darlin', don't leave. Uh-oh." He uttered a rolling belch then bent farther over and made a vile retching sound.

Noah didn't need a second warning. He scooped her into his arms, raced past the back of Dolly's Dress

281

Shop, and then stopped behind Corbett's Freight office and deposited her rather roughly on the porch.

He crossed his arms, and she could barely make out his features in the moonlight. "Explain."

She rearranged her skirts as she sat on the hard wood and hiked her chin. He may have rescued her and saved her from hurting herself again, but she didn't owe the preacher an explanation for her behavior. "No."

He leaned into her face. "Yes."

She swung her legs off the porch, then jumped up, forcing him to step back. "I don't have to explain my actions to you."

He heaved a heavy sigh, and she was certain he muttered something about patience. She needed to get home. She had a story to write, and her family had surely realized she was missing by now. Her papa would come looking, if he wasn't already. What would he think to find her alone in an alley in the dark with the minister?

The bigger question was what would he do to the minister?

She glanced back at the saloon. The screen door banged shut. The drunk must have finished his business and gone back inside. She and Noah were truly alone—and why did that thought excite her? She should be irate at his brutish bullying, but she was too thankful that he'd been there to catch her.

Wait a minute.

She crossed her arms. "Just what were you doing behind the saloon?" She thought of the spectacle he must have seen when she nearly fell the first time. Her cheeks flamed. Had it been light enough that he'd seen her unmentionables?

"Me? What were you doing hanging from the saloon window?"

Her mind raced for a logical explanation. Finally

she shrugged. "You know me." Her voice rose at the end.

He barked a laugh. "Far better than you can imagine."

She crinkled her brow. "Just what does that mean?"

His humor fled as fast as it had come, and he stepped closer. "Why do you take such reckless chances, Jackie? Don't you know you're not invincible? You could have broken your leg or your pretty neck falling like that."

The sudden tenderness in his voice caused a lump in her throat, but her defenses weren't yet ready to surrender. "Why do you care?"

His sigh was a gentle caress on her cheek. "Because I do, that's all."

She wished she could read the expression in his eyes. How did he care? As a friend? Or as a man who maybe. . . "You're the minister. It's your job to care for your flock."

He grunted, stalked away, and leaned one hand against a nearby tree. Intrigued, Jack followed. He wasn't acting very preacherly, but rather like a man—dare she hope—in love. She held her breath. He would have to make the first move. Otherwise she'd never know for sure that his feelings hadn't come about because of her own for him.

She blinked in the dark. Maybe in the daytime she couldn't admit it, but here, alone with him in the moonlight, she knew the truth—she'd fallen hard for Noah Jeffers.

It made no sense.

It didn't fit into her plans.

But hadn't Pastor Taylor said on numerous occasions that God had far greater plans than man could ever imagine for himself—or herself?

Could it be God's plan that she be part of Noah's life?

Her stomach swirled with the possibilities of it all. Her knees—which hadn't shaken during her ordeal at the window—now trembled so hard she thought maybe she ought to sit back down.

Noah spun around so fast, she didn't have time to move. She must have surprised him because he jumped, then grabbed her upper arms. "Yes, I care about you because I'm the minister."

As if she'd licked her fingers and put out a candle flame, her hopes dimmed.

"But"—he gave her a gentle shake—"there's far more to it than that."

"Far more to what?" She hated how her voice warbled.

"I do care about you—and not just as a minister."

She licked her lips and swallowed. "You do?"

He didn't answer, but his head tilted downward. Her heartbeat skedaddled upward.

"I may be a preacher, but when it comes to you, I've never been able to express myself like I've wanted. I shouldn't do this, but will you allow me to show you how I feel?"

Her headed nodded as if she were a marionette controlled by strings and had no will of her own. She was too intrigued—too hopeful—to refuse.

His large hands cupped her cheeks, and she marveled that this big, strong man was trembling. He stood there a moment as if indecisive or possibly cherishing the moment, and then he bent down, his lips brushing hers as lightly as a wisp of Emmie's hair.

Jack's heart thundered in her chest and ears. She slid her hands up Noah's chest, and he deepened the kiss. Her senses popped to life, and she pressed her lips harder against his. He moaned and grabbed her up, clear off her feet, kissing her as if there were no tomorrow.

And then he all but dropped her and stepped away.

She swayed, still caught up in her roiling emotions and passion. She wanted to say, "Amazing!" but his stoic reaction held her silent. Did he regret kissing her? Had she not done it right?

What did she know about kissing? She'd never done it before—at least not with a man. Her one and only kiss had been when she kissed Ricky, her old friend, just to see what it felt like—and it was absolutely nothing like what she'd just experienced. She placed her hand over her heart.

"I'm sorry." Noah's deep voice sounded far huskier than normal. "I shouldn't have done that."

Jack narrowed her gaze, a different kind of fire simmering. How could he stir up all these feelings she never knew she had and then say he shouldn't have done that? Was she unworthy of his affections? She hauled back and clobbered him on the arm.

The moonlight illuminated his shocked expression. Then he started chuckling. "I probably deserved that."

"You did." But she wasn't sure if it was because he'd kissed her or because he hadn't kissed her again. She stomped her foot. Oh! She was so confused—and she didn't like being confused.

He reached out and took her hand. "C'mon, I should get you home. Your folks are probably worried."

And she had a story to write and get to Jenny first thing in the morning. But she hated to go, leaving things as they were. Why had he kissed her? Should she tell him of her growing attraction to him?

Noah rubbed his thumb across the back of her hand, sending delicious chills racing up her arm.

"I didn't hurt you when I caught you, did I?"

"No, though you scared me half to death. Thank you for saving me from getting hurt, but you never said why you were behind the saloon."

"Neither did you." She could see his white teeth as he grinned.

"Read the next edition of the paper, and you'll find out."

He stepped close and lifted a hand to her shoulder, still holding the other one. There went her knees a-wobblin' again.

"Jackie, please stop taking such chances. You're not a kid who can shinny up trees anymore; you're a grown woman—a very beautiful woman—in skirts and petticoats, not overalls." His grip tightened on her hand and she glanced up. "You could have hurt yourself in that fall, and I dread thinking what might have happened if that drunk had actually gotten 'hold of you."

He dropped her hand and took hold of her upper arms. "Please stop taking chances with your life. It's too precious to put in danger. Promise me you'll be more careful."

Tears blurred her eyes at the tenderness in his voice. No man had ever treated her with such care and sensitivity except for Luke. Not even her best friends growing up—Ricky and Jonesy. She nodded, but what came out of her mouth surprised even her. "I will if you'll kiss me again."

He stared down at her as if shocked. Then he glanced around and backed her up into the shadows of the building. "I shouldn't."

"That's what you said last time." She tugged on his shirt, pulling him closer. After having a father who spewed his anger like a snorting bull and battered his wife and daughter, she never thought to find a man she could fully trust. One so gentle that he'd never hurt her. A man like Luke. A man who went around town doing kind deeds for people—just because he had a good heart. Noah would never treat her cruelly or lie to her or hit her.

He shuffled his feet, as if he might bolt away any moment. "I can't. It isn't right. I'm the minister."

"Shhh. . .even ministers have a right to happiness and to find"—dare she say it—"love."

He sucked in a breath.

Yes, she loved him. She'd been fighting it for days. She had no clue how it had happened so fast, but she loved Noah Jeffers, and though she wanted to shout it to the world, she'd keep that secret to herself and savor it for a while.

The crickets seemed to cheer him on. Off in the distance an owl hooted. "Please, Noah, kiss me one more time before we go in."

He chuckled. "You're a wanton woman, Miss Davis."

"No, not wanton, just a woman on the edge of a cliff, who's about to jump off."

He exhaled another heavy breath. "Me, too, darling. Me, too." He lifted her up and set her back down on the bottom step to Garrett's office. "This way I don't get a crick in my neck—not that I minded all that much."

She couldn't help giggling and boldly reached up and placed her hands on his shoulders. They were far wider and more solid than she'd imagined. She continued exploring, letting her hands wander around his neck where she fingered the hair on his nape. He tilted his face up, eyes closed, as if enjoying the moment. She gently tugged him toward her.

Dallas was looking less and less appealing with each second that passed.

Carly stared at Rachel then glanced at Garrett, hoping he would explain the courting thing. He just stood there with his hands in his pockets, a silly grin on his face.

Rachel's pale blue eyes went wide as her hand flew to her chest. "Not you two?"

Garrett's smile slipped, and he crossed his arms. "What's wrong with that?"

"Nothing. It's just a shock." Rachel glanced between Carly and Garrett, then shrugged. "I mean, it's just that I've never even seen you talking to each other. Have you prayed about it?"

"Well, no, not yet." Garrett kicked at the leg of the nearest chair. "Can't a guy take a gal for a walk without everyone gettin' in an uproar?"

"Of course, I'm sorry. But you didn't say anything about a walk."

Garrett had that confused look again. He reached up and scratched his temple, and Carly's gaze wandered up to his blond hair. Would it be soft like hers or stiff and coarse? "What's the difference in walkin' and courtin'?"

Rachel nearly choked on a laugh. "You've got to be kidding, Garrett."

He shook his head. "I'm not. A man doesn't take a woman walkin' around town unless he's interested in her. Too many folks would start talkin'."

"Well, I can see your point, but you need to seek God on something so serious." Rachel didn't smile. Carly shifted from one foot to the other. Did her friend think it wrong for her and Garrett to be interested in one another? Rachel had everything, not that she hadn't struggled in years past, and now Carly wanted the same thing, with the exception of such a big house.

"Is Andrew asleep?" Rachel asked, seeming suddenly sober.

"I'm not sure. I laid him in his bed after he belched." Carly crossed her arms. Did Rachel think she wasn't good enough for her husband's cousin? She grimaced, rejecting that idea. Rachel was right that they should pray about courting, but was there anything wrong with getting to know a man first and then seeking God about their future?

"Where's Luke? I thought you two took a stroll." Garrett reached for his hat, rolling the brim on one side.

Rachel stopped in the parlor entrance. "Oh, Terrance Gruber ran up and told Luke there'd been another break-in, but I didn't hear where. Sometimes I wish the town had stayed small like it was years ago. With growth comes problems." She nodded at each of them. "I'd better go check on the baby."

A tight fist clenched Carly's chest. Would folks blame her for this newest robbery?

She stared at the floor. Left alone with Garrett, she suddenly felt awkward. She knew how to talk to this man when her ire burned, but what did she say now?

"Well. . ."

"I. . ."

They both talked at once. Garrett smiled, and she relaxed a bit. He really was a handsome man.

"You go first," he said.

She shook her head.

He gently touched her arm. "Go on. I won't bite."

She shrugged and stared down at his dusty boot tops. They needed to be cleaned and polished. The end of his trousers had frayed bits sticking where he must have torn them. The man sure needed a woman to care for him, but was she the right woman? Dare she believe God had sent him in answer to her prayer?

"Carly. . ."

She glanced up at his use of her Christian name, liking the mellow tone of his voice. "You'll probably think it's silly," she admitted, "but I'm afraid folks will think I caused the break-in."

His eyes went wide. "Why would they think that? You've been here all evening, haven't you?"

"Yes, but folks talk, especially when there's an ex-convict livin' among them."

Garrett winced as if she'd hauled back and punched him.

"Surely you realize the gossip you'll be facing if you and I court. Have you considered that it could affect your business?"

He lowered his head, and she could see that he hadn't. She feared the side of his hat would be as curled as Tessa Morgan's hair on Sunday morning if he didn't stop scrunching it. She tugged it from his hands then stretched up and set it on his head. "Go home, Garrett. Thank you for asking me to court. I am deeply honored, but before we consider such a thing, you need to think it through—completely. Reflect on how a relationship with me could hurt your business."

"I'm thinking about changing businesses."

Carly wondered about that, but now wasn't the time to discuss it. A moth flittered between them. Garrett reached out faster than she could blink and caught it. A shy grin tilted one side of his mouth—his very appealing mouth. He held up his closed fist. "Guess I'd better go so I can turn this critter loose."

She nodded and crossed to the door. "If you're serious about us courting, promise me you'll pray about it—and that you'll only ask me again if God gives His blessing."

He stared at her a long while then inhaled a deep breath through his nose. "I will. I should have done it before, but I just—just got it in my head that we'd be good together and headed on down here."

With a boldness she didn't know she possessed, she reached up and cupped his cheek. A day's worth of light stubble tickled her fingers. "Thank you. You have no idea how much your offer means to me."

He pressed his hand against hers, turned it, and kissed her palm. Then he scowled. "Shoowy! We smell like baby spit-up."

Carly giggled and gently pushed him outside. Jacqueline and the pastor walked across the street, and Garrett greeted them. She closed the door, then hustled up the stairs, not quite ready to face another inquiry about her and Garrett.

Standing with her hand on her doorknob, she listened for the children. Only the sound of heavy breaths—and one nasally snort—could be heard. She smiled and entered her room. Leaning back against the closed door she thought of how her life might have taken a new road this evening—and she prayed it might be God's plan for her.

Kissing Jackie was wrong, no matter how good it felt. Surely it couldn't be God's plan for him. Berating himself, Noah hurried upstairs while Jackie went to say good night to her folks.

But he had to admit, kissing her—holding her close—had been the fulfillment of a long-held dream, and far better than he'd ever dreamed. His steps slowed. Imagine Jacqueline Hamilton Davis kissing him. He shook his head. Maybe it had all been a dream.

That was it.

He must be sleepwalking.

But if that was the case, he wouldn't feel so

guilty. He'd always admired Jackie's spunk and determination, even when it got her in trouble. He snorted a laugh—even when she got *him* in trouble. And she had. Plenty of times.

He closed the door to his room then dropped onto the desk chair. Bending over, he rested his elbows on his hands and forked his fingers through his hair. With the exception of a relationship with God, he'd never wanted anything as much as he desired a relationship with Jackie.

Was that wrong of him? Shouldn't a man of God be content to reach his whole flock and not be attracted to one pretty woman? One very beautiful woman who set his senses on fire and flamed his dreams. Dreams of a home—a loving wife—a family.

If only Pete were here, he'd tell Noah what to do.

The wind lifted a corner of the curtain, as if the Spirit of God drifted in. He needed to pray and find that comforting peace God always brought him, but part of his mind said he never should have come back to Lookout.

Yet in spite of all his initial objections, he realized now that a part of him had never left here.

He fell to his knees, head on the floor, and cried out to God. "Show me what to do, Lord. Help me to stay on the path that You want me to walk—and if Jackie isn't—" Just thinking the words gutted him. How could he say them out loud?

But to hold back anything from God was wrong. If he gathered Jackie up and held her close to his heart and refused to let her go, he'd be wrong. He had to give her to God—and if God chose to give her back, that would be the greatest day of his life.

Chapter 26

Jack strode into the *Lookout Ledger*'s office, relishing the familiar odors of ink and paper. She slapped her article down on top of the editor's desk.

Jenny jumped. She pushed her wire-framed glasses up her nose and scowled. "Can't you walk in all quiet and graceful, like most ladies?"

Ignoring her friend's intentional barb, Jack smiled. "I finally did it."

"Did what?"

"Got my scoop—the story I wanted that will land me a job in Dallas." As soon as she said the words, they tasted like curdled milk in her mouth. She'd stayed up half the night writing her article and the other half thinking about Noah's kisses and trying to decide what to do. Was she ready to give up her long-time dream for a man? Did she actually want to leave Lookout and go to a town where she knew no one?

Jenny glanced down and read the article. With an ink-stained finger, she followed the letters Jack had written. Jack looked around the familiar office. Papers littered the building, stacked in every nook and cranny, and the large black printer sat in one corner, looking alone and ignored for the moment.

Pulling off her glasses, Jenny eyed her, as if weighing the truth of the article. "You've actually confirmed that the railroad is coming? I've been trying to pin down that info for months, without a speck of luck. Who's your source?"

"I overheard the mayor talking with those two men he's been escorting all over town." Satisfaction welled up inside Jack, making her sit up straighter. She'd finally gotten her big story. There was a powerful feeling of success that she'd outsmarted the mayor, in spite of his avoiding her, and had learned what he'd tried so hard to keep quiet.

Yet writing this story, even though it was the biggest of her career, didn't excite her as she'd expected it would. What was wrong with her?

A vision of Noah illuminated by the moonlight drifted through her mind. She hadn't admitted it to Tessa or Penny, but she'd been attracted to him from the start. There was something about him that made her feel connected—as if they'd been friends for years instead of weeks. She couldn't believe she was in love.

"If that grin on your face means what I think, I'd say you've got a right to be proud. I've not heard hide nor hair about a hotel being built here. How does your ma feel about it?"

Jack sucked in her top lip. What would Jenny say if she knew that it was Noah on her mind and not the article? "I haven't told her yet. I don't know how."

Jenny lifted one brown brow. "You'd better tell her before the paper comes out."

"I will."

"Good job on this. It ought to stir up a lot of talk around town."

Jack nodded. "Probably so."

Jenny reached in a drawer and pulled out a letter, a tiny smile dancing on her lips. She held it as if it were something special, then handed it to Jack. "I admit to having mixed feelings about giving you this, but I have a surprise."

Curiosity bolted through her as fast as a horse off a starting line. Her heart flip-flopped. The wrinkled envelope addressed to Jenny Evans had *Dallas Morning News* imprinted in the upper left corner. She ran her thumb over the embossed letters, her hand shaking. Could this actually be the realization of her dream? Her gaze lifted to Jenny, whose mouth stretched into a wide smile.

"Go ahead, open it."

She pulled the paper from the envelope and nearly dropped it. She lifted the top of the page and began reading:

> *Dear Jenny,*
>
> *Thank you for your letter recommending Jacqueline Davis as a reporter for the* Dallas Morning News. *I have read over the clippings you sent and am impressed with Miss Davis's writing skill and creative talent for recording details while keeping the story interesting. Coming from a small town, she would have a fresh perspective on life in Dallas.*
>
> *I've discussed Miss Davis with my superiors, and we are prepared to offer her a position in our Home Living Section. Should she accept the position, she will be responsible for posting a recipe each issue, researching and discussing new and innovative products that women could use in their homes, and covering fashion trends.*

Jack's hopes sank. "What do I know of fashion? I'd never wear a dress if it was socially acceptable for a woman to wear pants."

"Just keep reading."

Not quite as enthused as a moment ago, she started reading again:

*If Miss Davis proves herself, as I believe
she will based on your recommendation, we
can discuss moving her into a more challenging
position in the future. Just one thing, I can hold
this position only until the end of the month, so
please inform Miss Davis to contact me at her
earliest convenience should she desire it.*

*As always, if you're in Dallas, Jenny, be
sure to stop in and allow me to take you to eat.
We have some delightful cafés here.*

Your friend,
Amanda Jones Bertram

Jack stared at the letter, trying to make sense of
her roiling emotions.

Yes—she had a job offer from a Dallas newspaper.

No—it wasn't the job she wanted.

Yes—there was the potential to one day become
a news reporter.

But did she truly want to leave her family? To
leave Noah?

In less than three weeks?

Jenny leaned back in her chair, her mouth twisted
to one side and brows lifted. Jack sincerely hoped her
less-than-enthusiastic response didn't offend Jenny.

"Tell me what's going on in that creative mind of
yours. I know the Home Living Section isn't what you
had your heart set on, but I halfway expected you to
be packing your bags by now."

She had no idea how to answer her friend. Stalling,
she blew out a heavy breath and read the missive again.

"Humph. It's a man, isn't it?"

Jack glanced up as her pulse jumped. "What?"

A knowing smile softened Jenny's face. "You've
met someone, and now you're not so sure you want
to leave town."

"How do you know?"

"What else would stop a determined young woman like you from chasing her dream once it's finally within reach?"

"What should I do?"

Jenny shrugged. "Only you can decide that." She suddenly leaned forward, eyes narrowed. "But tell me who the man is. I may be the newspaper editor, but you really slipped the wool over my eyes on this story."

Jack tried hard to control the embarrassed smile that twittered on her lips, but she couldn't. "It all happened rather fast."

"Surely it's not that Billy Morgan."

She shuddered at the thought of it. "Certainly not. Though if he had his way, we'd be married tomorrow. I can't seem to get it through his head that I'm not interested."

"Then who is it?"

"I don't know if I should say. I'm not sure where things are headed."

"And yet it's serious enough for you to consider not following your dream to Dallas."

"I suppose."

Jenny lowered her head for a few moments, then looked at Jack again. "I know you're independent-minded and don't care for folks telling you what to do, but if you have some young man interested, one who can support you and cares about you, that's a far better choice than working your feet and fingers to the bone, trying to sniff out stories for a paper."

Jack's mouth fell open. "I never thought I'd hear you vote for marriage over work."

"I've lived alone for a long while and had time to reflect on things. I love my work, but as you get older, you think more about marriage and children. If I could do things over, I'm not certain I'd do them the same, but that's water under the bridge."

"You're not too old to get married."

Jenny snorted a laugh. "I'm too set in my ways. Besides, we're not talking about me. What are you going to do?"

"I don't know."

"Maybe you should talk to your folks and get some advice. 'Course, neither one will like the idea of you running off to Dallas. And mind me, I *will* find out who your beau is."

Jack knew she would. Jenny was good at her job. Hadn't Jenny taught her all that she knew about reporting?

"I'd better get back home. Ma will be needing my help." She held the letter to her chest. "I can't thank you enough for this, Jenny."

Her friend swatted her hand in the air. "Glad to help, although I don't know what I'll do without you."

Jack smiled and stepped outside. The May sun shone bright, promising another beautiful day. Wildflowers had popped up along the edges of the boardwalk, adding color to the barren dirt street.

She felt as if she were being pulled in two directions at once, both having tremendous possibilities. The job in Dallas would mean a whole new life. A big city. New friends. New adventures.

But how could she leave her family?

How could she not watch Andrew learn to crawl? To talk?

And what about Noah?

She hadn't known him long, but he sparked something inside her that she'd never felt before. He made her want to be a woman for the first time in her life. To try hard to be a better person.

As she crossed Bluebonnet Lane, she couldn't help wondering which side of the tug-of-war would win.

Chapter 27

Jack was glad Jenny was such an early riser and had been at her office before breakfast. Waiting any longer to turn in her story would have been difficult. She reached for the doorknob of her house. A shrill scream suddenly rent the quiet morning. She spun around, frantically searching Main Street. Nothing looked out of place. A wagon was parked in front of the livery, but no one was on the street or boardwalk. What had happened?

Jenny burst out of the newspaper office, as did several other shop owners, each one looking around. It was far too early to be a saloon girl's phony squeal when chased by an eager cowboy. Besides, the scream had sounded real—as if someone had been harmed or frightened out of their wits.

Agatha Linus stumbled from between Dolly's Dress Shop and the Corbett Freight office. Jack hurried down the steps of her home, stuffing the letter from the *Dallas Evening News* into her waistband. She hiked her skirts and ran down the street, hoping her ma didn't see her.

Aggie wobbled, then reached for the dress shop's porch railing and collapsed against it. One hand covered her eyes; her head hung down. Was she crying? Hurt?

"Please, help me." She shuddered and dropped

onto the boardwalk steps.

Jack rushed to her side, as did Jenny and several others. "What's wrong, Mrs. Linus? Are you ill?"

She swiped her eyes with her fingertips then reached out her hand, and Jack took hold of it. "Oh, Jacqueline, it's dreadful. I—I fear my sister is dead."

Jack's heart jolted. It had been a long while since someone in their community had died. "Bertha is dead? How? What happened?"

"I'll get the doctor to come and check her," said Mr. Mann, who had been eating at Polly's Café and still had his napkin tucked in his shirt like a bib. He took off at a quick clip down the street.

Aggie shook her head. "It's all my fault, you see. I was feeling poorly and slept late. I should have been up to fix Bertha's breakfast. She does like her biscuits and jam of a morning."

Jack glanced at Jenny, who gave a shrug and quick shake of her head, as if she couldn't make any sense out of the connection between breakfast and Bertha, either. There had to be more to the story.

Jack glanced over her shoulder and noticed Tessa standing just outside the mercantile door. "Tessa!" She waved her hand to catch her friend's attention. "Could you run over and see if Luke is still at home?"

Tessa glanced across the street at them as if she didn't want to miss anything, then nodded. She untied her apron, tossed it inside the store, and hurried to the boardinghouse.

Jack patted Aggie's wrinkled hand. She was as thin as her sister was wide.

Aggie, normally a shy, refined woman, sucked in a hiccupy sob. "Oh, what will I do without her?"

Shifting her feet to a more comfortable position, Jack couldn't help thinking Aggie would live a more peaceful life without her gossiping sister, who constantly ordered her around, but as soon as the thought breached her mind, she cast it off as not Christian. Her heart ached for Aggie, and her chest swelled with compassion. The woman had lost her husband years ago, and now she may have lost her sister.

The thud of quick footsteps drew her gaze up, and Jack's pulse soared. Right behind Luke, Noah followed, looking concerned. His black eye had faded to a greenish-yellow tone, and the cuts from his fight with Billy had healed. His gaze collided with hers. She felt that connection—two separate beings that belonged together—soul mates.

"All right, move back, folks and let me through." Luke pushed his way into the crowd and squatted in front of Aggie. Noah stopped beside Jack, so close their arms touched when she moved. The back of his hand brushed against hers. Jack's throat clogged, making it harder to breathe.

"Tell me what happened, Miss Aggie." Luke pushed his hat back on his forehead, as if to see her better.

"I don't know. I came downstairs a bit later than normal and found Bertha lying on the kitchen floor." Her lower lip wobbled, and tears ran down her wrinkled cheeks. "Th–there was b–blood on the floor. My sister's blood." Aggie covered her eyes again, her shoulders shaking from her sobs.

Luke glanced up at Jack. "Take her back to our house, and let your ma tend her."

"No!" Aggie's hand snaked out and latched on to Luke's arm. "I need to be with Bertha."

Luke covered her hand with his. "Are you certain?"

Aggie nodded, and he helped her to stand. He caught Jack's eye, and she hurried to Aggie's other side.

"The rest of you folks go on back to whatever you were doing. You'll know soon enough what happened."

"I. . .I'd like the reverend to come along, Marshal."

Luke nodded at Noah, and he fell in step behind them. Jenny jogged up to Luke. "I want to come, too."

He shook his head. "Not right now, Jenny."

Scowling, Jenny caught Jack's eye, and she knew that her friend expected to hear every little detail later on. Jack gave her a brief nod, but for once, she had no desire to write a story. Shouldn't Aggie be allowed to grieve before the details were splattered across the paper for the whole county to see? Why had she never considered how covering the news might actually emotionally wound the people involved?

They cut between buildings and went in Aggie's back door. Though Jack had visited Aggie and Bertha with her ma and had been in the parlor previously, she had never been in their kitchen. On the counter, several canisters were overturned with sugar and coffee spilling out. The pantry door lay open, revealing a mess with containers and jars sitting haphazard on the shelves, while others lay strewn all over the floor. Something definitely wasn't right here. Bertha may not be the tidiest person around, but Aggie most surely was.

Noah's hand gripped her shoulder, and she peeked up at him. He nudged his chin across the room where Luke and the doctor were kneeling on the floor. Jack's heart nearly lurched out of her chest at the large, unmoving body on the floor. She backed up against Noah, silently drawing his support. Aggie stood alone, staring down at her sister. Jack crossed the room and put her arm around the older woman's waist.

She winced at the blood pooling beneath Bertha's head. The woman's hair had been fashioned into the untidy bun that characterized her, and her colorful dress spread out around her like a spray of wildflowers.

Doc Phillips held his fingers against Bertha's neck. He looked up and shook his head. Aggie gasped and turned toward Jack, sobbing on her shoulder.

After a few moments, Noah gently took Aggie's arm. "Let's go in the parlor and let the doctor and marshal tend your sister."

Aggie allowed them to lead her from the room, but just as Jack stepped across the kitchen's threshold, she heard Doc Phillips whisper, "Murder."

∽

Noah stood before a somber crowd of parishioners Sunday morning. He should be happy that more people had shown up this week, but he'd rather their motivation for coming to church be heartfelt rather than fear-driven. Three break-ins and a murder had folks quivering in their beds behind doors that had rarely been locked before.

"Agatha Linus asked me to personally thank those of you who attended her sister's funeral yesterday and for all the gracious condolences she has received. Let's remember to keep her in our prayers—as well as little Adam Howard, who fell and twisted his ankle yesterday. Lastly, congratulations to Luke and Rachel Davis on the birth of their second son, Andrew."

"And to you, too, Pastor," Dan Howard called out, "for saving the baby's life."

"Thank you, but that was the Lord's doing, not mine." He smiled. "Please join me in prayer." He directed a prayer heavenward, then opened his Bible. "In Jeremiah 29, we read, 'For I know the thoughts that I think toward you, saith the Lord, thoughts of peace, and not of evil, to give you an expected end. Then shall ye call upon me, and ye shall go and pray unto me, and I will hearken unto you. And ye shall seek me, and find me, when ye shall search for me with all your heart.'"

He stared at the faces in the crowd, hoping to touch some hearts today—to bring a lost soul to the Lord.

Jackie sat on the third row with most of her family, holding Andrew so that Rachel could sit with Mrs. Linus at her home. The peaceful scene of Jackie looking down at the baby, surrounded on both sides by wiggly children, created longings he shouldn't be having during a sermon. He caught Luke's stare, and the man lifted one brow as if asking what he was doing. Noah jerked his gaze away and focused on a scowling man in the back.

"God wants good things for us, folks. He truly does, but I know what some of you are thinking—what about Mrs. Boyd? How could God allow an innocent woman to be murdered?

"John 10:10 says, 'The thief cometh not, but for to steal, and to kill, and to destroy: I am come that they might have life, and that they might have it more abundantly.' God loves each of us, folks, and wants good things for us, but evil has entered this world. Evil lies in the heart of man. The scriptures say that 'all men have sinned,' but the good news is that we don't have to remain in sin. Jesus died to set us free—to forgive our sins."

Noah's heart pounded. He felt God's anointing on his message and believed it would bring change in someone's life. God had changed his life so much, and he longed to share the forgiveness and joy he'd received with others.

"We may never know why tragedies happen, but we have to believe in God and let Him strengthen us in hard times. Don't get angry at God when tragedy strikes, but rather run to His comforting arms. Know who your enemy is. And let me tell you, it's not your neighbor—or his goat that wanders into your garden, eating what doesn't belong to him." Titters circled the room, and heads nodded.

"Preach it, brother!" Doc Phillips hollered.

"Don't be a casualty of war." Noah leaned across the pulpit, trying to get closer to his parishioners. Outside the open windows, birds flitted in the trees, chirping and singing as if cheering him on. "God is amazing, folks. Can you believe that the One who created the world cares about you—each one of you? He wants you to seek Him in all areas of your life, not just when tragedy strikes.

"Are you struggling with an important decision in your life? What line of cattle to purchase? Whether to plant wheat or corn next year? Whether to marry that pretty gal who's stolen your heart?" His gaze skittered to Jackie then dashed away. Luke straightened in his seat and crossed his arms, making Noah not a little anxious.

He cleared his throat. "The point I'm trying to make is that God cares. He cares about every little detail of your life. He wants you to draw nigh unto Him, confess your sins, and let Him wash you clean. Don't make important decisions without God's guidance. 'But seek ye first the kingdom of God, and his righteousness; and all these things shall be added unto you.' Shall we pray?"

Abby and Alan were on their feet and pushing past Jack the moment Noah bowed his head. She lifted one foot to block their escape during the prayer, then her papa snagged each wayward child by the collar and stuffed them back in their seat.

Noah's deep voice gently rumbled through the

room. She loved the sound of his voice—so masculine and strong. His words—as if directed right for her—had pierced her heart. Most of her life she'd tried to control her circumstances. After living in a home so out-of-control when her first pa was alive, she'd sought to never be vulnerable again—and that meant being able to take care of herself. It meant making choices, even when it went against her ma, especially before Luke came into their lives. He brought stability and took care of them, but her independent spirit had already taken root. She'd done what had to be done—and never much considered if it was God's will for her life. Until now.

The tone of Noah's voice changed, drawing her from her reflections. "We'll be taking an hour-long break to enjoy the wonderful meal the ladies of our church have provided, and then the marriage of Rand Kessler and Christine Morgan will take place outside under the arbor." All eyes swung toward the engaged couple, and Mrs. Morgan blushed. Tessa sat beside her ma, dressed in a pink silk gown with enormously puffed leg-o-mutton sleeves and wearing a scowl. Jack hadn't seen Billy all week, but surely he'd attend his mother's wedding.

"If anyone cares to talk to me privately about today's message, just track me down. Y'all are dismissed."

Noah closed his Bible, and Jack couldn't help noticing that he glanced at her. She smiled. He gave her a brief nod then turned to shake Dan Howard's hand. Luke stepped into the aisle, carrying Emmie, and chased after Alan and Abby, who'd already made their escape and were no doubt headed for the food tables.

"Jacqueline, let me see that baby." Leah Howard pressed up the aisle against the flow of the crowd with seven-month-old Michael on her hip. The white-haired child grinned and reached for Andrew, his dark eyes dancing. Leah stood back, keeping her son from touching Andrew. Little Sarah held on tight to her mother's skirt and stared at the baby with wide blue eyes.

Jack couldn't help being a little jealous that the girl was so much better behaved than Abby. She held up her brother. "We're sure glad to get another boy."

"I bet your father and Alan are especially happy."

Jack chuckled. "You should have heard Alan's yell when he found out he had a brother."

Leah hadn't changed a lot in the decade she'd been married. Her blond hair was fashioned into a bun and pinned on the back of her head. Jack tossed her loose hair over her shoulder and glanced at Noah. Would he like her hair better if she succumbed to womanly standards and wore it pinned up?

Leah smiled. "Our new minister is quite a handsome man, isn't he?"

Jack tried to mask her surprise at Leah's direct comment. "I. . .uh. . .suppose."

Baby Michael grabbed his ma's nose, and she pulled his hand away and kissed it then lifted her eyebrows at Jack. "You suppose?"

Jack couldn't help smiling. "All right, I noticed."

Leah laughed, her blue eyes sparkling. She nodded her chin toward the door. "I sure am surprised to see those two together. I'd never have thought it—not in a million years."

Jack turned and looked. Voices lifted in friendly chatter, and clusters of people stood near the door, including Garrett and Carly. "Me neither, but they seem happy, and I'm happy for them."

"Well, it will be good to see the last boardinghouse bride married—if things lead to that."

Leah's six-year-old son limped toward her. "Ma, I'm starvin'. Can we go eat? I wanna play with Alan."

"Ma, Adam disobeyed me." Naomi, half a head taller than her brother, pushed Adam out of the way and stood in front of her mother. "I told him to sit and wait for you and pa, but he didn't."

"You two may go outside, but don't get into the food yet." Leah stared at her son. "Mind your sister, and be careful. You don't want to hurt your ankle more. I'll be right out."

Jack watched the duo head for the door. "I imagine your house is busier than ours—and things get pretty hectic at ours."

"Yes, things are pretty busy. Remember when I broke off my engagement to Dan because I didn't want to be a mother?"

Jack nodded. "Yeah, I do."

"Let me be a testimony that God can change hearts. Nine children—I never could have imagined I'd be happy with so many."

"At least you don't have twins."

Leah lifted her hand to her forehead. "Oh my. I thank the good Lord for that, but if He chooses to send a pair my way, I'll take them and be glad. Speaking of children, I should head outside and check on them all. The big ones keep good watch most of the time, but the little ones are fast and far too sneaky for my likin'."

"It's good talking to you."

Leah glanced over her shoulder as she made her way to the front. "You, too."

Andrew stretched and then muttered a squeak. Jack scooted out of the pew, just as Margie Mann strode toward her. Jack uttered a sigh and prepared herself for a lecture.

"Jacqueline Davis, what in the world are you

doing with a newborn in church? What was your mother thinking?"

Jack lifted her chin a smidgen and tried to control her temper. "She was thinking of Mrs. Linus and how to best comfort her on her sister's loss. She didn't sleep well last night, and Ma didn't want the baby to disturb her rest this morning."

"Humph. I never took my young'uns out until they was a full month old." She turned and sashayed down the aisle.

Picking up the spare diaper she'd brought in case Andrew decided to relieve his belly, Jack moved toward the front. Noah was there alone, staring at her with a soft smile on his lips. Her thoughts immediately shifted to the memory of those same lips on hers, and her pulse sped up. "Your sermons are getting better each week."

Noah chuckled. "Wouldn't be too hard to improve on that first one."

"Yeah, well, it *was* entertaining." She grinned.

He sobered and shook his head. "I still can't believe I preached about pelicans. I don't remember saying that at all."

She wanted to reach out and rest her hand on his arm but resisted. Church wasn't the place to show affection, especially to the preacher.

"You going to eat?"

"Yes, but I need to run Andrew back to Ma first."

He stared down at her, affection shining in his eyes. "Will you forgive me if I don't sit with you? It might be a bit overwhelming for the townsfolk this soon."

Disappointment weighted her shoulders, but she forced a smile. "Sure. I'll have to help Pa with the children anyhow."

He glanced toward the door and stepped closer.

309

"You know I'd like nothing more than to be with you, don't you?"

A lump formed in her throat, and she nodded. He smiled, then reached out and gently squeezed her upper arm.

Jack sighed and watched him go, affection for the kind, gentle man wearing down any remaining defenses she might have. She remembered Leah's words about how God had changed her heart and couldn't help wondering if He was changing hers, too.

Chapter 28

"That was a fine sermon, young man." The mayor slapped Noah on the back, nearly dislodging the plate of food from his hand. Mayor Burke waved an ear of corn, dripping in butter, at him. "I'm certain you saved some sinners with that one. You might make a preacher yet."

Noah could barely abide the holier-than-thou man, but if he wanted to keep peace, he needed to hold his temper in check. And when the truth of his identity was revealed, Mayor Burke would most likely be one of his harshest opponents. "Thank you, sir, but I don't save sinners. Only God can do that."

"Yes, well. . ." The mayor glanced past him, then waved his corn again and strode off. "Perkins, hold up there."

Lord, save that man's soul. Noah couldn't help smiling at how Mr. Perkins sidestepped the mayor and hustled back to the food tables that lined the edge of the church's back lot.

Noah wandered through the crowd, mingling with the townsfolk, getting to know people he'd only met before, but his gaze kept drifting down Apple Street, where he'd last seen Jackie walking away from the crowd. She'd looked so pretty in her light green dress, which swayed like a bell when she walked.

"Parson Jeffers."

Noah turned back, and Dan Howard strode toward him, his sleeping baby balanced in one of the liveryman's big arms. Noah had remembered the livery owner was one of Luke's friends, and his wife was one of the women who'd originally come to town to marry the marshal.

"Mighty good message today, Parson."

Dan was the only man in town Noah could look eye-to-eye with, and he had a pretty wife and a whole passel of children. Noah hoped one day God would bless him as He had Dan. "How's my horse doin'?"

"Good! My boy spoils him with a carrot every now and then."

"I'm glad. I need to ride him more."

A young boy about Alan's size limped toward them and halted beside Dan. "Pa, Ma says to come 'cause it's time for d'sert."

"I'm coming." He ruffled the boy's brown hair, then glanced back at Noah. "This here's a good town, Parson. Don't let Mayor Burke put a burr under your saddle. You're doin' just fine. You'll hav'ta come to supper one night soon."

"I'd like that—and I appreciate the advice." Noah nodded, and Dan returned to his family.

Soon he'd perform the marriage ceremony of Rand Kessler and Mrs. Morgan—his first wedding. His stomach swirled at the thought, but not enough to make him set aside the plate of delicious food. He spooned in a bit of mashed turnips, almost yellow from the butter that had been added. He never would have thought that he would preside over his first funeral and wedding, one day apart.

Leaning against the side of the church, he finished his food as he watched friends and families joining together on old quilts to eat and converse. The sun shone bright overhead in a clear sky, but not so much to make the day too hot to enjoy. Children raced around the outskirts of the crowd, chasing one another, laughing, and having fun. A boy held up a garden snake, and Abby Davis let out a shrill scream that turned heads. Noah chuckled. He'd rarely felt so at home in a town.

A peace and contentment he'd never encountered, other than when he first gave his heart to God, wafted through him. An acceptance that filled a hollow place deep within. He wanted to stay in Lookout. To live here. To marry Jackie.

But he needed to tell folks the truth about his past before he could realize that dream.

He just needed a little more time.

Jack hurried down the street after passing a fussy Andrew back to her ma. She hadn't wanted to go in Mrs. Linus's house so soon after seeing Bertha Boyd's dead body, so she checked on her ma from the front porch and passed her brother through the doorway. Jack had covered a lot of stories for the paper, but rarely did they ever include a dead person. Mrs. Linus must be brave to stay in the house after all that had happened.

Jack's stomach growled, and she picked up her steps. She could see the townsfolk gathered in the lot next to the church and sure hoped there'd be some food left. If she'd been smart, she'd have asked someone to save her a plate.

She couldn't quit thinking about Noah's message. Having always been independent and resourceful, she had a tendency to act without thinking. As a child, thanks to her willful streak, she'd done pretty much what she wanted. No wonder her mother had been so frustrated with her back then. Under Luke's guidance, she learned to find joy in pleasing her mother, but she still fought stubbornness and the desire to do things on impulse.

She believed in God, but she hadn't prayed about her future, other than a few frantic pleas for help or guidance on occasion, like when Andrew almost died. She hadn't sought God first in her daily life, but Noah had helped her see the need to change that.

How could she make such an important decision like going to Dallas or staying here to see how things worked out with Noah without God's guidance?

A man suddenly jogged out from between two houses. Yanked from her musings, Jack jumped. A nut brown hat was pulled down low, blocking his face, and he strode purposely toward her. The only times she'd ever been truly frightened had been in her own home when her other pa was alive and when her ma had been kidnapped by an outlaw, but with all the robberies and now a murder, her nerves had a hair trigger. Jack glanced around for a rock or stick for defense, but then she recognized the man's walk—Billy.

Horse feathers.

She didn't want to argue with him again about getting married. That would never happen. She moved away from him, hurrying her steps, but he broke into a run, then skidded to a halt, blocking her way. Jack sighed, her doubts rising about there being any food left except for Margie Mann's baked beets, which everyone but newcomers knew not to touch. Since she couldn't get away from Billy, she might as well be cordial. "Where have you been? I haven't seen you all week."

He pushed his hat up his forehead and grinned. "Did you miss me?"

Well, she'd walked right into that quagmire. "I

just noticed you weren't around. Why weren't you helping your ma in the store so she could get ready for her wedding?" Jack crossed her arms and tapped her toe. Her cordialness hadn't lasted long, but she had little patience with Billy, especially when he was standing between her and her dinner.

A frown replaced his smile. "I don't wanna be a storekeeper. It's boring."

"What do you want to do? If you don't run the store, how will you make a living?"

He shoved his hands in his pockets and lifted his chin. "I've got ways. And I got me a place to stay. I ain't goin' to that ranch."

Jack's stomach complained about its empty state. She stepped sideways, but Billy matched her efforts. "I want to eat, Billy, before the food's gone and the wedding starts."

"Come with me first. I got something to show you."

Jack flung out her arms, wishing he'd leave her alone. "There isn't time. I had to take Andrew back to Ma, and now I want to eat."

"Who's Andrew?"

Jack stared at him. "He's my new baby brother, remember?"

He shrugged, as if it were of no importance. She scowled and noticed his clothes. His tan shirt was wrinkled and stained, and his pants and boots dusty. "Is that what you're wearing to the wedding?"

He glanced down and swiped his hand across his thigh. "Ain't goin'."

"Billy! That's just plain mean. Your ma will be so hurt."

His steely blue eyes flashed. "She should have thought of that before she agreed to marry that man."

"What's wrong with him? He's got a nice ranch, and from what I hear, a big house. He can provide

315

for your ma. She won't have to work so hard—and besides, they're happy together. I don't understand you and Tessa."

He yanked his hands out of his pockets and shoved them on his hips. "Tessa wants to live in town, not all alone on that ranch—even if she's taken a likin' to one of the cowboys out there. And I don't want that man bossing me around. I ain't a kid no more."

Jack pinched her lips together. She didn't know what to say to him. She just wanted to eat. "I'm leaving now. All the food's probably gone already." She picked up her skirts and dashed to the left. When he slid in that direction, she darted back to the right—and almost made it.

He grabbed hold of her arm, jerking her to a halt. "I've got us a place, Jack. I want you to come see it."

She almost groaned out loud. "I can't. I need to help Papa watch the young'uns, and I—want—to—eat." She emphasized each of the last four words. As she pulled away from him, her hands came down hard on her waist, and she felt something stiff in her pocket. "Oh, yeah." She pulled out the bracelet Billy had given her and held it out to him. "Here. I can't keep this."

He stared down at the shiny silver bangle reflecting in the sunlight. "I don't want that back. I bought it for you."

"It's not proper for me to take presents from you. We aren't courting."

Billy's eyes narrowed. "You're gonna marry me, even if I have to force you."

Of all the nerve! She jerked her arm, but he wouldn't let go. She'd never been truly afraid of him before, but today, something menacing darkened his blue eyes. Still, she wouldn't be forced to do anything, especially marry him, not when she was within shouting distance of most of the town. She fluffed up her bravado. "No, I'm not. And don't forget my papa is the marshal. He won't take kindly to your threatening me."

He glared back. Then his gaze darted past her. His brows lifted, and he let go and smiled, albeit without his normal charm. "We shall see," he said through clenched teeth.

She needed to tell Luke about Billy's odd behavior, but she kept forgetting. Issuing threats about forcing her to marry was carrying things way too far. Stepping out of his reach, she peered over her shoulder to see what had distracted Billy. A man rode down the street, watching them. The relief she felt at the stranger's arrival made her knees weak. A beam of sunlight reflected off the star on his vest. A Texas Ranger.

"I gotta go, but this ain't over." Billy swung around and hurried back between the houses.

The ranger stopped his horse beside her and touched the end of his hat in greeting. He glanced in the direction Billy had fled; then his kind gray eyes looked her over. She couldn't see his upper lip because of his large mustache. "You all right, ma'am?"

She nodded and put the bracelet back in her pocket. She couldn't help wondering how forceful Billy might have gotten.

"I'm looking for Marshal Davis. Could you direct me to him?"

Jack smiled. "I sure can. He's my stepfather."

The ranger dismounted. "Martin Carlisle, ma'am. Me and Luke were friends in the army."

"It's a pleasure to meet you, Ranger Carlisle." She waved toward the end of the street. "I reckon you can hear all the noise. We're having a church social and then a wedding."

He fell in step beside her, leading his gray horse. Sweat ringed his old brown hat, and his clothes didn't look a whole lot better than Billy's. "Maybe I can get me a bite to eat at this social."

"I sure hope so. I was just on my way back there and was thinking the same thing."

"It's none of my business, ma'am, but don't let that man get rough with you."

Jack nodded. Billy's harsh grasp on her arm had hurt and reminded her of the times her first pa would sometimes grab hold of her if she didn't obey fast enough. When he was in a fair mood, he never paid her any attention, nor did he ever hug her or bring her a present when he'd been away. He had promised he would, and she always hoped he might, but he never did. Not once. He was a liar—a mean man who hurt women and children. She had a feeling whoever married Billy might suffer the same pain she had as a child.

The ranger walked beside her, leading his horse, his gaze focused on the crowd as they drew near. She glanced at the gun in his holster. Maybe she needed to start carrying a weapon—a derringer—because she'd never let another man treat her like her father had.

Noah stood on the outskirts of the crowd, holding an empty plate and talking to Mr. Mann. At least she didn't have to doubt Noah. She had at first when he wouldn't talk about his past, but many people had things in their past that hurt to remember or they were ashamed of. She rarely ever talked about her first father or what he'd done. At least with Noah being a Christian and a minister, she'd never have to doubt his word.

Carly stood on the edge of the field where folks had laid out their quilts and watched the children playing. The younger ones, their bellies full of their mamas'

cooking, played with less enthusiasm than they had when church had first let out. She watched Alan and Abby playing hopscotch for a few minutes, making sure the rambunctious children were behaving. Several older girls sat in a cluster together, chatting and making chains of clover flowers. She'd never once made one. Didn't even know how they hooked those long stems and white flowers together. She swiped her hand in the air at a pesky fly and chased it away.

As far back as she could remember, she had helped her mama wash clothes from sunup to sundown. Hauling water, carving soap chips, squeezing clothes, and hanging them up, then taking them down later to be ironed and folded. Even today, she couldn't resist shuddering when Rachel needed help with the laundry. She'd rather clean a privy.

Would life have been different if she'd had a father? Would her mama still have had to work so hard? Would she?

Pressing her lips together, she blew a heavy breath out her nose. She would never know—and wishing life were different wouldn't change the past. But she could hope the future would be different.

She scanned a crowd of men standing near the horses and wagons and found Garrett beside Luke. They stood with a half dozen others in a rough circle. One man raised his fist, and though she couldn't hear the words, she suspected they were talking about the murder. Everybody had been talking about it. From what Rachel had said, it was the first that had ever taken place in Lookout.

Garrett glanced in her direction and winked. She smiled back, feeling heat warm her cheeks that had nothing to do with the sun. Two women dressed in calico and sunbonnets walked between her and Garrett. One lady glanced at her and scowled, then leaned toward her friend and said something.

Her smile fading, Carly looked away, feeling the brunt of their silent censure. She zigzagged her way through the groups of families, back to the Davises' quilt, wishing Rachel had come or that Jack would return. She smiled a thank-you to Mrs. Castleby for keeping an eye on Emmie while she slept on the quilt.

After sitting and rearranging her skirt, Carly leaned her head back against one of the few trees shading the field. Her eyes drifted shut, and she yawned. Taking a nap right about now would be nice, but the wedding was soon to start. The steady hum of conversation lulled her into a limp state, and her whole body relaxed, her arms felt as heavy as leg-irons.

On the other side of the old oak tree, two women chatted about a recipe, but she tried to ignore them. She lifted up a heavy hand and swatted at a mosquito that landed on Emmie's calf. She sighed. If only she knew more people.

"What'dya think about that murder—and those break-ins? Ghastly, aren't they?" one lady behind her said. Carly stiffened.

"Yes, it's getting so that a decent woman's afraid to walk the streets of Lookout these days."

Carly rolled her eyes at the woman's exaggeration.

"Well, if'n you ask me, I think it was that female outlaw. All these appalling things didn't happen until after she came back to Lookout."

Carly gasped, their cruel words breaking her fragile hope. Unable to listen to any more nattering, she pushed up from the quilt. Her heart ached. Would these people never accept her? Couldn't they see she'd changed?

She scooped Emmie up in her arms and looked for Luke. She noticed Garrett instead, talking to Mr. Howard, and made a beeline for him. He smiled in her direction. Mr. Howard turned his head, looking right at her, and one brow lifted. But instead of censure in his gaze she saw surprise, then his mouth curved up in a grin. Too bad Leah had left earlier to go feed her baby. At least she and Carly had something in common.

Garrett leaned toward Mr. Howard, who nodded. Then Garrett walked toward her. His smile dipped. "Is something wrong?"

Carly shrugged, unable to explain her unease. He'd lived in this town his whole life. How could she expect him to understand how badly the woman's unjustified accusations had hurt?

"I thought I'd take Emmie home. The sun is moving toward our quilt, and I don't want her to get a sunburn."

"But what about the wedding?"

Carly shrugged. "I don't know those folks gettin' married, other than she owns the store, and he once hoped to marry Rachel and also your brother's wife—before she married Mark, of course."

Garrett leaned toward her and waggled his blond brows, his blue eyes sparking with mischief, somewhat soothing the pain the callous women had inflicted. "Don't you want to get some ideas for our weddin'?"

"You don't wanna marry me." Tears stung her eyes, frustrating her. She never cried—not even when Luke had hauled her to jail all those years ago. Not even when her brother sat in the cell next to hers, giving her the skunk eye and blaming her for his capture, for hours on end. Only Luke's threats to gag Ty and hogtie him made him finally shut up.

Garrett grabbed her elbow and hauled her toward the edge of the crowd. Folks gawked at her as if she'd done something wrong or was trying to steal Luke's young'un. Standing between two wagons, so that nobody could see them, he dropped her arm and shoved his hands to his hips. "Why would you say that? I wouldn't have asked to court you if I didn't intend on marryin' you."

Carly shifted Emmie to her other arm. The girl was small, but heavy.

"Let me hold her."

"No, I need to take her home. Could you tell Luke and then help him keep an eye out for Alan and Abby until Jacqueline returns?"

"Don't think I didn't notice you changed the subject."

A horse behind Carly nickered, as if asking for a handout. Why couldn't Garrett just let her go without causing a ruckus? "I prayed and thought God gave me the go-ahead, but I'm foolin' myself to think we could ever marry."

"Why?" His face crinkled up, making him look as if he'd been sucking on lemons. "Am I too old for you? Is that it?"

"What?" Carly blinked, confused at his question. In truth, he didn't look anywhere near forty. His shoulders and arms were muscled from lifting crates of cargo for years, and his blond hair wasn't thinning or turning white. He no longer favored the arm he got shot in or wore the sling. He didn't look overly old at all. "No. I've never thought that."

She nibbled on her lower lip and stared at the closest vehicle. The black paint of the spring wagon was partly worn off, revealing the grayed wood underneath. Stuffing hung out one corner of the padded front bench. Right now, she felt as worn out as the buggy. "It's just that. . .can't I tell you later? Emmie's really getting heavy."

He rubbed his nape, then scratched the back of his head. "I guess so."

"You'll let Luke know I've got Emmie and to watch out for the other young'uns?"

He nodded, but he didn't look too pleased. "Luke's talking with that ranger over there." He nudged his chin to the right. "Stay here for a minute and let me run and tell him; then I can carry Emmie and escort you back home."

Carly offered him a weak smile. "Thank you, but that isn't necessary. The wedding will be starting soon, and you need to be here."

"Just wait." He held up his hands, palms out, then backed away. "I'll be right back."

Carly watched him jog off, her heart already feeling his loss. She'd dared to dream of marriage and family—of having a permanent home—but she should have known dreams don't come true for people like her. Folks would always think of her as an outlaw. Hadn't those women proved that?

Batting her burning eyes, she wove between the haphazardly parked wagons and buggies, down the street toward the boardinghouse. She shifted Emmie to her shoulder to relieve her shaking arm and patted the child's back.

Maybe it was best for all if she just moved on to another town.

Chapter 29

Jack sat in the church pew for the second time that day, cocooned by her family. Holding Abby, who was nearly asleep, Ma sat on her left, while Alan leaned against Jack's right side, kicking one leg and pouting at having to come back to church again when he'd rather play with his friends. Luke proudly jiggled Andrew, alternating between staring at his newest son and watching the wedding. Even the ranger who'd come to see Luke had decided to attend the wedding after getting his fill of food and sat on the far end of the pew.

A sense of peace—of belonging—wrapped around Jack. How could she even consider leaving her family?

Noah's voice rumbled through the room as he read the vows to Christine Morgan and Rand Kessler, who each recited them in turn. Noah stood straight and tall, his voice confident, but she knew he was nervous about marrying his first couple. She closed her eyes and said the vows along with Mrs. Morgan—only she was saying them to Noah.

Somewhere in the past few days, she'd taken a turn. Dallas no longer held her fascination. Being an ace reporter in the big city had lost most of its attraction, although she hoped to continue to work for Jenny. She had written a letter to the *Dallas*

Morning News, declining the job, but she had yet to mail it. Part of her dreaded turning it down. The other part felt at peace with staying in Lookout, but she would continue to pray about it before making a final decision. And how could she possibly think of leaving town until things were settled with Noah?

Was she making a huge mistake? Throwing away her dream just when it was within her reach?

Or had her dream changed? Caring for Noah wasn't something she'd planned or sought after. It just happened—more quickly than she ever would have believed possible. From the first time her eyes had collided with his, she'd felt that connection. Almost as if he'd come to town just for her.

But that was silly. He simply came for the job and had no former knowledge of her.

"Would you please bow your heads as I ask God's blessing on this couple?" Noah's voice pulled her back from her musings. With one hand on Christine Morgan's shoulder and the other on Rand Kessler's, he ducked his head and started praying.

Jack caught a glimpse of the thick black hair on the top of Noah's head, and her fingers moved, aching to touch it. She blew out a heavy sigh. Her ma glanced at her, then closed her eyes again. Jack bowed her head. Why couldn't she concentrate on the wedding instead of Noah?

Because she had to know if she was just having her first severe case of infatuation or if she was truly falling in love. But how could one know the difference?

Noah was kind, brave, handsome, and made her feel things she'd never wanted a man to make her feel. He reminded her of Luke. Both men were honorable, truthful. Tall. But was she only attracted to Noah because he resembled Luke in so many ways?

She needed to talk to someone. Jenny was too

jaded. Penny had never been in love. And Tessa—well, she definitely couldn't ask Tessa. Noah said, "Amen," and Jack glanced at her ma. Maybe it was time they had a heart-to-heart talk.

"Mr. Kessler, you may kiss your bride."

Rand's smile was as wide as all of Texas. A rosy red stained Mrs. Kessler's cheeks. The groom ducked down, paused to gaze into his wife's eyes, then kissed her. Masculine cheers resounded throughout the room.

Jack looked at Noah. He was staring directly at her, a gentle smile pulling at one side of his mouth. She'd kissed that mouth. Her pulse leapt. And she hoped to do it again. Was it shameless of her to enjoy kissing him? To feel completely safe and cherished locked within the minister's strong arms?

No, not the minister—the man.

Noah.

The couple quit kissing, but their fervent smiles remained. Noah held out his hand toward the newly married couple. "Ladies and gentlemen, it's my pleasure to present to you Mr. and Mrs. Randall Leland Kessler."

The room filled with cheers and clapping. Abby jerked awake, staring with unfocused eyes. Andrew slept contentedly in his father's arms. Jack, overwhelmed with emotion, hugged Alan, but the boy pulled away.

"Don't we get to eat cake now?" he asked.

Carly changed out of her Sunday dress into her cooler calico. She peeked in the girls' bedroom to check on Emmie. The child slept contentedly, curled on top of her bed. She pulled the door almost shut, in case someone returned with the other children before Emmie woke up; then Carly tiptoed downstairs.

She half-expected Garrett to come knocking

on the boardinghouse door, but it was probably best he stayed at the wedding. It wouldn't look right for them to be home alone and nobody else around. Carly opened the front door, unable to hold back a contemptuous snort. People could hardly think much worse of her if they were blaming her for thefts and murder. She laid a hand over her chest. Knowing someone believed that about her cut her to the quick.

She dropped down into a rocker below the girls' open window, knowing Emmie would cry out for someone once she woke up. Not a soul walked down Main Street, although as usual, several horses were hitched in front of the Wet Your Whistle.

Closing her eyes, she pushed the rocker into motion and prayed about what to do. She longed to race upstairs, pack her bags, and flee the vicious gossip as if she were running from an angry posse. Faced with the chance of possibly losing Garrett, she knew without a doubt that she wanted to stay, to marry him, and raise a family, but how could she if folks continued to spread rumors? Her husband and children would suffer. Her whole body felt as if she were being split apart.

Tears burned her eyes, frustrating her even more. She swatted at them and wiped her cheek on her shoulder. "What should I do, Lord?"

She spent the next few minutes praying, but no answer came. Maybe she was making too big a deal of things. It had only been the two women talking, after all, and once the marshal figured out who was doing the break-ins and solved the murder, surely talk would die down. Until then, she could stick close to the boardinghouse. There. She felt better thinking things through and praying about the situation.

Loud cheers erupted from the direction of church. So the wedding was over. That meant folks would be walking down the street back to their homes. She opened her eyes, and her heart leapt into her throat.

Two cowboys stood just on the other side of the porch, leering at her. One was leaning on the rail. His mouth lifted in a grin, but his eyes remained cold. "Well, look what we have here, Buck."

The tall, thin man named Buck scowled at the other. "Why'd you have'ta go and use my name, Laredo? That was a dumb thang t'do."

Laredo rolled his gray eyes, then glared at Carly again. For the first time since her return to Lookout, she wished she was armed. But she hadn't carried a gun since her outlaw days.

"If it ain't our local jailbird." Buck smirked, sending shivers racing through her.

Laredo stroked his mustache. "We cain't have her kind in our good town, now can we?"

She pushed up from the rocker and rushed to the front door, nearly tripping as her skirts grabbed her legs. Scuffling sounded behind her, but she didn't look. She twisted the doorknob, then she was jerked into Laredo's arms. With one arm around her waist, he hauled her backward off the porch.

Help me, Lord. She couldn't let him take her and leave Emmie all alone. Her heart fluttered like the wings of a newly caged bird as he dragged her down the steps. She lifted her arm, then brought it down in a swift jab, elbowing him in the side. His breath whooshed past her left ear, but he didn't let go.

"Git her." Buck danced in the street, flapping his arms like a chicken with clipped wings.

Laredo lifted her off the ground, and Carly lifted one leg and kicked back. Laredo cried out and dropped her. The fall jarred her whole body, rattling her teeth. The smooth *shush* of a gun being drawn drew her gaze up. Laredo aimed his pistol at her chest.

Garrett sat in the church, as close to the door as he could. If Rand hadn't been a good friend, he would have skipped the wedding altogether. Why hadn't Carly waited on him? Why had she called off their courting when she'd been happy and hanging on his arm earlier?

Had she become upset because he'd been talking with some of the men instead of sitting on the quilt with her after dinner? Well, tough. He was a man, and men liked to see one another and catch up on the latest news about livestock and new inventions. She'd just have to understand that.

Instantly, he regretted his harsh thought and that he wasn't paying attention. He bowed his head as Noah offered prayer for the couple. Garrett had hoped his wedding would be next. It might have taken him by surprise to realize he had feelings for Carly, but once he did, there was no turning back. He'd just have to figure out how to change her mind.

He winced as he watched Rand kiss his bride. Too bad it wasn't him and Carly up there. He was tired of living alone.

Noah introduced the newly married couple, and everyone stood and cheered. Garrett dashed out the door. He could visit Carly, straighten things out, and then come back and congratulate the Kesslers.

He wove through the bevy of wagons, sending up a prayer. *Lord, You know I believe in You. I don't often ask You for help, but I'm asking today. Change Carly's heart. Let her see I'm serious about this marrying business. I promise we'll be in church each Sunday—'less we're sick.*

Eager to see her, he quickened his steps. He cleared the wagons, then noticed a commotion in the street in front of the boardinghouse. Two men were attacking a woman. He sucked in a breath. Not Carly!

Garrett broke into a run. *Help me to help her, Lord.*

He could handle two men—as long as neither pulled a gun. One man had his back to Garrett while the other wrestled with Carly. She elbowed the man, but he didn't let go. She reached up and grabbed hold of the man's hair.

Garrett suddenly darted between Polly's and Dolly's hideous purple house and the Castlebys' fancy home, as if pulled by an invisible hand. He slowed his steps, and an idea forged in his mind. He ran around the banker's home and in the back door of the boardinghouse.

Luke kept a rifle and extra gun in his bedroom. Garrett snatched the gun from its spot on top of the wardrobe where Luke had placed it after he first bought it. He hurried down the hall to the front door and slowly opened it, hating the time he wasted but knowing he needed a weapon if he and Carly were both going to survive.

The men had her almost to the end of the porch. Garrett raced through the parlor and climbed out the open window on the side of the house, then stepped out from behind a bush. Carly sat on the ground, her back to him, staring up at a gun.

"Laredo, look out." The thin man who'd been watching the other man struggle with Carly reached for his gun.

Garrett aimed and fired, completely missing his target. Thank the good Lord the man was a slow draw. Aiming with a steadier hand, he hit the man in the shoulder, just as his gun left his holster. The man yelled and fell to the ground, dropping his gun and grabbing his arm. Garrett's eyes swiveled to the other man, and his heart all but stopped. Laredo held his gun to Carly's head.

"Move, and she's dead, mister."

Chapter 30

Carly's gaze lifted to Garrett's. His beautiful blue eyes held an apology—and more. He was sincerely concerned for her.

The man he'd shot rolled on the ground and howled like a hunting dog. "He'p me, L'rado. I hurt."

She could feel her captor's chest rise and fall as his breathing quickened. With Laredo's arm crushing her just below her breasts, she could barely breathe. He loosened his grip for a second, then hoisted her up, closer to him than before. The gun pressed hard to her temple, forcing it sideways. Hurting. Bruising.

She didn't want to die.

She wanted the dream.

She wanted to live in Lookout and marry Garrett.

"That wedding's over. People will be swarming the streets any minute." Garrett's gaze and his voice hardened. "You'd best just let her go and take your friend and git."

Carly could sense the man's uncertainty. She could almost smell his indecision. She swallowed hard.

"My cousin is the marshal, you know. He won't take kindly to your harming that woman."

"She's nothin' but an outlaw—a jailbird."

Garrett winced, and Carly wondered why. But then she knew. He'd thought the same thing not so long ago. Had his feelings truly changed?

Her gaze snagged his, and she found her answer there. She couldn't explain how it had happened, but he'd come to care for her—and that made her want to live.

She wouldn't let this man steal her life and her future. She flicked her gaze downward, then back up to Garrett's, and did it again. He frowned. She wiggled one finger of the arm crushed to her side. His gaze dropped down.

Buck groaned. "I'm dyin'. I need a doctor."

"Shut up. It's just a shoulder wound." Laredo's unsympathetic words rushed past Carly's ear. "Get up. And get the horses."

"If he does, I'll shoot him in the leg," Garrett growled.

"Nooo, I cain't walk if'n you do that."

"I'll shoot him myself if he don't git up." Laredo moved the gun away from her head and pointed it at his cohort. "Get up, Buck, and hurry."

With the gun gone, Carly wiggled her finger again. Garrett watched.

She lifted her index finger.

Then the middle one.

And then her ring finger.

Suddenly she went completely limp.

"What the—" Taken off guard, Laredo loosened his hold, and Carly slipped free.

A gun blasted—then another. The stench of gunpowder rent the air, leaving behind a cloud of gray. Laredo yelled and fell back. Carly sat on the ground, head ducked down.

She was afraid to look.

Afraid Garrett would be dead.

Strong, gentle arms lifted her up, and Garrett pressed her against his left side, keeping his gun trained on her attackers. Her arms wrapped around his waist and held tight. He was alive!

"Shh. . .you're safe now." Garrett patted her back and pressed his cheek against her head.

Tears of joy poured from her eyes like a river, dampening his shirt. She never wanted to move.

"You're marrying me, and I won't take no for an answer." Garrett kissed her head. "What happened back at the church that made you say you didn't want to court me?"

She shrugged. He gently set her back from him, and shame made her duck her head. "Two women were talkin'. They said the r–robberies and m–murder were my fault."

Garrett stiffened and lifted her chin with one finger. "You listen to me, Carly. That's a bald-faced lie. People will always talk, but you don't have to take to heart what they say, darlin'. Maybe you were a robber a long time ago, but you've changed. God changed you and set you free from the past. You served your time, and now you're a free woman—in more ways than one."

She studied his face, encouraged by his sincerity. "You're right. I am a child of God. When I gave my heart to Him, He washed me white as snow. It's as if I never sinned."

Pounding footsteps and shouts sounded down the street and drew nearer. Garrett glanced that way, then nodded. "That's right. You're no more of an outlaw than I am."

Buck moaned, but Laredo endured his pain and failure in silence. Carly peeked at them, then saw Luke and a dozen other men running toward them. She hated for this time with Garrett to end.

He pulled her behind the shrub, where they were partially hidden. "It's true that I used to despise you, Carly. I won't lie. Your brother kidnapped Rachel, you pretended to be one of the mail-order brides, and for all I knew, you two planned everything just so you could rob the bank. God changed my heart. I don't know how or when, but He did. I care for you."

He didn't say he loved her, but they hadn't been courting very long. All she knew was that she felt the same. "After I got to know Shannon and Leah, I despised you and your brother for what you'd done to them." She shook her head. "How could you order your cousin three brides?"

Garrett grinned. The footsteps stopped, and the rumble of men's voices floated their way. "I wanted to get his mind off of Rachel, and if only one bride had shown up, he'd have just sent her packing. Besides, I wanted to give him a choice."

"It had the opposite effect, you know. Having those other women competing for him made him realize how much he still loved Rachel." Carly shook her head and smiled. "You're a rascal, you know it?"

"I know."

She smacked him on the chest, but then her heart stilled. He lowered his head and kissed her. Warm sensations zinged through her body, and she tightened her grip on his shirt.

A man cleared his throat, and they jumped apart. Carly lifted her hands to her blazing cheeks.

"Guess I'm going to have to lock you two up for public indecency." Luke grinned. "Care to tell me what happened?"

"We're getting married, and those two"—Garrett waved his gun toward the men on the ground—"tried to break us up."

Luke's brow lifted.

Garrett sobered, all teasing aside. "They attacked Carly. One man looked bent on hauling her off somewhere."

Carly ducked her head. "He said they didn't

need my kind here."

Garrett held the gun out to Luke. "Here, thanks for letting me borrow this. I owe you a few bullets, Cuz." He wrapped his arm around Carly and tugged her close. "It's *their* kind we don't need, darlin'."

∽

Jack longed to run down the street after the men and see what the gunshots had been about, but she couldn't. She and the rest of the women and children were huddled in a group behind the church, while their menfolk stood guard and waited for Luke and the other half-dozen men to check out what that gunfire had been about. The ladies talked in hushed voices, speculating on what had happened. Tired children fussed, unhappy at being corralled after sitting through church and the wedding.

And the bride stood patiently holding her groom's hand, while in his other hand he held a rifle someone had tossed him.

Jack remembered the stormy day her ma and Luke were married. A tornado hit right after the wedding, sending people scattering, and taking much of the store with it as it roared through town.

Leah Howard stood next to Jack's ma, holding her baby, the rest of her little ones hanging on to her skirt or standing nearby. "What do you suppose happened?"

"I don't know, but at least we haven't heard any more gunshots." Her ma lifted Andrew to her shoulder and bounced him.

"Maybe there was another break-in"—Callie Howard leaned toward Jack—"or murder."

"I hope not." Jack studied Callie. She was a pretty girl—only a few years younger than Jack. They'd played together some when they were younger, but Callie had generally been busy tending her siblings and helping her stepmother. Now that Jack had younger brothers and sisters, she had more compassion for the other woman.

Abby suddenly jerked on Jack's hand, trying to get free. "Let go, Sissy."

Ma latched on to Abby's shoulder. "You hold still, young lady, or you'll be in trouble when we get home."

Abby's lower lip popped out. Her brother, holding Jack's other hand, chuckled. Abby lunged toward him. Jack almost jerked her sister's arm out of its socket, trying to keep her away from Alan.

Her ma sighed. Jack knew she'd only planned to come to the wedding because Christine was such a good friend. Most women who'd given birth so recently wouldn't have.

"You look exhausted, Ma." Jack stared at her mother's pinched face. "You want me to hold Andy?"

"I rested all morning at Agatha's, but now that I've been on my feet awhile, I am getting a little tired, and I'm worried about Emmie and Carly."

"Those shots sounded as if they were close." They shared a worried look then went back to watching the road where they'd last seen Luke.

Carrying a rifle, Noah walked around the outside of the crowd with the men who were guarding the women. He looked uncomfortable with the weapon, and Jack wondered if he even knew how to shoot it. She could teach him, if he didn't. Luke had made sure she knew how to protect herself.

Her heart pounded harder, just thinking of standing close and teaching him how to aim a rifle. She thought about his kisses. They made her feel cherished, special. What would it be like to be married to a kind, gentle man like Noah?

Two men walked past Polly's and Dolly's house, waving their rifles. "All is well," one of them shouted.

The women exhaled a uniform sigh of relief and

started moving toward the wagons. Jack was ready to get out of the sun, as she was certain the others were.

Abby jerked again. "I wanna go see Papa."

Ma glanced down. "Stay with your sister. Your father is probably busy."

"Aww. . ." Abby pasted a frown on her face again.

As they passed the Dykstras' purple house, her ma gasped. Jack gazed down the road, her heart nearly jumping from her chest. Luke stood in front of their house, and two men lay in the street. But where was Carly? And Emmie?

She suddenly remembered the time outlaws had kidnapped her ma. Jack dropped her siblings' hands and broke into a run. She had to make sure Emmie was safe.

"Jacqueline!" her mother cried.

"Wait for me, Sissy!" Abby's little feet pounded behind hers.

&

"What happened, Papa?" Jack skidded to a stop beside Luke. She quickly studied the scene. Two wounded men sat on the ground. Doc Phillips was tending one of them, and the ranger squatted next to the other, questioning him while Jenny took notes. Garrett stood off to the side, pacing. The stench of gunpowder still clung to the air.

Luke snagged Abby's arm as she ran toward one of the strangers. "The children don't need to see this. Take them inside, Half Bit."

Jack winced at Luke's scolding. She should have thought of that herself. "Where's Emmie and Carly? Are they all right?"

"Inside." He nudged his chin toward home. "They're both fine."

She sensed there was more to the story, but maybe

Carly could satisfy her curiosity.

"Why's them two men bleedin'?" Abby asked.

Luke passed her to Jack, his brow lifted in an I-told-you-so smirk. She didn't waste time but spun around and headed toward the porch. Alan ran past her, but Ma snapped her fingers, and he jerked to a halt. He glanced back at the men. Luke merely pointed at the house, and Alan's shoulders dropped.

"Ahh. . .can't I watch? I'm gonna be a lawman some day."

"Go inside with your ma, Son."

Alan turned and dragged his toes all the way to the porch, kicking dust on his shoes. Abby wiggled to get down, and Jack set her on the steps. Ma held the door open, not giving either child the option of disobeying.

Jack blew out a breath. She wanted to watch, too, but Jenny would get the story—and Jack really didn't care, other than wanting to know why those men were shot so close to her home. She closed the door.

Carly came down the stairs and lifted a finger to her lips. "Emmie is still asleep."

"If you two wouldn't mind seeing to the other children, it's time for Andrew and me to take a rest." Ma brushed the hair that had come loose from her bun off her forehead with the back of her wrist. She looked exhausted.

"Can I help you with anything?" Jack offered.

Ma shook her head, but then stopped. "If you wouldn't mind changing Andy's diaper and putting him in a fresh gown, I'd appreciate it."

Jack took the baby. "Of course I don't mind."

"I'll tend to the other children. You just get a good rest." Carly took hold of Abby's and Alan's hands and led both children toward the stairs. "Just be mindful that Emmie is sleeping."

The kids clomped up the stairs only slightly less

noisily than normal. Jack smiled. "Carly's doing better at getting those two to obey her."

Her ma dropped down onto the bed and exhaled a sigh. She yawned. "I probably should have stayed home today, but I wanted to comfort Agatha and attend the wedding."

Jack laid Andrew on the bed. He raised his fist, brushing his cheek, and his head turned toward it, mouth open. He licked his fist, then scrunched up his face when he didn't find what he wanted. Jack chuckled and quickly fastened on a dry diaper. "I think someone is hungry."

"Not me, that's for sure." Ma shed her Sunday dress and petticoat and climbed into bed. "I hope I can stay awake long enough to feed him."

Jack handed the baby to Ma. "Don't worry about anything, because Carly and I will be here. You can rest all day."

"That sounds nice. Thank you." Ma's eyes shut as Andrew began his lunch.

Jack closed the bedroom door and hurried toward the front of the house. Since Carly and the children were still upstairs, Jack stepped outside and surveyed the scene. In her rush to get home, she'd forgotten the platter and pie tins she was supposed to bring home from the social. She walked over to the crowd that had gathered and watched. Luke had the two men on their feet. The tall, thin man was whining worse than Abby ever did, but the handsomer one kept silent, his head hanging down. She thought she might have seen them around town before, but she wasn't certain.

Knowing she needed to get back to help Carly, she headed toward the church, content to wait to hear the story from Luke. Halfway there, she met the Kesslers coming down the street in their buggy. The engaging smiles on their faces made them both look younger.

Tessa sat in the backseat, her face scrunched up in a scowl, arms crossed. She didn't even acknowledge Jack.

"Did you find out what happened?" Rand slowed the buggy.

"No, I had to help with the children, but two men over there have been shot."

"You know 'em?" Rand asked.

Jack shook her head. "Might have seen them in town before, but that's all. I meant to congratulate you two, but then the shooting stirred things up."

"Thank you." Mrs. Kessler turned toward her on the seat. "It was so nice of Rachel to attend after so recently having her baby."

"She wanted to. She is so happy for you both."

Tessa sent Jack a chilly glare.

"Well, guess we'll be on our way." Mrs. Kessler started to face the front then glanced back at Jack. "I'll be in town on Saturdays for a while to open the store—at least until I find a buyer." She peeked at Tessa, as if the thought of having to sell because her children didn't want the mercantile bothered her.

"I'll spread the word."

Rand nodded his thanks, smacked the leather traces on the horse's back, and the buggy rolled forward. Jack couldn't help wishing that she and Noah were the ones riding off together.

Resuming her walk, she shoved her hands in her pocket and felt the forgotten bracelet. *Horse feathers.*

What was she going to do with that thing?

Suddenly an idea burst into her mind.

She spun around and raced to catch the buggy. Thankfully, Rand had stopped it near the crowd of spectators. Jack jogged toward it and stopped on Mrs. Kessler's side of the buggy.

"Mrs. Kessler, I forgot something."

She turned away from the crowd and smiled.

"What is it, Jacqueline?"

She pulled the bracelet from her pocket, and the silver glistened in the sunlight. Tessa leaned forward to get a look.

Mrs. Kessler gasped and reached for the bangle. "Where did you get that?"

Luke walked up to Rand and shook his hand but obviously noticed Mrs. Kessler's reaction. He glanced at Jack, brows lifted, probably wondering the same thing.

"Billy gave it to me. He's still trying to get me to marry him, but I told him I can't. I don't care for him the way a woman does her husband. I tried to give it back, but he refused to take it and got angry at me."

Mrs. Kessler fell back against the seat, unable to take her eyes off the bracelet. Jack couldn't imagine what would cause such a reaction.

Rand put his arm around his wife's shoulder. "What's wrong, honey?"

She held out the piece of jewelry. "This was one of the items stolen from the mercantile the morning of the robbery."

Chapter 31

Jack paced the parlor, waiting for her parents to finish tucking in the children for the night. Carly and Garrett had gone out walking, and Noah had been invited to supper with the Manns. She needed to talk to her folks while everyone else was occupied. The newest edition of the *Lookout Ledger* would be available tomorrow afternoon, and she had to tell them about the new hotel.

What would it mean to her family? Would they still have guests come and stay? Would they have to close their doors?

She twisted her hands, hating to be the one to break the news to them.

The railroad coming to town was a good thing, since it would bring growth and new businesses, cut down on travel times, bring more people to town, but the hotel...

Too many things were changing. She dropped down on the edge of the chair. Maybe she should get a job where she'd make some decent money. The piddling she got for her occasional articles barely paid for a new dress twice a year.

Her folks entered the parlor and sat down together on the settee. Luke laid his arm around her mother's shoulder, and Jack couldn't help wishing Noah had the freedom to do the same.

"What's on your mind, Half Bit?"

"My guess is a man." A teasing smile danced on her ma's lips.

Luke swung his head toward his wife. "A man!"

Rachel elbowed him in the side. "Stop pretending you haven't noticed how they look at one another."

Luke's mouth turned up on one side, and he scowled.

Jack's heart pounded. She'd tried not to be obvious, but she had a hard time not looking at Noah when he sat across from her during meals. He must be who they were referring to, but then why would that make Luke unhappy? Did he object to her having a relationship with a minister? Who could be a better choice?

"So?" her ma said.

Jack folded her hands then unlocked them and straightened a crease in her skirt. She hated being the bearer of bad news. She glanced at her parents.

Luke leaned forward, knees on his elbows, intensely staring at her. "What's wrong? Did Noah do something that made you uncomfortable?"

"What?" Jack blinked, trying to make sense of his unexpected question. "No! He's never been anything but a gentleman."

"Then tell us. You've got our minds running rampant." Luke relaxed and sat back.

"I overheard something." Jack jumped up and resumed her pacing. "And Jenny's printing the story in tomorrow's paper. I wanted y'all to know ahead of time, so it wouldn't be such a shock."

Luke sat up again. "What did you do?"

Jack grinned and shook her head. "It wasn't me, this time." She thought of how she'd hung from the saloon window and then fallen again but wasn't about to mention that. "The railroad is coming to town. A spur track is being built from Denison to here."

"Oh, that's your news?" Luke exhaled a loud breath. "I already knew that."

"You did? How?"

"The mayor told me. Said he wanted to be prepared for more people coming to town and was going to ask the town council to approve hiring two part-time deputies."

"Truly?" Her ma gazed at Luke. "Then you wouldn't have to work so much." She reached over and squeezed his hand. "I love that idea."

Jack sat down again, stunned that Luke already knew. "Why hasn't the mayor announced it then?"

"He was afraid there'd be a run on land and that prices would soar."

Jack frowned. Had the mayor purposely kept the news quiet so that he could profit? She'd heard he'd recently bought several lots on the east end of town—right where the hotel was going. "Do you already know about the hotel, too?"

Luke rubbed his jaw. "I wouldn't be a very good lawman if I didn't investigate the strangers who pass through my town."

"Why didn't you tell me?" Jack sat back, crossing her arms and pouting, not unlike Tessa.

"Wasn't my news to tell. How did you find out?"

"Uh. . ." Jack swallowed hard. Nope, she couldn't tell him. "I. . .uh. . .used my investigative skills."

This time her ma sat up. "No more rooftops, I hope."

"No." Jack hated how her voice rose unnaturally. Even though she told the truth, guilt needled her for what she'd done. She needed to distract them before they questioned her further. "But if a hotel comes here, won't that put us out of business?"

Luke glanced at her ma, who nodded. "It might.

We've been talking about that and have decided it's time to stop taking boarders."

Jack's mouth dropped open. The house would almost feel odd without people coming and going. Where would Noah live? If he moved, she wouldn't see him as much. Wouldn't get to talk to him while he sipped his morning coffee. Wouldn't get to say good night each evening.

She listened to the crickets chirping outside the open window, already missing him.

"What's going on in that creative mind of yours?"

"I'm. . .uh, just shocked—and disappointed that you already know my news. I thought I'd gotten a big scoop—even Jenny was surprised. Who else knows?"

Luke shrugged. "Probably just the town council. Your story will be news to most folks."

Jack settled back in her chair. "Yeah, I suppose. But how will we get by without the additional income?"

"We're not destitute, Half Bit. The house is paid for, plus when your ma and I got married, I had most of my army pay saved and invested. With the railroad coming to town, Garrett's business will slack off. He and I are going to buy some brood mares and a quality stallion and start raising stock horses. We're already looking for a section of land that's not too far from town, where Carly and he can live after they marry." He took a deep breath, then continued. "Your ma has enough to do with just caring for the family and this big home. You sound disappointed."

"No. Just mulling things over." Suddenly a pleasing thought dashed through her mind. "If we aren't taking in boarders, can I have my own room?" She grinned and waggled her eyebrows.

Hope sparked in her ma's eyes, taking Jack by surprise again. "Does that mean you're not going to Dallas?"

They knew? About the letter? Were all her secrets public knowledge? She jumped up, flinging her arms out sideways. "Did Jenny spill the beans? Nobody else knew."

"No." Her ma bit the edge of her lower lip. "I went upstairs to check on Abby yesterday, and she'd gotten in your lap desk. She had the letter and was just getting ready to write on the paper." She ducked her head. "I shouldn't have read your letter, but I was too curious not to. I'm sorry for that, but"—she glanced up with wounded eyes—"how could you even consider such a thing without talking to us? Do you have any idea what it's like in a city that large?"

Luke patted her ma's shoulder. "Now, Rach, I've been to Dallas several times, and it's not a bad town."

The look her ma gave Luke could have boiled frozen water. "Whose side are you on?"

"Nobody's—I mean both of you. Jack's not an ordinary young lady."

"But she *is* a woman—and no woman should go off alone to a big city. Who would protect her?" Her ma blinked her eyes several times, then looked at Jack again with a watery gaze. "What about Noah? I thought something was developing between you two."

Jack fidgeted in her chair. She might have been oblivious to hurting her ma when she was young and half wild, but she didn't like it now. "I was going to tell you. In fact, that was one of the things I wanted to talk about tonight. I've decided to turn down the job offer and stay here."

"Really?" Ma smiled and wiped her eyes with the hanky she'd pulled from her pocket. "I know that must have been a hard decision since you've wanted to be a reporter for so long."

Jack shrugged. In truth, she hadn't made her final decision until she'd seen how upset the thought of her leaving made her ma. What job compared to love of family?

"So, does Noah have anything to do with your staying?" Ma asked.

Jack stared out the window into the twilight. "Maybe."

No, more than maybe—most definitely. But for some reason, she was uncomfortable saying so in front of Luke. He'd grown quiet, which meant he was stewing on something.

"You'd make a good pastor's wife."

"Ma!"

"Rachel!"

Both Jack and Luke spoke at once.

Luke stood and started pacing the room. "Don't you think it's a bit too soon to be talking like that?"

Rachel grinned. "It's springtime, and love is in the air. Look at the Kesslers—and Garrett and Carly."

Luke snorted. "And what about the Lord? Does He still have a say in our lives?"

Rachel fluffed the pillow Luke had been leaning on. "Of course. I've prayed about the man Jacqueline would marry for much of her life. I knew God would bring the right man in His timing."

Jack just stared at her mother. How could she be so confident? Was she actually voicing her approval for a union between her and Noah?

"All that matters is that you've prayed about your relationship with Noah and that you love him."

Luke grunted and ran his hand through his hair. What was wrong with him? She thought he liked Noah.

"I have prayed." Jack's gaze darted to her ma and back to Luke. His behavior was making her uneasy. "I—care for him."

Luke kicked a table leg, whether accidentally

347

or on purpose, she wasn't sure. Her ma gave him a curious glance. "And I believe he cares deeply for you."

"It's too soon," Luke said. "You've only known him a few weeks. How can you care for him that much?"

Jack shrugged again. "I can't explain it. From the first moment I looked into his eyes, I felt something— as if we'd been bound together for a lifetime."

Rachel hugged the pillow. "I know just what you mean. I felt that about Luke when I first met him, too."

"You were in first grade, Rachel. How can you remember that?"

"A woman just does." She batted her lashes and gave him a coy smile.

Luke finally stopped in front of Jack, and she had to lean back to see his puckered brow. "Has Noah talked to you?"

Jack opened her mouth to respond, but paused, baffled by his question. "Uh...we talk every day."

"That's not what I mean." Luke's hand lowered to where his gun normally rested, then he closed his fist. Something was definitely bothering him, but she had no idea what it could be.

Luke squatted and looked her in the eye. "You promise me—before you let your feelings for him grow any more—that you'll have a heart-to-heart talk with him. Tell him he'd better tell you everything—or he'll answer to me."

Jack glanced at her ma, seeing the same confusion she felt. Luke bounced up and strode out of the room and down the hall. What was the "everything" he was referring to?

The front door opened, and Noah strode in, his eyes shining. He shut the door, removed his hat, and noticed them. He walked into the room with a wide grin pulling at his cheeks. "Evening, I just got some rather exciting news—at least it seems that way to me."

Her ma lifted one brow. "Oh, and what is that?"

Noah sat down on the edge of the chair next to Jack's. She studied each detail of his handsome face. His eye was all healed except for a faint bruise, and a slight red mark remained just above his lip from the cut. His nose was perfectly straight, and dark stubble made him even more appealing. His beautiful eyes beamed. How could this kindhearted man be hiding a secret so bad that it would send Luke into a tizzy?

Noah leaned toward her. "The Taylors have decided not to return to Lookout. The town council offered me a permanent position and use of the parsonage."

He was staying! Jack's heart leapt for joy. She jumped up and almost hugged him, then remembered her ma was still in the room. "That's wonderful news."

Rachel also stood and clapped her hands. "Yes, that is. I'll miss the Taylors, but I know they've wanted to move back home for a long while. Do you mind if I tell Luke?"

Noah shook his head, and she left the room, leaving them alone. He reached out and took Jackie's hand. "Are you happy?"

∽

She looked happy but not delirious, as he'd hoped. When he first heard the news, he'd wanted to flee the Manns' home and run back here to tell Jackie, but he couldn't. He had to sit quietly and listen to what they expected: no more preaching about pelicans and the discussion about his salary, which was a decent amount plus the offer to use the parsonage. All the time, every part of his being was bouncing.

"I am happy." She squeezed his hand and smiled.

"But?"

She broke his gaze and shrugged.

"Don't you know what this means, Jackie? I have the support of the town council, a home, and a salary that I can support a family on—if we're careful."

"We?" She stared up at him, her blue eyes looking enormous.

Did she not yet know his heart? Or maybe she didn't feel the same. He knew little of women and their ways. Had he misread her?

He closed his eyes. He wanted to obey God and do His work, but if she didn't share his feelings, how could he stay here? He'd thought God was answering his dream and giving him this opportunity. More than he ever hoped for. Much more than he deserved.

But without her. . .

"I'm thrilled, Noah, but there's something I have to know. What is in your past that you don't want to tell me about?"

The moment he'd dreaded the most was here. He hadn't told the council about his secret yet. He wanted to talk to Luke first about how to approach it. They'd given him a week to decide, but he could tell they weren't happy that he hadn't made an instant decision.

"Noah. If you truly care about me and want a future together, there can be no secrets between us."

He sighed and nodded. "You're right. I'm just. . . scared, I guess."

She took hold of his other hand and gave him a sweet smile, but her eyes held a teasing glint. "You're scared of me?"

You have no idea. "Not exactly." He looked down and studied the floorboards. *How do I tell her, Lord? I don't want to lose her.*

There was no easy way. He captured her gaze, gaining strength from the love he saw there. Ten years had passed. Maybe she didn't even remember Butch.

"You're a good man, Noah. It can't be all that bad. What did you do?"

He shook his head. "It's not what I did but rather who I am."

The confusion in her gaze threatened to steal his boldness. He had to tell her before he lost his nerve. "I lived in Lookout a long time ago, and we went to school together."

Her eyes went wide, and he could almost see her sharp mind racing, trying to figure out the puzzle.

"I–I'm. . .Butch."

She crinkled her brow. Her eyes widened. She dropped his hands and stepped back, forming a chasm between them as wide as the state of Texas. He already felt her loss.

"Not Butch Laird?"

He nodded and ducked his head, hurt with how she'd spewed his name.

"How could you?" With a hand on her chest, she looked as if she couldn't catch her breath. Leaning forward, she narrowed her eyes. "How could you kiss me and not tell me such a thing? Was this just a cruel game you were playing?"

"No, Jackie—" He ran his hand through his hair, seeing his dream dying. "I care for you—I always have."

"That's a lie." She backed up clear to the piano. "You were mean. You picked fights and—and—you locked me in jail and left me there."

"I'm sorry about the past, but I've changed. Haven't you seen that?"

She shook her head. Tears ran down her cheeks. "Is Noah even your real name? Jeffers sure isn't."

"Yes, Noah is what my ma named me, but my pa never liked it and called me Butch. I adopted my friend Pete's last name when he came to mean more to me than my own pa."

Jack's chin quivered. "You lied to me. More than once, and that's all that matters. I thought you were above such things, but I was wrong. My first pa—he always lied. I told myself I'd never have anything to do with a cruel man or a liar."

She hurried past him, making as wide an arc as possible. He was losing her.

"Jackie—wait."

She skidded to a stop in the hall and looked to her left. His hope took wing. Would she hear him out?

Luke stepped into view.

"You knew!" Jackie's word spewed forth like snake venom.

Luke nodded, sorrow etched in his face.

"Why didn't you say something?"

"It wasn't my place, Half Bit."

Jack swung toward the stairs. She stopped on the fourth one and glared down. "I'll never trust either of you again."

Noah watched her charge upstairs, his dreams dashed. He should have told her sooner.

Much sooner.

Chapter 32

Jack lay in her bed, her aching eyes matching her heart. Her whole body hurt. Her tears were spent. How could he be Butch?

How could he not tell her?

The thing she feared most had come true. She'd lost her heart to a man just like her pa.

She stared up at the half moon. How could she have been so stupid?

How could Luke have betrayed her like that? Wasn't it his job to protect her?

She sucked in a breath and a dose of reality. Luke had tried since she first met him to protect her, but only the Almighty could truly do that.

But hadn't He let her down, too?

Jack sighed and listened to her sisters' breathing as they slept. How could she feel so alone with two others in the room?

Just when Noah had everything he needed to provide for her, she learned the shocking truth—he was Butch Laird, her childhood nemesis. And yet, even knowing that, she still loved him. She bolted up in her bed, her heart pounding. She honestly, truly loved Butch Laird.

The thought should have repulsed her, but it didn't. Hadn't she always been curious about him? Even tried to be friends once?

Noah or Butch—what did it matter when he

lied to her? She could never trust him now. Her tears must have restocked because they started again.

Father God, make this hurt go away.

She wiped her tears on her pillowcase and her nose on her sixth and last hanky. Lying in the dark, she continued to pray. *Show me what to do, Lord.*

How can I stay in Lookout now? I can't bear to see him again.

Should I take the Dallas job?

Jack jerked. She blinked in the darkness and noticed the moon heading toward the horizon. Had she finally fallen asleep?

Her eyes ached, and she lifted her hand to touch their puffiness. Her head hurt as bad as when she'd gotten that concussion, but it was her heart that was shattered.

A metallic *ching* sounded near Emmie's bed. Jack sat up and rubbed her eyes. Something banged and rolled across the floor. Had Emmie awakened?

As her eyes grew used to the darkness, the form of a man's body took shape. "Papa?"

A masculine curse filled the room, and Jack gasped. The man hurled himself toward her. Before she could untangle herself from the sheet, a hand clamped hard over her mouth. Whiskey-laden breath filled her nostrils. "Where's that bracelet?"

Jack's eyes widened in the dark. She turned and could see the man's face in the moonlight. She pulled his hand down. "Billy?"

"I need that bracelet."

"I gave it to your ma."

He sucked in a deep breath. "You stupid. . .you've ruined everything."

He turned away and pulled open a drawer of her dresser—her unmentionables drawer, yanking out one garment after another. She tossed the sheet aside and stood, her nightgown sliding down to cover her legs. "Stop it. I don't have the bracelet anymore."

He grabbed her jaw. "I bought that for you. Why'd you give it to Ma?"

"You're hurting me. Stop it." She grabbed his hand, but he didn't let go.

"Shut up, or I'll hurt you like that fat, ol' lady."

Jack gasped. "You killed Bertha?"

"All I wanted was some money." Suddenly Billy's other hand careened toward her in the moonlight. It crashed into her jaw, knocking her back on the bed. Pain mixed with darkness. She fought to keep a hold on her awareness.

From a distance, someone screamed. Abby. She had to help her sister—as soon as she plowed through this quicksand of darkness.

Noah sat on the edge of the bed, unable to sleep. His heart had broken and fallen in pieces all over the floor. His prayers seemed to fall on deaf ears. He'd had everything he wanted in the palm of his hand for a few minutes—but he'd lost it all.

He'd lost her.

And without her, nothing else mattered.

He jumped up and strode to the window. A cool breeze lifted the curtains, reminding him of things greater than himself. The wind had always put him in mind of God. Something you couldn't see but you knew existed.

"Did I hear You wrong, Lord? Wasn't it Your will for me to come here, to make restitution for my past offenses? To have a chance to start over with Jackie?"

He should have told her the truth from the start. She would have reacted the same, but it wouldn't have hurt so much.

Or maybe it would have.

"What am I going to do, Lord?"

He had to tell the church board who he was. He probably wouldn't have a job after that, but with things like they were now, maybe that was for the best. First thing in the morning, he'd go see them.

He stared at the moon and longed to talk to Pete. The old man always put things in their proper perspective. Noah knew what he'd say, though.

Don't be so hard on yourself.

Talk to your Creator.

Trust the Lord.

But hadn't he done all that and still lost Jackie?

He wanted to throw something. Wanted to get on his horse and ride until he reached the ocean. Wanted things to be like they were when he'd kissed Jackie in the alley.

But they never would be.

A frantic scream broke into his misery. He bolted to the door, stumbling on the chair he'd left out earlier. A sharp pain ratcheted across his knee, but he ignored it when another scream came. He scrambled down the stairs and slid to a stop outside Jack's bedroom door.

He'd overreacted. Abby was just having a bad dream. He could not go in there.

Something thumped hard on the other side of the door, and Abby screamed again. Emmie started crying, and he heard a muffled squeal. "Jackie?"

He reached for the knob. The squeals got louder as if someone called for help. He turned the knob and shoved open the door. Abby's screams reverberated around the room.

His eyes focused on a large shape bending over Jackie's bed—a man's shape. His hand fumbled to light the lamp by the doorway. His eyes rebelled at the sudden brightness, but he rushed forward. Billy Morgan stood over Jack. Her cheek was red, and she glanced at him with a dazed stare. What had Billy done?

All his pain rushed to the surface. In two quick

steps he grabbed Billy's arm. Noah hauled the man away from his beloved. He shook Billy hard. "What are you doing in here?"

Without warning, Billy went berserk—kicking, punching, cursing.

Abby's screams continued, and Emmie's wails grew louder. Noah dodged Billy's fist. He didn't want to fight the man again, but he'd crossed a line. He slammed Billy against the wall and held him there by his throat. Billy smashed his fists into Noah's cheeks. Rage filled him.

"Noah, stop it." Jackie's pleas barely pierced his mental armor.

"That's enough, son," Luke's stronger, deeper voice called to him. "Let him go, Noah. I've got my rifle."

He glanced toward Luke and suddenly realized how his rage had overpowered his senses. Just like his pa's always had. He opened his hand, and Billy slid down the wall.

"Papa, he killed Mrs. Boyd." Jackie slid off her bed and rushed to gather Emmie to her then carried her to Abby's bed and cuddled both frightened sisters.

Luke hauled Billy up. "You're under arrest, Mr. Morgan."

Noah took one last glance at Jackie and dashed out of the room. The worst thing he could have imagined had happened—he'd become his father.

~

The sound of songbirds tickled Jack's ears, and she stretched. She opened her eyes, surprised to see the sun had fully risen and both girls were already up and gone. Suddenly the horrors of last night rushed back.

Noah.

Billy.

What would Billy have done to her if Noah hadn't come to her rescue?

She shivered and sat up. Her eyes felt dry and scratchy—puffy from her hours of crying. And in the end, the result was the same. Noah was Butch—her worst enemy. The man she loved.

How could they be one and the same?

Why hadn't she recognized him?

He had the same black hair. The same dark, probing eyes. And Butch had been tall, but never as well-built as Noah. Somewhere over the years, Butch had lost his pudginess and bad complexion and mean streak and turned into sweet, gentle Noah.

As if someone had snapped together the final piece in a jigsaw puzzle, it all made sense:

That connection she'd felt—as if they had a past history—made sense now.

His familiarity with her—how he knew so much about her.

His odd comment about a possible headline: Town Delinquent Returns as New Pastor.

No wonder Noah couldn't stomach pork after his father had raised hogs. As poor as they'd been, it was probably all he'd eaten for years.

Some investigative reporter she turned out to be. The truth was right in front of her. He'd even tossed out clues to his identity like bread crumbs, but she'd acted like an infatuated schoolgirl blinded by reality.

But Noah had lied—and so had Luke.

She longed to do nothing except stay in bed all day, but she couldn't.

Yet how could she face him?

What could she say to him?

Nothing.

She forced herself up and trod to the washroom. She rinsed her face, holding the soothing water on her eyes for a moment. Then she looked in the mirror and gasped.

Her cheek where Billy had hit her was red. Swollen. She worked her jaw, wincing at the pain.

She dressed and brushed her hair, then wandered downstairs, her heart as battered as her face.

She searched for Noah in the parlor, then the dining room, but instead, she found her ma and Carly washing dishes. Emmie sat at the table in her chair, munching on a biscuit, and smiled at her. Jack pulled out a kitchen chair and flopped down, feeling one hundred years old.

Her ma slid a cup of coffee in front of her and sat down. The strong aroma drifted up from the cup, teasing her senses.

"How do you feel?"

"Numb."

"That will pass."

Jack made a derogatory snort. "Maybe in twenty years."

Emmie wrinkled up her nose and snorted, and Jack gave her sister a weak smile.

Her ma squeezed her forearm. Carly set a plate of biscuit, eggs, and bacon in front of her. All she could do was stare at the bacon. It reminded her of Noah. Of Butch.

She was in love with a liar and a man who had come within a hair's inch of bashing Billy to pieces last night—not that he didn't deserve it. Touching the sore place on her cheek, she realized that Noah had never actually hit Billy, but rather just held him away from her until Luke could get there. He wasn't like her pa, after all. He had self-control.

Andrew squeaked from the bedroom then let out a yell. Carly tossed down the towel she'd been drying dishes with. "I'll change his diaper and see if I can make him happy for a bit."

"Where's Luke?" Jack couldn't bring herself to call

him papa this morning.

"Down at the jail. He's writing up formal charges against Billy for breaking into his mother's store and also for Bertha's murder. Turns out those two fellows that Garrett shot saw Billy breaking into the store, and they did the other robberies, hoping he would be blamed for all of them." She shook her head. "Billy always was a troublesome boy, but I never expected him to be capable of such things."

"Me neither. Did you know he broke in last night because he wanted the bracelet back that he gave me?"

Ma nodded. "Luke told me. Hardest thing I ever did was staying down here with Andrew when you girls were screaming." She rubbed her palm over the top of Jack's hand. "Luke feels like he let you down. His heart is breaking, you know."

Jack's lower lip wobbled at causing him pain. "He should have told me."

"He couldn't. It was Noah's place."

"Luke could have said something before I started liking Noah."

"And just when was that? Seems to me you were smitten from the moment you met him."

Her ma didn't play fair. Jack stared into her black coffee—coffee that reminded her of Noah's eyes. She squeezed hers shut and pushed the cup away. "Do you think God sent Noah here for us to be together?"

"I think it's highly possible, but I think God also had another purpose. This town needs a minister."

Jack blew out a mocking breath. "Not one that lies."

"Why are you fighting this so much? You know you love Noah. Are you going to let him get away just because of your stubborn pride?"

Jack glowered at her ma. "He *lied* to me—just like my first pa."

"Everyone lies at one time or another, not that

I'm making excuses for him, but when was the last time you lied?"

Jack winced. "How can I trust him again?"

"I don't condone his lying, but he was scared."

"Of what?"

"Of people rejecting him just because of who he was. Do you honestly think anyone who'd known him as the town bully would receive him as pastor? People harbor long memories of those who hurt their children or destroy their property." Her mother slid the plate of food closer to her.

Something suddenly made sense. "That's why he was chopping wood and painting the store—he was trying to make up for the bad things he'd done." Jack's heart ached. She'd treated him so cruelly.

Ma nodded again. "And I think he waited to tell you who he was because he was afraid of how you'd react."

She hadn't considered that. If she'd known from the start who he was, she probably would have snubbed him—might not have even gone to church—and she'd have missed his thought-provoking messages. She broke off a piece of bacon and put it in her mouth, enjoying the flavor.

"I don't know what to do. I'd be lying if I said I don't care for him, but how can I face him again after how I reacted last night? I wasn't very nice."

"You were hurt—and reacted accordingly." Her mother sighed and played with the corner of the towel she'd used to dry dishes.

"What's wrong?"

The look that engulfed her mother's pretty face scared Jack, but she didn't know what she should be afraid of. "What is it?"

Her ma's pale blue eyes looked straight into Jack's. She swallowed hard, knowing she wouldn't like whatever her ma was going to say.

"I'm sorry, sweetie, but Noah is gone."

A cruel fist squeezed Jack's heart and wouldn't let go. "What do you mean he's gone? Has he already moved to the parsonage?"

"No, he left town."

Jack jumped up so fast the chair fell backward and banged on the floor. "No! Where did he go?"

"Uh-oh," Emmie said and pointed to the chair. Jack picked it up but remained standing.

"Sit down, sweetie."

"I can't. What am I going to do? Why did he leave?"

Her ma stood and came to her, pulling Jack to her chest. "He said it was better for everyone if he did. Better for you."

"I was wrong, Ma. He's a good man."

"Yes, he is. He's not the troubled youth he used to be. God took that wild boy, washed him clean with the blood of Jesus, and formed him into a man of character. A man who loves you."

And she loved him. So help her, she did. How could she have been such a stubborn fool?

She'd let her pride—her refusal to forgive—steal something precious. Her vendetta toward her pa had killed her chances with Noah.

Forgive me, Lord. Help me forgive my pa for all the mean, hurtful things he did.

Jack hugged her ma then stepped back. "You said Noah was headed home? Back to Emporia?"

She nodded. "I think the only person Noah has in the world is Pete, the man who took him in."

Jack backed away, her determination swelling with each breath she took. "No, Ma, he's got us, too."

She spun on her heels and ran into the hall.

"Where are you going?"

"To don my trousers."

Chapter 33

Noah walked his horse down the dusty lane. He was looking forward to seeing Pete again, yet each step Rebel took was a step farther away from Jackie. He missed her with every speck of his mind, body, and soul. He didn't know how he'd go on.

All he'd wanted was a chance to prove he'd changed. He'd fooled himself into believing she loved him, but she never truly had any faith in him—she didn't as a child, and she didn't now.

He'd finally found a place he thought he could call home. People had started accepting and befriending him. Trusting and respecting him.

And he'd lost it all.

Lost his chance to tell the townsfolk of God's love.

Lost the woman he loved.

Tears stung his eyes, and he tilted his head toward the heavens. "I've failed in every way, Lord. Forgive me."

He reined Rebel off the road into a patch of grass and dismounted. Kneeling, he cried out to God. "Forgive me for leaving the town You sent me to. Forgive me for failing You. Make this burning ache go away, Lord."

Yet maybe he deserved the pain. Hadn't he hated his own father? Caused trouble for his schoolmates and the townsfolk each time his pa had beat him?

Hadn't his mother and sister died because he'd been too scared to leave them and ride for the doctor?

He was an utter failure.

"No, son, you are forgiven. You are deeply loved. Forgive yourself."

A sob gushed forth from the deepest recesses of his soul as he turned loose of the pain of his past and let the words of God wash over him.

Soothing.

Comforting.

Healing.

He was a child of God. His pain had momentarily blinded him so that he'd listened to the lies of Satan. But he wasn't a failure—he was a man of worth because of Christ's blood, which was shed for him on the cross. He was fully forgiven.

As the reality of the truth set in, Noah relaxed in the peace that only God can bring a troubled man. After the sleepless night before, he closed his eyes, weary from battling his fears but confident now in God's love. He may always love Jackie, but now he could give her to the Lord. He closed his eyes, and sleep overtook him.

The sound of rifle fire jerked him awake.

The rifle shook in Jack's hands. "Get up from there, Reverend."

"Jackie?" Noah stared at her, his eyes still foggy from sleep. "What are you doing?"

"You ran out on me, and I'm not letting you get away that easily." She forced her voice to sound gruff when all she wanted to do was wrap her arms around Noah and kiss him silly.

He lumbered to his feet and rubbed his eyes. "Am I dreaming? Or did you really just shoot at me?"

She could see his apprehension—and no wonder after how she had acted. She slid the rifle into the scabbard that hung from the horse and saddle she'd borrowed from Dan Howard. Bolstering her determination with a quick prayer, she turned back to Noah. "I'm sorry. Your confession last night took me by surprise—and I never liked surprises."

He took a step toward her. "I'm sorry, too. I should have told you sooner, but first I wanted you to get to know me as I am now. I've changed. God changed me."

"I know." She closed the space between them, tears stinging her eyes and making Noah's face blur. "Can you find it in your heart to forgive me?"

He exhaled a cough of disbelief. "Are you serious?"

She smacked him on the arm. "Of course I am. Do you think I'd ride all this way if I wasn't?"

"Yeah, I do, if you were truly bent on shooting me." He grinned and rubbed his arm, something enticing now burning in his gaze. "You pack a wallop for such a little thing."

"I'm an expert shot, too, so don't forget it."

"All right." He ducked his head and toed the dirt. "I'm really sorry, Jackie. I just didn't think you'd give me half a chance if you knew who I was."

"We'll never know now, but I want to put it behind us. Do you have feelings for me or not?" She was tired of mincing words. "And are you going to forgive me or not?"

"Yes." He stepped closer and ran the back of his finger down her cheek.

"Yes, what?"

"Yes, I forgive you, and yes, I love you."

That was all she needed to hear. Jack lunged into his arms, and her lips met his. He lifted her off the ground, nearly squeezing the air from her lungs as he showered her with kisses. The kisses took a turn, desperate, frantic—and then he pulled back, his breath heavy on her cheek.

"I love you, Jackie—I think I always have."

"I love you, too." She ran her hand across his cheek, marveling at its roughness. "It just took me a bit longer to realize it."

Noah's warm smile tickled her stomach. To think she almost gave him up because of her own stubbornness and refusal to forgive. He lowered her so that she could stand.

"Are you ready to go back home?" She fingered a button on his shirt.

"Where is home? I quit my job, you know?"

"I know the marshal real well, and maybe I can persuade him to 'encourage' the council to hire you back."

Noah lifted her off the ground again and kissed her, then he spun her around, hugging her tight. "Thank You, Lord!"

She sent her own prayer winging its way heaven bound. *Thank You, Father, for helping me see past my hurts and for giving me another chance with Noah.*

Epilogue

Jack repeated the vows in her head after Noah stated them. His black eyes caught hers, and he winked, sending shivers of delight through her. In front of the church, Carly gazed at Garrett with adoration and promised to love, honor, and obey him.

Jack winced. She wasn't 100 percent sure about that *obey* stuff, so she skipped that word. Maybe she and Noah could write their own vows before their wedding next month.

She could hardly wait. The two weeks they'd been courting had dragged by slower than a slug. But she'd seen the wisdom in waiting and getting to know each other better—that and they had to wait until another minister could come and marry them. At least Noah had his job back, and most of the town had forgiven him after their initial shock. Nothing stood in their way now—no barriers from the past, no hurt feelings, no unwillingness to forgive.

"Join me in praying for the bride and groom." Noah bowed his head, his deep voice lulling the room into a hushed reverence.

Jack breathed her own prayer, overflowing from her abundantly grateful heart. *Thank You, Lord, for helping me forgive my father and giving me Noah. He's a good man.*

One day soon, she'd finally be a bride.

ABOUT THE AUTHOR

Award-winning author Vickie McDonough believes God is the ultimate designer of romance. She loves writing stories in which her characters find true love and grow in their faith. Vickie has published eighteen books. She is an active member of American Christian Fiction Writers and is currently serving as ACFW treasurer. Vickie has been a book reviewer for nine years as well. She is a wife of thirty-five years, mother of four sons, and grandmother to a feisty three-year-old girl. When not writing, she enjoys reading, watching movies, and traveling. Visit Vickie's website at www.vickiemcdonough.com.